The Vivian Inheritance

The Vivian Inheritance

Jean Stubbs

St. Martin's Press
New York

Library of Congress Cataloging in Publication Data

Stubbs, Jean, 1926-
    The Vivian inheritance.

    I. Title.
PR6069.T78V5   1982   823'.914   82-17020
ISBN 0-312-85068-9

First published in Great Britain by Macmillan London Ltd.

First U.S. Edition

10 9 8 7 6 5 4 3 2 1

To the first seven years,
and the last twenty-one.

Acknowledgments

I thank yet again those tireless and imaginative providers of research books: Bob Gilbert of Gilbert's Print and Bookshop, Truro, Cornwall; D. G. Willcocks of Longs Booksellers, Poulton-le-Fylde, Lancashire; the staff of Helston Branch Library, and Paul Bannister of the Library Van. I thank Helen MacGregor for a Victorian novel called *The Manchester Man* which provided background details of Chetham's Hospital; and Terry Coleman for his study, *The Railway Navvies*, to which I became addicted, and for which I am truly grateful. I thank John Treloar of Wendron Forge, Cornish engineer, for talking to me about pumping engines, and suggesting places in which I might see, and books in which I might read about them. I thank my grandson Nicholas Mathys – though he may not in later years thank me! – for the merry portrait of Herbert Howarth. I thank my editor of many years, Teresa Sacco, for frank criticism, generous praise and constant encouragement. Finally, to my husband: the man who went so far as to give me a micro computer word-processor and printer to lighten my load – and who must have felt at times that the Wyndendale railroad was being dug out of *him* – thank you, Felix!

Contents

Part One

Legacies

1	Victory!	15
2	The Cornishman	30
3	News	45
4	Deep Workings	52
5	Disaster	64
6	A Digan for the Bucca	74
7	Designs	82
8	On the Eve	96
9	The Locked Heart	109

Part Two

Alliances

10	Resurrection	129
11	Playing Games	145
12	Father and Daughter	163
13	The Wyndendale Railway	174
14	Coming Out	187
15	Picks, Shovels and Gunpowder	201
16	A Fine Lady Upon a White Horse	207
17	A Great Occasion	217

Part Three

Destinations

18	New Growth	229
19	Victors and Vanquished	238
20	A Breath of Fresh Air	251
21	An End and a Beginning	266
22	All Aboard!	281
23	Many a Spoiled Breakfast	290
24	Grand Designs	305

Forget not to shew love unto strangers:
for thereby some have entertained angels
unawares.

The Epistle of Paul
to the Hebrews, xiii. 2.

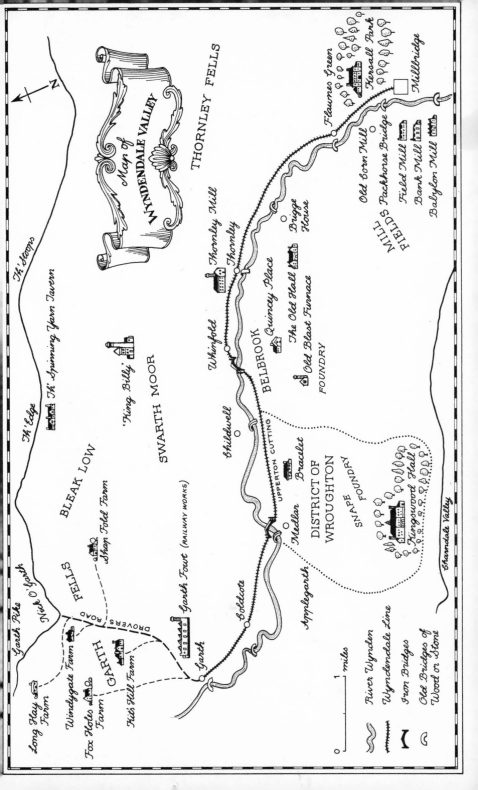

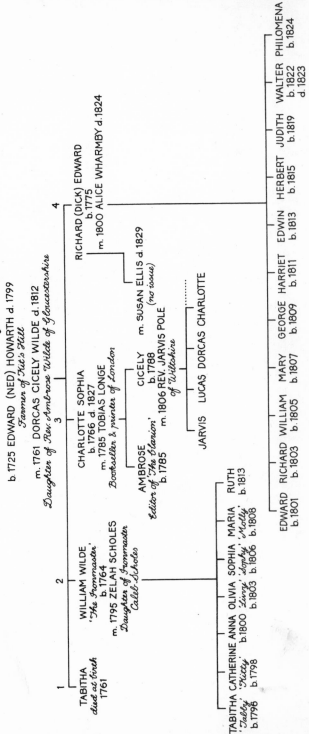

The Howarth Family Tree

b.1725 EDWARD (NED) HOWARTH d.1799
Farmer of Kit's Hill
m.1761 DORCAS CICELY WILDE d.1812
Daughter of Rev. Ambrose Wilde of Gloucestershire

1
TABITHA
died at birth
1761

2
WILLIAM WILDE
'*The Ironmaster*'
b.1764
m.1795 ZELAH SCHOLES
Daughter of Ironmaster Caleb Scholes

3
CHARLOTTE SOPHIA
b.1766 d.1827
m.1785 TOBIAS LONGE
Bookseller & printer of London

4
RICHARD (DICK) EDWARD
b.1775
m.1800 ALICE WHARMBY d.1824

AMBROSE
Editor of 'The Clarion'
b.1785

CICELY
b.1788
m.1806 REV. JARVIS POLE
of Wiltshire

m. SUSAN ELLIS d.1829
(no issue)

JARVIS   LUCAS   DORCAS   CHARLOTTE

TABITHA   CATHERINE   ANNA   OLIVIA   SOPHIA   MARIA   RUTH
'*Tabby*'   '*Kitty*'   b.1800   *Livvy*   '*Sophy*'   '*Molly*'   b.1813
b.1796   b.1798   b.1803   b.1806   b.1808

EDWARD   RICHARD   WILLIAM   MARY   GEORGE   HARRIET   EDWIN   HERBERT   JUDITH   WALTER   PHILOMENA
b.1801   b.1803   b.1805   b.1807   b.1809   b.1811   b.1813   b.1815   b.1819   b.1822   b.1824
                                                                                    d.1823

The Vivian Inheritance

Part One

Legacies

1815-1818

ONE

Victory

June 1815

Bells, bells, bells, bells. They are ringing in every town and village throughout the country, for the long war with France is over and won, the Duke of Wellington is England's hero, and the field of Waterloo will stamp its name upon all future decisive contests.

For the past four years poor mad King George the Third has been declared unfit to govern, and frequently restrained by a straitjacket. So the stout Regent, though no more fit to govern than his father, and regularly constrained by a corset, will preside over the ensuing scenes of drunkenness and gluttony. His subjects, loyal and disloyal, have forgotten their differences in order to celebrate the occasion. Maypoles are being taken down and repainted, weathercocks freshly gilded, banners and flags set flying from window and steeple. Poor folk and rich will dance in their finery. Every guild will decorate a cart to join the local procession. Travelling professionals, combining loyalty with profit, will walk high wires, tumble and juggle, tell fortunes, sell sweetmeats and novelties and infallible medicines. For those who take their amusements violently there will be dog and cock fights, boxing and wrestling matches, bull and bear baiting. Beggars will exhibit their sores, and freaks their monstrousness. At every inn drinkers will sing 'God Save the King' as long as they can form the words and carry the tune. Bellringers, restored by ale at intervals, will pull their arms and shoulders into a multitude of aches, and before the day is done are certain to distort the changes. From head to foot, this jubilant island will be all beer and bonfires.

★　　　★　　　★

In Wyndendale, Lancashire, the very essence of this triumph was distilled at the end of June in the year 1815. Lord Kersall, as titular head of the valley, had thrown open that part of his private grounds which he reserved for important public events. Every local squire and personage of any note in the nine-mile length of Wyndendale was treating his servants and dependants to food and fun of some sort. But down in the iron realms of Cunshurst, Upperton and Snape the ironmaster had bested everyone as he always did.

The medieval market town of Millbridge was the valley's acknowledged capital, and its growth had absorbed a village or two in the last fifty years, but it was not as large even now as William Howarth's iron kingdom. Indeed, the Borough Council were thinking of renaming that vast district, which once was nothing but mean farms, millstone grit and water. The question of its baptism was only one of many thoughts which preoccupied the ironmaster. At ten o'clock that summer morning he was standing at the windows of the long library in Kingswood Hall, arms folded and brow dark, trying out names and looking down at the small public park he had recently given to his people.

'Kingsfield?' he asked himself softly. 'Kingsmere? Kingshill?'

A warm white hand upon his sleeve reminded him of present duties. He met his wife's dark gold eyes with some anxiety. Did she love him? he wondered. Were he to ask her outright she would reassure him. But the tranquillity of Zelah Howarth's body and mind, the quiet joy which illumined her face upon occasion, owed little to the ironmaster and much to God. For she had long since found her Maker to be more reliable than her husband, and sensibly invested her trust in Him instead.

'The solicitor hath been here above half an hour, love,' she said without reproof, 'and all the family is waiting for thee.'

'What, is brother Dick come on time for once?' asked William.

His tone was rich, good-humoured, pleasantly bullying: the tone of a man who treats everyone as his equal but reminds them they are not.

'With all his brood?' cried the ironmaster, smiling broadly to show that he did not mind his brother siring five boys and two girls, while he himself had only daughters. 'In the farm wagon?' Laughing uproariously at the thought of such a spectacle.

Even at fifty, his teeth were still sound and good. He was the handsomest of men, all black and grey like the metal he commanded, and the fire in his heart and belly was as hot and true as the fires in his many furnaces. But his wife's Quaker upbringing forbade her to join in such mockery of honest folk.

'If thou art ashamed of his wagon thee should have sent a carriage,' she replied coolly, and her tone reminded him that this was no occasion for mirth.

Humbly he bent his head in acquiescence, proffered his arm, led his wife forth. What a mansion he had built, on expectations long since fulfilled, on self-belief long tried and proven. Yes, *Kingshill*, he thought suddenly, for that brings in the whole of the slope and echoes the name of the house. So ironmaster and lady paced the stately hall and stood in the doorway of the dining room. Their hospitality was a form of grace, and their guests rose as if for royalty. William inspected them, chin resting on his starched collar, black silk stock well in evidence.

To his left, uncomfortable on their gilt and satin chairs, were the Howarths of Kit's Hill: Dick and Alice, both ruddy and thickset, surrounded by seven little rustics in dyed mourning and with an eighth imminent. William smiled benevolently.

To his right, his niece Cicely, her husband the Reverend Jarvis Pole, and their four children: gentlefolk but poor. He smiled sympathetically.

Turning towards him gravely, his nephew Ambrose

17

Longe, bachelor and London journalist: thin, brown and over-intelligent. William inclined his head a little.

In the background as always, Caleb Scholes the Younger: Zelah's brother and William's former partner in Belbrook Foundry, now sole owner of that same ironworks: a small affair devoted to the production of domestic utensils, further up the valley. A hearty nod from the ironmaster, befitting both relationships.

Facing him, Nicodemus Hurst, respectable family solicitor of Millbridge. William extended a cool hand, which was briefly shaken.

Then five of his seven fair daughters came forward to embrace him, for he liked to be seen to be adored. His eldest, Tabitha, could not be with them. She had married almost a year ago and was shortly expecting her first infant. His youngest, Ruth, scarcely sixteen months old, was in her nursery.

One other member of the Howarth family was missing: his sister Charlotte who had died under peculiar and distressing circumstances, and whose Will was about to be read.

The ironmaster handed his wife to her seat at the foot of the dining table, and enthroned himself at its head. Mr Hurst, on his right-hand, cleared his throat in a pernickety fashion. His little sheaf of papers rattled in the collective silence.

The mahogany surface mirrored twenty-five attentive faces. Their images were pensive, pale, thrown into relief by the night of their clothes, testifying to the depth of their grief. The ironmaster's countenance became wintry, bleak, as he listened to the opening words.

'This is the Last Will and Testament of Charlotte Sophia Longe of Thornton House, Millbridge, Lancashire, Widow of Tobias Longe, late of Lock-yard, London . . .'

William pursed his lips against affliction, for she had been his only sister, his earliest friend, his closest confidante, his greatest embarrassment, and still remained an enigma to himself and everyone present. He saw his pained disbelief in her death reflected by each adult, for all had loved Charlotte and none had understood her – except perhaps that political idiot Jack Ackroyd, who had been hanged, drawn and quartered for their joint treason almost three years ago.

'. . . I, being on the Eve of Transportation for the Term of Seven Years Hard Labour to New South Wales and in Delicate Health and therefore not Expecting to Survive the Rigours of my Sentence and yet Trusting in the Mercy of Almighty God . . . '

On the eve of transportation, and what an eve! Her lover executed in the most diabolical manner, though stoical, just that one shout as he felt life torn from him and he from it. Her mother Dorcas Howarth, dead of grief within a fortnight of the sentence being passed. Her family disgraced. Herself turned grey almost overnight. And then those months aboard the convict hulk, so aptly named *Retribution*, until the Christmas of 1812, while they awaited the completion of necessary work on the *Isabella*. The ironmaster had done what he could, but even power and money can penetrate only so far. And Charlotte was already weak and ailing in body, sick with grief.

The full details of her voyage had been culled from a reliable source, but William decided not to confide them to anyone but Zelah. The prison quarters wet, close, stinking of ragged and sick convicts. The storms which delayed the already delayed voyage. Outbreaks of fever and scurvy. Even attempted mutiny by the men. For which three were flogged to death. Well, not exactly flogged to death for that was not permitted, but they had all died after their floggings. By the time the ship docked in Botany Bay in the autumn of 1813 Charlotte was carried out on a stretcher, and the women convicts were sent off into the interior, taking their sick and dying with them. This painful news had come painfully back by the same long road, to reach them when England rejoiced at last.

Poor lass! Poor Charlotte! Gently-bred and gentle of nature. It was all the fault of that ranting radical Fleet Street hack Toby Longe. His sins had lived after him, and his widow had paid for them.

'. . . I leave my home of the past twenty years, to my son, Ambrose Longe, to do with as he pleases . . . '

Thornton House had been in the family, on Dorcas's side, since it was built in the reign of Queen Anne. What would the fellow do with it? Sell it and take the proceeds back to London with him probably! That would be a minor scandal. Far better to put good tenants in it, draw the rent and keep it together, as William himself had done so far in case Charlotte returned. Still, no reason for that now. And yet, and yet.

'. . . my two small private incomes, inherited from my great-aunt Tabitha Wilde and my Dearest Mother Dorcas Howarth, whom God hath Safe in his Keeping, to my daughter Cicely Pole . . . '

Now that was a different kettle of fish altogether. Cicely was a tender-hearted young woman. Very like Charlotte to outward view, but happily not of Charlotte's political persuasion. See those tears, never too far from the surface and ready to spring with compassion? She had chosen a good husband in Jarvis, or rather Dorcas had chosen him. And, sorrow notwithstanding, that income would make a difference to them. Not a great deal. Perhaps fifty pound a year, all told. But a needy clergyman would find it a small fortune. He must advise them on better investment. And with poor Lottie dead and that Luddite scandal buried with her, Jarvis Pole stood a fair chance of becoming rector of St Mark's in Millbridge. Old Robert Graham was swollen and lame with dropsy. A preaching piss-pot, as someone unkindly said. Give him a couple of years at most, and the living could be slipped from uncle to nephew without a word spoken. Jarvis would be a better rector than old Robert in every way. He was a better man.

'. . . and All my Capital to be Held in Trust for my Grandchildren and the Interest to be spent upon their Education until they be of such Age as to Inherit . . . '

For once, Nick Hurst and he had seen eye to eye on the

subject of capital. Given Charlotte's former circumstances there would have been none, but Dorcas's death had made her quite a wealthy woman. Comfortably placed, as folk said. And they could not let that spendthrift son of hers whim it away. Aye, Ambrose might well curl his lip. He knew what they had been at!

'... to my Good Friend and Servant of many years, Polly Slack, the sum of One Hundred Pounds...'

Polly would be well advised to invest that money before Ambrose parted her from it. William would tell Nick Hurst to hold the legacy until he had had a word with her. He remembered Polly first entering the Longe household when Ambrose was born, back in '85. And the girl had been with them through thick and thin, and mostly thin, ever since. To give Ambrose his due he had taken Polly back to London with him after the trial, to keep house for him. House! Some scurvy rooms near the Fleet, William supposed. Anyway, they were as thick as thieves together. He supposed it was not his business if Polly chose to hand over her legacy to Ambrose. William had suspected her of knowing more about Charlotte's political activities, and of the Jack Ackroyd affair, than she admitted. Though the authorities had questioned her pretty sharply, and got nothing for their pains or hers. Stupid, they had said. William was not at all convinced of that.

'... to my physician, Dr Hamish Standish ... to my brother-in-law Caleb Scholes...'

Remembrances, small but in excellent taste, for past kindnesses to Charlotte and her two children. Kindnesses! Either man would have married her at the drop of a hat, any time in the past twenty years. Come to that, Nick Hurst had been sweet on Charlotte too. She had probably given him his memento when he visited her professionally in Lancaster Jail, to draw up the Will.

All three men had courted her, and she had kept them graciously at arms length. Penelope and her Suitors, Ambrose had dubbed them. He had a neat wit. Well, he needed wit, he lived by it! Oh, granted, none of those

21

gentleman callers was a brilliant light, but they were all decent men in decent professions. Lottie could have been a beloved wife instead of Jack Ackroyd's mistress. She could have become a respected member of the community instead of a felon. Dear God, what had she seen in Jack Ackroyd? A misfit, if ever William met one. Son of a weaver, adopted son of an academic, with a head full of radical rubbish and a mouth full of Latin quotations. And he had lived two lives: one as headmaster of Millbridge Grammar School, the other as Charlotte's lover and political accomplice. Well, he had got his deserts. Hanged, drawn and quartered. And serve the damned chap right!

An ornament here, a picture there, a particular set of books elsewhere. That was like Charlotte, who could abstract herself for hours and days, and then become thoughtful and tender in a moment. He could see her clearly: not sorrowful and grey in her chains as she had been at Lancaster Jail, but dry of wit, warm of humour, teasing, magically aware. Lottie. Lottie.

The ironmaster's eyes were bright with tears. His throat ached.

'... and to my niece and god-daughter, Mary Charlotte Howarth of Kit's Hill, Garth Fell, Lancashire, my gold locket...'

Which was Mary? He scanned Dick's row of children. Ah, Mary, of course. The elder girl. That thin red-headed lass with the pale skin and sulky mouth. Wherever had she got such unfortunate colouring? The Howarths were all wheaten, the Wildes glossy as crows. Probably from her mother's side. Alice, formerly Braithwaite-Wharmby, the nut-brown maid from Windygate farm. Now fifteen years a wife, and neither nut-brown nor maid any longer!

'... in WITNESS Whereof I have hereunto set my Hand to this my Will this ninth day of September, 1812....'

Craning his head slightly, William could see the fine Italian hand, adopted by Charlotte from her mother Dorcas, stalking across the page. So that was that.

Noiselessly, the ironmaster's secretary entered the dining room, to stand unobtrusively by the long doors. His manner and timing were perfect: two of the reasons why William employed him.

The meeting was moving gently to its close when eight-year-old Mary Howarth suddenly burst into a passion of tears. Everyone started out of the trance induced by Mr Hurst's modulated voice. Alive, unable to reach her daughter, scolded in whispers for her to behave herself. Dick Howarth, scarlet with embarrassment and grief, lifted and dropped his hands helplessly, torn between loyalty to wife and child.

At a sign from Zelah up rose the ironmaster's second daughter Catherine, a silvery girl of seventeen summers, and bore the small mourner away to be dried and comforted. The secretary, standing courteously to one side, managed to convey disapproval of the lapse without seeming disrespectful. The assembly, as though given permission, was fractured with coughs and comments.

'Our Mary,' said Dick in explanation, 'were right fond of our Lottie.'

'Mary weeps for us all, my dear,' said Zelah kindly, and made everything well again.

The ironmaster cleared his throat and consulted his silver watch. Majestically, he crossed the room and pulled a bell-rope: watched by all eyes. Servants appeared, and opened white-and-gold doors to the rooms beyond.

'Shall we take refreshment together?' asked Zelah, smiling.

William was walking away from them. His secretary hurried at his side, reading out the programme of the day, which began with a public ceremony in Snape Market Place at one o'clock, when the ironmaster was to carve the first slices of roast ox and order the festivities to begin. His part in this family proceeding was now over. His wife would see that their guests were watered and fed. He was free to put away the thought of death, to get on with the business of the world about him. His love and grief for Charlotte

23

were sincere, but the moment was all. Effortlessly, he wiped his sister from his mind.

'What word from Swarth Moor, Tom?' he asked, in his tone which was half-threat and half-friendship.

'Not too good, I'm afraid, sir. They tried to drain Prospect mine again yesterday, but Edgeworth says it filled up like a bladder.'

'The Cornishman will sort that out for us,' said William, sounding more convinced than he felt. 'Where is the damned fellow?'

'We've heard no more, sir, since his last letter a week ago, in which he said he would be here before the end of the month.'

'Well, he's a confounded nuisance. But he'll drain Prospect for us. And the others. You'll see, Tom. He's the best there is at this game. The only trouble is that everyone else knows it. Can't get the damned fellow to name a date. Before the end of the month, indeed. It *is* the end of the month, Tom!'

'Should I send word to the Royal George, sir, to see if he's arrived there?'

'No, deuce take it! What use would he be today? The valley's like a damned great fair from one end to the other. Why should I invite him to come and loll about here at my expense? No, let him stay where he is and cool his heels for a bit. That'll teach him to speak of the end of the month. End of the month!' Then he switched, coming at once upon his secretary's thoughts. 'And what are they all saying about my bargain over the colliery, Tom? Eh? Saying that Ralph Kersall sold me a pup?'

'Something of that sort, sir,' the man replied lightly.

'Something a damned sight worse than that, if I know them! They're mean-spirited, Tom, and small-minded. They have no vision to sustain them. I have two mottoes, Tom, which you would do well to observe. Never accept an easy way out of a difficulty. Always accept a challenge.'

The secretary said nothing. He had heard the ironmaster hold forth a thousand times, and none of the advice applied

24

to him, nor would he be tolerated did he choose to follow it. While William, glancing sideways at this dependable dependant, clapped one big hand heartily upon the narrow shoulder as they walked together. For he liked the idea of good fellowship between master and man, and even more did he like to be seen exercising that rare virtue.

'At any rate, I look after my people better than Kersall does,' said the ironmaster, as though he answered some invisible accuser.

This was true. His ironworks was run on Quaker lines, with a sound system of apprenticeships, a workman's benefit society, its own medical staff and a health scheme. Hillside Estate was owned by William's company, who built the sturdy cottages – each with its patch of garden and a pigsty – and rented them to employees for between a shilling and one and sixpence a week.

Recently, the ironmaster had branched into communal recreation. With his encouragement, Snape Botanical Society had been formed, whose members rambled for miles upon a Sunday afternoon, collecting specimens of wild flowers. A cricket club was in the process of evolution, with the help of a subsidy to purchase equipment. The Company Offices were compiling a library of books, to be lent to skilled and learning workmen. There was a school, a church and a chapel for the nourishment of mind and soul, and plans for building more as the population grew. Whatever the ironmaster forgot his wife remembered, and he was always generous when petitioned.

'Look after your people,' William said, 'and they and their children will belong to you!'

His easy manner was popular among them. To see him in his grandeur, pausing to kick a football which had gone astray, cheering the teams from the edge of a field he had donated, was a heart-warming spectacle. He had a way of righting some fallen toddler, of patting a brave lad on the head and giving him a ha'penny for treacle toffee, of asking a little lass the name of her doll, which delighted folk.

Whereas the valley's feudal overlord, faced by these new strident masters of industry, was retreating into a more graceful past. Old Humphrey Kersall had died the previous spring, and Ralph was not the fighter his father had been. The Kersall blood, once that of well-born adventurers, was thinning. Their luck was running out, their hold loosening. They kept themselves to themselves, stayed within the charmed circle of the aristocracy, pursued eccentric hobbies, built follies and improved their gardens.

'Finished,' said the ironmaster. 'The Kersalls are finished. That's why the idiot sold me those three mines. He hadn't the guts to try to drain them himself! Eh, Tom?'

Daring the secretary to contradict him.

'Well, let us see what the post has brought,' said William, sitting down at his desk at last. 'For once I step outside the front door today I shall not be back until night!'

Wherever the ironmaster went his people either set up a quasi-throne for him or built a rostrum. Today he was furnished with both. Only the Howarths' lustrous black reminded folk that they had sustained a sorry loss. Otherwise they played their parts with decorous enthusiasm. When William took off his tail coat and rolled up the sleeves of his fine white shirt, as though he were a workman about to embark upon a dirty job, the crowd laughed outright. And when he cracked a joke as he sharpened his butcher's knife and eyed the huge roast ox, they fairly roared appreciation. Simply to be present was to participate in a glorious event: as though a god had descended from Olympus and mingled with mortal men.

The boiling parts of the beast were stewing in a vast iron pot, upon which was stamped the two-headed mark of Belbrook Foundry, justifiably famous for its municipal cauldrons. And to this humbler feast came the poor, carrying jugs that they might receive their fill of beef juice and a lump of meat. Every baker in the district had worked throughout the night to provide the stalls full of free bread. Every brewer had rolled out every available barrel of beer.

And all at the expense of the ironmaster.

The ox being tasted, and pronounced delicious, the Howarths led the way to the new public park where an entertainment had been arranged for them, and a covered pavilion erected against rain or sun, whichever chose to weep or shine upon the occasion. There they sat attentively while twenty children in their best clothes danced round the maypole.

Then the newly-formed Upperton and Snape Choral Society sang, accompanied by Cunshurst Brass Band: both companies zealous but somewhat thin in ranks and sound.

The tenor, Arnie Bracegirdle, pleased the ladies most, for he was a handsome fellow and his message poured forth on the summer air. '*Their sound is gone out into all lands, and their words unto the ends of the world.*' And the ironmaster shook his head and wiped his eyes at its brevity and beauty.

But then a giant stood up, Isaac Lawler who worked in the cannon foundry, and his voice thundered across the turf and reverberated the little bells on the striped awning. Massive he was in all respects, and he hectored them and the universe. '*Why do the nations so furiously rage together? And why do the people imagine a vain thing?*'

Inspired by such compelling questions the chorus launched themselves into '*Let us break their bonds asunder....*' And William smote his knees in joy and admiration for he loved a good round barrage of music.

Then they followed Handel with Haydn, and sang the Gloria from his *Mass in Time of War*, and finished with Purcell's fifth anthem from Queen Mary's funeral music, '*Blessed are they that fear the Lord*', and smiled triumphantly as the applause rose in volume.

And the ironmaster clapped his hands and stamped his feet and asked if Isaac Lawler would sing once more, which the giant obligingly did, though very scarlet of countenance. But however embarrassed he might be about his sudden eminence his voice did not betray him. A Vulcan of a bass, it growled out its eternal questions: mighty, sonorous, godlike. And William nodded, and wiped his eyes again, for he understood this. It was about power and glory and endurance. Faith, hope and charity were all very well and he paid them lip service and pocket service too, but the power he understood. So that afterwards his people smiled and said to one another, 'Eh, didn't he enjoy himself? God bless him!'

Then the family went the rounds of the fairground, where oranges were two for a penny-ha'penny; and William, seeing some children short of halfpence, threw down a sovereign and bought up the whole of one woman's wares, and bestowed them widely. He avoided the boxing and wrestling matches because Zelah abhorred violence, and their daughters were too young and gently-bred to enjoy such displays. So they were escorted home to take tea and rest in the privacy of Kingswood Hall, before changing into finer finery for the evening banquet and firework display.

But the ironmaster himself joined a crowd of his workmen to watch a purring match. Right from the beginning he was there when two colliers, stripped to their drab tights and vaunting their bulging muscles, glowered at one another while watchers laid bets.

The two men wore brutal, brass-nailed, iron-toed clogs with which to kick and tear the other's flesh; and would throttle as they kicked, in the Lancashire fashion. Being well matched, neither would give way for a long time. And the spectators sharply drew in breath, and bit tongues, and winced and groaned and licked their lips, as each vicious blow went home. Until one collier fell to the ground at last and could not rise, and both were red with each other's blood and their own, and their faces mere obliterations.

Then the victor smashed his sticky clog into the victim's side, and they heard his ribs snap like stalks. And saw there was nothing more to be had out of either man, and walked away sated.

'That were a bit of all right, then, eh, Master?' said

William's neighbour, hands in pockets, holiday hat to one side of his rough head.

And William replied, as he would have answered one of his father's farm labourers in his youth, 'Aye, it were that, Fred!'

But not in the least condescendingly. Man to man. That was what they loved about him. And yet there was a line they could not, would not have crossed. For he was the ironmaster, after all.

TWO

The Cornishman

The man who had played a part in the ironmaster's thoughts that morning was, that evening, stepping down with his fellow-passengers from the Manchester–York Flyer. The great day in Millbridge was done, leaving only its litter behind. The last bonfire guttered on a hill, the last firework exploded, the last drunkard tumbled into his ditch. Descending from the magical to the mundane, entertainers quarrelled over their takings, packed their belongings, and prepared to move on. A few late revellers howled and cat-called in the sleeping High Street. And in the quiet market square scraps of paper scuttled before the night wind.

'Half-an-hour for refreshment, ladies and gentlemen!' cried the guard, consulting his watch.

The coach-driver came down stiffly from his perch. The ostlers led away the tired horses and harnessed a fresh team. The landlord smiled and bowed in that oblong patch of light and warmth which was his doorway. The landlady smiled and curtsied before that munificence which was her supper table. Maids and manservants hurried to and fro, carrying plates and dishes. A fire roared up the chimney-back. Ladies departed in search of chamberpots. Gentlemen lifted their coat-tails and turned their backsides to the hearth. And the ironmaster's consultant engineer made himself known.

'Mr Vivian, of course, sir!' the landlord said, as though the Royal George had been waiting a century and a half to meet this particular guest. 'We've given you Number Six, sir, overlooking the gardens at the back. Very quiet and comfortable. Shall you join the company, sir, or take supper in your room? Arthur'll fetch your luggage up.'

Hal Vivian was unusually tall for a Cornishman, but he had the dense black hair and rich complexion of his race. His air was that of a person who is used to travelling. His speech that of an educated man.

'He can take this up if he likes,' said Vivian, holding out a modest portmanteau. 'It's all I have. And all I need, come to that!' And he grinned at the landlord. 'I'll sup down here by the fire, Mr . . .?'

'Tyler, sir. Benjamin Tyler.'

'You keep a fine old hostelry, Mr Tyler.'

'We do our best, sir. I think I can say we have something of a reputation hereabouts!' Smiling, well-pleased.

'Aye, so I have heard. Well, Mr Tyler, I'll take a portion of your good wife's pie before it is all ate up!' Of the glazed brown delicacy.

'Plenty more where that come from, sir. Sit you down. Florrie! Look after this gentleman, will you? He's got more time than the others. What about a bottle of claret to go with the pie, sir? We keep a fair cellar here. A fair cellar, I think you'll find.'

'I leave it to you, Mr Tyler. I trust your judgement entirely.'

Then he turned to a lady sitting near him and made some remark which brought her to smiling attention, and also attracted the interest of the man opposite. Within moments the little party was laughing together as they had laughed often in the coach on their way here. For the Cornishman travelled the length and breadth of the country, and had a story in his head for every occasion. Moreover, being a bachelor in his early twenties with a vigorous business and a healthy delight in life, he was much in demand with the ladies. Mammas cast favourable eyes upon him. But papas shook their heads and smiled slily, sensing that this fox would not be caught if he could help it. And any girl who thought that a pretty bosom and a pair of slim ankles might fetch him to his knees was sadly mistaken.

The landlady cut the pie with a generous maternal hand,

31

and laid a slice before him. The landlord carried up the bottle as though it were an infant, dusting it tenderly before drawing the cork, pouring a taste into Vivian's glass, watching the young man sip and smile and nod in appreciation. Then the Cornishman again addressed himself to the company, leaving his wine and pie untouched. Until the guard brought forth his dictator of a watch, and the coach party gathered themselves and their cloaks and coats together for the next stage, leaving a legacy of crumbs and silence.

Now he could eat and drink at last with relish.

'Your health, Mr Tyler!' he cried, as the landlord hovered at his elbow. 'Will you join me in a glass of this venerable wine, or are you too busy to stop and talk?'

'No, sir, I'm more or less free now. That was the last coach to come through afore the London-to-Carlisle at a half-after-six tomorrow morning. I'll take a glass with pleasure, thankee.'

The Royal George had ceased its bustle and was being made ready for first breakfast.

'You're the gentleman as Mr Howarth was expecting, aren't you, sir?' asked the landlady, moving between table and fireside, setting the room to rights.

'I am indeed, ma'am. And shall be on my way to Snape tomorrow morning, with the help of a horse from your stables.'

Landlord and guest sat and drank in a comfortable silence, and Hal Vivian looked all about the room as though he would search the very corners for knowledge. Then, jerking his chin at the blackened beams above their heads he said, 'How old is he, Mr Tyler?'

'He, sir? Mr Howarth do you mean?'

'No, no. I beg your pardon. That's a trick of speech I learned from my father. I mean, how old is this hostelry, Mr Tyler?' Smiling.

'Oh, the old George? Built in the reign of King Charles the Second just afore the Plague, sir. 1664. Called The Royal Oak then, in honour of the King's escape, like. But when the first Hanover come to the throne it was changed to The Royal George. And, excepting for two new signs being painted, the George it's stayed ever since.'

'I love these old houses,' said Hal Vivian with great simplicity. 'If you have no objection, Mr Tyler, I have a few letters to write before I go to bed, and should like to write them here in the warm.'

'There's a fire laid in your room, sir. We could light it in a minute and no bother.'

'I'd sooner stay here. I like the feel of the place. It will keep me company in the small hours. I'm a fanciful fellow, Mr Tyler!'

'Just as you please, sir. Arthur'll be here if you want anything.'

'If you set a pot of coffee by the fire I can look after myself.'

But this the landlord would by no means allow. For what would become of the Royal George's reputation if it were ever known that a wakeful guest had been left unattended?

So, at well past midnight, the Cornishman sat with his portable writing desk upon his knees: a clever little contraption which he had produced from the depths of the portmanteau. And he began to deal with his correspondence. The long clock ticked sedately on. Hal Vivian scratched away, shedding letters to right and left: not a few at all, but a dozen or more. Orders, answers, advice, requests: some of them accompanied by sketches of machinery or plans of mine-shafts, adits, workings. Until the sentinel Arthur fell asleep from sheer weariness, a white napkin over one arm, and was only brought back to consciousness by the sound of coals falling. And saw the Cornishman replenishing his fire from the scuttle. His tasks were evidently done, but he sat back in his chair, legs crossed and hands clasped behind his head, musing.

His social manner dropped, he seemed gentler, less robust: a different man entirely from the cheerful companion of the coach journey, or the genial traveller who chatted with the landlord. His eyes were very pale and

33

fine, crystal-grey and contemplative. A smile hovered on his mouth as though he remembered something which both awed and delighted him.

'Whatever's he thinking of at this hour in the morning?' Arthur wondered, before he dozed off again.

Such images, known and conjectured, past and present and future, practical and fantastic. Such a world of marvels passing before his eyes. And he the man to try to realise all of them, and young enough to believe he could do so.

Though he could not have slept more than three hours the Cornishman rose early, ate and drank frugally, rode down the valley smartly, and found himself in the presence of the ironmaster as that gentleman read his newspaper at the breakfast table.

'Mr Vivian!' cried William, jumping up at once and extending his hand. 'We have been expecting you daily. Why did you not send word you had come? I should have ordered a carriage to fetch you.'

Equally cordial and at ease, Hal Vivian replied, 'Why, I could ride here as fast as I could send word, sir. And since I did not arrive in Millbridge until near midnight I would scarcely have disturbed you or your lady,' bowing respectfully to Zelah, 'at that hour.'

'Wilt thee sit down and join us, Mr Vivian?' Zelah asked.

'I have broke my fast, madam, but a cup of coffee would not come amiss, I thank you.'

The ironmaster's daughters made way for him with hospitable little cries. To hear their exclamations, one would think that a summer morning's ride of seven miles was an expedition to Peru. A footman brought up another chair. A fresh place was laid at the oval table in the window-bay. The sun shone pleasantly upon white napery and girls' faces. Everyone smiled upon the Cornishman.

'You will never remember my daughters' names, Mr Vivian,' said the ironmaster, as the young man sat down among them. 'For they have those with which they were baptised, diminutives of the same, and pet names which they have acquired with time. However, let us make a start! Upon one side of you is our fourth daughter, Olivia – Livvy – also called "Patch" – short for "Crosspatch". Childish squabbles dubbed her so. Quite unfairly, for she is now very sweet is our Livvy. Yes, you may give me a kiss, love. There, that's enough! I am besieged even at breakfast, Mr Vivian!'

Highly pleased. And God help any of them who did not so besiege him at frequent intervals.

'On your other side is our fifth daughter, Sophia – Sophy – otherwise "Sunny" – her nature is such. Sitting beside her mother is our sixth daughter, Maria – Molly – and "Tinker"!' A mischievous grin from this child. 'Sitting opposite you are our second and third daughters. Catherine is so grown up that I will not divulge particulars – she may be leaving us shortly, in any event. . . .' Kitty's colour became so brilliant that Zelah silenced further remarks with a warning look. 'And, Anna – pretty Nancy – alias "Pusscat"! Our eldest, Tabitha, married last year. Our youngest, Ruth, is up in the nursery. We reckon to be rather good at providing ourselves with beautiful daughters, do we not, love?'

His delight in his family was evident, but he fell silent for a while. There were no sons, that was clear, and the ironmaster minded the omission. Hal Vivian judged the lady who was presiding over the table to be in her forties: not a hopeful age for child-bearing. She was now taking over the conversation, presenting it in a new form to her husband as she would present a delicacy: purely to see if he would like it, would accept it. Most wives did this, and the Cornishman had observed their blandishments with varying degrees of contempt. But Zelah Howarth had made an art of management which in no way diminished her dignity nor that of her husband. He observed that though she used the Quaker speech she addressed him by the more usual prefix.

'My husband tells me that thee comes from Cornwall, Mr Vivian. My father, Caleb Scholes the ironmaster, hath

35

many business connections there. Where is thy birthplace?'

'Oh, I was not born there, madam. My father was, but like many Cornishmen he made his fortune away from home. My birthplace was in Liverpool, I believe.'

'And thy father was born...?' Zelah urged him gently.

For the ironmaster continued to stare moodily at the tablecloth, and had a visitor not been present would have buried himself in the *Wyndendale Post*.

'My father, Santo Vivian, came from Menheniot, near Liskeard.'

'Why, those names are poetry, Mr Vivian!' cried Zelah.

And her five daughters echoed her opinion.

'So you're really a Lancashire man, like myself,' said William, catching onto an aspect that related to him.

Hal Vivian seemed reluctant to agree, and Zelah sensed this.

'Oh, I cannot think of thee except as a Cornishman, Mr Vivian, for that is how thee wast presented to me!'

'Aye, but if his father did not stay there,' William argued, prepared to make difficulties, 'and he was not born there....'

The girl of fifteen, who had been introduced as Anna, now grinned mischievously and said, 'I suppose, Mr Vivian, that a Cornishman is much like a Scotchman, and the noblest prospect he sees is the road that leads into England!'

At this William threw back his head and laughed until the teacups tinkled in their china saucers. Whereat Anna looked triumphant, Zelah worried and relieved, and Hal Vivian paid the girl rueful respect. For she had diverted the ogre, which had evidently been her purpose. She smiled most charmingly at him now, and he smiled back to show that he forgave her for twitting him so openly.

'You see why we call her "Pusscat", Mr Vivian,' said the ironmaster jovially. 'A lightning dab of that pretty paw and we cower before her!'

'But we are what we feel ourselves to be,' said Zelah, firmly on the side of her guest, 'and Mr Vivian is a

36

Cornishman.'

Her tone was honeyed. Her meaning was clear. All the girls fell to questioning him about Cornwall. While the ironmaster protested that it was but a joke, and anyone knew that Vivian was an old Cornish name.

'Was thy mother Cornish, Mr Vivian?' Zelah asked graciously.

'No, madam, she was a Lancashire woman, born and bred. She died when I was a young lad of eleven.'

They saw that the remembrance was a painful one, and Zelah said something about the value of companionship between father and son after such a grievous loss.

'He was my best friend in all the world,' said the Cornishman, 'and the best father any son could hope for. He could not replace *her*' and here he paused momentarily, 'but she was our only lack.'

A silence threatened to ensue, which was warded off by the ironmaster pushing back his chair and throwing his newspaper to the carpet.

'These women are never satisfied,' cried William heartily, 'until they have picked a man's brain, broken his heart, and learned his history into the bargain! Come, Mr Vivian, you and I will talk of more serious matters.'

And he laughed again, that loud and cheerful sound which sent all sorrows packing, and threw his arm round the Cornishman's broad shoulders, and led him forth to earn his living.

The secretary laid out a map of the Wyndendale Valley upon the long table in the library, and stood by with a sheaf of papers containing facts and figures. Ill at ease, but determined to stay in full command of the situation, was Edgeworth, the ironmaster's chief engineer. He was a lean man of truculent disposition, who found engines more interesting than people. The ironmaster kept himself apart, in the splendour of his age and authority, proposing to set one man against the other in order to obtain the best results.

Introductions were made. Vivian and Edgeworth

nodded briefly and shook hands with abrupt courtesy. They were on their mettle and they knew it. William Howarth had taken an expensive risk, and they must make it pay if they could.

'Put Mr Vivian into the picture, Ted,' said the ironmaster amiably, and prowled towards the window, hands behind his back, listening.

Edgeworth's manner was as plain and forthright as his countenance, and the Cornishman guessed that he came from a poor family and had fought for his opportunities. But William obviously enjoyed his sardonic humour, and emitted a deep *Ha*! at certain dry remarks.

'This is a map of our valley, Mr Vivian,' Edgeworth began, 'with Millbridge at one end and Garth at t'other. Going from rich to poor, as you might say! Here's Snape Foundry on one side of the river. Further up on the other side is the coalfield known as Swarth Moor. This here coalfield is about five mile long, from Childwell to Whinfold, and two mile broad, covering four big estates and a number of small 'uns. With ten collieries on it, run mainly by Liverpool and Manchester business companies as'd soon cut your throat as shake your hand!'

A laugh from the ironmaster.

'Otherwise owned by one or two old squires and fat clergymen as'd also sooner cut your throat, etcetera...'

Another laugh. Edgeworth was encouraged.

'Now Mr Howarth has just taken on the lease of the biggest colliery from Lord Kersall – who either owns or has interests in most of the other mines. That's the piece, shaded in red, by the side of the Charnock Fault. Tarbock Colliery it's called. And Mr Howarth's architect who has a precious sort of mind,' Hal Vivian guessed that Edgeworth did not like him, 'tells us that Tarbock means "the brook where the hawthorn trees grow" – and very wet and thorny it is!'

The ironmaster's laugh was a ghost of its usual self.

'Lord Kersall's family has worked this colliery since 1784 and done well out of it. It were a colliery owner's dream to start with – good outcrops, shallow workings, quality coal – but then the seam run out and they had to go deeper. Lord Kersall's master-borer put down over one hundred bore-holes on the downthrow side, and found coal at two hundred and forty fathoms. So they sunk a new shaft – which ain't cheap!'

He was forgetting his resentment, and began to talk to the Cornishman as to an equal who would understand his difficulties.

'The bloody pit filled up like a pig's bladder! So they cut another sough – another adit – and that cost more than tuppence! And it were summer-time, and a miller dammed the sough water for his mill, and the bloody sough blocked. And there were so much blackdamp in it that the men wouldn't go down to work! The pumping engine couldn't drain it, and the new pit flooded worse nor ever.

'The water were coming in at the rate of a million gallons a day! At one point it boiled up! *There's* the new sough, all five hundred and forty feet of it, joining the old sough seven hundred and fifty feet from the mouth. And it crosses the Charnock Fault – which makes it merry hell to maintain!'

The Cornishman was nodding, registering each fact, chin in hand.

'Then they reckoned they'd spent time and money enough, and they put the pit up for sale. Twenty acres of it. And advertised it all over the place. But nobody would bite – and I can't say as I blame them! – until Mr Howarth come up with an offer. . . .'

Here the ironmaster strode from his window to speak his piece.

'I, too, have eyes and ears and master-borers, Mr Vivian,' he said briskly, genially. 'And way down Tarbock is a treasure-house of coal, if only we can get to it! But I was not to be fobbed off with a waterlogged pit, and so I told his lordship – he and I are old friends, by the by – that if he put up the whole colliery, together with his pumping engine and all other materials, I would be interested to take the problem off his hands. I made an offer which appeared generous, but was in fact merely a little fortune to catch a greater one!'

Edgeworth could not allow this. It was not in him to baulk at the truth, and he had no love or skill for diplomacy.

'Come on, Mr Howarth! Tell Mr Vivian what the other pits was like! That's only fair. Lord Kersall couldn't get a damned one of them dry, now could he? There's nigh on five hundred million gallons in Prospect alone by now! It's like trying to drain the River Wynden. And I advised against buying, and I still say it were a wild offer! A wild offer, sir!'

And he smote the plan in disgust.

'Then why do you think I made it, man?' cried William, voice and temper and colour rising.

'Because you could never refuse a risk, Mr Howarth, I reckon!'

This was so close to the truth that they fell silent for a moment. Then the ironmaster recovered.

'Mr Vivian, I have got to my present position by taking risks. I have had my failures, of course, but I have never made a *bad* mistake. There is an instinct in me that says Tarbock shall not fail!'

And he folded his arms and thrust out his bottom lip, while Hal Vivian sat reading the notes.

'Of course, the life of a pit is short,' William broke in, unable to keep quiet. 'We shall be sinking other shafts as well as this!'

'The place is like a bloody colander already!' said Edgeworth gloomily. 'The plan they give us warn't complete. It only goes back fifteen year! They acted like bloody pirates – all loot and no records!'

'Mr Vivian,' said the ironmaster, ignoring his chief engineer, 'it is only Prospect pit we are considering at the moment. Not any others.'

'Prospect!' muttered Edgeworth, and clicked his tongue.

The Cornishman said, fascinated, 'And was Lord Kersall

attempting to drain this pit with a sixty-three inch rebuilt single-acting Smeaton engine, working bucket-lift pumps? I am not surprised at the results, sir! Only that such an engine still exists!'

'It is in good condition,' said William defensively, then hurried to amend his statement. 'But of course I know we shall need another. I saw an advertisement in the *Wyndendale Post* this week for a secondhand seventy inch Watt engine from a mine in Charndale. Only a few hundred pound!'

'It'll be clapped out,' said Edgeworth, 'and the price of fetching it here would double the cost.'

'Kindly hold your tongue, sir, while Mr Vivian gives us his opinion!' cried the ironmaster, incensed. But could not resist leading the Cornishman to an opinion which coincided with his own. 'I believe that if we convert the old engine from bucket-lift to plunger-lift, and have another and newer engine working alongside, the problem is solved.'

The Cornishman looked fully at William, and his eyes were so light in his dark face that they glittered like rock crystal. The ironmaster was momentarily discomposed by the intensity of this gaze, which was both piercing and abstracted. As though Hal Vivian were thinking, 'Who is this fellow to tell me my business?' And yet simultaneously to answer, 'Well, he is not worth my while, after all.'

'I thought you asked me here, sir, to give a considered judgement on the matter,' said Hal Vivian coolly. 'If you merely wanted your own ideas corroborated I should have thought it cheaper to ask a friend.'

In a flash of temper William replied, 'Well, now you mention it, sir, I did think your fee somewhat exorbitant for so young a fellow.'

'My fee is in proportion to my company's skill and reputation, sir. And now you have got me here you will pay it, whether you take my advice or no,' said the Cornishman.

'I don't care a tinker's damn about the fee,' William

growled, realising that he could lose this argument. 'You are too sensitive, by far. Give us your advice, sir, since that is what you are here for.'

'I shall need to inspect the colliery before I commit myself fully, of course,' said the Cornishman composedly. A glint in his pale eyes spoke of ill news gladly given. 'But you will need a large new pumping engine. There is no cheap answer to an expensive problem, sir.'

The ironmaster turned about and strode over to the window.

'Very well, Mr Vivian,' he said, grim but amenable. 'You know more of these matters than I do. Each man to his own profession. How much, approximately speaking, might such an engine cost?'

'Well, you could save money by constructing some or most of it at your own foundry. On the market it would be in the region of six to eight thousand pounds. And you can add another two thousand for the house, stack and boiler-house. Which does not take into account the cost of erecting the engine, digging the road and site, and so on.'

Unwisely, Edgeworth cried, 'I told you, Mr Howarth! I said! Now didn't I? That's good day to ten thousand pound afore we start!'

'And you may need new tramways on the site,' the Cornishman continued smoothly, as though the atmosphere were not already smouldering. 'Perhaps a locomotive-engine to draw your coal-wagons?'

The ironmaster burst into one of those calculated rages with which he usually subdued all opposition.

'I am not a nincompoop, sir. I know that the purchase of a new engine puts money in your pocket. A fee for consultation. Another for designing the damned machine. Yet another for supervising its erection. And a fat annual retainer atop of that.'

The Cornishman rose without haste, handed back the notes to William's secretary, and straightened his waistcoat.

'If we cannot converse in the manner of two gentlemen,

sir,' he observed quietly, 'I may well go about my business and leave you to your own devices. I am not in your employ, sir, unless I choose. And then only temporarily.'

He stood face to face with the ironmaster, unimpressed and unafraid. They were much the same height and William found the experience slightly disturbing. He was accustomed to dominate men physically as well as mentally. Slowly the crimson flush left his neck and forehead. He smiled shamefacedly, laughed splendidly, and shook Hal Vivian by both hands.

'I like a man who knows his own mind,' said William. 'You are free to go where you wish, to look into anything you please. Ted here will show you round.' Patting Edgeworth's shoulder. 'And Tom keeps all the facts and figures.' Nodding amiably at the secretary. 'They are both clever fellows in their fashion. Use them, Mr Vivian, use them.'

He waved dismissal. The secretary left the room as unobtrusively as he could. Edgeworth tramped sturdily out.

'Sit down, Mr Vivian, sit down,' said the ironmaster genially. 'I accept your advice, and shall be pleased to offer you the hospitality of Kingswood Hall for as long – and as often – as is needful. I shall send to the Royal George for your baggage immediately.'

'Sir,' said the Cornishman, smiling but inexorable, 'I should prefer to stay at the Royal George. I find it more conducive to good work if I can retire at the end of each day to neutral ground. I must refresh my energy if I am to spend it properly. You are most kind in your offer, sir. It grieves me to refuse you.'

'Refuse?' said the ironmaster.

He tried the word over on his lips. It was strange to them.

'And if it is agreeable to you, sir, I should like to pass the rest of the day at your colliery. I can report back to you this evening, if that is convenient.'

William's lips were still stiff from their encounter with that extraordinary refusal.

'You will dine with us?' he asked uncertainly.

'I shall be delighted to do so, sir.'

'We dine at a half-past six o'clock.'

'I shall be punctual, sir.'

'And you will then return to Millbridge?' Unbelieving.

'With your permission, sir.'

'With or without my damned permission!' grumbled the ironmaster, but smiled to himself as well. 'Off with you, Cornishman!' he cried. 'Here, take this note; it shall be your passport.'

And he scrawled the freedom of the realm upon a sheet of paper, and signed it very large as became a man of power.

'Good day to you, Mr Howarth,' said Hal Vivian, bowing.

And made his departure in great style.

The girl skipped back smartly from the library door, at which she had been listening with glee, and dropped a deep and demure curtsey. The Cornishman recognised her as being one of the older daughters, but their names and faces eluded him. So he bowed in an abstract fashion, being full of his victory, and forgot her immediately.

But Anna came up out of her curtsey and stood looking after him. All the ironmaster's daughters had inherited their mother's colouring in various degrees, from richest gold to ash. Anna's hair was silver-gilt. Her eyes slanted a little at the corners. Her nose was pert and turned slightly upwards at the tip. Her mouth was soft, pink and determined.

So she stood there, very pretty, very impudent, very sure of herself on that bright summer morning. And watched Hal Vivian stride victoriously away.

'I shall marry that man,' said Anna Howarth to herself.

THREE

News

The *Wyndendale Post* had been the valley's principal newspaper for over sixty years. Anybody of consequence read it, reported their social gatherings and business successes to it, and savoured the sight of their names in its ponderous columns. No other journal had challenged its supremacy as a local paper. And with the confidence of established power, the Tory *Post* permitted such Whigs as came of respectable families to air their grievances in the correspondence section. Thus it felt able to declare itself an Independent paper, though everyone knew that Kersall money backed it and the Kersalls dictated its policy.

Office and printing-shop were to be found at No.12 Market Place, Millbridge, where the *Post* had begun life with a dim bow window and a small tin sign. Time and prosperity had transformed these into a handsome stone front and a gleaming brass nameplate. And whereas early editors had been inky hacks, Arnold Thwaites was known to dine with such of the lesser gentry as found a use for him.

On the opposite side of Market Place, at No.17, was the late Miss Warburton's sweetshop: a mere sliver of a building, sandwiched between Buckley's Millinery and Unsworth's Family Grocers. This had been empty for above a year, and two or three Millbridge shopkeepers had toyed with the notion of renting it for storage. But being only one room wide and three stories high, with a dusty attic and damp basement, the premises were inconvenient. And since Miss Warburton had lived in genteel poverty all her life, her house had decayed with her and needed

45

considerable restoration before it could be used. Then at last, in the winter of 1815, there were signs of activity. Shutters were fetched down and windows thrown up to air the place. The roof was repaired, floors renewed or strengthened, panes of glass replaced, shelves and cupboards built, and the little shop painted inside and out.

All this was done with such secrecy that each shopkeeper suspected his fellow of expansion, until it was rumoured that the premises had been taken by two gentlemen from London. This caused a flutter of interest, without chagrin, for No. 17 as a single business was not large enough to offer competition worthy of the name. They might be hatters or shoe-makers! said Braithwaite's Gentlemen's Outfitters charitably. A small confectionery or muffin shop! suggested the lordly Millbridge Bakery. Another sweetshop! cried all the children hopefully. For they had loved Miss Warburton whose scales were loaded in their favour.

At any rate no one minded and everyone speculated until that blustering March day when the wagon of furniture arrived. The youngest apprentice on the *Post* was straightway stationed at the window to report progress. While Owd Bob, the master-printer, interpreted his commentary over the noise of the press.

'Two iron bedsteads, single. Two jugs, basins and chamber-pots. One deal table. Four rush-bottomed chairs. One rag rug. . . .'

'Ah! Them two gentlemen is a-camping on the premises at present!'

'One clerk's desk and high stool, one drawing table. . . .'

'Some sort of office, then.'

'Bales o' paper – eh up!' As the mystery cleared. 'Dammee!' cried the youngest apprentice, forgetting himself. 'if it ain't a. . . .' For being shunted, edged, pushed and cursed through the front door of No. 17: secondhand at the very least, unsophisticated without a doubt, but ready to go the moment its handle was cranked. . . .'

46

'A printing press!' shrieked the apprentice.

And they all came running.

'Some jobbing printer?' said one. 'Nay, they told us they was gentlemen!' said another. 'Specialists in small editions?' said a third.

Then they were transfixed by the sight of the new owners themselves, who had sauntered over from the Royal George, unnoticed. They were dandified young men: one not particularly tall, the other decidedly short. Their fawn top hats were set at a killing angle. They made an art of gesture with their malacca canes.

'*He* looks familiar,' said Owd Bob, peering at an immaculate back.

The workmen were now hanging the answer to a final question, and the *Post* staff watched in silence. The sign was not as grand as their brass plaque, but it swung jauntily in the wind, full of pluck and impudence. Beneath it hung a miniature trumpet, and in black and gold upon a green ground was emblazoned a challenge. The *Clarion*.

At that precise moment the gentleman in chocolate-brown broadcloth, whose linen was an ode to purity, whose black stock was an elegy of mourning, turned deliberately round. And seeing the clutch of astounded faces at the window of the *Post* raised his hat with a flourish and made a bow of exaggerated courtesy.

'By gum!' said Owd Bob, confounded. 'It's bloody Ambrose Longe!'

The ironmaster was not concerned with such tittle-tattle as the letting of obscure shops in Millbridge. Nor, once the Will had been read, was he concerned with his nephew. And Ambrose, master of the gesture and keeper of greater secrets than William dreamed of, preferred to announce his presence and intentions like a thunderclap. So the news was served up to William at breakfast, in the shape of a letter attached to a handbill, and caused him to cast his porridge spoon back into its bowl with disastrous results.

'Good God, what is this all about?' cried the ironmaster.

'Great heaven, why should this be?' he exclaimed, stamping round the morning room and bringing his Maker to account.

Anna rescued the sheets of paper from beneath the table with a quick pounce, and presented them to her mother. Zelah read them and passed them to Kitty. Rapidly, silently, each daughter possessed herself of the news. Then letter and handbill were put on William's side plate, and six golden heads bent demurely over their porridge again.

'It is monstrous! Unthinkable!' cried the ironmaster. 'You shall not receive him if he calls, Zelah. You girls will not so much as acknowledge his presence. I shall cut him dead in the street.'

'William, sit down and eat thy breakfast, love,' said Zelah tranquilly, 'or thee will suffer from indigestion all day.'

He smote his fist into the palm of his hand. His colour rose high.

'As if there had not been enough trouble from that branch of the family! Mind you, I do not blame poor Charlotte. She was the tool and victim of both Toby Longe and Jack Ackroyd. And that son of hers promises to go the way of his father. How has he raised the money? Has he sold Thornton House? I will not have it sold without my knowledge.'

'It is not sold,' said Zelah peaceably, 'and the present tenants are there until Michaelmas. And Ambrose says in his letter that he and his partner will live over the printing-shop on the rent money from Thornton House, until the newspaper is established.'

'Established? A treasonable rag like that! Live over the shop? He will be arrested and transported for sedition, more like.'

'I think not,' said Zelah. 'The paper is classed as Independent.'

One of Ambrose's many sly digs at The *Wyndendale Post*.

'And he hath written thee an open and an honest letter, love, hoping that we shall stay good friends though our opinions differ.'

'Differ? I should say they did! I shall support the *Post* up to the hilt. I shall not buy one single copy of *The Clarion*. I shall not allow that damned radical rag in my house!'

'But Ambrose is sending thee complimentary copies for twelve month, hoping thee will give his views a fair reading. And in *our* family' – she meant the vast national network of Scholeses – 'we read all newspapers. My father subscribes to journals of every persuasion.'

'Aye, well, he is more liberal in these matters than I,' William said drily, making liberalism sound like a peculiar vice.

Her little silence was eloquent. Then she spoke as drily in return.

'So thee will not meet thy sister's son halfway?'

'No, I shall not. I disown him. Charlotte's last political escapade nearly drove us from the valley. I had to resign my magistracy!' The injustice stung him. Tears came to his eyes. 'I was almost driven from my birthplace. Torn from my very roots!' he said heart-rendingly.

'I left my birthplace and my roots when I was twenty,' Zelah observed coolly, 'and all our daughters are like to do the same. And we survive. Besides, thee never visits Kit's Hill, and we never see Dick except there is a baptism, a wedding or a funeral.'

The ironmaster looked deeply at her and adjusted his silk stock.

'I have work to do,' he said reproachfully, and gave her a token kiss upon the cheek and left the room, full of moral indignation.

As soon as he had gone his womenfolk ordered fresh toast, and began laughing and chatting together, passing Ambrose's letter and handbill round the table, discussing this new project vivaciously.

'We must drive into Millbridge, Mama,' said Anna, 'and find out what is happening, and tell Cousin Ambrose our news. For will he not wish to report father's new Cornish pumping engine in his *Clarion*?'

49

'Oh, that old engine!' cried Molly, weary of the topic. 'Papa goes on and on about it, and Mr Vivian's letters make him stamp and shout.'

'Well, now he can stamp and shout about *The Clarion* instead,' Sophy suggested pertly, and avoided her mother's glance of rebuke.

'But Papa said we must not communicate with Cousin Ambrose!' Kitty reminded them, coming from her dream of the young Quaker merchant to whom she was engaged.

'Oh fig!' cried Livvy irreverently. 'He was only roaring round.'

'My dear girls,' said Zelah firmly, 'there is no question of visiting your cousin without your father's permission. But I do think Papa should let us explain to poor Ambrose why he is being cast out.'

Her daughters smiled at each other complicitly.

'It should not take you too long to get permission, Mama,' Anna remarked. 'Should we order the carriage and put on our best bonnets?'

On the official opening day No. 17 was crammed with well-wishers from attic to basement. People and packages jostled on the stairs. Bottles of claret jingled against jars of printer's ink, and only the press was silent. Ambrose Longe, already in his shirt-sleeves, stood by the new apprentice. The lad had been told what to do, and threatened with unmentionable retribution if he did it wrongly. He looked red and nervous by the side of his elegant master.

'Ladies and gentlemen! Friends! If you please!'

They hushed themselves and each other, from floor to roof. Those on the top storey craned over the well of the stairs to catch the editor's speech. And he lifted up his face that all might see him, and spoke out as though he were used to addressing a crowd.

'We are here today,' he cried, 'to witness the marriage of Honest Policy with Goodwill to All Men! For far too long the Wyndendale Valley has been pap-fed with such news as its overlords chose to nourish it. From today the valley shall have a fair choice.

'My partner, Jeremy Tripp, and I, have declared this paper to be Independent in policy, because we intend to report objectively. We shall keep an open mind. We shall not stoop to the usual mud-slinging and tale-telling practised by party newspapers. You will *never* read what we have been *told* to say. You will *always* read what we have seen for ourselves, and know to be true. And though we are in deadly earnest, you shall not find us dull or stuffy. We shall entertain as well as inform you. In short, your breakfast tables will be enlightened and enlivened at once.'

His manner became perceptibly less cavalier.

'The name we have chosen is a good name, a resounding name, a name for present and future, and a name we hope to be proud of. But I shall toast another name first. That of a magnificent weekly journal, published in the teeth of danger and adversity during the final decade of the eighteenth century, conceived by my late father Toby Longe, edited by my mother the late Charlotte Longe. The memory of whom and of which I keep locked in the most precious and private depths of my heart. Ladies and gentlemen, I give you – *The Northern Correspondent!*'

They raised their glasses and sipped in reverent silence.

'And now I ask you all to join me in wishing long life, good friends – and a few lively enemies' – there was some laughter at this – 'to *The Clarion.*'

'To *The Clarion!*' they cried joyfully.

'All right, Alfie?' Ambrose asked the apprentice.

Then, loudly, dramatically, 'Let her *go-o-o!*'

The lad applied himself to the handle with maniacal zeal, and clattered out the first copy.

There was a great cheer as Ambrose held up the sheet, which was the size of a small table-cloth, still damp with ink.

'Hurrah!' they all shouted.

As though the *Clarion* were a ship, now successfully launched.

FOUR

Deep Workings

The Cornishman had undoubtedly got the better of the ironmaster at their first meeting, and William Howarth accorded him respect for that. Indeed, an expert was no use to him if he could not stand up for himself, and therein lay a paradox. For the ironmaster, in his bitter lack of a son, would make favourites of talented young men, finding in them the seeds of his own greatness. And for a while all would be sunlight and encouragement. Then the quasi-son either failed to prove as gifted as William could wish, or his gifts demanded more independence than William chose to allow. And whichever way the matter fell out all was thunder and disenchantment.

Many such youths had been picked up and dropped again in the past fifteen years or so. The iron road of William Howarth's career was littered with the bodies of failed sons, while ever ahead of him stalked that desired, that elusive creation of himself, and would not be found.

No one had ever asked Zelah Howarth whether she wanted a son. She accepted the children she was given, and if the omission of an heir caused her personal grief then no one knew it.

For the time being, Hal Vivian had unwittingly stepped into the phantom's shoes and was staying the course remarkably well. Like the ironmaster he persisted in having his own way, and the breakfast table at Kingswood Hall, scene of each morning's post and newspapers, resounded with tales of the Cornishman's impudence and extravagance. The Howarth females steeled their nerves and consumed their porridge, knowing that when their lord had sputtered and grumbled to a close he would rise and leave them: to give orders, to accede to requests, to concur with suggestions made by the Cornishman. For the fellow knew very well how to appeal to his patron's pride, and would subtly offset the expense of the new pumping engine by praising its power and quality.

The conception was mighty, the fruition slow, the labour prodigiously hard. But this engine had long been one of Hal's dreams, and until he met the ironmaster had remained a bubble of the mind: a thing of wonder to be mused on when work was done and flames licked upwards on the chimney-back. Then, of a sudden, here was William with enough money to play business roulette. And here was he with an idea which would cost more money than anyone had cared to spend so far. And between them was a waterlogged mine which would benefit from such an alliance. But of course there were problems, beginning with the size.

'I considered a seventy inch cylinder to be adequate, myself,' cried the ironmaster, glaring at his minions, 'but should not have been surprised by the suggestion of an eighty inch. Even, knowing this fellow, I might imagine him capable of advising a ninety inch.' Here he paused for effect, while his audience looked and listened obediently. 'But what does he want? He wants the round century! One hundred inch! I never heard of such a monster. In fact, I believe he has conjured it up expressly to annoy me. Why, simply to cast that size of cylinder alone would require a degree of skill far beyond the ordinary. That much I know – and so, apparently, does he.' Hooking on his spectacles in order to read the letter more clearly. 'He says here that he believes it could only be cast – *only* mark you – at Coalbrookdale. Setting aside the cost and trampling upon my personal pride, he suggests *Coalbrookdale*. Is Francis Darby the only ironmaster and Coalbrookdale the only ironworks? How would he feel if I said, "Well, Mr Vivian, you are a very clever fellow, but I prefer to consult Mr Whatisname of somewhere else because he is the *only* man who can design an engine." How would he like that sort of remark? Eh?'

And so on. Venting his majestic displeasure upon the heads of his subordinates, since the culprit was not there to be chastised.

Hal Vivian continued to be independent, to appear without being summoned, to leave without being dismissed, and to make a sanctuary of the Royal George on his flying visits. Regal commands from the ironmaster, by post and messenger, could impede but would not stop him. He begrudged even the time taken to argue his case.

'I have too much to do, sir,' he would say impatiently. 'I cannot quibble over details.' Then observing the cloud upon Jove's brow, the sparks of quarrel in those hard black eyes, he would cry, 'Shall I go elsewhere, then? For I give you my word that this is the first and finest hundred inch engine in the country, perhaps in the world. And if you miss the chance of taking it then someone else shall have the glory, ironmaster. I know it is unique.' Spreading his hands protectively over his paper masterpiece. 'I know it!'

He was possessed and he could not be moved. He would not compromise one inch of his creation. At times like these his Cornish blackness became impenetrable, and his eyes as cold and pale as the winter sea.

'He's mad. I'm certain of it,' said the ironmaster, exasperated by Hal Vivian's obstinacy. 'I never met such a fellow. He must have been nursing this grandiose idea for years, waiting for some fool to buy it. Well, I am that fool. But how the deuce I got into such a situation I am at a loss to comprehend.'

William was like a man given a gold sovereign, who must try it again and again with his own teeth to make sure it is genuine. And as often as he sank his teeth into the Cornishman, without making any particular impression upon him, so often did he come to assert that Hal Vivian was a genius: thus implying that he himself was an enlightened and generous patron. And he began to defend the cost of the venture. For Ted Edgeworth had been right.

£10,000 was only a beginning.

The first months of 1816 were not especially severe, yet spring seemed reluctant to arrive. Even in mid-May the morning fields were white and crisp with frost, the hilltops venerable with snow. Piercing winds stabbed the tender buds. New-born lambs, cast upon hostile fells, perished before a shepherd could reach them. Leaves fluttered in black rags upon the trees. In June there were cruel squalls of rain and hail, and the hay harvest failed.

But long before the engine was assembled, in that bitter summer of 1816, local newspapers were agog for information. To these reporters of industrial progress William was grossly unfair: according the *Post* every facility, allowing the *Clarion* only such crumbs as it could pick up. No blame then to Ambrose Longe if he were forced to employ spies and thus throw light upon the darker side of the ironmaster's concerns.

So, though the *Post* announced WYNDENDALE WILL HAVE THE LARGEST PUMPING ENGINE IN THE WORLD! and followed this reckless declaration with ecstatic details, mostly inaccurate, the *Clarion* struck a different and a more challenging note. MEN ARE CHEAPER TO HIRE THAN HORSES!

'Ironmaster Howarth is regarded as an Enterprising Man in this Valley, having Created the whole of our newly-named District of Wroughton from Wasteland. He also enjoys the Reputation of being a Good Master, but apparently his Conscience stops Short at Tarbock Colliery, where they are Building a new Engine-house.

Yesterday we saw such Scenes of Slavery as we thought had been Abolished in this Country. Working for Twelve Hours at a time, Teams of Men were tethered like Beasts to unwieldy Slabs of Stone, and required to Haul them up the slopes of Swarth Moor. It was the Building of the Pyramids all over again! Only the Lash was absent – unless you count the Whips of Hunger and Necessity.

Why does Ironmaster Howarth not use Oxen or Horses for this Task? Because, we are told, Horses are Dearer to Feed! Dearer to Feed? Great God, are we to Mount these Towers of Babel upon Raw Backs and Empty Bellies? Is Ironmaster Howarth Trimming his Costs – which we understand to be Prohibitive – at the Expense of the Poorest in Our Midst. . . ?

And so on. Ambrose's partner, Jeremy Tripp, had illustrated this diatribe with a wickedly like caricature of William presiding over a pair of huge scales. The ironmaster was depicted as being made of iron. In one saucer of the scales rested bags of gold; in the other, a heap of ragged labourers had been flung higgledy-piggledy together.

On the morning this article appeared, Zelah Howarth decided that henceforth William must be persuaded to breakfast apart from them. But in the Royal George, lately arrived from Manchester to inspect progress, the Cornishman laughed until tears came to his eyes. Which made them seem more crystalline than ever.

'Monarch' was to be the official title of the great engine, but long before it was an entity the colliers referred to it as 'him' and nicknamed him 'King Billy'.

Every part of the monarch was both massive and heavy, and not all could be made at home. The hundred inch cylinder was cast by master craftsmen at Coalbrookdale, and when it had cooled they held an impromptu luncheon party for thirteen people inside its hollow hall. And cylinder and case together weighed thirty tons, and must be carried from Shropshire to Lancashire by water and land. Belbrook cast seven boilers, each thirty feet long and ten feet in diameter: and each boiler required twenty dray-horses to haul it, and a hundred men to act as brakes on the iron capstan ropes astern. The main beam and case were transported separately, since their combined weight came to six-and-forty tons: and each had a team of thirty horses and an attendant army to hold it back.

In this, the coldest June ever remembered, King Billy was assembled. To see such Gullivers being coaxed up the steep wastes of Swarth Moor was to see mankind at its Lilliputian best. What swearing and urging and terror, what shouting and straining, as the giant showed signs of crushing those who would create him anew. What triumph as the mighty part arrived in its proper place.

The ironmaster had decreed that both engine-house and boiler-house should be built of local stone, and great blocks of this gritty rock had been hewn and man-hauled to the site. While day after day, all day long, Albert Birtwhistle sat aloft with his bottle of beer and his red spotted handkerchief full of thick sandwiches, and directed the laying of stones one upon the other: perceiving instantly which slab would fit where, and being paid one shilling a week extra for this peculiar skill.

The ceremonial July day dawned grey and cold as November. But tar barrels burned on the hill, and church bells rang in the vale, and Wroughton Brass Band played rousing tunes to the waiting crowd. The engine-house could hardly be seen for bunting and evergreens.

The ironmaster had been liberal, as usual, with bread and beer for the multitude, wine and fine food for the gentlefolk. Now he stood at the head of his family, with his wife upon his arm, looking collected and handsome. King Billy's trial run, the previous day, had taken the edge from his anxiety, but the occasion was still momentous.

A pink silk rose bloomed upon the crown of Anna's new straw bonnet. The twirl of her parasol set the wintry weather at naught, but its fringes would jig in the wind. Nor did the ironmaster's third daughter shiver in her worked muslin gown, though her silk spencer did little to keep her warm. She was looking for the Cornishman, who had conceded to the cold by wearing a pale-grey overcoat trimmed with grey fur, and cuffed wellington boots. Her father was similarly attired. But all the ladies chose to be fashionable, even if it meant catching their deaths in the north-easter which bore down upon the assembly.

High stood King Billy in his four-storey keep, on the black stretch of Swarth Moor. Down below, five thousand faces were uplifted, to see the Cornishman emerge from a little door in the topmost storey and walk solemnly to the edge of the platform. The huge bob was poised motionless beside him, so that one marvelled at his daring to go up there alone in the shrivelling wind, with only a Colossus for company. They gave him a preliminary cheer, and listened for the words he shouted into the gale. First, the name of the shaft.

Then, 'I name . . . this engine . . .'

A valve was opening. The great bob was descending.

Hal Vivian stepped back, and cracked a bottle of the ironmaster's finest champagne across its iron snout.

Crying, '*Monarch!*'

The ghost of a 'hurrah' eddied in the wind, and was answered by a roaring breath. Eyes and ears were poised for a few seconds lest this be all. But again King Billy dipped his doughty bob, and drew a thunderous inhalation. And another, and another. Then they jumped and clapped and cried 'hurrah' again, and whipped off their hats in homage. For that little figure up on the towering platform, whose own hat had blown off, had created something far more powerful than himself and them. He had conceived an iron god before whom they inwardly knelt. The tears in his pale eyes were not entirely due to the wind.

Eight times in that first minute of his life did the monarch thrust deep into the rushing waters of the earth, and with each lordly sip at the gulf fetch up nine hundred gallons. His thirst was unquenchable, noble. Every hour he poured almost half a million gallons into the waiting launders: every day ten millions. Working without cessation, tireless in his cups, until the little ocean was drained dry.

Among the few who watched objectively was a dandified man of middle height, with a thin brown clever face and narrow dark eyes. And by his side lingered his companion, sketchbook in hand, who smiled and joked as he glanced continually from subject to drawing.

'Well, it is a splendid piece of engineering, Jem,' said Ambrose Longe, 'but they had no need to raise up an altar to it.'

'Oh, but they must,' said Jeremy Tripp. He spoke in rapid bursts, much as he drew. 'People must worship something, you know. They long to marvel. They need to see the power and the glory before their very eyes. If God and the Devil were able to make regular appearances there would be no more atheists. Trouble is – values are invisible.'

They made to depart from the festivities, but were waylaid by Kit's Hill Howarths in great numbers.

'Eh up!' cried Dick, face aglow with pleasure. 'You're knocking the stall over! How arta, lad?'

He held out his hand, first to his nephew and then more shyly to Jeremy Tripp. Alice nodded and smiled, uncertain whether to curtsey as well. Her presence at family gatherings was an embarrassment to herself and everyone else, and she longed to get back to her dairy. But Dick, like his father before him, cherished good fellowship and would continue to greet his relatives with affection.

'Going to write a nice piece about our William, then?' said Dick.

Ambrose knew that he did not read the *Clarion* or he would not have asked.

'How are you all?' he answered heartily.

For his mother had been fond of them, and in her memory he made conversation.

'Fair to middling,' said Dick. 'You should come and have your Sunday dinner with us sometime, shouldn't they, Alice?'

'You'd be more than welcome,' said Alice loyally. Distressed.

'Most kind,' said Ambrose, resolved never to set foot in Kit's Hill. 'Hello there, Mary. How you grow!'

'Grows sulky, more like,' said Alice in her natural voice.

'For goodness sakes, Mary, put a blessed smile on your face.'

'Leave her be,' pleaded Dick, shamefaced, for he loved this awkward girl, and only in his arms and under his protection did she flower a little.

'Say hello to your Cousin Ambrose,' Alice commanded.

The child moved her lips, looking sternly at him with grey-green eyes. She had inherited Charlotte's milky skin, and on her small white neck glowed Charlotte's locket. Ambrose's heart contracted at the sight of it. Inwardly he chided himself; outwardly said something un-complimentary about the weather. Dick's face lost its radiance.

'We'st all be clemmed this winter if t'hay harvest is owt to go by,' he said. 'Eh, I don't know, Ambrose,' and the name sounded exotic, foreign upon his chapped lips. 'It looks like one step forrard and two steps backard, all the time.'

'If we can help...' said Ambrose spontaneously, though they lived like mice, and from day to day, themselves.

Which brought back Dick's grin and a hearty disclaimer. But the conversation languished, which they all regretted.

'Are you still letting Thornton House, then?' Dick asked, for want of anything better to say.

'Until our poor fortunes increase – yes.'

'Well, if you're hard up, why don't you sell it?' Dick asked, who had no ties with Charlotte's home.

'I could,' said Ambrose, more lightly than he felt, 'and yet I would not like to lose it entirely.'

Then seeing that the ironmaster was coming that way he made a smiling excuse, and parted from them.

'We must have a word with our William,' said Dick cheerfully.

At which message of doom Alice gathered her brood together, and took a fresh grasp of the baby.

Mary lagged behind the family group, frowning and biting the side of her forefinger. For the Longes had

60

intrigued her from the first, being outsiders like herself. So she gazed crossly, yet wistfully, after Ambrose, until her mother called her to heel again.

The Cornishman had at last retreated from his admirers into the privacy of the engine-house, where Anna followed him.

'What can I do for you, Miss Howarth?' Ted Edgeworth asked.

And though he wore his best clothes in honour of the occasion he was wiping his hands on a lump of cotton waste, which his wife would not have been pleased to know.

'My father said Mr Vivian would show me the engine-house,' the girl replied composedly.

Had Zelah been present she would have known by the set of her child's mouth that Anna was in a wilful mood. Edgeworth merely noted that she looked pinker and prettier than usual.

'Nay, this is no place for a young lady, Miss Howarth,' he chided her gently. 'Go on back to your Mam. You'll only get your frock covered in muck. There's nowt but steam, oil and noise in here.'

'But I wish to know how the engine works, Mr Edgeworth,' she persisted. 'And my father said I could. Mr Vivian must have forgot.'

Ted Edgeworth sighed, and cast the cotton waste away.

'Stand you here, then,' he warned her dreadfully, 'and don't move. King Billy'd gollop you down like a teacake if you got too close.'

He went to give the Cornishman a piece of his mind. But as Hal Vivian was ignorant of the matter, and inclined to the same opinion, they shared a quiet grumble instead.

'. . . and he's said and done no more about putting them safety rails round the engine, like you suggested, neither.'

'Aye, he is the very devil of a fellow for cutting corners, and they are always cut at somebody else's expense. Well, let us get this visit over. What possessed him to allow her to come?'

'Eh, he canna say nay to his womenfolk. All them girls is sweet as sugar atop, like their Mam, and right bulldogs underneath – like him.'

Anna had flattened herself obediently against the wall and was watching King Billy with respectful eyes.

'Well, Miss Tibby,' said the Cornishman with careless good nature, 'do you wish to become an engineer?'

'You cannot tell one from another of us, can you, sir?' she answered, and her voice shook a little with love and chagrin. 'I am not Tibby but Anna. And what should I know about engineering until someone shows me round and explains it to me?'

In spite of a mild annoyance he was touched by the girl's tone, but could not for the life of him understand why she had come, since she was obviously nervous of the pumping engine.

'Then, Miss Anna, I will endeavour to instruct you. Keep to the wall of the tower, take my arm, and do exactly as I say. One heedless action on your part could send you to your death. King Billy is no gentleman, and would not stop even for a lady.'

'He is no gentleman, certainly,' she replied, restored to pertness, 'for he smells abominably of hot oil.'

Then she spoke no more, but compressed her lips in fortitude; while the Cornishman, once launched upon his subject, needed no encouragement. He assailed her ears and brain with facts and explanations. And what with the thunderous breathing of King Billy, difficulties of comprehension, walking up and down three flights of stairs and being made to feel giddy at the sight of the ground below, Anna paid dearly for this first rendezvous. But she shook off discomfort with one twirl of her parasol as she got safely outside, and thanked him politely.

'There is no need to escort me, sir,' she said with some urgency, as she espied her sisters searching for her. 'I see my family only a short distance away. And I would not trouble you further. So, good-day to you, Mr Cornishman. And good-day King Billy!' – with a pretty grimace at the monarch in his high tower. 'I thank you, sir, for showing me round. Shall we not see so much of you now the engine is built? Pray come and visit us anyway. We have such splendid parties! And you are very welcome . . . oh, lor'!'

She was gone, running like the wind so that she might saunter up on Livvy and Sophy from behind, and make believe she had looked everywhere for them in the crowd.

It was fortunate that she did not hear Hal Vivian's farewell, for he said absentmindedly, 'Good-day to you, Miss Kitty!' And turned away to adore the latest love of his life, who seemed about to drain the very wells of the earth without assuaging his kingly thirst.

FIVE

Disaster

For a few months King Billy was the pride and wonder of Wyndendale, then he began to show signs of displeasure. First of all, one of his cast-iron balance bobs broke suddenly, without warning. The *Post* reported the damage as 'negligible', but quoted Edgeworth as saying that had the bob broken at the gudgeon, and part of it fallen down the shaft, then the engine would have sustained terrible damage. In the meantime all pumping had stopped while repairs were being carried out.

The *Clarion* agreed that the safety of the engine was paramount, and the public need not concern themselves with the fate of two greasers, who had been knocked down the shaft and maimed for life!

At this point the ironmaster entered the fray through the columns of the *Post*, protesting that the two workmen had been compensated in full measure, according to his rule.

The *Clarion* apologised profusely, mentioned the exact sum of money regarded as adequate recompense, and compared it with the cost of installing the pumping engine. They hoped that the ironmaster's generosity might not tempt other workmen to fall down the shaft on purpose, and live a life of idleness and luxury at his expense!

But William had to endure more than the *Clarion*'s impudence. In a fit of economy he had suggested iron instead of the customary wood for King Billy's main rods.

'Even if we use Danzig pine we shall have a bill as long as my arm. And you speak of the best Riga timber, Mr Vivian?' he had cried, incensed at the Cornishman's latest idea. 'Think of the transport alone, sir! What? Some two dozen tree trunks, each seventy-foot in length, to be fetched sixteen thousand miles from the Pacific Coast and round the Horn? Pshaw!' And he struck the estimate with the flat of his hand. 'No, no, let us use our commonsense and cut the costs – as Ted here is always advising us to do. Let us make the rods of iron, and make them here at home. You are fond of innovation, Mr Vivian. What do you say to that?'

Hal's eyes seemed to look into the depths of the proposition.

'I am not against it, sir,' he said cautiously, 'but we should have to make extraordinarily strong couplings.'

'So we shall. What do you say, Ted?'

'I don't like it,' said Edgeworth flatly. 'I'm not as fond of progress as you and Mr Vivian are. We've allus used wood. We know wood. And I think it's best to spend money now, sooner than be sorry for saving it later on.'

'Surely the superiority of iron over wood is indisputable?' William cried. 'Look how successfully we have substituted the one for the other in a hundred cases.'

'Wood wears slower and gives you warning,' said Edgeworth. 'You never know when iron's going to snap.'

'Wood rots, and iron does not,' William argued.

'Iron rusts,' said Edgeworth, having the last word.

'I think it is worth trying,' said Hal Vivian, having made up his mind. 'I can find no fault in the theory at any rate; but we must take every precaution to see that there is no special strain put upon the main rods.'

So they had been cast and assembled at Snape, and for the best part of half a year done noble service. Then on a cold February day in 1817 one of them broke. Fortunately, the engine man was alert and in the right place at the right time. He threw up the equilibrium switch and prevented a disaster.

Pumping operations were again at a standstill. The monarch stood idle upon his hill, with his minions swarming round him putting him to rights: a sobering sight for any owner. The ironmaster sent note of the fact to the Cornishman at his Manchester office.

Within the week another main rod fractured, and again King Billy stood idle. Then a third and a fourth rod went. Each time the man attending him had been lucky or skilful or both, but William was now profoundly disturbed and sent an urgent request for help and consultation. Meanwhile the engine was mended once more.

'That should be all right for the time being,' said William, shaken. 'Did you say that the rods hadn't been properly balanced?'

'Aye, Mr Howarth, and how that came about I don't rightly know.'

'So long as you have seen to it.'

'I have. And quite a few couplings gone and all, Mr Howarth.'

'God damn it, we made couplings strong enough to brace a ship.'

'Then we'll have to make 'em strong enough for two ships, sir. Shall we wait until Mr Vivian comes, or start up without him?'

'Oh start up,' said the ironmaster, but without enthusiasm.

Hal Vivian arrived in the valley quite literally posthaste. Travelling from Bristol, he had paused in Manchester only long enough to change his linen and pack a couple of clean shirts. He drank his coffee standing, reading the news from Millbridge, and was off on the overnight coach from Market Street.

He endeavoured to sleep on the way, but his dreams were so vivid as to wake him again and again. His companions also slept uneasily, moaning and turning, occasionally opening their eyes to stare blearily about them. The sound of wheels rumbled in the Cornishman's head. Now and then he raised the blind to look out. A brilliant moon lit the frosty landscape, the sky was velvet and diamonds, the window icy to his touch. Up on the box, in the cruel cold, the coachman drove them through strange places to their journey's end, and the guard watched over them.

Awake, he fell to musing on the patchwork of events. Anna's winsome face appeared at intervals, chiding him as it were for his lack of attention. He knew now what she wanted of him. He did not want her, except in the way a man wanted a pretty girl. On the other hand he did not want any woman in particular, but supposed he would marry sometime. Anna might do as well as anyone, better perhaps, for she was the ironmaster's favourite daughter. Marriage was, or should be, a sensible pact made for life with the partner most likely to last the course. He could tire of beauty, but the acquisition of a father-in-law who liked and encouraged him, who could provide money for those ideas which might perish for want of a patron, was something worth the having.

Yet the girl reached him at times, filling him with tenderness and delight. On his previous visit she had learned the old names for the plunger lifts on the engine, solely to please him, to engage his attention for a little while.

'House, tye, rose, crown, lily, violet, puppy.'

Making play of a matter which was serious to her, registering each change of his expression.

'Going up or going down, Miss Anna?' he had asked, teasing her.

She consulted the slip of paper in her pocket before answering him in triumph.

'Going down, sir. *House* is at the top and *puppy* in the sump. Poor puppy,' she added inconsequently, 'why should he be at the bottom of that great shaft, I wonder?'

Which made him laugh, momentarily love her, want to swing her up and whirl her round and kiss her pink protesting mouth. But even a mild flirtation would bring about serious consequences, so he was careful to keep his distance.

Upon his eighteenth birthday, his father had given him a guinea and an introduction to a lady of mature years and great discretion.

'Don't you go asking every girl to marry you,' Santo

warned him. 'And while you're waiting, my handsome, pay for your pleasure.'

So Hal Vivian had lived from day to day, believing he kept emotion in its proper place. His heart was as ungrown as that of a boy who loves his mother and regards girls as a distraction from vital matters.

What truly disturbed him was the behaviour of his pumping-engine. Those iron main rods. Damned dangerous. Suppose King Billy, in a fit of royal rage, made a proper job of it? He blamed himself for being swayed by reasons of economy. He should have sided with Ted Edgeworth who might not be a genius but was a sound engineer. Now, too late, he saw that iron rods were a liability. They must be replaced.

Best Riga wood? Out of the question, for reasons of time as well as expense. Well, they need not go so far afield. British Columbia was nearer. European pine nearer still. And yet – the cost of replacing the rods at all, in a shaft close on three hundred fathoms deep – Christ Jesu! Oh he should have held out for timber rods. He should have listened to himself instead of to the ironmaster. When he stayed true to his own vision he was never wrong.

He fell uncomfortably asleep, and in his dream he saw himself, very small and distinct, riding from Millbridge towards King Billy who was silhouetted upon the hill of Swarth Moor. For a moment he thought the mighty engine was idle, but then the doughty bob condescended to dip. A good engine should be able to vary its strokes; as few as one a minute, as many as ten or more. He began to count, to put his finger as it were upon the great pulse of the machine.

In the monarch's keep he could see the engine-man lying asleep; a freckle-faced lad, mouth slightly open, a red kerchief wound about his neck. Fools! To put a boy on duty who didn't know an engine from his arse! And he looked into the heart and mind of King Billy, who sensed the weakness of those iron rods and was exerting tremendous pressure on them, since they were not worthy of his

68

performance. Ah, the power and arrogance of that inhuman judgement.

Then the Cornishman rode and rode upon the frosty landscape. The reins were icy to his touch. His breath smoked on the diamond air. His shouts became silent shapes. He knew he could not get there in time. And all the world lay asleep with the engine-man and could not be wakened.

'Throw up the switch, lad! Throw up the switch!'

The monarch scythed through rods, threw off couplings, launched himself upon self-annihilation.

'Puppy, violet, lily, crown, rose, tye. . . .'

'He's coming indoors too fast!' shouted the Cornishman.

The lad opened his eyes for the last time.

The pump-rod shot into the house with such force that the spring-beams broke and the roof of the engine-house lifted into the air.

And the Cornishman shouted. And shouted.

The gentleman opposite was tapping him upon the knee to recall him to life.

'What? What? What?' cried Hal Vivian, as though he were poor mad King George himself.

'Sir! Sir! You have woke the entire coach with your cries!'

The dream floated slowly down-wind.

'I beg your pardon, sir,' said the Cornishman, starting.

He stared round at the little carriage full of shocked faces.

'I beg your pardons, all. I have had the devil of a bad dream.'

He took out his brandy flask and drank to warm himself; subdued, ashamed, but more than all else afraid.

'Are you ill, sir?' asked the gentleman opposite, in quiet concern.

The Cornishman's complexion had become livid, his eyes unnaturally bright, and still he shuddered with cold though the brandy branched like fire through his veins.

'No, no, sir. I thank you. It is an affliction which runs in my family. Pay no attention to me. I shall be well enough presently.'

For his mother, who had nothing of earthly value to leave him, had bequeathed her gift of dreaming true, and he was full of terror.

At Millbridge, though his body ached with travelling and his stomach protested at its long abstinence, he had small mercy on himself. Only the determined kindness of Florrie Tyler made him sit by the fire, and drink a measure of hot coffee, and eat a little toast. This he despatched absentmindedly, rapidly, while asking if there was news from Tarbock Colliery. The landlord said he had heard nothing recently.

'Would you order a horse to be saddled for me at once?'

'Why, sir, it's hardly light yet. And shouldn't you stop and rest a bit? You look proper poorly,' said Florrie Tyler.

The shaking had come upon him again like an ague.

'It is nothing, madam. Nothing,' he said between clenched teeth.

And as soon as the horse was ready he clattered out of the Royal George yard like one possessed, and headed for Swarth Moor.

A thin brown gentleman, who had come to breakfast with the editor of the *Black Dwarf*, as that famous radical journalist passed through the town, turned round and looked after the Cornishman.

'Trouble somewhere, locally?' asked Mr Wooler, relishing hot chops.

'Trouble of the most expensive kind! If that damned white elephant of the ironmaster's has trampled any more natives underfoot the *Clarion* will have something to say about it, or my name is not Ambrose Longe!'

'. . . four o'clock this morning, he did it,' said Edgeworth, unshaven and red-eyed. 'He come indoors too fast, Mr Vivian, and went clean through the roof. Broke his spring-beams. God alone knows what the damage is. They're just fetching the engine-man out.'

Their breath smoked on the bitter air.

'Was there a lad on duty? A young lad wearing a red neckerchief?'

'Nay, not as I know of. It were Lewis on duty. Ever since that first rod broke I've hand-picked them engine-men. Eh there, Bob!' As a group of silent workmen put the first body on a home-made stretcher. 'That's Lewis, ain't it?'

'Should've been, Mr Edgeworth. Lewis must have asked one of the lads to take his turn instead. He were newly-wed last Saturday. . . .'

'Newly-wed?' Edgeworth shouted, beside himself with sudden rage. 'He's bloody fired! Tell him if I set eyes on him I'll kill him my bloody self!'

'The lad was asleep,' said the Cornishman, empty.

One man pulled a ragged blanket over the freckled face. A red triangle of cotton was knotted rakishly round the young neck.

'He's dead now,' said the man.

'He's not the only one, neither,' cried Edgeworth, stamping up and down in the cold. 'King Billy don't blow his top without taking payment for his trouble.'

The Cornishman looked as he would when he was old, with wintry eyes and colourless face.

'Have you told Mr Howarth yet?'

'Not yet,' said Edgeworth in a lower tone. 'I'm taking toll first, so's I've got the full story for him.' He glanced at Hal Vivian and then away. 'I don't fancy doing it neither,' he added honestly.

'I'll tell him,' said the Cornishman, digging his hands deep into his pockets.

Edgeworth was relieved.

'It'll come better from you than from anybody, Mr Vivian.'

'It is right and fitting that I should tell him.'

'We should have had wood for them rods, Mr Vivian,' said Edgeworth urgently. 'God forgive me if I'm speaking out of turn, but we *must* have wood. I can't be responsible

71

for any more bloody cast iron.'

Hal Vivian nodded curtly. His own mind had been made up hours ago.

'It'll cost a fortune,' said Ted Edgeworth. 'And all the while he's standing idle them pits are filling up. Where will it all end?'

The two men stood by the fireplace, preserving a silence which was by no means companionable. The ironmaster had fallen into his old habit of trying to bully his way out of a situation.

Hal Vivian had replied, with considerable temper, that it was his patron's proposal to use metal which had caused the trouble in the first place. With sound timber they could have been sure of reasonable wear and tear. But this damned touchy cast iron fractured on an instant. The ironmaster's economy would prove to be a most expensive mistake.

Whereupon William broke into a furious diatribe against insolvent idiots with high-flown notions who expected other men to foot the bill.

Folk got what they paid for, the Cornishman replied hotly. If he wanted a cheap job he should have gone elsewhere. But he was so eager to save a few hundred pound that he was like to lose a few thousand.

The silence after this had journeyed past some point of return. Still the ironmaster frowned into the bright fire. Still the Cornishman stood his ground, though pallid with an exhaustion which was both physical and emotional. Zelah's knock on the library door came as a reprieve, and they turned towards her as if for counsel.

'My dear?' said William simply, too proud to show what he felt.

Another woman might have pleaded for goodwill or offered sympathy. Zelah chose to be practical.

'Thou hast had no breakfast, William,' she said in her usual tone, 'and Mr Vivian hath been travelling all night. Come with me, both of thee, and eat in peace and privacy.'

The two men hesitated, glancing at each other, strained and sorry. The ironmaster stirred from his immobility. The Cornishman felt her comfort reach his heart, though still he was unsmiling.

'Is thy news so grave, Mr Vivian?' Zelah asked him directly.

'Aye, madam. There has been a great accident in the engine-house. We do not yet know the full extent of the damage.'

'Were any workmen hurt?' she asked, concerned.

'A lad who was on watch is dead. Others are being fetched out. And some fool, in an effort to douse the fires quickly, threw water upon one boiler – which burst. How many are dead and injured we cannot tell, but it will be a fearful matter.'

Her face changed, and she said out of sorrow, 'Oh, that is cruel news indeed. For an engine may be mended, but lives can never be returned.'

Then they were ashamed, remembering that men had been of no importance in the arguments and anger of the past hour, and followed her from the room like children – strangely humbled.

SIX

A Digan for the Bucca

Four dead and a dozen injured, coupled to the leading article in that morning's *Clarion,* had decided the ironmaster's course of action. Hands clasped in magisterial fashion behind his back, chin thrust stubbornly forward, he listened to his chief engineer without wavering one degree in his intention. He would be seen to take part in this tragedy, to care. He would inspect the shaft in person.

'Well, I'm telling you once and for all, Mr Howarth, that it's a bloody daft idea,' said Edgeworth frank and forthright as ever. 'There's no royal road to inspecting a pumping shaft, and no way we can make it easy on you, neither. You'll swing down in a hoppet with us, and three hundred fathoms is a hell of a long way down. You'll wear a fustian suit and a backskin and a sou'wester, along of the water running down your neck and back. There's a downcast draught like a nor'-easter even in the summer. In mid-winter you can reckon on it freezing your arse off.

'The tub's unsteady, and you can't get a straight drop, along of the equipment in the shaft. So you have to push yourself from side to side, and if you lose your grip or your balance there'll be another funeral.

'We'll be there a long while, and if you get starved or weary then we'll have to fetch you up early. That wastes time and makes two jobs out of one. Even if you stick with us you can do nowt but hinder us. So think on! Eh! I might as well save my breath to cool my porridge. . . .'

The little group of men hanging about the damaged engine-house gave the ironmaster a thin cheer as he prepared to go below. He answered them with a paternal nod, a confident salute. Though the sight of the shallow hoppet, made from half a wooden barrel and fitted with four wrought-iron straps and hangers, gave him reason to pause.

'I towd thee,' said Edgeworth infuriatingly, divining his master's thoughts. 'Here, grab a hold of that chain, Mr Howarth, and keep holding it as if your life depended on it – which it does. All set, Mr Vivian?'

'It's a little like boating, sir,' said the Cornishman cheerfully, steadying his patron. 'But we boat in the air instead of on the water.'

'Lower away!' Edgeworth ordered, unimpressed by this description.

Open torches, slung from the hoppet chains, now became their only light in an underworld which cared not an atom for human frailty. Impossible to believe that man had wrought all this in the cavernous depths; endless iron columns of pump pipes, plunger-poles, rods, clacks, door-pieces, ponderous balance-bobs. And the mighty cylinder, whose piston was as thick as a man's body, brooded in the dark.

Rarely had the ironmaster felt as vulnerable. He clung to the chain with such assiduity that he bore the mark in his palms for days after, as the little craft rocked and eddied upon the dank air; while Edgeworth and Hal Vivian inspected the damage, and clicked their tongues in exasperation and disbelief.

'I'm going to speak out for once,' said Edgeworth, who never did anything else. 'It's no use doing another patch-job, Mr Howarth. Just take a look at these here rods. You'll be throwing good money after bad if you use cast iron again. I want good honest wood, like what we should have had in the first place. Are you with me, sir?'

'Yes,' said William between his teeth, holding on for dear life.

'Are you ready, again?' Edgeworth asked. He tugged the chain and shouted, 'Lower away!' Then, 'See them couplings, Mr Howarth?'

'I see them, man.' Trying to concentrate.

'Rubbish, that's what they are, sir. Not in theirselves perhaps, but in King Billy's estimate. Rubbish!'

'Smashed them to bits, has he?' said William, in despair as they jerked and swung further into the abyss.

'Aye, eight of 'em, sir. Eight! Gone like matchwood!'

'What sort of shape is he in? Badly damaged?'

'Astonishingly good under the circumstances, sir,' said the Cornishman, acting as mediator, for Edgeworth delighted too much in his master's plight to be objective. 'But I fully agree with Mr Edgeworth that we should remove all the iron main rods and replace them with timber which will take the strains and stresses. *Good* timber.'

Torches flared and smoked. Shadows leaped. The iron cathedral towered above, sheered below them.

'There is no question,' said William sharply, 'of importing fancy timber. We cannot wait several months while some blasted ship floats twenty-five tree trunks in our direction.'

'There must be decent wood somewhere in England,' said the Cornishman, equally firm.

'Oak!' cried William, fending off a great pumping pipe which loomed at him out of the dark.

'Pine is my choice, sir. Oak would not be pliable enough.'

Hal Vivian spoke implacably now, for they really could not go through this danger and expense twice in succession.

'Hold hard, Mr Howarth!' said Edgeworth with relish, tugging the chain to indicate a further descent.

'One moment, Ted,' said the ironmaster, as they came to a jangling halt. 'If we are all agreed to replace iron rods with pine rods, is there any need to see-saw up and down this damned shaft?'

Engineer and consultant looked briefly and significantly at one another. A wry smile flickered across Ted Edgeworth's face. That of the Cornishman was closely kept.

'No sir,' said Hal Vivian amicably. 'If we are so agreed,

then your men can begin clearance work right away, and Mr Edgeworth and I will take a closer look at the engine after that.'

'Well, I will give the order,' said William, recovering some of his equanimity, 'and that will put heart into my men, for an idle pit is a sorry problem at any time – but in the depths of winter is a cruel one.'

Ted Edgeworth could not resist saying, 'Well, I was against you coming with us, Mr Howarth. But now I'm glad you did, after all.'

With his capacity for shutting out that which displeased him, the ironmaster had switched to another line of thought. Snape was casting ordnance for the British navy, which gave him some leverage in its corrupt backyards. At Deptford, with a personal visit and a few palms buttered, he might pick up a couple of dozen first-class pine trunks intended for mainmasts. Get them squared off, too. And a visit to London was always entertaining.

Edgeworth gave two tugs on the chain and they began to ascend. The nearer they got to that pinhole of daylight the higher William's spirits rose. It was like him to make a disaster seem like a triumph, and yet this experience had been sobering. The smile on his mouth gradually faded.

'Aye, it is hard and perilous work, being a shaftsman,' said Hal Vivian, divining his patron's thoughts.

'If you think this is hard work, Mr Howarth,' said Edgeworth unwisely, 'you should see what the miners put up with, down Prospect.'

His pride aroused, the ironmaster replied impulsively, 'I intend to do so. Make arrangements at once.'

But Hal Vivian, having compassion on him, said, 'Tomorrow will be soon enough, sir. We have been down here longer than you think.'

As William endeavoured to conceal tremors of cold and exhaustion.

At Prospect Mine the three men descended into the pit, as did all colliers, by the ladder-road, preceded by the fireman. Alf Rowbottom had trimmed his candle closely so that the flame might give forth the purest light, and he carried a bundle of similar candles with him.

To climb St Paul's would have been considered an eccentric and dangerous business, worthy of public interest. But every day in the course of their usual work, thousands of miners descended and ascended perpendicular ladders, the length of which would scale St Paul's more than three times over.

The ironmaster was weary, and yet was enjoying himself, for he had kept up with these younger men every step of the road, until their way was stopped by a roaring torrent which cut off the deepest part of the mine. Here they sat and ate their dinners at its brink.

'I see you do not use the safety lamp, sir,' said Hal Vivian, munching his bread and cheese with good appetite. 'And yet it was invented all of two years ago. I marvel you were not among the first to realise what an excellent device it is.'

Mocking the ironmaster gently, since he was in a mellow mood.

'Rowbottom will tell you why,' William replied, gesturing in the direction of the fireman, who was sitting a respectful distance apart.

The man's words came indistinctly at first, hobbled by crumbs.

'I've worked here, man and boy, for sixteen years, and I say *Sod the safety lamp!* Begging your pardons, masters. Why, I can test for gas with this here candle, Mr Vivian, and judge to an inch how much firedamp there is, from a bit of a whiff to firing point. Give me a safety lamp and I don't know where the hell I am. Begging your pardons again. It don't light up as well as a candle, and it won't tell me owt. Afore I knew it, I'd be laying on t'bloody ground, half-suffocated. Here, I'll show thee why we're sitting where we are, masters.'

He walked away from them, further down the cavern, cupping the naked light so that the flame flared steadily over the cover of his palm. Then he crouched to the floor, calling on them to watch.

'See her grow blue from the spire, masters? That's gas. Keep your eyes on her. Bluer still, and see how the spire points up'ard and up'ard? And bluer yet, and longer and sharper the point? There, that's enough. D'you see what I mean? Besides, them lamps can blow up!'

This demonstration concluded to the satisfaction and education of his audience, the fireman sat down again and finished his beer with a loud smack of the lips.

'So much for progress,' said Edgeworth, proved right again.

The Cornishman was silent: his mind twisting and darting through the world of invention in which he lived.

'If we lower men into a pumping shaft in a hoppet,' he ruminated, 'why should we not lower them into a mine, and so save legwork? Why not design a deeper carrying-vessel with safety rails? A man-cage. . . .'

'Enough!' cried William, in dry good humour. 'Let us get one of your brainchildren mended before we entertain the notion of another.'

Then the Cornishman knew he had been forgiven for William's mistake. Edgeworth made a grimace of sympathy.

'That's King Billy's beer!' he observed, of the Stygian waters before them. 'Get him to rights again and he'll sup it for breakfast.'

'How much deeper does the mine go?' William asked, diverted.

The fireman shrugged his shoulders as they looked to him.

'From where we stand now, master? It'd be like clambering down Swarth Moor Edge or t'Stoops.'

'So deep?' mused the ironmaster.

He was glad he had come here and seen for himself how matters stood. Today, he had shown all who laboured for him that he was prepared to understand the extent of their labours, to dress like them, to tread the ladder-road with aching legs and eat his dinner in the brooding dark, to accept the same risks they took daily. They would remember that, and like it.

The *Post* had been informed of his intentions. The *Clarion* could hardly ignore his gesture. Well, they would have something worth writing about, for once.

He reached for the coarse striped shirt and short jacket, and laughed as his fingers blackened his pampered flesh. The heat down here was almost tropical. Sweat ran down his broad back, hung in drops upon his broad chest.

'You've getten some muscle on you, master,' said Rowbottom respectfully.

'Farrier's muscle,' William replied proudly. 'And I can still swing a sledgehammer with the best of them.'

Hal Vivian smiled to himself, but the smile was affectionate. His father, Santo Vivian, had approached old age in the same belligerent fashion.

'All muscle, boy,' he would say of his thickening body.

'All suet pudding, more like!' Hal's mother would reply, smiling.

The Cornishman had saved a token from his repast, and now placed it on a little spur of rock overhanging the rushing waters.

'Leaving a bit for the fairies, Mr Vivian?' Edgeworth asked, grinning.

'I did not know you were so fanciful!' cried the ironmaster.

Hal Vivian kept his tone deliberately light, but was serious.

'All man-moles are fanciful, sir. And rightly so. I should have trembled to speak in such a lordly way as you did of King Billy, and in the monarch's own shaft. I have far more reverence, sir, than that.'

'Why, what might his majesty have done?' asked the ironmaster in mockery, donning his jacket ready for the ascent.

'Oh, cast you down to the sump. Rocked the hoppet. Any manner of fine and fiendish tricks which he keeps up his iron sleeve.'

Edgeworth laughed, but uneasily.

'Do *you* hold with this nonsense?' William asked his chief engineer.

Edgeworth hemmed and hawed, and mumbled something about not being as superstitious as a Cornishman – though he had been known to address King Billy as if the engine were human, and superhuman at that.

'Why, are the Cornish more superstitious than other folk?' William said idly, amusing himself.

The fireman had kept his own counsel so far, squatting on his heels as miners do, squinting sideways at his companion flame. Now he spoke up, his eyes glinting in his blackened face.

'Nay, master, there's sperrits underground. You'd know if you worked here. We know them, master, and fear them too – in a proper sort of way. There's my bit o' snap for them, and they're welcome to it!' Putting his morsel by the side of the Cornishman's offering.

'Well, I'm damned,' said William, amazed. 'How do you come to worship such pagan things when there is a Christian Gód above – or so I am told in church of a Sunday?'

'Nay, I've nowt against God above,' Rowbottom answered sturdily, 'and I go to Chapel and pay respect to Him and all. But underground, master, there's summat else. And we do well to know that.'

Both the ironmaster and his chief engineer felt slightly uncomfortable about this information, since they had nothing left with which to appease these earthy influences.

'Mice or rats will eat that bread and cheese,' said William, defending himself.

Rowbottom shrugged. It was not for him to decide.

'Come, sir,' said Hal Vivian, smiling. 'You will be forgiven this once. But on another visit it would be wise to remember.'

'A sop for Pluto?' suggested the ironmaster.

'*A digan for the bucca* is what we Cornish say.'

SEVEN

Designs

Spring 1818

Hal Vivian stood drinking coffee and reading his letters. His greatcoat was unbuttoned, which suggested that he had that moment arrived from somewhere else; it had not been removed, which meant that he would shortly be away on another trip. In the Manchester house, which served as both home and office, his secretary and his housekeeper each strove to gain his attention: the one concerning an invitation from the ironmaster, the other on the state of his laundry and stomach.

'. . . Mr Howarth of Wyndendale. Giving a coming-out ball for his daughter on the twelfth of next month. Wishes you to attend. Unluckily, clashes with the Birmingham date. Both very important clients. . . .'

'. . . don't know how many to pack if I don't know how long you'll be away, now do I, sir? And there's a hot meal ready this minute, which I'm sure you've ate nothing proper since you left on Sunday. . . .'

'I shall answer you both in a moment. One moment, if you please!' cried the Cornishman, for the letter he had just opened was penned in a lady's hand, and a faint disquiet seized him as he read.

Sir, Pray do not take it Amiss that I write to you Direct. It is but as one Engineer to Another! Though perhaps you have Forgot me Quite or Else remember me as Miss Tibby or Miss Kitty or Any Other of my Sisters! No matter. King Billy has behaved so Civilly since y^r Last Visit that it is close on Twelvemonth since you came here. The proximity of Two Events Emboldens me to

Suggest that they might be Enfolded in One. I speak of y^r annual Duty Call on the Monarch of Tarbock, and the Coming of Age of y^r Humble Servant. Y^r Official Invitation will follow. This is but an Idle Thought on My Part, but I shall not be Half so well Pleased if My Grand Ball lacks the Presence of that Gentleman we All think of as *The Cornishman!* Pray do come! Y^{rs}. Anna Howarth.

Hal Vivian thrust the note in his greatcoat pocket while he considered how to reply to such an advance, and gave his attention to matters of immediate importance.

'Clashes with the Birmingham dates? Then it cannot be. In any case, I do not think it wise – no matter. Tell Mr Howarth I am deeply obliged, and so on and so forth. Three shirts, if you please, Mrs Craven, and as I catch a coach within the half-hour you must eat the dinner yourselves. Pack me a basket. I shall be travelling overnight. . . .'

Anna's note lay forgotten in his pocket until his housekeeper found it a week later, while brushing the greatcoat; and acting upon its crumpled and discarded appearance, dropped it into a wastepaper basket. So it was never answered.

The silence with regard to her own plea, the impersonal reply to her parents, humiliated the girl. Her position, even in such a warm and loving family, was curiously isolated. Tabby and Kitty were married. Livvy and Sophy were inseparable siblings. The other three were mere children. While Zelah, who could usually be relied upon as a confidante, was encouraging a young Quaker banker to pay court to Anna.

So she suffered bitterly, and in a solitude which might have touched even the green heart of the Cornishman, had he known of it. But he was in hot pursuit of the new Goddess of Steam, perpetually offering her tributes that other men would pay for, and content with his single lot. Yet fate would have it that the Birmingham coal magnate died of an apoplexy prior to their appointment, leaving his estate in disarray, his heirs quarrelling, and Hal Vivian with the project of a tramway locomotive on his hands and no one to buy it.

The Cornishman was a restless fellow, and as rain drummed on the roof and his fingers drummed on the breakfast table, he bethought himself of the ironmaster of Wyndendale whose present wagon road at Tarbock Colliery was a scrubby affair. The grey of his eyes became cloudless, crystalline. Within five minutes his office boy was trotting down the street to enquire about fast coaches, his housekeeper was packing the modest portmanteau, and his secretary fetching out the Howarth file. Within an hour Hal Vivian had gathered his drawings and estimates together, jammed his beaver hat on his head, and run all the way to Market Street to catch the Leeds tally-ho.

At Kingswood Hall the evening was sweeping inexorably on. Pale and pretty in her cream silk dress with its lace overlay, Anna Howarth stood with her parents to greet their guests. Polite and pretty, she glided and spun about the shining ballroom. Her little programme was pencilled with illustrious young names, her dowry and face and figure were under close appraisal. She was possibly the most miserable person present, and would have remained so had the Cornishman not arrived at a late hour.

'Mr Henry Vivian!' the footman announced, with courteous disapproval, and the grand assembly rustled in amusement.

For there stood a consultant engineer, astonished at the spectacle, and totally unprepared for a festivity which had never registered with him. His informal dress, his untidy charm, his abstract air, rendered him up to well-bred mockery. Under one arm he held a scroll of paper, under the other a long wooden box. He was out of place, but did not abase himself in consequence as many men would have done. Rather did he wake up to the fact, accept his position, set down his box and papers beneath a potted palm, and

84

advance towards his host and hostess with all the dignity he could muster.

Anna, pretending to smile behind her fan like the rest of the ladies, glided up looking slightly haughty, as if he were any late and unimportant guest. But loved him with her eyes.

'I fear I arrive unexpectedly, and at a most inopportune time, madam,' he said honestly, bowing over Zelah's hand.

'Thou art always welcome, Mr Vivian,' she answered warmly, amused.

'And after all you were invited. Though perhaps you had forgotten?' said the ironmaster.

His tone was dry, but he loved the man for being himself, for ignoring social niceties.

'It is – as thee knows – our daughter Anna's birthday,' Zelah reminded him, as he stood bewildered.

'Of course!' he cried, kissing her hand again in gratitude. 'My felicitations, Miss Anna, on this splendid occasion.'

Staring round in wonder. For the celebrations seemed excessive.

'It is not *any* birthday, sir,' said Anna, drawing herself up. 'I am eighteen. I have come out!'

Both parents hid their smiles and looked gravely to the Cornishman for his answer. He cleared his throat. He embarked upon deception.

'Although I was unexpectedly delayed, and did not have time to change, I have not come empty handed, Miss Anna!' For this would serve as his excuse. 'A gift from one engineer to another!' he suggested, remembering the phrase from somewhere or other, and picked up the wooden box, and offered it to the delighted girl.

Her small hands delved, touched wood and metal.

'A mere toy,' said Hal Vivian proudly, 'which would not appeal to any young lady but Miss Anna – who was kind enough to show quite an interest in engineering when I was here last.' Then seeing her in slight difficulties. 'May I? He is not too heavy, Miss Anna. But you should be careful how you bring him forth.'

Those nearest to them began to laugh and whisper. Others smiled or coughed or raised their quizzing glasses. He was truly outrageous, this tall gipsy of a fellow, with his sooty lashes and sea-water eyes, and his ridiculous gift. For Anna was holding a model steam-locomotive.

She looked up at its creator, she looked down at the little engine, with equal adoration. The last year had brought her to the peak of young beauty. And he, astonished, bewitched, bowed low and humbly before her.

Zelah became grave with knowledge of her daughter's heart, but William was jubilant. The situation could hardly have suited him better.

'Thrice welcome, Mr Vivian!' he cried hospitably. 'We care not how late or informally you come. You are a very busy and important man,' glaring round the assembly until every watching face expressed some degree of respect, 'and we are fortunate to have you here.'

'Hast thee eaten, Cornishman?' asked Zelah, as hospitable as ever, though a slight cloud overcast her countenance.

'I – do not think so,' he answered, unable to remember.

'Well, there is but one more dance before supper,' said William, 'he can wait that long. You do dance, I suppose, Mr Vivian?'

'I am no expert, sir,' said the Cornishman, now out of his depth.

'Then Anna shall teach you,' said the ironmaster splendidly, 'and see that you eat a good supper after!'

'My dear,' Zelah reminded him, 'Anna is having both the dance and the supper with young Barclay.'

'Oh, Barclay is a good fellow. He will understand,' said William carelessly. 'Take care of our Cornishman, Anna. It is the least we can do for him, after all his endeavours to get here, would you not agree?' And he gave his daughter a wink of conspiracy. 'Here, I will take care of this gift of yours – whose potentialities I feel you cannot fully appreciate as yet, despite your talent for engineering. Mr Vivian' – meeting his eyes deliberately – 'is this another of your expensive and kingly notions?'

Then the Cornishman warmed towards him, knowing that William guessed the reason for his visit, but would not betray him.

'Aye, sir, it is an idea I have played with because I loved it. And none but a man of wealth and vision could afford it, for it is unique.'

'Then we must guard it jealously, and speak of it later, sir,' said William, smiling.

Away swept Anna with the Cornishman, and spent one of the happiest hours of her life: guiding him with many giggles and great difficulty through the steps of a quadrille, then with no difficulty at all through the abundant delicacies of the supper table. While the ironmaster mused on the possibility of gaining a son-in-law by means of his steam-engine; and Zelah was left to apologise to young Barclay.

Plans for the engine lay upon William's library table in the morning sun. They were Hal Vivian's first chance to assert himself since the events of the previous evening, which had belonged to Anna. He had even lodged overnight at Kingswood Hall, to his own astonishment, and accepted the loan of a nightshirt and cap from the ironmaster.

Though the ball heralded a social weekend with a houseful of guests, William considered his part in the entertainment as done. The rest might disport themselves as they pleased at his expense, but he chose to breakfast early with the Cornishman and summon Ted Edgeworth to join them afterwards.

'More money, Mr Howarth,' said the chief engineer, shaking his head dolefully.

'Well, it is not your money, Ted,' the ironmaster replied, in jovial mood. 'And has not King Billy proved his worth in the last year?'

'Oh aye. He works like a good 'un, but we're nowhere near meeting costs yet, let alone making a profit.'

'Early days, early days. Mr Vivian, you will be pleased to

hear that his majesty has not only drained Prospect and the rest of our pits, but actually dried up a few neighbouring ones – for which service we shall be paid a gratuity.'

'Cheese-parings!' said Edgeworth dispassionately.

'They shall become cheeses when *I* own them,' said the ironmaster grimly, 'but that remark stays between the three of us.'

'This engine, Mr Edgeworth,' said the Cornishman, who respected his judgement, 'will be cheaper, faster and stronger than the horses it will replace. Here are my estimated figures. . . .'

'Oh I believe you, Mr Vivian. But Mr Howarth here is throwing money about as if King Billy fetched it up with the water. Afore we can run this engine, let alone buy it and sort its little problems out, we shall have to lay down a new wagon road. The old wooden 'un won't take a machine of this weight and size and power.'

'We could lay iron strips along the top of the wooden rails,' William suggested, and then glanced guiltily at the Cornishman who did not like to be advised.

'I should not do that, sir,' said Hal Vivian firmly. 'I strongly recommend a new iron tramway – else you are doing half a job.'

'Very well, Mr Vivian,' peaceably, 'Belbrook will be glad to supply the rails, and do it at rock-bottom price too.'

'I'd like to know what's under them old sleepers and all,' Edgeworth mused. 'If they're ballasted with coke breeze or slack we're all right. But that colliery did everything on the cheap, Mr Howarth. If they've cut their costs on the ballasting we've got to replace that, on top of the rest.'

'We have the sale of the horses and the old rails to set against expenses, Ted,' said the ironmaster, always optimistic when his desires were concerned.

'I can't see us making a fortune out of two dozen knackered beasts and a load of old firewood,' said Edgeworth sarcastically.

'You have no vision, Ted!' cried the ironmaster, savouring his own.

'No,' the engineer agreed, 'but I've got plenty of commonsense, Mr Howarth, and you're putting in a deal more than you're getting out.'

But his eyes softened as he picked up the model engine and admired its workmanship.

'This must've taken a few hours,' he remarked, of the polished mahogany and beech, the brass fittings. 'Is model-making a bit of a hobby with you, Mr Vivian?'

'I thought it a good idea to show the buyer what he was ordering,' said the Cornishman, off guard. And flushed as he saw William smile. 'But it is not a working model,' he added with regret. 'I had neither the tools nor the skill to create that. And my apprentices did the tedious parts, for the benefit of their experience and my time. But I admit to enjoying myself, designing and making this fellow.'

'We must call it *The Cornishman*,' said William gracefully.

'Aye, it's a grand little engine,' said Edgeworth, setting it down carefully. Then he faced his master. 'I might as well shut my mouth. I see you've made your mind up to it, Mr Howarth.'

'Subject to certain considerations,' said William judiciously.

The engineer stood back from the library table as if to show that he, at any rate, had thought of every objection and might well be about his business. He permitted himself a final warning.

'You know we're going to have to put down *stone* sleepers for an iron tramway, I suppose, Mr Howarth?'

The ironmaster's chin lifted to take the blow.

'In for a penny, in for a pound, Ted,' he said gallantly.

Edgeworth nodded. Once to the Cornishman, once to the ironmaster.

'So long as you know what you're letting yourself in for,' he said maddeningly. 'Don't come complaining to me when the bills mount up.'

There was a few seconds' silence when he had gone. Then both men looked at each other to assess the state of their minds and hearts.

'I tend to overlook such matters as time and money,' Hal Vivian confessed. 'Mr Edgeworth is more than a good servant to you, sir. He is also a good friend.'

The ironmaster relaxed, and inspected his latest acquisition in miniature – eyes keen and bright.

'I am aware of that, Mr Vivian, and I honour him for it. I will take more impudence from Ted Edgeworth than from most men. But it is not your business to trouble about money. That is my prerogative. Yours is the production of ideas, and unless I am much mistaken they are somewhat ahead of their time. Let us sit down and talk awhile. I will order coffee for us. What were you saying last night about the consequences of the steam locomotive reaching into the future?'

It was the first time William had treated him as an equal, and Hal Vivian found himself talking freely. He moved from one logical step to another, then took an imaginative leap into the dark, expanded upon themes which other men would have dismissed as the ravings of an idiot. The ironmaster lay back in his armchair, eyes half-closed, hands clasped on his chest, and listened.

'Oh, there will be problems which we cannot even visualise as yet. But think of our present system of hauling coal from mine to dock, on an iron tramway, drawn by horses. Then imagine a more powerful locomotive than this one, drawing wagons which can carry both goods and *people* faster and further still. Imagine, not a mile of wagon road or tramway, but a railroad running the length of this valley. Imagine other such railroads connecting throughout the kingdom. All manned by steam-driven locomotives which would be faster, larger and cheaper to run than the present stagecoaches. Think of the benefits to public and private communications. Of speeds which seem well-nigh miraculous!'

Hal Vivian's coffee had gone cold. His coffee always went cold while he talked or worked. Now he drank it hurriedly, confused by his own eloquence.

The ironmaster stirred in his long reverie and spoke from a younger and more vulnerable self.

'Mr Vivian, it is thirty years or more since I travelled to London by one of the first Royal Mail coaches, and – without your special knowledge, and our present expertise – argued that a stage coach powered by steam might be a possibility.

'We change roles, Mr Vivian, with the years. Perhaps you do not believe that? Perhaps you think that in thirty years' time you will be exactly as you are now, but richer? Not so. If you succeed in your aims your business will have grown beyond you, and taken you over. If you fail, no man will lift a hand to help you. Once I was much as you, Mr Vivian. I wanted to be a blacksmith. For seven years I was a blacksmith. Then I wanted to be an ironmaster, in partnership with Caleb Scholes at Belbrook. Then I must be ironmaster in my own right, master of Snape. Then I invested in other concerns, played a part in public life. And so on, and so forth. Until I come full circle, to find whom? Not my former self, but a young man much as I was. I find him in you. Do you mind my asking how old you are, Mr Vivian? Would that seem too impertinent?'

'I am five-and-twenty, sir,' said the Cornishman stiffly.

The ironmaster's face was open, gentle.

'God bless my soul,' he said to himself, 'how the years fly! You have grown old, ironmaster.'

The Cornishman was touched. So had his father, Santo Vivian, sat in the long winter evenings at the Manchester house – narrow black eyes glinting at the fire, big hands folded over his belly. While Hal's mother moved quietly to and fro, untiring, unhurried. And old Santo would look up, follow her with his eyes, quizzically, fondly.

'What's to do, my bird?' he asked, sometimes detaining her with an imperious hand that she might speak to him.

'Leave me be, Santo, else your supper'll be spoiled,' she would answer briskly.

He would be as pleased with that retort as if she had embraced him.

The ironmaster sat in silence for a while longer. Then, almost shyly, he said, 'Have you ever seen round my ironworks, Mr Vivian?'

Again it was old Santo to the life.

('Did I tell you about the time the roof caved in at Wheal Mary?'

Aye, twenty times, dear father! But you shall tell me again if it so pleases you, with words and gestures known to me from boyhood. And all I ask is that I can exchange a secret smile with my mother – without your seeing us!)

So the Cornishman replied, 'Why no, sir, I cannot say I have. Not in detail, that is. Only in a cursory manner.'

'Should you like to?' asked the ironmaster humbly.

'With all my heart, sir,' cried the Cornishman.

'I should like a word with thee, William,' said Zelah Howarth at bed-time, combing her grey-gold hair.

'Yes, my love?'

'Thee knows that Anna is in love with the Cornishman?'

'I should have thought that was obvious to anyone, my love.' Humorously. 'Well, I have done my best for the minx. I am buying his steam locomotive, and laying down a new tramway at Tarbock.'

Zelah watched her lord in the dark looking glass, and began to plait her hair dexterously as she spoke.

'I know nothing of thy business, William. It is of Anna that I wish to speak. Do not evade me, love.'

He took a turn about their bedroom, resplendent in his velvet dressing gown, his Turkish slippers, unable to see a way out of the conversation. Zelah's fingers wove rapidly. She fixed his image in the glass and spoke to it directly.

'Thee must not bind Hal Vivian to thee by means of Anna.'

The ironmaster's face showed that he felt the smart of her honesty. She was sorry for the hurt but did not repent the truth.

'I? Bind him?' William cried. 'It is Anna who will bind him, not I. Speak to your daughter, not to me.'

Her fingers trembled over their work, but she finished one ashen rope of hair and began upon the other, still speaking to his reflection.

'Do not think I begrudge the love thee bears him,' she said gently. 'It was not given to us to have a son. But it hath pleased Providence to make some recompense with Hal Vivian, and thee should be content with the affection and respect he bears thee, not seek to draw him too close. Anna is headstrong, and a favourite of thine. At present Hal sees a father in thee, not a father-in-law. I do not think he wishes to marry. I do not think he is ready to marry. But you and Anna together might well persuade him against his better judgement. I beg thee not to encourage her in this.'

'The case does not arise,' said the ironmaster, choosing to misunderstand her. 'Hal and I are bound by our mutual interest in Tarbock Colliery. Nothing else.'

But she would not allow him to compromise.

'He hath no interest in Tarbock, except thee buy the engines he designs. If he could not persuade thee to buy them then he would persuade another, with as good a heart as he musters for thee. But at all times he is his own master, and lives his own life. He does not belong to thee, nor to Anna, but to himself.'

'You do not like him!' William cried, furious.

Zelah wound three silver hairs round the second plait, and her hands sank into her lap.

'I love the boy,' she said quietly, 'but I love him as he is, not as thee and Anna would have him.'

The ironmaster paced the carpet, silenced. In a corner of himself which only she could reach he knew she was right. But all the rest of him rose up and fought to keep the dream he cherished – scarcely a day old – of a chosen son-in-law who would inherit his kingdom. It was too precious to set aside.

'Well, there is something in what you say,' he replied in a softer tone, 'but I think it is his youth you judge, and not himself. Great Heaven, Zelah, how is he different from any other young man? And yet young men grow older. They change. He will settle down. As I did.'

Zelah's silver-framed mirror reflected sadness, and the acceptance of her husband's weaknesses.

'I do not disagree. But we must speak of the present. He is young and ambitious, unready for close ties and deep affections. He gives the best part of himself to his work, and any woman who loves him must make do with what is left. In time, perhaps – unless he hardens – someone will stir his heart and mind. But that time is not yet, and Anna is not that woman.'

He threw up his arms then, as though in defeat.

But added, 'Suppose he decides to marry rather than burn – and I have seen the way he looks at Puss-cat. What then, my love? Are we to forbid the match?'

The silver image in the silver glass answered him.

'Thy mind is made up, William. Thou wilt do as thou wilt.'

'And after all,' he blustered, feeling unkindly treated, 'you had the choice of Tibby's husband, and of Kitty's also!'

'They were mature men, ready for marriage, and they love and care for our daughters as husbands should.'

'Well, now it is my turn to choose,' he said pettishly, but glanced at her quickly as he spoke, fearful of her reaction.

She did not reply. Gracefully she rose, and moved out of the mirror's oval range, leaving it to reflect a great room empty of people.

'Art thou angered with me?' the ironmaster asked softly, lifting her hand and putting it to his lips.

'Nay, not angered,' she answered. 'Saddened, William. And fearful for our child's happiness.'

'Thee would not leave me?' he whispered.

For she had done so once, and the mark of it was on him for life: a talisman had he but known it, which he did not.

'I love thee, Zelah,' he said, into her dark gold eyes.

'And is that thy answer to everything, William?' Ironically.

'Thee knows how much I love thee,' he said, drawing her to him.

'Oh, thou child!' cried Zelah, for he wanted comfort from her.

And he was as safe as any of her children, nourishing himself with the nectar and ambrosia of her love, sleeping afterwards with the splendid exhaustion of a child, and a smile upon his mouth.

Zelah watched an hour or two longer in the night, and prayed that another child of hers might be spared the hurts of love. Yet accepted that she might not, and could thank God just the same.

EIGHT

On the Eve

December 1818

In the great houses and on the prosperous farms in the valley, the twelve days of Christmas were celebrated in style. Gentlemen feasted their servants, farmers their labourers, and even the humblest on these estates could expect to fill their stomachs for once. But in the slums of Millbridge and the valley towns, where people lived but did not belong – in the workhouses where no one cared – the poorest of all remained unwarmed and uncheered.

At Kingswood Hall, as might be expected, the festivities were full of splendour and rich in Christian charity. Preparations began in the first week of November, when Zelah descended to the vast kitchen to see that puddings were made according to the Scholes family recipe. Quite a ceremony attended the mixing of them. Even the ironmaster must stir the heavy mess of black fruit, reeking with brandy, and make a secret wish. And all his daughters naturally fell to teasing one another, and trying to guess their inmost desires, with much shrieking and giggling. But mincemeat and plum cakes called for no particular celebration, and were stored away to mature unnoticed. While the geese on the home farm, unaware that they were destined for the ironmaster's table, honked and ate to their heart's content until their necks were summarily wrung.

Then there was much plotting, whispering and consultation over suitable gifts: involving expeditions to Millbridge to buy or order elaborate presents, and patient handiwork at home on more intimate offerings. And this year the Cornishman, instead of eating his dinner alone at Manchester, had accepted an invitation to join the family.

After his initial overnight stay at Kingswood Hall, and the emergence of a closer understanding with the ironmaster, Hal Vivian had sent for his modest luggage from the Royal George, and never again stayed there as he had done.

He was to create two steam-engines which worked in partnership. *The Lancashire Horse,* equal in power to fourteen horses, would draw twelve wagons of coal at an average rate of three miles an hour up an incline railway. Here they were disengaged, and *The Cornishman* conveyed the wagons down to the river to be put aboard barges.

While Hal Vivian busied himself with design and execution, William set a little army of labourers to dig up the old wooden railroad at Tarbock, and lay stone sleepers for the new one. His financial advisers were alarmed, his managers dubious, but the ironmaster would not listen to them. For the first time in his life he was taking risks for the sake of someone other than himself, whom he regarded as equally important. His affection for the Cornishman was by no means disinterested, but it was deeper than any he had previously experienced. He was prepared to sacrifice much, even part of himself, to pay homage to it. He no longer reckoned entirely in terms of profit and loss.

Gradually, painlessly, Hal Vivian was growing used to being part of an ordered household, to joining a social circle of some distinction. Though he fought instinctively to keep his freedom, in such little ways as arriving and departing unexpectedly and arguing with the ironmaster over detail, he was being weaned away from his bachelor life.

Cautiously, delicately, little by little, William Howarth played his future son-in-law onto the family shore. Holding her breath, Anna watched and waited. For father and daughter were alike. Beneath that silver-gilt head ticked a practical mind. Within that porcelain fragility lay the ironmaster's fibre. She did not overstep the limits of friendship. Showing the self-control of her mother, the determination of her father, she kept back her need to love and be loved. Wisest of virgins, she held her lamp trimmed and ready: much as honest Alf Rowbottom crept and sounded his way through the darkest caverns, with a vital flame held close to his breast.

And at last all their patient preparations had borne fruit.

'It is the Eve!' cried Anna Howarth at breakfast, and smiled on the Cornishman who had arrived the previous night.

'It is the Eve!' echoed five-year-old Ruth, in imitation of this lovely elder sister.

'Who else is coming this year, love?' asked the ironmaster, busy with hot chops. 'Tibby or Kitty?'

'Neither, my love. Tibby must take her boys to the Freames this year, and Kitty is too close to her time to travel. I should have liked to be with her, but there was so much to do here. . . .'

'It is an extraordinary thing,' cried the ironmaster, ignoring the plea in his wife's voice, 'that you and I, love, could not produce a single son – and Tibby has two already.'

But the old seminal ache had gone. Hal Vivian sat at his table more and more frequently. All should be well.

'And are you going to help the girls to fetch the yule log home, Hal?' William said cheerfully, laying down his knife and fork.

'Oh pray do, Cornishman!' cried Ruth, who showed all the pretty vices of a favourite. 'For it is such fun, and the gardener's boy does the heavy work. And the children cheer as we go through Snape. And because I am very little I can ride upon the log!' And she came over to him, and twined her arms about his neck, saying, 'I shall marry you, Cornishman, by and by.'

Anna bent her head over her plate in a pleasing anguish. For how she would have loved to say and do the same.

'Ruth!' said Zelah, 'go back to thy place and do not tease Mr Vivian so. And do not address him as *Cornishman* but in a more seemly manner. No, William, do not let her come to thee instead! How am I to teach the child if thee will laugh at all her naughtiness?'

'I shall help to haul the yule log home,' said Hal Vivian, laughing with the rest of the family at Ruth's self-assurance and impudence, 'and Ruth shall ride upon it. But I do not think I shall marry her – yet!'

He spoke in a droll fashion, and in spite of himself he glanced at the silver-gilt head opposite to gauge Anna's reaction. She knew he looked at her, and would not return his look. And in that moment he felt as though a great tide tugged at his feet and would pull him under.

In his generosity and pride, the ironmaster had instituted the Eve of Christmas as a Howarth family occasion. So by six o'clock everyone except Ambrose Longe was standing round the fireplace in the main hall, while manservants carried in two yule logs: one being the charred remains of last year's offering, the other a gnarled green trunk which the girls had borne homeward that afternoon.

'We chose a green one, Papa,' Anna announced, 'so that it should last all the longer.'

'Do you know this custom, Hal?' William asked genially, as the wood was placed upon the stone hearth with great ceremony and ignited.

'Aye sir, for I was in North America one Christmas, where they have serving-men dressed as Spirits of Mirth from an older time. And there they sing the Wassail Song, and proclaim a toast to the log.'

The ironmaster cried, 'Then give us that toast, Cornishman!'

His glass steaming with a noggin of *Lamb's Wool*, Hal Vivian stood before the assembled Howarths: apart from them, yet almost one of them.

'I charge the log that it shall burn brightly and well upon the hearth of this hospitable mansion!' he cried. 'And may it shed a glow of warmth and friendliness throughout the coming year!'

'Hurray to that!' shouted Dick, beaming and ruddy.

'Aye, hurrah to that!' echoed the ironmaster. 'Come

forward and raise your glasses, all of you.' Motioning to the servants to join them. 'Here's to the Eve! May we have the happiest Christmas of our lives!'

Then the staff gave three cheers for Mr Howarth, another three for Mrs Howarth, three for the young ladies, and three more for the season. The glasses were refilled, and vast platters of mince pies were passed round as a preliminary appetiser to the feast which would follow. By this time each of them had consumed a fair quantity of hot ale, roasted crab apples, toast, nutmeg, sugar and eggs, and were feeling convivial.

Above their heads, suspended from the massive chandelier, hung and swung the kissing-bough: a dark glossy globe of evergreens, gleaming with ribbon, blushing with apples, bejewelled with mistletoe berries.

Hal Vivian kept quiet in the corner by the fire. The drink made him warm and faintly tipsy after his exertions of the afternoon, and he would have preferred them to let him be. But Anna's voice came through the fuzz of conversation, the haze of firelight.

'Why, what a wanderer you are, Cornishman – bedazzling we poor homebodies with your foreign customs.'

She was teasing him as usual. Mockery was the only bridge they dared cross together as yet.

'Aye, madam, *my* home is the next hostelry along the road.'

'How I envy you your freedom, sir! Were I a man I should travel the whole world.'

'You would find it a most uncomfortable place, Miss Anna. No maid. No hot chocolate. No pianoforte to play. Aches in your bones. Fleas in the blankets. Bugs in the beds – if you were fortunate enough to find a bed at all – and a general disregard for honest soap and water. Your nose would be in a perpetual state of wrinkle.'

She knew her nose was charming, and smiled radiantly upon him.

'But you do not understand me at all, Cornishman.

Young ladyhood has been thrust upon me. I am not what I seem.'

She stood as near him as convention allowed, and the warmth of the fire brought out some subtle personal fragrance. He could see the life pulse beating in the hollow of her throat, the delicate line of neck and bosom where the pale satin of her gown met the paler satin of her flesh. He knew that she longed to be possessed. He longed to possess her. Bemused by her presence, he entered upon the perils of flirtation.

'You astonish me, madam. I had thought you to be *everything* you seem.' And he looked the compliment directly, meaningfully at her. 'Would you rob me of all illusion? Is Miss Anna Howarth merely a vagabond in elegant disguise?'

She laughed very high and excitedly, but needed to persuade him that they were of one mind.

'Sir, I am quite serious in what I say. There are two Annas, if you will. One you see before you, who is the ironmaster's third daughter. The other, I – but only I! – know well, so you must take her on trust. And though she has never been tried, she would welcome the discomforts of true adventure. For very often, Cornishman, her life seems small and dull and unimportant.'

He paid her real attention now.

'Should *you* like to be a woman, Cornishman?'

'Lord, no!' he answered too quickly, shocked by the notion. 'I thank God I am as I am. A woman's life is mostly penances!' But he caught himself up at this point, feeling he had got into deep water, and added lightly, 'Which is why we cosset and adore them so.'

'You disappoint me, Mr Vivian,' said Anna in her mother's tone, frank and sweet. 'I had told you a truth. I did not expect to be silenced with flattery.'

In the short pause which ensued he knew he must decide whether to go on or to go back. His mind was turbulent with fear and admiration. She had made him see her, instead of any pretty girl with a rich father.

'I beg your pardon, madam,' said the Cornishman. 'I had not meant to insult you. And since truths should speak to one another, let me tell you in all earnest that *I* am not what I seem, either.'

At this moment of mutual fascination, a small passing Howarth, some two-and-a-half years old, tumbled over Anna's feet.

He was a typical Kit's Hill product: apple-cheeked, sturdy of body and limb, with grey-green eyes and thick fair hair. In one hand he held a mince pie, which he was concerned to save from destruction. With the other hand he grasped Anna's satin skirt in order to steady himself.

'What a multitude you are,' said the Cornishman, with all the astonishment of one who had been an only child. 'Whose lad is that?'

'My uncle Dick's youngest, to date. Name of Herbert, sir.'

Once more upon his feet, Herbert studied his pie with some anxiety, but finding it unscathed he fetched it to his mouth and took a bite. The feel of Anna's gown pleased him. His smile was lavish, his affection spontaneous. He clutched both gown and pie afresh, and began to lever himself into her satin lap, spraying her with crumbs as he cried imperiously. 'Want Umpy-Dumpy!'

'Herbert wishes me to ride him upon my knee, and recite Humpty-Dumpty,' Anna translated, between laughter and chagrin.

The boy, now settled to his entire comfort and satisfaction, crammed the rest of the pastry into his mouth and shouted through it, 'Umpy-Dumpy! Umpy-Dumpy!'

'Put him down and give him another pie,' Hal Vivian counselled, and his eyes glinted with amusement. 'He looks the sort of fellow who would rather have a pie than a rhyme any day.'

He stopped a maidservant who was going by, and divested her of some of her wares. 'Here, Herbert, take a couple. One for each hand, my lad.'

The child obligingly accepted these offerings, biting first

at one and then at the other pastry to make sure of both. But on Anna's attempting to put him down he stiffened his back and legs, flushed with determination, and called upon Humpty-Dumpty as though that unlucky egg were his champion.

Anna made a grimace at the Cornishman, who could not help laughing. And she, seeing the funny side to this situation, joined him.

'Well, let the fellow stay upon his throne,' said Hal Vivian. 'Providing we feed him he shall not come between us in spirit.'

He spoke lightly, tenderly, seriously, as she had not heard him speak before. He looked fully upon her, as he had not done before. She had aroused his desire and his interest. And relief was at hand.

Catching sight of their situation from the other side of the hall, Alice Howarth gave her elder daughter a push and a frown.

'Go and fetch our Herbert, and look sharp about it,' she ordered. 'You should have more sense than let him run off like that. He's sitting on your cousin's lap and you know what he's like when he gets excited.'

Thoughts of Anna's expensive satin gown ruined by a flood of excitement dismayed Alice utterly. Her eyes filled with tears. She was pregnant for the ninth time, and though she produced babies with enviable ease she was nearing forty and had too much to do.

'Go on with you! And think about somebody else besides yourself for a change,' she scolded, and slapped Mary's arm.

The girl was now eleven, close to puberty and abnormally sensitive. Her milky skin turned not scarlet but white with resentment. The only feeling Mary ever had in common with her mother was a fear of being invited to Kingswood Hall. To cross the polished parquet floor was purgatory. She felt that everyone was looking at her and laughing at the incongruous spectacle she made.

She knew that her brown wool dress and stout clumsy

shoes were ill-looking and ill-fitting. Sophy and Molly, a year older and a year younger than herself, were wearing identical pale green and white striped dresses, with emerald velvet sashes. Their black silk slippers were strapped criss-cross fashion in the Spanish style.

Meanwhile, young Herbert Howarth became aware of trouble to come. In his enjoyment of the moment he had forgotten an old weakness, nowadays rare indeed but still liable to disgrace him – his bladder.

'Oh Lor'!' Anna whispered to herself, and clutched Herbert to her lest he expose their joint shame.

He, only too glad to remain unnoticed, finished his third pie with some misgivings: seeing his doom approach in the shape of a hostile sister, who gazed on him with knowledge and disdain.

'You haven't, have you?' Mary hissed, trying to communicate with the lost one, and to seem unperturbed by the company he was keeping.

'*No!*' lied Herbert, with more confidence than he felt. 'Stay wiv Anna. Umpy-Dumpy. Pie.'

Anna tried to weigh up the advantages and disadvantages of her present plight, while smiling upon both cousins.

'He is very well with me,' she said, pacifically.

'I,' Herbert announced, growing worried, '*like* Anna.'

'Mary Howarth!' Alice shrilled across the assembly. 'Do as I say!'

Mary swallowed nervously and made a grab for her youngest brother.

'No – o – o – o!' he wailed desperately.

Everyone was now alerted, and need not have been, but Alice could never handle delicate situations. She began to push her way through the guests, alternately apologising to them and calling to her errant son.

For, naughty though he was, still he was her baby.

'No – o – o – o!' cried Herbert, all bravado gone, fists in eyes.

'Why not, love?' asked Alice, shoving Mary aside with

one elbow, holding out both arms to the child. 'Why not come to your Mam?'

He peered through his fingers, which were all tears and crumbs.

'Little bit wet,' Herbert confessed.

The amused uproar that followed covered the embarrassment of the protaganists. Zelah hurried forward, laughing with the rest, trying to set her sister-in-law at ease for the hundredth time, knowing there could be a thousandth and never the slightest gleam of communication.

She also thought of her daughter, who had evidently been treading sacred groves with the Cornishman and would be painfully exposed to good-natured ridicule. But Anna, seeing that all was discovered, threw back her head and laughed as heartily as the rest, and the Cornishman laughed with her, but very kindly, and admired her spirit.

'I think you had best come upstairs with us, and change, love,' said Zelah, relieved at finding one person less to comfort.

Then, as Alice dissolved into tears and Herbert joined her, she sent her daughter an expressive look.

'Canst thee help me with these poor people, who are our guests?' the look asked Anna.

'I beg you to excuse me, if you will, Cornishman,' Anna said, smiling on him. 'I have an urgent matter to attend to. Perhaps we shall speak with each other again?'

'Madam,' he cried, quite won over by her grace and gallantry. 'I shall be waiting for nothing else, I do assure you.'

He bowed low before her, kissed her outstretched hand, and coming up from his obeisance looked into her eyes with deliberate intent. Anna blushed beautifully, curtsied deeply, looked back at him in heady understanding, and ran away to catch up the sorry procession now moving towards the staircase.

'Oh do not punish him, Auntie,' Hal Vivian heard her

say, as she put her arm round the sobbing culprit, 'for he is a dear little fellow, and could not help it.'

A remark which somewhat softened Alice's woe, since she agreed with it on the whole. But Herbert roared as though he had fallen off that mythical wall, and nothing and no one would ever put him together again.

The Cornishman now became aware of a profoundly disturbing gaze just two feet to his left.

'Well, miss?' he said automatically, jokingly. 'Have you nothing better to look at than me?'

The girl stared at him, and considered his question.

'I suppose not,' said Mary Howarth, blighting him.

Although Hal Vivian normally inhabited some world other than this one, and could hardly have been called vain, he was nevertheless piqued by her reply, and set out to show her she was wrong.

'But I am generally thought to be good company,' he cried.

The faintest lift of her stern brows was his only reward.

'Let me find a nice large mince pie for you,' he said courteously.

'I'm not our Herbert. All stomach!' she replied witheringly. Then, hearing her lack of polish in contrast to his own manner, she modified her tone. 'I don't eat much. Ta, all the same.'

'You look as though you ate very little, Miss...?'

'Mary. They named me after me Grandma Braithwaite. That cousin over there,' pointing to seven-year-old Dorcas Pole, 'is called after our Grandma Howarth. I wish I was, but Mam never liked her, you see. She's dead now, Grandma Howarth, but I can remember her. And me Aunt Charlotte that give me this locket – it's the only nice thing I've got – I remember her. But *she's* dead, and all....'

She noted Cousin Dorcas's white embroidered muslin dress, her white pantaloons showing the requisite two inches of lace.

'That's one of Cousin Molly's old frocks,' she said keenly, bitterly. 'Aunt Zelah hands everything down, but my Mam won't have any of them. She says they're not right to wear on a farm. That's why I've got this 'un on. It were cut down from one of hers. It looks like it, and all! Proper scarecrow! I'm sick of looking like a proper scarecrow!'

She pretended to be smoothing a fold of the rough wool, but her eyes were charged with sudden tears. The Cornishman was touched, and some of the tenderness he felt for Anna flowed over this homely waif.

'Come and sit by me, Miss Mary,' he said in his most charming manner, 'and I will tell you a story about a boy who went to the famous Bluecoat School in Manchester, where they wear a particular uniform. It is a fine school, but the uniform is a little hard on the boys once they are outside the gates. For the city and grammar school lads call them names, and pelt them with stones. . . .'

'That boy's you, isn't he?' said Mary, impaling his fancy.

'I see I must be truthful with you, miss!'

'Well, it's best, isn't it?' said Mary with diverting honesty. 'Then we all know where we are, don't we?' And wiped her eyes dry.

For the second time that evening, Hal Vivian first gasped and then laughed at unexpected frankness in one of the female sex.

'Miss Mary,' he confessed, 'I am about to tell you the story of my schooldays.'

'Do you know,' she answered, as nicely as she could, 'I think I fancy eating one of them mince pies, after all.'

By the time Anna returned, half-an-hour later, the Cornishman and Mary had entered upon a conversation which he would quickly forget, but she would always remember. Given encouragement, as Dick said, the girl could shine. And shine she did, most luminously. Her woes were fast receding in the joy of the moment. Her awkwardness disappeared with animation, her sulky face was transfigured, her clumsy costume was revealed as mere disguise.

Anna raised her eyebrows significantly at Zelah.

'What a flowering in *that* little wilderness,' she remarked.

'Then give her a little more time with him,' said Zelah, smiling. 'She who hath a garden should not grudge a bloom.'

The two women looked upon one another with complete understanding.

'Should I entertain Aunt Alice?' Anna asked lightly. 'That shall be my secret Christmas gift to Mary. In fact, I will do anything for anyone at the moment – apart from taking Cousin Herbert upon my lap again!'

NINE

The Locked Heart

Recollection of his schooldays had released an emotional spring, and that night the Cornishman dreamed of his boyhood.

He was alone on the Stockport highway in the twilight of a winter afternoon, hurrying to reach the shelter of Ardwick Green before dark fell. At six-years-old his mother judged him sensible enough to be sent upon short errands, and in his hand he clutched the object of one of them – a packet of Bohea tea. Like any lad he hopped and whistled and talked to himself as he walked and ran, and marked off personal signposts on the way: Ardwick Bridge, the cattle barrier, the poplars on the village green, the first glimpse of the lake beyond. Nearly home. Just ahead of him stood the grand red-brick villas, built by Manchester businessmen who chose rural peace after a day's work in the city. The chimneys of Bewsey House sent comfortable spirals into the lambent air. Within those walls was peace and safety, toast and tea, his mother's smile, old Mrs Vivian's welcome. Once there, he was safe.

He opened the garden gate into an old nightmare.

Lost. Lost in a network of strange courts and cramped alleys. His nostrils dilating at odours putrescent, offensively sweet. Beset by a sense of life's hostility, of hopelessness. In a panic to be out of the place he stopped at the nearest house and tried the latch.

The door opened onto a long passageway at the end of which he could see a woman stirring a cauldron of stew over the kitchen fire. As he strove to identify her in the gloom she turned to look at him: standing silently, spoon in hand. And he saw it was his mother. Joy and terror were mingled, for he longed to be enfolded in those beloved arms, and yet knew that she was about to ask the impossible of him. In his fear he shouted, 'No! No! No!' And so woke himself – groaning aloud, his cheeks wet with an old grief, his heart heavy with an old foreboding. But after a while slept again. And dreamed again.

The room was ancient and tranquil. Through the oriel window came shafts of light in which the motes danced and spun. They glistened on vast oak tables and ponderous chairs, touched to life the dark and dingy oil paintings of dead divines. For this was Easter Monday and the trustees sat in council over a crowd of poor, worthy and clever boys from whom they would select a few, to be educated and maintained at the expense of the College until they were apprenticed.

Over the wide chimneypiece hung a portrait of the school's shrewd and benevolent founder, Humphrey Chetham. Upon one side of the grate was carved a cock, said to crow when it smelled roast beef (and there were those who said they had heard it do so); on the other, a carved pelican fed her young with her life-blood.

'Let the boy and his mother step forth,' cried an official voice.

Hal felt her hand close round his, and gave it a squeeze of comfort though her own was trembling.

'Where are the necessary papers? Where is the witness?' demanded the warden, very dry and formidable.

'Be careful you tell him the truth, and nothing but the truth,' whispered a voice behind them, 'for he sees and knows everything.'

'Is the lad of good character?' the warden was saying. 'Is he of legitimate birth and baptised in the Christian Church? Is he healthy and strong? Is he intelligent and willing to work hard? And are his parents so poor that he cannot be educated without we help him?'

Hal's father now came forward carrying an armful of scrolls, and to his horror the boy saw that they were plans for pumping-engines.

'Are these the proofs of the family's poverty, honesty and industry?' the warden was saying.

To all these questions old Santo Vivian was beaming and nodding, though as one of the boy's parents he could not be a witness, and the papers he put on the table were proof of the family's prosperity. Hal's terror communicated itself to his mother and she put her hand to her mouth, afraid. The trustees unrolled the plans.

The hush in the room was absolute.

The warden leaned forward across the oak table and spoke directly to the frightened child before him.

'You are not what you seem,' he cried, in judgement.

And changed into the ironmaster.

'Confess!' shouted the board of trustees.

'Confess!' roared Humphrey Chetham, coming out of the portrait over the chimneypiece.

'Confess!' crowed the cock from the ample grate.

His mother did not answer, and he saw that she was carved of wood like the pelican on the fireplace, and her life's blood was dripping on the polished floor.

He rose and dressed, avoiding servants and family, and walked the winter garden in solitary thought. And wherever he looked he found corruption and decay. Rooks had abandoned their nests in the elms, and the bare black trees could no longer hide industrial Wroughton. The nightmare was upon him, laying waste all hope and promise, bringing with it a debt from the past.

Laughter and beauty faltered and hung back at the sight of this human desert. Then strolled on, a little more slowly than usual but still smiling, and slipped an arm in his.

'It would seem that your Christmas is not merry, Cornishman,' said Anna cautiously.

For she had slept all night in the swansdown of their mutual understanding.

'I have had a bad dream,' he replied stiffly, 'and am not myself in consequence.'

Skilled in the art of managing a difficult man, she ventured to lead him imperceptibly back to the house, to quieten his mind.

'When we were children, and had a bad dream, my mother pretended to turn it into a dandelion clock and blew it clean away.'

He smiled a little then, but a moment later had relapsed into his black mood.

'*My* mother used to say that there was fat sorrow and lean sorrow,' he replied sombrely. 'The rich find trouble more easy to blow away. Our early years would not be moved so lightly, for we were poor.'

She was silent, thinking the problem over. He did not withdraw his arm since that would have been discourteous, but he kept it wooden and unresponsive and she knew this.

'So you dreamed of lean sorrow last night, did you, Cornishman?' she asked, looking into his dark face.

Reluctantly, he nodded.

'And can that sorrow never be healed, though it is long past?'

'No more than a brand can be erased, I do believe.'

He spoke coldly, and saw tears of hurt in her eyes.

'I do not mean to sound unkind,' he said, part penitent.

They sauntered on, arm in arm: she unsatisfied, he just as wretched for a different reason. But her ebullient spirit would not be quenched for long. He had talked tenderly to her the previous evening.

'Last night, you told me that you were not what you seemed,' she began again in a sprightly tone, and contrived to dry her eyes without being noticed. 'And were about to explain yourself when Herbert misbehaved. And afterwards I saw you speaking so gently to my cousin Mary that I did not care to interrupt – for her life is difficult. So I never heard your tale, in consequence, and this morning I am ate up with curiosity, sir!'

He felt the softness of her arm through his sleeve, the resilience of her young body moving to his pace. The winter sun gilded her hair. Her gallantry in face of his hostility touched him. He longed and feared to confide in her. But shied away for the moment, choosing instead to tease her with another matter.

'Anna, I am in the very devil of a quandary,' said Hal Vivian more cheerfully, allowing himself to dwell in her hazel eyes.

Her buoyancy was restored, her smile brilliant.

'How so, sir?'

'If I confide in you, you must not tell your father, madam.'

Anna's pink mouth, dropping open with excitement, was an enticing spectacle. She squeezed his arm and promised never to tell a living soul – though threatened with torture and slow death.

'What a nonsensical girl you are, miss,' he said reprovingly, but amusement warmed him. 'In strictest confidence then, I have been offered the most astonishing opportunity in South America.'

Her face lost all its colour and vivacity and he could not bear that, for she stood between him and chaos. So he caught up her hands and fetched them to his mouth and kissed them tenderly.

'It would only be for a year or so,' he promised. 'I should come back again. But it is such a chance – the chance of a lifetime, Anna.'

'And what of me?' she cried, pulling her hands away and thus showing considerable strength of character, for her fingers were entranced by his kisses. Still there was a female war to be won. She must not be led astray by a single encounter. 'A year or two, you say? As though that were nothing! Are my feelings not to be consulted, Cornishman? What of me, sir?'

He was stern with her, for he must be sure.

'Were you honest with me about travelling the world?' he demanded. 'Did you truly mean what you said about enduring discomfort and virtual homelessness? Or were you flirting with me, as women do when they seek to bind a man to them at any cost to themselves or him? If so I have no further time for you. But if you wished to be a fellow-wanderer. . . .'

The title sounded so right in Anna's ears that she went up on the toes of her little black slippers to kiss him. And he, never having experienced youth and love and beauty all wrapped up in one girl, abandoned his principles and crushed her lips and waist until both he and she were dizzy.

'Mercy on us!' cried Anna, getting her breath back. 'It is either all or nothing with you, Cornishman!'

They walked on together, delighted with themselves, in that moving and ridiculous way lovers are delighted at nothing.

'South America, then?' he challenged her.

'South America,' Anna answered with conviction. 'No hot chocolate! No maid! No pianoforte! An abundance of fleas, bad odours and bed bugs. But we shall have to tell Papa first, of course.'

'Of course.'

Exasperated, adoring, she cried, 'Have you not forgot to ask me something, Cornishman?'

'What should I have forgot, madam?'

Smiling, for he loved to bait her.

She made a sound of disgust. Then seeing her parents coming from the house, well-wrapped against the cold, she ran towards them pulling him with her by the hand.

Crying, 'We have something to tell you!

Thus compromised, Hal Vivian was forced to make his declaration direct to the astonished ironmaster.

'I do beg your pardon, sir, for this sudden. . . . Anna has such a way of hurtling into situations. . . .'

Then resolved his future and his past in one brief brave speech.

'Sir, I want to marry Anna, but there is something you should all know before you give me leave.'

They sat in Zelah's private parlour. And again the Cornishman confessed, 'I am not what I seem.'

There was a little silence, then Anna lifted his hand to her lips and kissed it. She looked lovingly into his pale eyes. She made her own declaration.

'Nothing you tell me will alter what I feel for you. Nothing will be too dreadful for me to hear or to understand. If there is anything to forgive, then I forgive you before you even speak of it. Whatever you have done wrong, we can right it. Whatever you have omitted we can replace. I love you, and that is all that matters, now and for ever.'

He began to talk, stumbling at first. Then, as the knowledge left him, more easily but no less sadly and heavily.

'Before I speak of her, of my mother, I must tell you that I love and honour her, and always shall. I am sick and faint at the notion that any might wrong her, even by so much as a thought. If she were here you would need only to look upon her to know her truth and goodness. You above all must not blame her, for you are the only ones with whom I have entrusted her history.' He looked at them directly, saying, 'I am not Santo Vivian's son!'

Then he looked away again, through the window, and through the leafless trees, finding the courage to tell his tale.

'Santo Vivian, God rest his soul, was our shield and buckler against a world of poverty. Heaven alone knew how much he did for us, how much we needed him. But he was not my natural father. He adopted me years later, when he married my mother.'

The Easter Monday sun shone upon the wigged heads of the trustees, and dappled a burly grey-headed man who stood witness for the boy.

'Come forward, Mr Vivian,' said the governor. 'Would you oblige the board by answering the following questions?'

He glanced at the little sheaf of papers before him. He meant to be impartial but his tone deferred to these particulars.

'Are you Santo Vivian? Head of the engineering firm of VIVIAN & COMPANY, off Deansgate, Manchester? And presently resident at, and owner of Bewsey House, Ardwick Green, in the suburbs of Manchester?'

'I am, sir.'

'And is this your housekeeper and her son Henry, who have resided with you and your mother, Mrs Redvers Vivian, for the past four years?'

'It is indeed, sir.'

The woman dropped a curtsey to the board. The lad bowed.

'And were you the person who particularly recommended this boy Henry, as being worthy of further education?'

'I did, and do, sir.' Very emphatically.

'Which his mother, being reliant only on her wages and her health and strength, is unable to afford?' A nod from Santo. 'We have here your housekeeper's marriage lines, the boy's registration of birth and certificate of baptism, and an excellent character reference from Mrs Redvers Vivian who is unable to be present.

'Apparently, however, there is no satisfactory history of the five years previous to her employment with you. By your own admission she was in dire straits, and had been so ever since her husband disappeared prior to the boy's birth, in Liverpool – which is in itself no good recommendation, though accidents do happen. Neither can she produce any relative, or friend or employer from that period in her life, to vouch for her. Poverty is no disgrace, but such mystery surrounding her poverty may well be. We have no wish to distress anyone, Mr Vivian, but the requirements of the benefice insist upon the honesty and integrity of *both* parents. We feel there is some reasonable doubt in this case. We wondered whether you could assist us to clear it?'

The middle-aged man seemed to grow in stature and dignity as he confronted the tribunal. He had laid aside his genial self and answered formally as behoved the occasion.

'Sirs, anything I can tell you will be but hearsay. For it is what Annie – as we call her – told mother and me. Her husband was a jobbing carpenter, and by all accounts a good husband. I never heard her say no word against him. And they'd been wed a long while, sure enough. Like Sarah, in the Bible, the Lord had blessed her late in life. And this handsome lad was to be their first and only child.

'Her kin turned Annie out when she was wed, and his kin was dead already. Work was hard to come by, and wages low. They thought to better themselves, so they up and came to Liverpool where a carpenter might make good money on the ships.

'They looked to make an honest living and found naught but bad fortune. Annie had sewed their savings into a gown she wore, to keep them safe. But while they slept one night in poor lodgings that gown was stolen, savings and all. And soon after she lost her husband as well. Come winter, she had neither man nor money nor a friend to turn to, and the child expected at the coldest time of year. How she made out, well, I don't know.'

And he shook his head to himself, forgetting his audience.

'Where was I to?' he asked himself, and then picked up the thread of the tale again. 'Well, her worst enemy – and I don't know of one – could never say Annie was a lazy woman. She'll work until she drops. So somehow she makes out. And if there was but one cup of milk to drink and one crust to eat, the boy would have it – my word on that.

'Then somebody tells her there's more money and work to be found in Manchester. Though how they make that out I don't know, for I've seen folk starve here same as anywhere else. But what does Annie do but pack up their worldly goods, which went in one old shawl, quite comfortable. And she took her bundle in one hand, and her boy by the other, and off they started – from Liverpool to Manchester is some way, I tell you – until she sits on our back doorstep at last, with her poor head – so!'

Here he unconsciously mimicked the extreme weariness

of the supplicant. Then was brisk again.

'So we took them in and fed them both. But Annie wouldn't eat unless we gave her work to pay for it. So we did. And then they stayed. And now we can't think how we did without her.'

The housekeeper stood composed and pale before her inquisitors, wearing her best black wool gown in honour of the occasion, and her Sunday apron. Her linen cap was freshly washed, starched and pleated. Round her neck was a frilled muslin kerchief, passed down by a kind employer and skilfully mended. Though no longer young she was still comely, with her shining brown hair in braids under her cap, and those clear grey eyes which her son had inherited. Her hands were not beautiful, but capable and neatly kept. She seemed a modest little wren to have produced such a vivid and handsome lad, with his dark good looks and graceful bearing. Though Santo Vivian evidently thought otherwise. His admiration counted against her respectability.

He knew it. The shrewd fellow. He changed his tune.

'I know what idle minds might think, and idle tongues might say,' he continued in a sterner tone. 'Though I never once heard Annie speak ill of anybody. I doubt she'd even *think* ill of them, though she had cause. I've never seen a better mother nor a better teacher. She taught the boy his letters, and I taught him his sums. And he's a credit to us both, and so I tell you. He'd be a credit to this school, if he was let. Some handsome scholar you lose if you turn him away!'

The room was very quiet and intent. He gathered himself for a final burst of oratory.

'You say you want proof? Well, what better can you have than the proof before you? There's proof that an honest man wed Annie, and proof before you that she's a tidy woman with a fine son. And something else I tell you,' glowering at the tribunal. 'If so be that honest carpenter was here now, he'd knock down the pack of you for thinking ill of her. And if the founder of this school, Old

Humphrey Chetham, was alive today – he'd hold the man's hat while he did it.'

Whereupon he shook his head once or twice, as though regretting his loss of temper, and sat down glancing guiltily from time to time at his housekeeper.

There was a considerable pause while the board conferred together. Then their subdued whispers changed at last into smiles. . . .

Anna held out her hand, and the Cornishman put it to his lips. His face was bleak, his pale eyes full of tears.

'That was what she did when they accepted me for a place all those years ago,' said Hal Vivian. 'Took my hand. And kissed it. And wept.'

After a moment he said, 'But that is only half the tale' – and so continued.

'I was but seven years of age. I knew that Mr Vivian was angry on my mother's behalf, that there was some shame connected with my father's disappearance, but I chose to put the knowledge away from me.

'My education began. I went home to the house at Ardwick Green for my holidays. I learned my lessons and made friends and fought enemies, like any other lad. I was accepted by the other pupils as one of themselves, honoured or mocked by outsiders – it did not matter which – for being a Blue coat boy. For the first time in my life I belonged somewhere and was somebody, in my own right. And I thrived.

'A year or two later old Mrs Vivian died, and Santo Vivian came over one Saturday to see me. It was a summer afternoon, I remember, and he got permission to take me out. I loved the man, and he loved me. No doubt about it.

'He told me he had long loved and honoured my mother and wanted to marry her, but she would not without I gave my full and hearty consent. In his goodness and humility he asked me if I would like him to adopt me, to give me his name, and to become my father.

'I replied, "Oh yes, sir, if my own father were dead."

'He stopped dead himself for an instant, and then went into such an explanation as you would give an adult. He said that my real father had been gone for over seven years, and could therefore be considered legally dead.

'Being a sharp little fellow, I asked him if I should have to leave Chetham's Hospital, since my circumstances would no longer be poor. He was flustered. He must have been amazed how much I understood, how much I had remembered. But he answered me in full. He had seen the governor, Mr Terry, and they both agreed that it would be a pity to alter my course at this stage. So Santo Vivian would pay for my schooling. Thus giving my opportunity, but not my place, to some other poor but clever boy who needed it as much as I had done.

'I expressed myself as being well pleased with this notion. And now all points were cleared to my precocious satisfaction, I assured him that there was no man I should like better as a father than himself. After which statement we got back to our usual good fellowship, and he filled me full of treacle toffee.

'So I, who had been a poor and fatherless nobody without a future, became the son of Santo Vivian with all the world before me.

'I believe that the next years were the happiest I had ever known. Then my mother died suddenly. Her heart, so great in every other respect, failed her. She who had been our centre left us empty. I was eleven years old at the time, and again it was high summer. Santo Vivian heaped her coffin with roses of every hue, for they were her favourite flower. I cannot now smell the scent without I am reminded of her, and of that day. All my memories are in some way darkened like this. It is as though destiny marked me.

'The two of us, father and son, now set up a bachelor existence together. Bewsey House was sold. We moved into rooms over the firm's house in Deansgate. We engaged a housekeeper – who is still with me – to look after us. And, boy though I was, we made VIVIAN & SON the beginning and end of our lives. Until I met you, Anna, it was all I had. And all I wanted or cared about.'

She held his hand tightly and said in her pretty, inconsequent way, 'She was called Annie, then? Much like me?'

'No, that was a pet name he had for her,' the Cornishman replied hurriedly. 'Though it is true her name was much like yours.'

She had caused him to disgress, and motioned him to continue, watching his face, listening with loving attention.

'Four years ago,' said the Cornishman, coming to the nub and pain of his story, 'I inherited Santo Vivian's entire estate. And on going through his papers I found my mother's marriage certificate.

'All my old terrors returned to haunt me; no one who has been poor in purse and hope would wonder at them. What had become of that unknown father, who vanished in Liverpool before I was born? I belonged to him in no way but the one of begetting, and yet he rose in my mind like some wretched ghost demanding expiation.

'Then strangely enough, a short while after, you made your first business appointment with me, sir' – inclining his head at the ironmaster – 'and though I had never been in this part of the world before, the name of Wyndendale seemed curiously familiar. I was puzzled to know why, until I dreamed – as I sometimes do – where to look for it. And on my mother and father's certificate of marriage I found that same name. They were married near Millbridge.

'I never allow anything to come between me and the work I am on, so it was upon the conclusion of my business here that I ventured to pursue my private enquiry. I found the chapel, and I found something else as well. My father's name on a humble stone in the chapel yard. He had died nearly eight years before I was born. . . .'

Now he looked at them fully, and said, 'So who am I?'

And the silence was longer than it had ever been.

The ironmaster cleared his throat. He was a man of the

world. He begged pardon of the ladies first, but put forward his theory with some confidence.

'Well, lad, it seems to me that Santo Vivian *was* your father. And for some good reason – who knows what? – could not marry your mother and so set matters right, until the old lady died.'

'How should you be so fine an engineer, if he were not your father?' Anna cried triumphantly.

'If I had been his son,' said Hal Vivian, 'he would never have let my mother face that tribunal, nor lied to cover his own sins.'

Then Zelah spoke the truth that troubled him.

'Then thee must believe that thy mother put her trust in a man who abandoned thee both?'

He inclined his head.

Zelah said, 'Let her rest in peace. And thee rest also, Hal. For Santo Vivian put right thy wrongs, and was thy father before God, and thou art still his son – and still the Cornishman.'

Anna went on tiptoe to kiss one tear from her future husband's cheek, and embraced both parents tenderly.

The Cornishman laughed, somewhat tremulously, and brushed his hand across his pale eyes, and marvelled at the face of fortune.

'And yet,' he said, 'I wish – whatever mystery they had reason to conceal – that they had not lied for me.'

'We were taught, as Quakers, to look beneath the surface for the truth,' Zelah replied. 'And beneath thy mystery I find only two people that loved thee, and would even perjure themselves to help thee. Count thyself blessed, Cornishman.'

'You are very good,' said Hal Vivian, shaking both her hands. 'You are very like her. Except that she was humbly born.'

'And her name was Annie, much like mine!' cried Anna, entranced like a child with this joyful turn of events.

'Her name was Hannah,' said the Cornishman, smiling. 'Hannah Garside.'

The ironmaster became aware of chaos.

'When were you born, Cornishman?' he asked abruptly.

'On the second day of January 1793.'

'So *thou* art Hannah Garside's child,' said Zelah.

As though she had always known.

She looked at her husband, who looked at no one. The young couple stood immobilised in one another's arms. William Howarth rose, and walked slowly over to the window. He spoke with his back to them, staring into the winter garden.

'Then I can end your tale, Cornishman.'

The ironmaster drew breath from the very well of himself. He lifted his chin, braced his shoulders, and turned to meet the other man's eyes.

'Hannah Garside was my housekeeper at Flawnes Green. Was more, far more, than that to me – was very dear. Was my unwedded wife for upwards of five years.'

He glanced hurriedly at Zelah, but she was unsurprised, and any sorrow she had suffered from this knowledge had lost its sharpness.

'Hannah left me in the summer of 1792, giving me as reason the fact that I had met' – he looked now directly at Zelah – 'my present wife.'

Gently, Hal Vivian released himself from Anna's light embrace. His pallor was startling, his eyes winter-grey. But the likeness between him and the ironmaster now stood out, salient, wonderful.

'I had no knowledge, believe me,' William continued steadfastly, 'that she was with child by me. She left without warning. She wrote me a letter of loving explanation. Which I still have. Which you may see if you wish. For you have that right. . . .'

Though the moment was terrible beyond words, it was also beyond words wonderful. For the ironmaster was thinking as he looked and looked upon Hal Vivian, 'This is my *son*. My only begotten *son*.'

'I never heard from Hannah, nor of her, again. Until today.'

He spread out his arms in supplication, to show his sorrow. He knew that nothing he could do would ever be enough. He waited.

The Cornishman remained standing, staring at his father. Anna's mouth opened on a soundless cry. Zelah came over to her and clasped her, but the girl stood rigidly upright, unregarding, unmoving.

Hal Vivian said, almost inaudibly, 'So we have suffered to no purpose, in the end – she and I.'

The statement was so damning that it left the ironmaster with nothing to offer but reparation. He cleared his throat, which had become congested.

'You have a right, Hal, to my name and a part of my fortune,' he said awkwardly. 'I shall acknowledge your claim.'

And in all this the feelings of his wife and daughter were forgotten. The girl looked into some dark future of her own imagining. The mother patted her hand.

Then the Cornishman's heart and tongue were unlocked.

'Devil take your name and fortune, sir!' he cried. 'I would not touch either with a dirty stick. Have you understood nothing in all this? I am *proud* of the name I already bear. I wish it sprang of Santo Vivian's loins, instead of from his generous heart. And as for fortune – I can make that for myself. And the better without your help – who would have hampered and confined me to your own sphere.

'As for acknowledgement, I beg – nay, I command – that you tell no one. Ever. I charge you with this, upon your honour, sir. I charge you to say nothing of our relationship. For I would have none of you!'

But give the lad time, the ironmaster was thinking. Give my son time. And he will come round. Think of the power, the money, the future I could offer him!

As though he divined his father's thoughts, the Cornishman's eyes became colourless in their intensity.

'Sir, I have no need of you,' he said deliberately, 'except as an example of the man I should not care to become.'

Then he turned to Anna, and took her gently from her mother's embrace, and kissed her cold hands and cheeks, and communed with her as with a child who is grievously hurt.

'My little love,' he whispered. 'There is so much strength and hope and courage in you as would have healed and brightened all my days. Use it now for yourself. And you shall be well again, Anna.'

She clung to him, sobbing and inarticulate. He kissed her for the last time upon the lips, and gave her back to Zelah, who met his farewell halfway.

'I have so much for which to thank you,' he said hurriedly, 'and so much to regret. You too will have been damaged by this knowledge of me. I beg your pardon and your forgiveness most humbly. Think of me kindly, if you can.'

But Zelah answered, 'Nothing hath been said which I did not know, Cornishman. For thy mother confided in Dorcas Howarth, who helped her in the way she wished, and kept her secret safe until I stumbled on it. So let me kiss thee for thine own sake, and for thy mother's also. As Mrs Dorcas said so wisely, thou art a part of us after all. . . .'

Part Two

Alliances

1820-1825

TEN

Resurrection

Summer 1820

The Millbridge night was sultry, haunting the nostrils with mingled scents and odours from the dusty day. Now the white-headed woman, who had rested and refreshed herself after the long journey from London, ventured forth into Market Square. She had travelled as lightly and familiarly as the Cornishman, bundle in hand, accepting discomforts and delays, aching bones and an empty stomach, listening to the complaints of her fellow passengers with a half-smile and an abstracted air. Judged by her clothes and the condition of her hands she was a working woman. But her voice and bearing were those of a person of distinction, and her eyes shone with intelligence in her fine worn face.

There were few folk about at that hour, which seemed to suit her, for she turned her head aside and shrank into herself when anyone approached. But none gave her a second glance, and shortly she felt able to saunter slowly down the length of the High Street, looking all about her. There was a curious sadness in her quiet inspection, and at certain houses or places she paused for a while in reflection. Then walked on, and up the other side, until she was back at the Royal George, where she sat upon a bench outside the hostelry and considered some problem.

'Couldn't you find it, missis?' asked one of the stable lads, poking his head over the half-door. Then he spoke to someone behind him. 'Here, take over for a minute, will you, Len?' And so came out into the evening air. 'I'll show you, missis. You can all but see it from here. But it's tucked away, like.'

In his kindness he took the woman's arm and led her to

the archway at the end of the yard.

'There!' he said, pointing. 'In between Buckley's Millinery and Unsworth's Family Grocers. You canna miss it.'

She thanked him and tried to give him something for his trouble.

'Nay, put it back in thi pocket,' he said. 'I can do summat for nowt, can't I? I tell thee what, I'll stand and watch thee. If I see thee going wrong I'll call out. Right?'

She had no choice but to walk up to the door she had twice passed on purpose. She looked up at the black and gold sign, trembling. She kept in the shadow, out of range of that lighted window. She hesitated.

'That's the *Clarion*, missis!'

In despair she lifted the knocker and rapped softly. The noise of the printing press overrode this modest sound, and she stepped back, relieved that no one had heard her.

'Hammer on t'window!' the lad shouted.

She knocked louder now, afraid lest the stable boy come over to help her, and thus add to her explanations.

Simultaneously, a masculine voice shouted up the stairs, 'Open the door, for God's sake, Polly!'

While a female voice shrilled down the stairs, 'There's somebody at the door, Mr Ambrose.'

The woman listened to their voices almost in terror, and picked up her bundle from the step. Had her inexorable friend not been watching she would have run down the street.

'Will you open that damned door, Polly? I'm busy.' Annoyed.

'So am I.' Exasperated. 'I got more to do than run up and down stairs, night and day.' Relenting. 'Oh, all right, then. I'm a-coming.'

'She's coming,' cried Ambrose Longe cheerfully.

The front door bounced open, revealing a lighted passage and stairway, cluttered with packets of paper, jars of printing ink, and leaning piles of books in every state of repair.

'Well?' Polly enquired sharply of the shadowy figure.

'Pray don't be afraid,' said the woman, shaking. 'It is only me. It is Charlotte Longe.'

And she pushed back the shawl from her white hair, and smiled as best she could.

Polly's scream stopped the printing press, and her master ran out into the hall, clutching a spanner, crying, 'What is it? What is it?'

Charlotte put out her hand to steady herself on the door jamb, and then remained perfectly still in the shock and joy of seeing him. For he could have been his father, running out from the old shop in Lock-yard, struck dumb by the sight of another ghost. Ambrose Longe's lips framed the word 'mother'. His mouth was as white as his face. While Polly threw her apron over her head and gave forth the most heart-rending sounds of terror and delight. And a stray dog, which had been slinking by, sat down upon its haunches and howled in unison.

'Forgive me,' Charlotte said, almost inaudibly. 'I should have wrote. I should have prepared you in some way. It is as though I came back from the dead. . . .'

The voice and phrasing were well known, but her appearance choked Ambrose. He laid down the spanner on a box of type, put his arms round her, and wept. Charlotte, too, trembled and cried, endeavouring to stroke his head and to pat Polly's shoulder at the same time. And the dog bawled at the moon.

'What a . . . deuced hour of night . . . to call on us,' said Ambrose, recovering sufficiently to dry her tears and his own, to find humour in their present situation. 'Come inside, mother. Hark at that damned hound! Come in, come in, or we shall have the constable upon us – not for the first time, eh? Oh, stop your row, Polly! You sound like the entire tribe of raped Sabines.'

'Shame on you, Mr Ambrose!' the servant cried indignantly, wiping her eyes and nose on the apron, daring first to touch Charlotte's hand and then to shake it jubilantly.

A black kitten squatted in the darkness of the passage, gazing on their reunion with yellow eyes.

'You was always an unexpected sort of person,' said Ambrose gleefully, 'but this beats all. How light and thin you are!' Holding her at arms length, regarding her with loving concern. 'Why, you are more spirit than flesh, Mrs Charlotte.'

'She allus was,' cried Polly, feelingly. Then caught up a broom and flourished it at the kitten, who showed signs of bedewing a bundle of newspapers. 'Get on out of it, you little varmint!'

'He looks like the kitten we had at Lock-yard,' said Charlotte unbelieving. 'You remember our old Wilberforce?'

'Aye, and this fellow is one of the late Wilberforce's grand-bastards – Wilberforce the Second.'

She nodded, and set down her bundle in a corner of the hall, and this action told him more of her life in the last seven years than hours of conversation. This was all she had. She could carry it herself. And wherever she put it was home for the moment. Ambrose hurried on that he might not think of her past plight.

'Did you know that Cicely and Jarvis are living at the rectory now? That he is the new rector of St Mark's?' She shook her head and smiled in slow delight. 'Their family has doubled, of course, since you left England. One daughter is called *Charlotte* – now then, no more weeping, no more tears. . . .'

'They are tears of gladness. Oh Ambrose, I had thought I should never cry again. I have got out of the way of such a luxury. . . .'

'Here, come upstairs to the parlour, such as it is, and Polly will fetch us some tea. Do you want tea? Are you hungry?'

'Not hungry, no. But I should like some tea. I cannot get over the pleasure of drinking good tea from a china cup.'

'Polly! Tea! Now where should I begin?' As they mounted the narrow staircase. 'Your brother, the ironmaster, is roaring away down at Snape. Richer than ever. Father of what appears to be his final daughter, Ruth; the only dark one of the lot of them, but, like all the others, uncommonly pretty and shockingly spoiled. Not that I see much of them. I fear we disagree over the policy and politics of the *Clarion* – what do you think of the *Clarion* eh?' Grinning with pride. 'And Uncle Dick is upholding the Howarth traditions at Kit's Hill. I can never remember how many children he has. Every time I hear of them Aunt Alice has another. All stout and hearty, except for that peevish godchild of yours – Mary, is it? I hardly see them either. And have you heard about my partner, Jem Tripp? Fantastical fellow. You will like him mother, and he worships you already, by repute. You are quite a famous martyr in the best radical circles, you know. Did you realise that?'

She shook her head and smiled.

'Here we are,' cried Polly, clattering in with an assortment of chipped crockery on a tin tray. 'Lucky to find a cup with a handle to it. Proper topsy-turvy place this is. Like that old rabbit warring in Lock-yard when I first come – afore we got it sorted.'

'So I see,' said Charlotte, not minding. 'But what has become of my china and silver, Polly? Where are all our things?'

The maidservant jerked her head significantly, but did not answer.

'In Thornton House, just as they always were,' said Ambrose. 'The place is let furnished, and provides us with a regular income. I could not afford to live there and run the *Clarion* as well. And yet I could not bear to part with it completely.'

'I am glad of that, my dear, though you were welcome to do as you pleased.'

'It's a good thing as I kept your nice clothes, and all,' said Polly, eyeing Charlotte's grey gown with contempt. 'I'd be sorry to see myself in somethink like that, let alone you, Mrs Longe.'

'Well, it does not matter for the moment. I have worn far worse than this. So that I am clean and covered. . . .'

'Carried 'em all over the place, didn't I, Mr Ambrose? Down to London and back up here again. And there's not a bit of moth in any of 'em. Even after we thought you was . . . did you know you was supposed to be. . . ?'

'Yes. Do you know that you have risen quite literally from the dead, my dear?' Ambrose asked, and she inclined her head.

'But not until I embarked upon the voyage home,' she added. 'They had confused me with a Mrs Laing, which was not surprising. We were both at death's door when we landed in Botany Bay. And out there they lose sight of names, of individual fates. We are sexes and numbers. Such and such a woman dies out of a group. What matter whether she is Mrs Longe or Mrs Laing? In all probability they both will die. And then we travelled far inland. It was not exactly the place,' said Charlotte, with a trace of her old dry humour, 'from which to conduct a proper correspondence. Fortunately, they were not prepared to quarrel over my reappearance seven years later, and so allowed the ghost to depart.

'A letter would have reached England no sooner than I did. So I came unannounced to your old lodgings off Fleet Street, where I was welcomed by Bob Jackson and his wife in such a fashion as to confuse me utterly. They gave me news of you, but could tell me nothing more. I should have wrote. But somehow I could not. . . .'

'So long as you are here,' said Ambrose, marvelling.

And now they were able to converse in a calmer fashion. Charlotte put her feet on the fender, nursing her cup in both hands, staring into the grate full of old ashes, sipping hot tea.

'I have a thousand questions to ask,' she said, as in a dream. 'So you have not married, Ambrose?'

'Who the devil should *I* marry?' he asked amiably, crossing his legs and leaning back in his chair. 'Who would marry *me*?'

'Nobody in their right minds,' said Polly acidly.

Charlotte smiled on them both.

'My return poses a problem,' she observed. 'I am alive, and my Will is therefore revoked. I must ask your forgiveness.'

'You can have my hundred pound back, and welcome,' said Polly, 'if only you'll take me out of here, Mrs Longe, and into a half-decent house as I can keep tidy.'

'Oh that,' said Charlotte of Polly's legacy. 'I shall not be troubling anyone to return small gifts, and I am sure Cicely needs her little income far more than I do. But the money in trust – how clever of Nick Hurst to think of it – that I shall require while I live out my second life. My grandchildren must wait a little longer for it. When does the present lease of Thornton House come to its end, Brosie?'

'Michaelmas, I believe.'

'Then may I borrow it back from you, my dear, and pay you rent?'

'Borrow away,' he said lightly, 'and in lieu of rent give me leave to call on you often. I had far rather the house belonged to you, and I had access to it, than it belonged to me and I was responsible for it.' He turned to Polly, who stood gazing at Charlotte, hands folded in her apron. 'And shall you depart then, Jezebel?' he asked.

'Nothink against *you*, Mr Ambrose,' she said automatically.

'Nothink for me either,' he said philosophically. Then, remembering, 'By God, Mrs Charlotte, I have a couple of bottles of claret put by. How tired are you?'

'She's tired out,' said Polly grimly, 'and where she's to sleep in this pigsty I don't know.'

'Oh, I can sleep anywhere, but I am not in the least weary. I am quite ready for a private celebration. And it is far too late to visit Cicely or anyone else. Let us have a party!'

'And we'll stay up all night, and talk ourselves hoarse,' cried Ambrose, delighted. 'Shall we? Just like old times?'

Charlotte threw back her head and laughed like a girl.

'Oh, it is so strange, and so miraculous to see you,' she said from her heart, 'that I could not sleep if I tried. Let us watch out the rest of the night together.'

'There's that dratted kitting again,' said Polly, as a black shadow hurtled past her. 'He will do his business in the coal scuttles!'

'Wilberforce had a perfect passion for coal scuttles too,' said Charlotte.

'Mrs Longe,' said Polly, rummaging at the back of a cupboard for wine glasses, 'don't this place put you in mind of Lock-yard?'

'Very much so,' Charlotte replied smiling. 'I find I have drawn a circle round time, and come back to my beginnings.'

Ambrose filled the glasses, and as he raised his to toast her return her image swam before him. Blurred, she seemed younger. Her radiance defied the marks of privation. Her fine white hair became an aureole shining about her head. She sat there, transfigured by his unshed tears; a legend come to life.

The return of Charlotte Longe was as triumphant as her exile had been dishonourable. This was partly due to death or retreat among the Old Guard of Millbridge society, who had frowned upon her; partly because the radical movement was quiescent in a time of growing prosperity; largely because she had atoned for her sins.

The change in Charlotte was great and went far deeper than appearances. She had died and been reborn, was in a way touched by immortality. Nothing more awesome could happen to her. From being cast down so low she was infinitely raised up; her ruined hands were a symbol of reparation. And if neighbours and friends felt awed and delighted by the emergence of this latterday Lazarus, how much more so did her family who loved her.

The ironmaster of course gave her a reception worthy of his status, and invited every Howarth to attend. Since he could hardly ignore his nephew, he and Ambrose exchanged a cool handshake and resumed their former relationship of mutual dislike and polite conversation. Cicely and Jarvis entertained her to a ceremonial supper party at the rectory, and invited her old beaux: Caleb Scholes the Quaker, Dr Hamish Standish and the solicitor Nicodemus Hurst. Lastly, out of humility but with all the more warmth, came the invitation to Kit's Hill brought by Dick Howarth on market day.

In all these meetings the men accorded Charlotte a respectful wonder which kept them slightly apart. But the women came closer and embraced her with a deeper understanding, having sister strengths of their own which had not been so sorely tried.

The celebratory visit to Kit's Hill, soon after harvesting, had been momentous for all concerned. And though Alice had never minded Charlotte's cleverness, which was unvaunted, still the day was fraught. As she organised her servants and children for Sunday dinner, her orders mingled curiously with old hurts, unforgiven and unforgotten.

'Any road, Charlotte's not like your mother, and thank the Lord for that,' said Alice bitterly. 'Sitting in the best parlour chair with her back like a blessed ramrod. (Susan, that beef'll be dried to curl if it ain't basted.) And her nose in the air as if the place smelled nasty. (Have you fetched up that elderberry wine yet, Margery?) And her eyes all over the house as if a body hadn't enough to do without being found fault with. (How many times do I have to tell you to put the plates to warm, Mary?) And fetching her own knife and fork with her, as if ours was mucky. (George, keep that spit turning or I'll turn you, you naughty lad!) And village folk bowing and scraping as if she was Queen. (Annie, are you going to lay that table or shall us eat off the floor?) I never could make out why your dad thought so much of her.'

'Nay, nay, what's to do, my lass?' Dick said soothingly, putting his arm round her and making her stop in spite of herself. 'What are you mithering about? Susan cooks dinner every day of the week, and has done for the past twenty year. And mother's dead and gone, and was allus nice to you. You canna deny that. What's up wi thee, Alice?'

'Nice to me! Aye, that's the rub,' said poor Alice, quivering. 'She went out of her way to be nice to me. As if I weren't as good as other folks. . . .'

'Mrs Howarth,' said Susan, who had been with her since Alice was a bride, 'you're looking a bit dark under the eyes. Why don't you go and lay down for an hour? Like master says, dinner'll be all right. We'st manage on us own.'

'Aye, tha's getten a bit of a yonderly look about thee,' said Dick kindly. 'Come on and I'll take thee upstairs, love. . . .'

For they suspected she was fruitful again.

Left to herself, Susan basted the baron of beef, gave Mary a smile, Annie a nod, Margery a push, and George a meaningful look. The dinner moved majestically forward.

And after all, there was nothing to be afraid of. Alice's heart spoke for her as she kissed and hugged Charlotte, feeling quite conscience-stricken, and finally held her at arms length, crying, 'Eh, we're that glad to see thee. And you don't look a bit different.'

Which lie Charlotte took most kindly, as it was meant.

'She's the same as ever, only better,' cried Dick loyally, lovingly. 'Give us a kiss, Lottie. Eh, that's capital, that is!'

He sounded so like their father that Charlotte's eyes glistened for a moment. And she looked about her, as she always did nowadays, as though she would take her surroundings into the deepest part of herself for safekeeping.

'And very welcome to you two gentlemen, and all,' Dick continued, shaking the hands of Ambrose and Jeremy. 'We kept on an-asking of them to dinner, Lottie, but they never come here until now.'

'They were too shy, Dick,' said Charlotte, and her dry humour made everyone laugh, including Alice.

'Why, wherever has our Mary got to?' cried Dick, reddening with concern as he saw his wife's frown. 'She were here a minute ago.'

'Begging for notice, like she allus does,' said Alice sharply.

'Nay, she's that fond of our Lottie. . . .'

'We shall see her presently,' said Charlotte, smoothing matters over, 'and there are three small strangers here whom I must meet.'

'Aye, come and inspect t'troops,' cried Dick, relieved.

So she turned to the ranks of Howarths, and asked particulars of everyone, from nineteen-year-old Ned who was said to be courting, down to toddling Judith whom she took upon her lap straightway; while Edwin and Herbert pulled at her sleeves and demanded to hear about Australy.

'I know what it is,' said Alice, who had been brooding over her eldest daughter's disappearance, 'she don't want her dinner, and she's gone off hiding.'

'Well, leave her be,' Dick pleaded. 'She'll snack at a bit of bread and cheese later on.'

All the joy had gone from his face.

'Why should she be treated any different from the rest?' Alice demanded. 'She does it a-purpose. . . .'

Charlotte heard this dialogue without appearing to listen. Jeremy had taken out his sketching book and was drawing cartoons to amuse the older children. Ambrose was making them all laugh with his imitation of the Mayor of Millbridge. Susan and her two little serving maids were setting up a tower of hot plates. Dick and young Ned detached the baron of beef from his lordly spit. The pageant of a Lancashire yeoman's Sunday dinner was about to begin.

Hidden away in the hayloft, Mary sat, eyes closed, face stern with grief. The gold locket she had worn so proudly was crushed in the palm of one hand. The world of fine clothes and good manners had once again proved too much for her to handle. She was still there two hours later when her father's ash-grey head appeared at the top of the ladder.

'Now then, my lass,' he said lovingly, to the forlorn figure stuck all with straws, 'there's somebody come all the way from Millbridge to see thee. Aren't a coming in?'

She shook her rust-red head obstinately.

'Aunt Charlotte wants to talk to thee,' he said comfortingly. 'We've had us dinner, and a capital dinner it were and all. You missed summat there. And we're having a right old time in the parlour. Ambrose and his friend are a proper pair of comics, I can tell thee. And your Mam's laying down for an hour or two, and I've saved thee a slice of apple tart – I know you relish that...'

Stroking her untidy hair.

She laid her face against his shoulder and wept aloud.

'I've broke my locket chain, Dad!'

Opening a damp hand to show him.

'However did you come to do that?'

For the locket was most precious to her.

'I – pulled it – off.' In shame and misery.

'Eh, Mary, Mary. You hurt yourself worse nor anybody else, lass. That were a daft thing to do, weren't it?'

She nodded and sobbed.

'The chain will mend,' said Charlotte's voice lightly, from below, 'and does not really matter. The finest gold locket in the world is not as valuable as a cup of stale water, in some of the places I have been. Everything in life is relative. . . .'

She was mounting the ladder nimbly, laughing and talking to allay Mary's shyness.

'You need not fear that any more of us are joining you,' she said, achieving the summit. 'The parlour is a theatre. No one would leave those two jesters of mine for a fortune. Well, brother Dick,' shaking out her skirt, 'I can still climb a ladder, can I not?'

'Aye, that you can, Lottie,' grinning with pride and pleasure, 'and you seem heartier than you did afore you left here.'

'It was the dry heat of Australia,' she said, making herself a nest in the hay beside them. 'My lungs are sounder than they have ever been. It was kill or cure out there, and I chose the latter. Let me see that chain, Mary.' Seeming to examine it closely, though she was paying more attention to the girl. 'Ah, as I thought. You have but wrenched open a link. I could almost mend it myself; but perhaps it is better if I take it with me, and ask Mr Sutcliffe in Millbridge to put it right. Then your father can pick it up on market day.'

Mary said humbly, 'I'm very sorry, Aunt Lottie. I didn't mean it.' Then in one of her strange passionate little outbursts she cried, 'It means more to me than owt in all the world, except my dad – and thee.'

Charlotte smiled, and said as though the idea had just occurred to her, 'You should stay awhile with me when I move house in the autumn. Would you let her come, Dick?'

Had his daughter not been absorbed in contemplation of Charlotte, Dick's awkwardness would have betrayed the plot. He was no dissembler.

'I daresay she can,' he said in a stilted fashion, like an actor who is badly learned in his lines.

'Should you like to, Mary?'

The girl was illuminated for a moment. Then her light dimmed. She shook her head vehemently.

'Well I'm danged,' said Dick, annoyed. 'Whyever not?'

'I think your mother will be quite agreeable to it,' Charlotte offered, perceiving deeper reasons than mere contrariness.

The girl said stiffly, glancing sideways at her father, 'Folks'll laugh at me, that's why.'

'Will they?' Charlotte asked. 'Why should they?'

Her father's presence restrained and shamed her. She could not betray him.

Charlotte clasped Dick's arm and gave it a slight squeeze, lifted her eyebrows and asked him a silent question.

'I'll go back t'theatre then,' said Dick, comprehending.

The sound of his boots retreated across the cobbled yard.

'Now, Mary,' said Charlotte kindly but directly, 'we can either waste each other's time and patience or come to the point at once. If you do not intend to visit me, nor to give me your reasons for staying away, then I will leave you alone. No offence meant and none taken, as Grandfather

Ned used to say. If, on the other hand, we can talk together openly and mend matters, then let us do so like old friends.'

Mary spoke hoarsely, rapidly, not looking at Charlotte.

'I'm feared folks'll laugh at me like they do at Kingswood Hall.'

'Who laughs at you there? Not your cousins, surely? I cannot imagine Aunt Zelah ever countenancing such unkind behaviour.'

Mary said, head drooping, 'I heard one of the servants say as we was clodhoppers. And we are. Our lads don't care because there's allus plenty to eat, and Dad don't notice. But Mam don't like going there, neither. Only, Uncle William – he *will* have us!'

Charlotte sat, hands clasped round her knees, and listened. With the profound but touching egotism of the oversensitive, the girl had observed and recorded every minute incident. Her disjointed phrases became eloquent. Imagination transformed petty faults into major crimes. Her persecutors were all Torquemadas; her suffering was martyrdom on a heroic scale. Silent once more, she bit the side of one forefinger and scowled, unsure how this narrative might be received.

'But Mam says as I make much out of nowt,' Mary added shyly.

'Do you think she is right?' Charlotte asked.

Mary considered the question.

'A bit,' she admitted. Then she flashed out in her own defence. 'But though it mayn't *be* as bad as that it *feels* as bad.'

Charlotte nodded, but said, 'Others are responsible for what they say or do, but only you are responsible for what you feel. A great many powerful and important people said I was a traitor, and punished me like a traitor, and made me suffer. But I did not feel a traitor, nor believe I was one, nor did I punish myself. I believe that is why I did not die. It is one of the most difficult lessons of life to learn,' she added, 'but like all lessons it can be learned.'

Mary brooded, plucking straws from her calico skirt.

'If there's summat I hate more than folks laughing àt me it's folks feeling sorry for me, else preaching at me,' she said ungratefully, and she glowered at Charlotte because she loved her.

'You are sufficiently sorry for yourself,' said Charlotte frankly. 'Further sympathy would be out of place.'

The girl was silent, finding no reply to this. Her thin face, without the guard of its frown, was defenceless. The struggle between pride and need were clearly marked in her expression. She tried again.

'I'd come and stop with you forever, if you wanted me, Aunt Charlotte, but I haven't got no nice clothes.'

'Oh, that could be quite easily arranged,' said Charlotte equably, 'unless you are too proud to ask Aunt Zelah. I am not. She must have cupboards full of clothes to spare, with all those daughters.'

The thought of Kingswood Hall finery brought a glow to Mary's eyes and cheeks.

'Mam would never let me wear them here,' she said tentatively.

'Not at the farm. No. That would hardly be sensible,' said Charlotte diplomatically, 'and we should not hurt her feelings by mentioning the matter, should we?'

Mary shook her head emphatically, seeing what was at stake.

'So shall we go and ask her nicely if you may come and visit me as soon as I have moved to Thornton House?'

'How long for?' Mary asked anxiously.

'Let us see how we get on together,' said Charlotte.

Mary pursed her lips, pondering the implications of this remark.

'Yes,' said Charlotte, reading her, 'it is quite a change to be made responsible for the course of your own life, is it not?'

She tossed the little locket and chain lightly up and caught it again, dropped it into her pocket, stood up and held out her hand.

'We shall do some mending, you and I,' she said,

143

seriously and yet with a gleam of fun.

'What?' cried Mary, scrambling to her feet, crestfallen at the prospect. 'Sewing, Aunt Charlotte?'

'Lord, no! I was always a fool at that. I meant that we shall mend each other.'

Soon after Michaelmas, on a soft October morning, Charlotte moved into Thornton House with Polly Slack. Shortly afterwards, Ambrose stayed so late one night, talking politics, that it seemed more sensible for him to occupy his old bedroom rather than risk walking up the street in the early hours. For Millbridge had its share of footpads. On the next occasion he was accompanied by his partner and three bottles of claret, and Charlotte assigned Cicely's old room to Jeremy Tripp. This happened quite often. Then the kitten committed an offence on a bundle of *Clarions* which were awaiting distribution. Ambrose kicked him down the front steps, carried him down the High Street by the scruff of his neck, and dumped him on the parlour floor of Thornton House. Where, swiftly recovering his dignity, Wilberforce retreated to the safety of Charlotte's skirts and spat defiance.

'You had best leave him with me,' she said, amused and sorry. 'His habits are not entirely his own fault.'

Polly poured a saucer of milk for their new lodger, and set it before him on the kitchen flagstones, looking very sarcastic.

'You know what's happening, I hope, Mrs Longe?'

'I do not mind,' Charlotte replied, smiling. 'He has no home of his own, and cannot make one for himself.'

She was not speaking of Wilberforce, the tip of whose tail moved frondlike as he lapped.

ELEVEN

Playing Games

New Year's Day 1822

> Kingswood Hall,
> Wroughton,
> Wyndendale,
> Lancashire

Dear Mr Vivian,
Tho' we can hardly Forget the last Occasion upon w^h we Met, still Time sh^d have Softened the Turbulence of our Emotion & certain Problems Demand that I Communicate with You once again.

'King Billy' has given no Cause for Complaint since the Rods were Changed, but the Cost of Maintenance & the Expense and Difficulty of Moving him from One to Another Shaft has been Immense. Ted Edgeworth, whose Opinion both You & I Respect, believes the Engine to be Something of a White Elephant & Thinks we sh^d do As Well or Better with two Smaller Engines. Naturally You shall be the Judge of this & I sh^d be Most Grateful if You c^d give us the Benefit of y^r Personal Advice instead of Sending y^r Admirable Assistant.

Lest You think this a Slur upon y^r Undoubted Talents I Hasten to Say that y^r Tramway & Both Engines have Run Economically and Without Fault – and I do Wonder whether or not y^r True Genius lies in That Direction! Perhaps You will Recall a Conversation on this Very Matter, early in Our Acquaintance, w^h we might Discuss Further?

I have Another Request to Make w^h may Interest You. I Understand that 'The Times' Newspaper has been

Using a Steam-Driven Press for the past Eight Years & I Wondered whether You had Designed – or had Access to Designs of – such a Machine, since I Wish to Purchase one for a Worthy Newspaper Editor in Millbridge. I Make this latter Enquiry in the Strictest Confidence & I look forward to Hearing from You Shortly. I Hope you will find it in y^r Heart to Visit Us again. Time passes. Think Kindly of Us. Y^r Friend – if You will Permit me to be so. William Howarth.

Zelah had written her personal message in the form of a postscript.

How often have I Remembered Thee in my Prayers! Come to See us, Cornishman! My Husband and Anna have been Estranged since that Sad Time, and she hath found Most Solace in the Bosom of my Family & after Much Thought on Her part and Theirs hath been Accepted by the Society of Friends – the Only One of our Daughters to have Adopted my Faith. Being Human as well as Mortal we can but Suit our New Condition to our Old Selves & Anna hath Decided that her Way of Life lies in the Field of Action. She Sailed for India upon a Mission of Mercy some Months Ago. My Husband cannot Reconcile himself as yet to her Decision & perhaps I, too, w^d have Chosen Another Road for Her. But I Believe she hath Cast herself upon the Waters of God's Mercy & a Greater Journey lies ahead of Her than we c^d surmise. I hope Thee too hast found peace, Cornishman. Thy Loving Friend. Zelah Howarth.

The Royal George, give or take a coat of paint, never seemed to change. The fire vaulted up the chimney-back and flickered in the brasses. Glazed brown pies and cold meats sat invitingly on the sideboard. Pert maids set the same blue-and-white plates. Man-servants bore away coats and cloaks, and carried steaming silver-covered dishes to the table. The old hospitality was extended to all.

As though time had stopped in the field of Waterloo, the Cornishman stood again on the threshold and was greeted in the manner of yesterday.

'Mr Vivian, sir! Good to see you again. We've given you your old room at the back, sir. Shall you be having supper with us or are you off to Kingswood Hall straight away?'

Hal Vivian shook the landlord's hand cordially, and bowed low to the landlady.

'I shall sup here tonight, Mr Tyler, and hire a horse tomorrow. After breakfast will be soon enough.'

'You're looking well, sir. A bit on the yellow side, if I might take the liberty of saying so – but hearty.'

'I have been much abroad, in feverish places, Mr Tyler.'

'Quite so, sir. Your old seat by the fire, sir? A slice of Florrie's pork pie, sir, and a bottle from the cellar to go with it? Right you are, sir!' Then, almost gleefully, over his shoulder. 'Just like old times, sir.'

But time, so kind to blackened oak and the spirit of the hostelry, had frosted the landlord's head, robbed the landlady of her buoyant step, and brought Hal Vivian to maturity. He who had once been defensive about his youth now viewed the approach of thirty with some philosophy. His dense black hair bore two or three silver threads. His pale gaze was shrewder, less contemplative. He gave the impression of being honed and polished by experience, of being gathered within himself to some pitch of concentration which many strive to acquire, which few achieve. A man of granite now, and coldly handsome.

'Just like old times, sir!' cried Benjamin Tyler, beaming.

But the Cornishman, smile as he might, was only too aware of the passage of time and the changes it had wrought in all of them.

Time had not dried the *Clarion*'s wit which was shed on Whigs and Tories alike. It had ceased lampooning the ironmaster. Perhaps he gave it no cause, or possibly Charlotte did not like the idea. So there was peace between Thornton House and Kingswood Hall. And in any case, on this damp March morning, the *Clarion* had other fish to fry.

'If Mr Howarth's not expecting you at any particular time, Mr Vivian,' said the landlady, inspecting his breakfast table, 'you might like to see Lord Kersall go up in his balloon this morning, from the Park. I've got the handbill somewhere. I think it's a shilling to get in, and sixpence for children. All the money to go to one of his lordship's charities. There should be quite a crowd, sir.' A smile hovered on her mouth and was quickly suppressed. 'His Lordship's been a bit unfortunate with his balloons. I'm a-feared a lot of them there'll be hoping to see it go wrong. Praise be, he's come off lightly so far, though with every limb in plaster at one time or another, and bandaged like a baby. But once they let him up he's off again, even though his poor lady goes down on her knees to ask him to stop. All in the name of science, he says, though what science there is in falling out of God's sky a-flaming like a rocket I never could see.'

'The deuce he does!' said the Cornishman, impressed as always by man's boundless enterprise. 'I admire his tenacity, Mrs Tyler. Well, an hour or so will make little difference to my meeting with Mr Howarth. I may stroll along to watch the ascent and cheer Lord Kersall on. But let us hope for better weather than this.'

'Rain afore seven, dry afore eleven,' said the landlord, coming in from his doorway. 'You're looking more yourself this morning, Mr Vivian, if I may say so.'

'Aye well, I slept soundly, Mr Tyler. I always do under this roof. And there is, for once, no immediate pressure of business upon me. Oh, speaking of pressure in another sense – do you happen to know what gas his lordship uses in the balloon?'

'I don't rightly know, sir, but he makes it in a machine, and it takes them the best part of two days to fill the balloon.'

'Hydrogen gas! He should try coal gas. There is plenty to hand. It is easier and quicker to use, and cheaper by far. Yes, I shall certainly walk over there to take a look.'

'We'd go us-selves if we could leave the George, eh Florrie?'

She nodded, and still with the suppressed smile said, 'It should be worth watching, sir. One way or the other.'

Lord Kersall may not have had much luck but he certainly had a large and faithful public. Folk flocked in their hundreds from miles around, cheerfully paying their shillings and sixpences in order to see him blown up or away. And every outdoor labourer kept an eye on the heavens, hoping to be horrified free of charge. His shortest flight had landed him on the Turnpike Road, narrowly missing the Leeds tally-ho as it trumpeted its way into Millbridge. His longest, due to exceptionally high winds, had swept him over the Pennines and onto the beach at Scarborough – setting back the health-cures of several elderly ladies. His most spectacular accident came in the form of an explosion. Each time, the gods who had so unkindly used him most miraculously rescued him. He rose spluttering from ponds, clambered out of trees, rolled down grassy slopes, still clutching his telescope to his dauntless breast – and ordered another balloon. An object of private mirth and public entertainment, he was also the greatest single benefactor to charity in the valley; and when his bubble of fancy danced upon air, every Wyndendale widow rejoiced.

Today was no exception, and Hal Vivian found a lively crowd in high good humour. It had taken thirty-six hours to inflate the balloon with hydrogen gas, made according to the old method with a portable furnace and boiler. Above the grassy knoll the varnished silk globe, striped in lemon and magenta, shimmered and bobbed in a most engaging manner. The rim of the creaking wicker car was some four feet deep, slung about with sandbags of different sizes, each bag having its weight neatly painted upon it. A grapnel and guide rope hung over one side. Eight stout lines tethered the craft to the ground. Comments from all sides, both humorous and serious, enlightened the Cornishman.

'By Gad, she's a queen! What would you reckon? One hundred and thirty feet round?'

'Nearer one hundred and fifty, I'd say. Squire Brigge was telling me . . .'

'How fast can it go, father?'

'That will depend on the wind, my lad. Anything from five to fifty miles an hour!'

'By Gow, you could go a fair way in that 'un!'

'He must be thinking of crossing t'Atlantic Ocean!'

'Dropping into it, more like!'

'. . . and about forty thousand cubic feet of gas, I should say . . .'

'Scientific instruments, my dear chap. This is a scientific trip.'

'They're putting plenty of provender aboard, I see. There's the footman with a picnic basket.'

'Champagne, too. Has he ever had cause to celebrate?'

'Father, they're lifting a dog and a cat into the basket.'

'Poor bloody beasts . . .'

'Your pardon, sir,' said the Cornishman to his neighbour, 'but which of the gentlemen is Lord Kersall?'

'Silk top hat. Glossy boots. Cream pantaloons. Blue cutaway coat. And one forefinger to the wind, sir,' said Jeremy Tripp, sketching away.

'I thank you, sir.' Watching the cartoon take shape.

'Don't I know you, sir?' asked a gentleman in brown on his other side. 'Isn't it Mr Vivian, the Cornish engineer?'

'Indeed! And you, sir?'

'Oh, we haven't met officially, sir. I am a newspaper editor in Millbridge, but perhaps better connected in the eyes of the world through my uncle William Howarth, the ironmaster. I remember seeing you when I was breakfasting with a friend, in the Royal George some half-dozen years ago. My name is Ambrose Longe, sir.'

'Your servant, sir.'

They bowed in unison.

The Cornishman, naturally but mistakenly, connected these facts with one part of his mission.

'You must be the gentleman for whom Mr Howarth is ordering the steam-driven printing press, Mr Longe,' he said cordially.

Jeremy Tripp's pencil stopped in midstroke. Ambrose stuck his hands into his pockets and gave a long low whistle. The partners looked at one another sarcastically, eyebrows raised.

'The old bastard,' said Ambrose. 'I knew he wouldn't let us be.'

'Have I made some error?' the Cornishman asked, disturbed. For he recalled the ironmaster's insistence upon secrecy. 'Are you not the editor of the *Wyndendale Post*?'

'No, sir, the *Clarion*. But you can rely upon our discretion. In any case, my uncle only speaks to me on Christmas Eve.'

All this was said lightly, though the news was a body blow.

'He never speaks to me at all,' said Jeremy, beginning to sketch again. 'I am not invited on Christmas Eve.'

'Deuce take it!' said the Cornishman ruefully. 'What on earth possessed me to speak first and think after?'

'Providence, Mr Vivian,' Ambrose replied, 'which takes care of fools and madmen. We are forewarned, and therefore forearmed.'

'Are you thinking of buying a steam-driven press, sir?'

'Thinking, sir? Yes. Buying? I doubt it.'

'I have no doubts on the matter at all,' said Jeremy. 'We can't afford it.'

'I daresay such a printing press would turn out hundreds of copies an hour, Mr Vivian, wouldn't it?' Ambrose asked wistfully.

'Thousands, Mr Longe.'

Both partners whistled.

'We should have to stay up all night to turn thousands out on our present machine,' said Ambrose thoughtfully.

'Well, we don't sell thousands anyway,' said Jeremy, 'and nor do the *Post*, so they must be thinking of expanding.'

'Wooler used to sell twelve thousand of *The Black*

Dwarf.'

'That was a widely-published paper.'

'Gentlemen,' said the Cornishman, on his hobby-horse in spite of his embarrassment, 'how can you sell more papers without producing more copies? At the moment you are boxed in, and cannot expand even if you would. With a steam-driven press the future is limitless. The newspaper of tomorrow does not think in terms of a few thousand but of tens of thousands. It produces more copies and produces them more cheaply, which enables you to gain a wider circle of readers.'

'Then the newspaper of tomorrow,' said Ambrose drily, 'must have rid itself of the burdens which hamper it today. With a stamp duty of four pence a copy, a duty of three shillings and sixpence on each advertisement, a duty on paper, and a considerable sum of surety against action for libel, the newspaper is struggling against greater odds than old-fashioned machinery.'

'In fact,' said Jeremy Tripp, 'the ironmaster must be expecting the *Post* to cut into our market to get back some of his investment. There is a limit to the number of readers who can afford the present price of a weekly paper in one small valley.'

A cheer from the crowd interrupted them, and they all craned to see the event they had come for.

Lord Kersall was being assisted into the wicker car. There he faced the crowd, solemnly raising his hat. One gentleman stood forth upon the knoll, holding a firing pistol in his hand. Eight lackeys poised themselves to cut the cords. A third man spoke a few words into a megaphone, but the wind came up suddenly and blew his voice away.

'They know nowt about t'weather,' said one old fellow with a wooden leg, 'or they wouldna let him go off in a wind like this 'un.'

'It's only a bit of a breeze, father.'

'Don't you tell me my business, Dolly. I warn't thirty years at sea, man and boy, hunder the *Hadmiral Lord Nelson*'

– lifting his voice so that his neighbours could hear him – 'and don't know a freshening wind when I smell one. They might have blowed this here leg off wi' chain-shot at *Trafalgar* but they didn't blow my weather eye out. . . .'

'Hush up, father. Everybody's listening!'

'. . . and I say it'll be blowing a gale inside the hour, and they're a set o' gawps to let him. . . .'

A pistol shot cracked through these ruminations, the crowd shouted, 'He's off!' and the balloon nipped upwards with astonishing velocity. Everyone cheered themselves hoarse, because they could see that Lord Kersall was going to be unlucky again. Raptly they watched the silk toy being sucked and swept across the sky, waving their hats and giving full rein to their imaginations, until it was no more than a bright dot scudding over a darkening landscape.

The little group of supporters on the knoll stood looking gloomily after it.

The old sailor said with infinite satisfaction, 'I towd thee!'

Whilst Ambrose Longe burst out laughing, threw his hat into the air, caught it, and clapped it once again on the side of his head.

Two onlookers now detached themselves from the throng: the white-haired lady shading her eyes to observe them, the girl pointing in their direction with her parasol.

'So that's where they got to,' said Ambrose to himself. Then, 'Come, Mr Vivian, let me introduce you to my mother and my cousin!'

All three men, by this time, had laughed and joked together and were in the mood for friendship. The two parties began to walk towards one another, but the girl was too impatient. Holding the crown of her poke bonnet with one hand, waving her parasol with the other, she ran across the grass and was castigating them before she was in earshot.

'. . . wondered where you had got to, and were looking everywhere. We very nearly missed the start because of you. And I thought, and I told Aunt Cha so, that you were

153

inconsiderate.' The word evidently pleased her and she embroidered upon it. '*Most* inconsiderate.'

She had recognised the Cornishman and added apologetically, 'Oh, pray forgive me, sir, but it is all their faults.'

'We will postpone this domestic squabble for another time,' said Ambrose grinning. 'Mr Vivian, this impulsive young lady with the tongue of vinegar is my cousin, Mary Howarth. Mary, this is Mr Henry Vivian, the famous engineer.'

'Your servant, Miss Mary!' cried Hal Vivian, laughing, bowing over her gloved hand, at his charming best.

'But we have met before, sir!' Mary cried, who never forgot a kindness. Besides, though elderly, he was handsome. She drowned in the sea of his eyes until Jeremy nudged her. Whereat she dropped a curtsey, and tried to seem unaware of him.

Time had clothed her raw bones, polished her rough hair and rougher manner, and was on the point of transforming her from bud to flower. But she was still given to violent affections, sudden changes of mood, and occasional fits of temper.

Charlotte, coming up at her own pace, held out her hand frankly to Hal Vivian, and was greeted with respect. They began to talk of ballooning, while Mary twiddled the handle of her parasol and watched the Cornishman covertly.

'Ambrose's father saw the first manned flight from Moorfields in London, thirty years since,' Charlotte was saying. 'I missed that occasion by a matter of months, but we attended a number of Mr Lunardi's subsequent flights, and he was a most daring man. Some newspapers, I recollect, nicknamed him "Mr Lunatic". . . .'

Here the men became witty at Lord Kersall's expense.

'What a devil of a wind,' said Ambrose, noticing Mary shiver in her finery. 'Perhaps we had better escort these ladies home.'

'Must you depart for Kingswood Hall straightaway, Mr

Vivian?' Charlotte asked. 'May we not offer you a glass of sherry first?'

Mary was radiant. Ambrose and Jeremy exchanged glances. The Cornishman hesitated.

'I think it might be somewhat inconvenient for Mr Vivian, just at the moment, mother,' said Ambrose easily. 'He has an appointment with the ironmaster which he must keep.'

Mary became as overcast as the sky.

'But I have so much enjoyed our conversation,' said the Cornishman, sincerely, 'that I should like to meet you all again.'

'Then we shall arrange it, sir,' said Charlotte cordially.

Hal Vivian bowed to the ladies, shook hands with the gentlemen, and departed at a brisk pace. The Thornton House party followed at leisure.

'Our family scandal seems to have been smoothed over,' Ambrose said, proffering his arm to Charlotte.

'So it would appear. I never met Mr Vivian before, of course.'

'What do you think of him?'

'I should think him well worth knowing. He runs deep. But, Ambrose, how like he is to William except for the eyes. How could they have missed – how could *anyone* have missed – the resemblance?'

'Ah, but you never see what you don't expect. I didn't myself. Besides, he was far more inconsequent then than he is now. Time has given him the presence and gravity of the ironmaster. Did you know Hannah Garside?'

'Scarcely at all. She was always self-effacing, quiet and dignified. She left Millbridge half a year before I returned to it.'

'So Mrs Dorcas held all the secrets?'

Charlotte smiled in answer.

'By the by,' said Ambrose carelessly, carefully, 'the ironmaster is up to his old tricks again.'

And he told her the substance of Hal Vivian's conversation.

'How very naughty of William,' she replied lightly.

'You do not take the threat seriously?'

'How, seriously? Seriously, I believe he intends to give the *Post* an immensely strong lead over the *Clarion*. But what is the point of being able to produce thousands of copies without a market for them?'

'This stamp duty is iniquitous,' Ambrose cried. 'It virtually inhibits a free press. And splendid though Richard Carlile is, he has not moved the government yet. There is a long struggle ahead of us.'

Charlotte said absently, '*The Northern Correspondent* was only tuppence a copy, and we sold twelve thousand a week.'

'That was Wooler's figure for *The Black Dwarf*, and he probably sold even more after the Peterloo Massacre. Poor Wooler. It was a deuced good radical paper. The best.'

'You should take care,' said Charlotte, reading his mind, 'not to attempt to make the *Clarion* another such paper as yet. You may play games upon the political border, as you do, Ambrose; but cross that line into the open country of radicalism at your peril. They have not forgot what we were and what we did. Besides, the country is enjoying some prosperity at the moment, the first for many years; they will not thank you for telling them tales of unease. But it is in times of quiet such as these that the seeds of radicalism grow. When Tom Paine wrote *The Rights of Man* he planted ideas which have since taken root. We are in the winter of man's rights, but spring will come.' Then she said, 'How much would a steam-driven printing press cost, Ambrose?'

'So much that I did not think it worth enquiring.'

'It cannot be more than a few hundred pound. If I could afford one would you and Jeremy let me make a present of it to the *Clarion*?'

He stopped, delighted but uncertain.

'Even if I did,' he said cautiously, 'what purpose could it serve in the present state of affairs?'

'It would be an investment for that newspaper of the

future the Cornishman envisions,' she replied, smiling. Then she caught back the smile. 'No,' she said, 'I am not being entirely truthful. I should like working people to read what you write for them. With the time saved by steam printing, you could condense the important matters of each week into a weekly chronicle, and publish that separately.'

'And give it away?' he cried. 'Or charge them the sixpence or so that it would cost me – which is still far beyond their means?'

'Oh, you give it away,' said Charlotte smoothly, 'since no one can prevent that. But you charge tuppence for the straw that goes with it, and that tuppence will cover your expenses. There is no stamp duty on straws; and there is nothing illegal or seditious about selling them.'

'Dear God!' said Ambrose softly; and chuckled. 'We shall be watched, nevertheless,' he warned her. 'Our reputations, as you say, are timber ready for burning. I don't want you endangered by association.'

'Then you must be clever and discreet,' said Charlotte, smiling, 'but as open as possible. Have a good reason for everything.'

'What – a – deuced – cunning – woman – you are, Mrs Charlotte!' cried Ambrose with sincere admiration.

'I hope I am more than that,' she replied. 'But as it has pleased Providence to bring me back to a world which plays games – then I must play as well as I can.'

Whether by happy chance or subtle purpose, Zelah Howarth was alone that March day when Hal Vivian arrived at Kingswood Hall. Again he felt time had stopped, as she rose smiling from her chair by the fireside, holding out her hand, making excuse for her husband's absence. They drank tea together in great harmony, and spoke of everything and everyone, with due consideration, without lingering upon any single person or event. It was as though she took up the chronicle of his life, turning the pages over from past to present, and said to the new clean sheet, 'Today is here, Cornishman. Use it well, and use it fully.'

So by the time William arrived upon the scene Hal Vivian was easy in his mind. The two men shook hands courteously, spoke lightly, glanced warily. A distance lay between them which the Cornishman intended to keep. Still, he had come. The ironmaster's eyes were humble with love.

This was to be their social pattern henceforth; devotion upon one side, cool acceptance on the other, and Zelah as peacemaker between them. They managed pretty well on the whole, though William had much to bear; one matter being the *Clarion's* decision to buy a steam-driven printing press. In this affair he suffered especially, since he could hardly discuss it with either his wife or his sister, and must fume alone. Moreover, Hal Vivian chose to advise both parties and to be on friendly terms with both households. Whereat William suffered again. But he continued to hope for a deeper understanding, and nowhere showed more delicacy than in the matter of King Billy, which he left to Edgeworth.

The monarch now stood idle in his stone tower, high on Swarth Moor. March winds riffled the harsh grass and tuned up the deserted bell pits. And the Cornishman stood holding his top hat behind his back, viewing that first great dream with sombre pride. While Edgeworth, looking at his dark face, thought, 'How like the old man he is, by Gow!'

Aloud, he said, 'We've had no more trouble with the rods, Mr Vivian, but iron couplings is another matter. He shives through them like bread and butter. And every breakage means shutdown, and a special part to be ordered and made. When you didn't reply to Mr Howarth right away he thought you weren't coming, so he bought a couple of second-hand sixty inchers. They're nowt very grand, but they do a steady job.'

The Cornishman said stiffly, 'King Billy can do the work of *four* fifty inch engines, and saves the fuel and manpower that they would demand.'

'It's not his performance we're criticising, sir, it's his maintenance. I know what he did at the beginning, and it were a bloody miracle. But he don't have to do miracles every day of the week, he just needs to keep going – and he's not so good at that.'

The Cornishman cried, 'He is unique!'

'Aye,' Edgeworth agreed, 'he is that. A bit ahead of his time, as you might say. And I have to admit that I've got a soft spot for the owd lad. I see as he's kept oiled and greased as if he was a babby. But not everybody feels the same way. He's got hisself a bit of a reputation.'

'I heard about last year's explosion in the boiler-house. That was hardly his fault.'

'Three men scalded to death,' Edgeworth noted in passing. 'Yes, I know what you mean, sir. Every engine has accidents and breakages of one sort or another in its working life. It's his size as is against him. Folks are feared of him. I've stood by a driver many a time, when King Billy were put up to ten or eleven strokes a minute, because the man were as white as a clout and quaking like a leaf.'

'Superstition!' cried the Cornishman, eyes grey with contempt.

'You can call it what you like, sir, but it don't alter what folks feel. They say he's a killer. I don't go so far as that. But whatever goes wrong with him he never hurts *hisself.* They've got a saying about him, you know. "Billy does the breaking, but nobody breaks Billy!" Do you mind that time when he broke eight couplings? I could have sworn he'd smashed hisself to pieces, but there wasn't hardly a mark on him. Now you add it all up and you can only come to one conclusion. He's like a race-horse between the shafts. No good to anybody, including hisself.'

The Cornishman gave an elegy of a sigh. He wedged his hat firmly on to foil the advances of the March wind. He turned himself about.

'Then mask him with grease, top to bottom, nook and cranny. Board the windows. And put him up for sale,' he ordered.

'And what price do you reckon he'll fetch on t'market?' he asked drily.

The Cornishman shrugged.

'That's what I thought,' said Edgeworth. 'Whatever we can get.'

'Not if you advertise him properly and well,' cried Hal Vivian, jealous for his offspring. 'Tell them what he is. The first hundred inch pumping engine in the country, perhaps in the world. A marvel of the Steam Age.'

Edgeworth said, almost reproachfully, 'Aye well, that's *your* tune, Mr Vivian. Let's hope to find another business gentleman willing to pay the piper, like what Mr Howarth did.'

The little dark shop at No. 17 Market Place was so crowded that the Cornishman had to stay in the doorway, in order to watch the first edition of the *Weekly Recorder* come off the new printing press. Ambrose, shirt-sleeves rolled above the elbows, hands on hips, nodded in a friendly fashion. Jeremy Tripp sat smoking a cheroot, legs crossed. The new apprentice, giving up his pose of nonchalance, had lapsed into a delighted grin. At the far corner of the shop Hal Vivian saw other members of what he privately termed 'The Longe Set': Drs Hamish and Jamie Standish, Edwin Fletcher the headmaster of Millbridge Grammar School, the Reverend Jarvis and Cicely Pole and their two elder sons, and Charlotte who smiled at him triumphantly. Behind him, bitterly chiding herself for lateness, came the girl Mary; that comical mixture of woman and child, who could not make up her mind to be either as yet.

Like the *Clarion*, the *Recorder* was printed on a single sheet the size of a small tablecloth, and Ambrose had chosen the most controversial article of the week to launch it. Dr Hamish Standish had at last found a champion in the cause of better sanitation.

DUNGHILL MARKET TOWN!

Filth, Poor Drainage & Bad Housing have turned the Principal Town of Wyndendale into a Breeding-ground of Disease. Dr Hamish Standish, Director of the

Hospital, and private Practitioner, addressed the Council – not for the first or last Time! – on the condition of the Poor in Millbridge. He believes that last Summer's Epidemic of Scarlet Fever could have been Lessened, and possibly Averted, by Cleanliness, Sweet Water, Good Drainage and Better Housing. The Time is fast Approaching when Diseases will not be a Prerogative of the Poor but a Scourge to Rich and Poor Alike!

Dr Standish Urged the Council to set up a Special Commission to look into the question of Public Health, paying Particular Attention to the Poor Quarters of Millbridge. He Described the Old Town as being 'at the Centre of a Dunghill' and Strongly Advised the Council to supply Free and Regular Quantities of Chloride of Lime, for Use in All Drains and Privies, and to Ensure that Poor Households were Lime Washed from Garret to Cellar every Year.

Ironmaster Howarth reminded the Council that he had been Asked to give an Estimate for supplying Millbridge with Iron Pipes some Twenty Years ago, as the Wooden Pipes were even then Unwholesome and Inefficient, but had Heard No More about the Matter. . . .

The apprentice was making up packets of the *Recorder*, and tucking a little bundle of straw into each packet. Outside No. 17 a horse and trap waited. Lines of communication between the newspaper and the working men's radical groups had been established, the entire length of the Wyndendale Valley. A lift of the eyebrow, a particular handshake, a significant expression, meant that people of like mind were to be trusted. Someone at each outpost waited to distribute the *Recorder*. Any man who had tuppence to spend could buy a straw and receive a free copy of the paper; or four poor men could put their halfpence together; or an inn-keeper could buy it for the benefit of his customers.

'I wonder what Ambrose has set in motion – apart from

that remarkable machine?' Edwin Fletcher mused.

'Who can guess?' Charlotte answered soberly. 'But I should be sorry to see either of them stop.'

TWELVE

Father and Daughter

From that first stay at Thornton House in the autumn of 1820, it was obvious to Dick Howarth that Mary had no desire to return to Kit's Hill, and that Charlotte was willing to keep her indefinitely. The pull of love between father and daughter was strong. Afraid to admit the truth they kept up the pretence of an extended holiday.

The prospect of Christmas without her upset him so much that Mary capitulated in mid-December, and promised to accompany him the following Saturday, provided she could return to Millbridge in the New Year. He acceded to this request, privately hoping that bad weather and family feeling would make her change her mind once she was back. He was wrong. Alice said Mary had become stuck-up. The younger children feared her quick tongue. By the middle of January they were all relieved to part from each other. And though Mary wept when he left her in Millbridge, Dick suspected that her tears flowed more from relief than sorrow.

In the beginning the girl held her tongue, kept in the background, and spent much time admiring her new wardrobe of cast-off clothes from Kingswood Hall. Perhaps the only member of the household with whom she felt entirely at ease was the cat Wilberforce who shared the warmth of her forbidden bed, permitted passionate hugs and lavish kisses, and winked at her monologues with lazy yellow eyes.

Then she took courage and sallied forth to try her luck

with the household. Only to Charlotte did she show open affection and respect. Ambrose and Jeremy roused her impudence, though secretly she adored them both, but the two young men gave better than they got. Ambrose mimicked her sullen silences, Jeremy caricatured her.

'Mary thanks with a scowl, and is joyful with tears,' Jeremy suggested once when they had had enough of her turbulent spirits.

'So we like her with loathing, and scold her with cheers!' Ambrose finished, laughing.

'That's not nearly good enough, Mr Longe.' Reproving.

'All I could manage on the spur of the moment, Mr Tripp.' Grinning.

'Well, it's a rotten poem.' Mary retorted, but thought it a model of wit and cleverness.

Polly, as housekeeper, accepted her. But would be sharp when necessary, and insisted upon the girl maintaining a high standard of behaviour towards the servants.

'For if you're a *Miss Mary*, then you behave like a *Miss Mary*,' she said. 'And the next time I hear you being cheeky to Prue I shall tell Mrs Longe, miss! Servants is people, and don't you forget it.'

Apart from looking sternly over her reading spectacles when Mary was being more than usually bumptious, Charlotte let her find herself in her own time.

Mary learned not to pout or cry at these reproofs. She began to think before she spoke. Her smile ceased to freeze within her at the moment it was wanted. She no longer stood in doorways, frowning slightly, rubbing one slipper on her clean stocking, hindering the servants' passage to and fro.

Still the bond between Mary and her family held. Alice's tenth child was expected in April, and as the eldest daughter Mary was expected to take her share of the responsibility. Between her father's love and her mother's jealousy she was taken back to Kit's Hill in the March of 1821. She returned in October, thin and red-eyed, brought by a silent Dick. Charlotte took her in again without comment, and this time Mary's education began in earnest.

'The Wizard of the North, Walter Scott, shall be the first to lighten your literary ignorance, miss!' cried Ambrose, presenting her with two leather-bound volumes. 'You can wallow in poetry with *The Lady of the Lake* and have all kinds of adventures with *Guy Mannering*. This should improve your mind and temper prodigiously, and enable us to conduct an intelligent conversation. Well, what do you say, miss?' As she dropped both books in her excitement. 'Did I hear sweet thanks or your usual snarl of deprecation?'

'Thanks is swank,' Mary retorted, for it was hard to learn the social niceties as well.

Nevertheless she did not cease to try mastering everything at once. Command of language, spoken and written, was expected in this household as a matter of course. Charlotte taught her penmanship, showed her how to keep a daily journal of her thoughts and actions, and instructed her in Latin and Greek. Jeremy gave her lessons in drawing and arithmetic. They were careful to praise as well as blame her, but in no way was she let off their hook. She did not mind. She loved them and wanted to be one of them. As her imagination expanded and overflowed, so did Mary. The winter passed unnoticed. Even Christmas was overlooked. Then spring came again. The old bonds were retied.

Twice in the past fortnight Dick had called when market day was over, ruddy with the Red Lion's ale and windy weather, and taken tea in the front parlour though its gentility stifled him. Each time he asked Mary in a jocular fashion if she was coming home with him. Each time she shook her head obstinately, but clutched him as he prepared to leave, and sobbed out that she loved him and missed him. On the third visit he brought her a bunch of bright ribbons, and she could not deny him.

Mary was now in her fifteenth year, no longer a child though she could still behave like one, and she knew her value in the terms of Alice's reckoning. The eldest daughter of a yeoman farmer, halfway to womanhood, should be her mother's right hand – unpaid labour in the dairy and farmyard, a nursemaid to the children. She suspected that once home, this time, she might never be allowed back.

Her behaviour that Saturday evening reached such a pitch of peevishness that Charlotte banished her to the kitchen. From there she was expelled by Polly for being rude. Whereupon she flung upstairs to her own room, refusing to eat her supper or say goodnight to anyone. Temporarily, life offered her comfort in the shape of Wilberforce, into whose flicking ears she confided her terrors, into whose flinching fur she poured her tears. But this was too much for any cat to bear, so he left her, a prey to every fresh fear she could conjure up.

In the early hours of the morning her troubles expressed themselves in slow suffocation, and she woke, wheezing and shrieking for air, scrambling in panic out of her bed to reach the sanctuary of Charlotte's room. Her pitiable state aroused the household. Ambrose threw a greatcoat over his nightshirt and ran down the High Street for medical aid. Such homely remedies as Charlotte could remember from the bronchial days of her childhood were swiftly applied. Polly steeped dried rosemary in a basin of boiling water as an inhalant, and clapped a mustard plaster on Mary's heaving back for good measure.

Dr Standish did not arrive alone, as usual, but brought with him a long red-headed young fellow in his twenties, and both of them in a hasty state of dress.

'You have no objection if my nephew stays, I hope, Charlotte?' Hamish asked. 'He is a student at the Edinburgh School of Medicine, and will be coming to Millbridge as my partner when he graduates.'

Then he turned to his patient, for Mary was catching at each fugitive breath as though it were her last.

'Stand aside, if you please. We need space and air about us.'

He drew up a chair and sat opposite the girl, holding her hands, looking into her terrified eyes.

'Now Mary,' he said, very calm and comfortable, 'I want

166

you to listen to me. The worst of this attack is over. Do you understand me, lassie? It is nearly over. You do not have to try so hard to breathe. Let yourself go into each breath as if you were letting yourself down into a deep pool of water. Down and down. And rest a while in that good water. And up again, as slowly as you can. . . .'

The little circle stood in sympathetic silence as Hamish gradually exercised control over Mary's breathing. He concentrated entirely upon her, simply holding her hands in his, telling her over and over again that she was getting better.

The sounds which had been inward screams for help now faded. Each draught of air became easier and longer. Several minutes later she gave him a trembling smile of relief.

'She'll be as right as rain now,' said Hamish to Charlotte. 'Put her back to bed. Prop her up with a couple of bolsters so that she can sleep in a sitting position. Someone should stay with her in case she feels uneasy in her mind. For that was a sharp attack, lassie, was it not?' And he touched her cheek with the back of his hand, very kindly. 'Do you have them very often?'

Mary shook her head carefully and then nodded.

'Now and again?' Hamish interpreted. 'Well, you shall tell me about it tomorrow when Jamie and I call in. This is my nephew Jamie, Mary!' Indicating the young man. 'Folk say he looks the very image of me. They take us for brothers! Would you not agree?'

A hiccupping breath indicated that Mary saw the joke. For between the bald thickset doctor and his lanky red-haired nephew there was not the smallest resemblance.

'Do you mind if he comes with me tomorrow, to see you?'

Quite a strong shake of the head.

'I think she's made a favourite of you already, Jamie.'

The young man bowed, and Mary gave him quite a coquettish smile, though still somewhat concerned to draw breath after it.

'Then we shall take leave of you good people,' said

Hamish courteously. 'You did right to send for me, Charlotte. . . .'

She accompanied them down the stairs and he took her arm in a confidential fashion, bringing his face close to hers as he spoke.

'Asthma. Did you not know? Very highly strung. Keep her quiet for a day or two. What age might she be? Fourteen and a half? Well, something has upset her badly. I think you should discover what it is, if you can.' Then he turned to his nephew, crying, 'Come away home, Jamie. Let us run down the High Street before Millbridge sees the absence of our hats and gloves. That would never do. They will endure their sanitation with the utmost fortitude, but let no one forget to tie his cravat correctly.'

Charlotte watched them hurry away, and sniffed the air with gratitude. It smelled of the open drains which Hamish Standish constantly deplored in public council. But it also spoke of mist and early morning, reminding her of childhood.

She returned upstairs to draw Mary's curtains upon the first metallic light of day. The girl was lying against a mound of pillows, her storm abated. Her eyes followed Charlotte's with quiet despair.

'You'll send me back for good, now,' said Mary factually.

'I shall do no such thing, miss,' Charlotte replied briskly, coming to sit by her, noting the marks of strain with quick compassion. 'Indeed, if you have suffered such attacks before, you should be in a milder climate than Kit's Hill can offer.'

Mary plucked at a rose-knot on the crocheted coverlet. One thin shoulder lifted and dropped, but the gesture was not sulky.

'It's my dad, you see,' she confided. 'He misses me, and I miss him too. Oh, but I do want to stop here. If he lived with us I should have all as I wanted.'

She paused, wondering whether this was a considerate

remark. Charlotte helped her out of the difficulty.

'None of us has all that we want. Nor should we. There would be nothing to strive for.'

'And then there's my mam. She's expecting another. They'll want me back home for good, and I can't see a way out. That's what flummoxed me. I'm feared of going back, to tell truth.'

She spoke with a resignation and a knowledge older than her years.

'But you've been proper good to me, Aunt Charlotte,' she said. 'And so's Cousin Ambrose and that Mr Tripp.' Anxious to give everyone their due. 'They're a right pair of comics.' Her grey-green eyes were peaceful now. 'Even Polly – though she don't half tell me off at times. Still, she tells Cousin Ambrose off and all; she don't half rattle *him*. I have to laugh.' And she gave a gasp of amusement, recollecting some particular incident. 'Yes, it's been a right treat,' she said. 'I have enjoyed myself.' And added, 'I'm sorry I was a pisey cat now and again.'

They sat in smiling loving silence for a while, then Charlotte said, 'What happens at home when you have these attacks?'

'Dad sits up with me. . . . Aunt Charlotte?'

'Yes, my love?'

'I don't half fancy that Mr Jamie. I'm glad he's coming tomorrow.'

'I rather thought that was the case,' said Charlotte lightly, 'in spite of being short of breath, and garnished with a mustard plaster.' Mary giggled. 'Now do you think you might sleep awhile?'

'I daresay. And even if I don't I'll be all right. If you leave the candle I'll lay awake and have a bit of a ponder. You go and get your sleep. Never mind me.'

Charlotte thanked her gravely, and hid a smile.

'And you needn't mither about me, even when I'm back at Kit's Hill,' Mary assured her. 'I can't expect to laike about here for ever. And I'm not the same as I was; I shall manage better now. Not all the time,' she added honestly, 'but some of it, any road up.'

Then Charlotte smiled no longer, but bent over and kissed her, and the kiss was a salute.

'Nay,' said Dick, troubled, 'we never fetched a doctor to her. We thought it were bronchitis, like you had when you was little.'

'Dick, my dear,' said Charlotte carefully, for this was a delicate subject, 'I know that you and Alice are the best of parents, but perhaps Kit's Hill is not the best of places for someone with Mary's kind of constitution. It was so with me, if you remember.'

He turned his unfashionable hat round and round in his big hands.

'Mary's hearty enough,' he said sturdily. 'Nowt wrong with her. Just a bit on the nervy side. She'll grow out of that.'

Charlotte wondered why, having survived seven years' transportation, she should still find family life so difficult.

'Dick dear,' she said directly, 'will you not let me keep her for the winter months, at least? Our parents sent me here to live with Aunt Wilde when I was much the same age as Mary, and for similar reasons. It is no reflection upon you and Alice – merely commonsense.'

'Alice needs her,' said Dick obstinately. 'It's Mary's duty to help her mother, and bide at home until she gets wed.'

'But Mary is not the slightest use to Alice,' Charlotte persisted, though still gently, 'and has never been helpful with young children. Indeed, if we are to be perfectly frank with each other, she thoroughly dislikes them.'

Dick had inherited their father's mouth, and seeing its line of hurt Charlotte was wrung with recollection.

'Dick dear, I know how much you love her. But father loved me as much, and let me go.'

He looked up with a sternness which always disconcerted those who thought him an easygoing fellow.

'And what good did Millbridge ever do you, our Charlotte?'

She saw the abyss into which they could fall if they began to argue and explain. She walked over to the window, and stood looking out at the melée of the High Street on market day.

'I have gone about the matter in the wrong way,' she said quietly.

'The proper folk to bring up a child, to my mind, are its parents,' Dick continued, feeling he had made a telling point. 'They know best.'

Charlotte had the uncanny feeling of standing outside life, of seeing the easy lies by which people live. She would not acquiesce.

'I wish that were true,' she replied, calmly and deliberately, 'for then there would be no evil in the world.'

Taken aback, he cried, 'There's no evil in Alice and me!'

'No,' said Charlotte. 'You are both good people.'

And left him to live with that statement.

'I want what's best for Mary,' he pleaded.

'No. You want what *you* think is best for her.'

He blurted out, in his fear of loss, 'If I don't take her back now she'll never leave of her own free will. She don't want to come home.'

'You think so?' Charlotte asked, facing him.

'I know it,' said Dick.

She regarded him with some wonder.

'And still you would take her?'

He could not answer, smoothing the brim of his old hat.

'Dick, you will never lose her if you let her go,' said Charlotte. 'But lose her you will, if you hold on.'

He cried angrily, 'You'll set her against us, giving her different ideas.'

'No. You will set her against yourselves by withholding what she needs, by preventing her development. Remember us as we were. Our parents did not force William to be a farmer, nor you to be a scholar, nor me to

171

cough out my lungs on Garth Fells. They dealt with each of us separately, according to our wants and dispositions.'

He shook his head vehemently. She had done all she could.

'Then take her home, my dear,' said Charlotte. 'She is ready.'

She rang the bell for Polly, and they waited for Mary in silence.

The girl looked ill and withdrawn. She was wearing her cut-down fustian dress and clumsy shoes. Clutched to her flat chest was a paper parcel containing the rest of her Kit's Hill wardrobe. Another package hung from one hand by a loop of string.

'I left the other things put by, Aunt Charlotte,' she said. 'But I've taken my learning books.'

Charlotte could not trust herself to speak. She gave Mary a hard hug and a tender kiss, nodded to Dick and turned away to the window again. For a long time after the farm trap had rumbled down the High Street, she remained looking after them, and aching.

Dick glanced sideways, several times, at his silent passenger. Her behaviour was exemplary. She did not sulk, frown, complain or wriggle pettishly in her seat. She sat upright, in a way which reminded him of Dorcas when she was making the best of a bad job. And she stared in front of her with a dumb sadness which reproached him.

'They're all looking forward to seeing thee again,' he offered.

His heartiness was empty. She attempted a smile.

'We've all missed thee, lass.'

She compressed her lips so that they should not tremble.

'Mam don't allus show her feelings. But I know she missed thee.'

Mary nodded harder, and tears spilled down her cheeks.

'Nay, that's no way to carry on,' he said, wounded.

She sobbed, 'I know. I'st be better in a while.'

There was a stone in his breast. He faced some inner

tribunal. They were almost at Coldcote, only two miles from home.

'Dosta not want to come back, then?' he asked directly.

She would not answer, but wept bitterly into her paper parcel. He reined in the horse, which waited patiently, head bent. He wiped his face on his sleeve and stared into the past for counsel.

'Nay,' he said finally, as Ned would have done. 'I wouldn't force a poor beast, let alone my own flesh and blood.'

The answer both robbed and rewarded him. He turned the horse's head towards Millbridge.

'I don't know where it went wrong,' he said to himself, 'but wrong it is, and wrong it allus will be. And we must stand by it.'

Mary, gulping back her sobs, cried, 'No, Dadda, you don't have to. I'st be all right. I'st be all right.'

He put his arm around her but drove on.

She cried against his shoulder all the way there, saying, 'But I love *you*. I love *you*. I love *you* . . . .'

It was the strangest and most beautiful drive back home he had experienced in years. Not since he was a little lad, sitting behind his parents in the wagon, had he seen such stars and such a heaven. Clear and cold and brilliant, the moon skimmed across the sky, behind chiffon clouds, transforming the wastes about her into mother-of-pearl. He let the horse find its own way, and marvelled.

He knew he had done the right thing, because past and present became one. He felt split and whole, wretched and joyful, new made. As he turned the corner of the lane, and saw the lights of Kit's Hill before him, he paused for a final communion.

'Dost know t'answer', he asked of the silent universe. 'Because I'm buggered if I do!'

THIRTEEN

The Wyndendale Railway

The ironmaster's letter had been a serious ploy to draw his son back into the family circle. He had already decided to sell King Billy, and could have bought his steam-driven printing press without consulting Hal Vivian who did not deal with such machines directly; but the conversation about a railroad was of great and mutual importance.

By the time they sat down to talk in the late spring of 1822, the first rail of a public line was being laid between Stockton and Darlington. Both men knew that George Stephenson, the company engineer, was working on a superior steam locomotive – one which would draw more wagons further and faster than any so far – and was suffering the full range of criticism from polite doubt to open abuse.

The idea had flowered in their own heads a long while ago. Now they discussed the matter with the freedom of dreamers who have nothing to lose, nothing to risk, because everything is as yet nebulous.

'The transport in Wyndendale is quite inadequate for the present flow of goods,' said the ironmaster. 'All our businesses are in a bottleneck. We cannot sell fast enough, and we cannot expand. What we must have is cheaper and faster haulage. Now I am certain that if we can put forward a reasonable plan for a railroad – running, say, from Snape to Millbridge – I can persuade a dozen Wyndendale businessmen to back the project.'

'Are we considering carrying passengers as well as goods?'

'I think we should give ourselves that option, yes. Though folk will be slow to trust themselves to such a novelty, and there will be few travellers at first.'

'And we intend to work the railroad entirely by steam locomotion?'

William consulted the ash on his cigar, and tapped it free.

'We shall have to feel our way there. Perhaps we should consider using horse-drawn wagons part of the time. A horse drawing a wagon on iron rails can draw heavier loads faster than a horse on the common road. What we shall be up against is popular prejudice – no doubt of it – but we must start as we mean to go on, and damn their eyes, say I!'

In that moment they were father and son, and knew it. On such rare crumbs did the ironmaster banquet.

'Well, we are not alone, sir,' said the Cornishman cheerfully. 'Mr Gray's *Observations on a General Iron Railway*, which he wrote two years since, is now in its fourth edition, and he envisions a national network of railroads to link the principal towns. Taken from that viewpoint, what is one small line in Wyndendale?'

'We shall find that one line trouble enough,' William prophesied.

The Cornishman's eyes were almost colourless in their intensity.

'And what happens next, sir?' he asked.

'I sound out various rich and influential men, form the nucleus of a committee, and give them the general idea to mull over. If they seem amenable you will be appointed, on my recommendation, as the Consultant Engineer. You then survey the territory, outline a probable route – we shall have some argument over that, I imagine – and specify what must be done. An Act of Parliament must be passed before we can set so much as a spade in the earth, but that is my part of the business . . .'

The buttering of official palms. Pressures put to bear in the right places. Old debts recalled. The bullying of subordinates and the flattery of superiors. A favour here and there.

'. . . and that being achieved, as I intend it should, our

company must put out tenders and appoint contractors. After which you will superintend the building of the railroad, and be answerable to the company for its progress.'

'What of the steam locomotive?' Hal Vivian asked. 'Are we to put it out for construction, or build our own? There should be more than one, in any case. Two. Perhaps three. But one will be enough to begin with,' he added quickly, fearing to jeopardise his own concerns.

'What would home construction entail?' asked William, watching him.

'A railway works. Skilled mechanics. Special tools and machinery – which we shall have to make. And land to spare so that we can grow and become completely self-sufficient. We can start with one building shed. But in the end we shall save ourselves time, money and convenience. And eventually, as the railway system develops nationally, we may well be asked to construct locomotives for other lines. So it will be prestigious and profitable, as well as useful.'

The ironmaster understood that only one answer would be acceptable.

'Then we must look out for cheap land,' he said.

He thought carefully about his next question.

'What will you do about your own business, Hal? We may as well be straight with each other from the start. There can be no coming and going when you please. This venture will demand total dedication for an unspecified number of years. Less than that will not be enough.'

He recognised the expression on the Cornishman's face. It meant that he was prepared to give if he could get.

'Assuming that all goes as we hope, sir, I would be ready to make a partner of my Manchester manager, and give him the responsibility of running VIVIAN & SON while I am occupied here. I shall keep in touch with the business, of course, but I set no time limit on my absence from it. Time does not matter. I shall lodge at the Royal George, and work day and night until our present plans come to fruition.'

William's face rivalled the June sunlight.

'In return,' said the Cornishman firmly, 'I wish, firstly, to design the steam locomotive. . . .' Here, love made him falter, and William knew that the design already existed, was in his overnight bag waiting to be produced. 'Secondly, to have a say in the choice of contractors. Thirdly, I want no cheese-paring as to costs – though I will keep them within reason. If we need – as we are bound to – bridges, cuttings, tunnels, I shall brook no argument. And I design those or supervise the design of them. Agreed? In writing?'

'Agreed,' said William, grimly, proudly. For this was his son. 'And in writing if you wish, though my word should be good enough.'

'I prefer to be businesslike, sir. And I am ready to put down a thousand pounds of my own money towards the railway works, to show my confidence – to be invested in company shares, of course.'

'Anything else?' William asked, with some irony.

'Not for the moment. We can review matters as the occasion arises.'

'You drive a deuced hard bargain, Cornishman,' William growled.

'I am a deuced hard worker, Ironmaster,' said Hal Vivian, smiling.

They had set their shoulders to the wheel of progress, and it moved forward slowly, ponderously, inch by inch. William had no difficulty in forming that first committee. Commonsense dictated that these new industrial kings must find a new mode of transport, and they did not lack or begrudge the capital investment. But the idea of a steam-powered machine hurtling across Wyndendale at twelve miles an hour came as something of a shock.

'Why, that's faster than the Royal Mail coaches!' cried

Arnold Harbottle, one of the richest cotton-mill owners in the valley.

'My locomotive will go twice as fast as the fastest mail coach, sir,' Hal Vivian replied. 'I fully expect it to reach twenty mile an hour. I was simply suggesting an average speed.'

They stared at him in shocked astonishment. They laughed and shook their heads, rubbed their chins, stuck out their bottom lips and winked at one another. They eyed the Cornishman as if to ask him whether this was some joke they did not understand.

'I am perfectly serious, gentlemen.'

After a short silence, Fred Shawcross the coal magnate said, 'Well, I think you'd best keep them sort of notions to yourself, Mr Vivian. We've got to put this Bill before the public and Parliament. If you stand up and start talking about twenty mile an hour. . . .' He was embarrassed even to mention the figure. 'Well, it'll discredit *us* – and *you* might find yourself in a straitjacket!'

William and Hal exchanged philosophical looks.

'Fred's right,' said Arnold Harbottle. 'I think we ought to set the speed at eight or nine mile an hour. That's more than fast enough. I should have thought a man could suffocate at twenty mile an hour, with the wind catching his breath, like.'

'We'd better retain a good counsel to speak for us, and all.'

'We shall have the best counsel available,' William promised. 'I shall see to that.'

'And *sensible* folk,' Shawcross continued, stressing the wisdom of this mythical multitude, 'are going to ask if it's safe, or if it's likely to blow up. They're going to worry about the noise and speed, whether it'll frighten their cattle or their children, make their womenfolk miscarry and their hens stop laying – that sort of thing. They won't like smoke and sparks flying about, neither. And, besides, look at the amount of iron Mr Vivian thinks we shall need. Even at the roughest estimate it's past all believing. Around sixteen hundred ton for the rails alone! Why, if everyone takes to making railroads the country'll run out of iron. Those are the sort of questions you'll be asked. What are you going to say?'

'Aye, and it's very well for Mr Vivian to talk about making the railroad of wrought iron,' cried another magnate, 'but it's more than twice the price of cast iron, and with that amount you're thinking in terms of £20,000!'

They nodded and growled among themselves, like so many bull mastiffs, over the bone of hard cash.

'Gentlemen,' said the ironmaster in tones of silk, 'we run our concerns and make our money by having the courage and vision to take risks. Our railroad is an investment in the future; a future which, at the moment, few can visualise. We must expect to be obstructed, insulted and generally misunderstood. On the other hand, we stand the chance of making anything from reasonable to quite outstanding profits.

'Now, are you prepared to sail into unknown seas, or sit on shore and watch? To bait Leviathan with a hook, or content yourselves with catching sprats? To trust in your own experience and beliefs, or be frightened off by ignorance and popular prejudice? For I say that if you lack faith and courage you are of no use to this venture. We can only succeed if we stand firm and stand together. There is much to be done, gentlemen. Those who prefer to sit and dream had best stay at home! Now let us put the question to the vote. Are we for or against?'

The motion to proceed was carried unanimously.

'And now you shall choose the name of our company,' said the ironmaster benevolently.

He threw them this sop because he had had most of his own way with the meeting, and did not in any case mind about a name. And the Cornishman held his tongue for the same reasons.

The committee ruminated.

'Well, we're on our own,' said Arnold Harbottle thoughtfully, 'and it's our valley, and we're not going anywhere else that we know of. How about The Wyndendale Railway Company?'

They tried out the title, quietly and enjoyably. They glanced at each other for agreement. They nodded towards their chairman who banged his gavel down smartly upon the table, like an auctioneer hearing the final bid.

'Well chosen, Arnold,' said the ironmaster. 'And, of course, the railroad itself would then be called The Wyndendale Line. Good. Very good. We must drink to it!'

Sedately, the secretary walked over to the bellrope. Excitedly, the committee members began to talk all at once. Triumphantly, the ironmaster and the Cornishman exchanged smiles. An initial hurdle had been cleared, a fragment of history made, that afternoon.

Surveying began at once. The time of year was propitious. From first light to last, that summer of 1822, Hal Vivian rode from place to place, and trod the territory foot by foot with his two young assistants, studying the features of Wyndendale as a lover might study his mistress's face.

The inhabitants of the valley found his attentions unwelcome. True, there had been a public meeting and public support had been given, but when they realised that the railroad would literally be on their doorsteps a public outcry began.

The surveying party was ducked in ponds, shot at by farmers and gamekeepers, driven out by dogs, and treated with every form of dislike and disrespect. The mere sight of a theodolite seemed to bring out the worst side of human nature. In the end, the Cornishman was forced to hire an ex-boxer to accompany them – who used his fists to great effect, until the opposition brought forward a bigger and a younger man to trounce him.

Zelah and the landlady of the Royal George endeavoured to regulate Hal Vivian's meals, with small success. Florrie Tyler supervised his breakfast to ensure that he started the day right. Zelah reminded him, gently but frequently, that a good dinner was served at Kingswood Hall in the early evening. But he preferred to carry a few sandwiches in his pocket, to stop at an alehouse for bread and cheese and beer, to knock at a farmhouse door and buy a cup of milk and a slice of hot meat pie.

Late at night, he would sit over his solitary supper, reading his notes. Afterwards, follow his old routine of writing letters, drawing plans, making sketches. And to bed for a few hours' sleep, in which the problems of the day resolved themselves, and fresh ideas came. And up again before the bootboy had rubbed his eyes awake.

William Howarth showed himself to be master of more than iron. He did not intend the Bill to be rejected, for that would mean loss of time. So he sounded out possible enemies as well as possible friends, converted them when he could and skirted them when he could not.

From the first, Lord Kersall was discovered to be a deadly opponent when it came to protecting his privacy. He threatened to oppose the Bill, tooth and nail, if the railway came anywhere near his game coverts. He persuaded all the local squires to sign a petition to that effect, and pressured the editor of the *Post* into writing a leading article against the idea of steam locomotion: after which William's relations with that newspaper were somewhat ambivalent.

The ironmaster did not quarrel with anyone, but he kept a long memory for all those who had tried to foil him, prepared to make them pay for it at some future date. His patience was rewarded in July of 1823 when royal assent was given to The Wyndendale Railway Act.

Immediately, the committee went into action. On Hal Vivian's advice tenders were put out for different sections of the railroad, so that one contractor could not monopolise the project. As the offers came in the wrangling began, because Hal Vivian knew many of the firms involved and would have considered their merit as well as their price, but the committee were only concerned to cut costs.

In the end two main contractors were appointed. One, greatly respected by Hal Vivian was Tom Hosking, a fellow Cornishman, who would bring his own standing army of navvies with him and begin construction from Millbridge. The other contractor, Len Babbage, was in charge of the line from the far end of Wyndendale. He had offered the lowest estimate, and Hal Vivian knew why. The fellow would hire agents with a reputation for keen dealing; who would employ gangers with a reputation for toughness; who would take on a rabble of navvies with no reputation at all, and exploit them. The Cornishman foresaw many difficulties, but had to be content with the so-called democratic decision.

Now all the secret deals, investigations and chicaneries of the past year became manifest. The obvious site for the Railway Works was in the poorest and consequently the cheapest part of the valley. Progress had caught up with the humble hamlet of Garth at last, and was about to merge it into the industrial landscape.

So far its stony ground and hungry inhabitants had been sacrosanct simply because they were of no material value. The nearest squire lived at Medlar, two miles away. The nearest magistrate was further yet, in Wroughton. And the only people of consequence in the parish were five yeoman farmers on the fells and one needy parson. So they were unable to resist when the Wyndendale Railway Committee bought up five hundred acres of land, at a farthing per square yard.

To be fair to the invaders, no one else had ever offered anything, and the Company was prepared to employ anyone who could wheel a barrow, pick up stones or heft a spade. Which they were all glad to do. The autumn of 1823 would be remembered in years to come as the time when every man in Garth was employed, and his family ate their fill of porridge and potato pie, and sprinkled sugar on their suet pudding.

That autumn also brought the navvies to Wyndendale for

the third time in forty years, and those who could remember these wild and lawless heroes capped each other's tales of terror. But their previous visits had been brief, confined to one small area and a single gang. This time hundreds of navvies poured into the valley to work along a nine-mile route. The people grumbled, and those who could write sent letters of protest to the local newspapers. But even in their worst nightmares they could not conceive how the face of Wyndendale would be altered, nor that its rough surgeons would plague the valley for nearly a decade.

At Garth, Len Babbage's gangs cleared and levelled two hundred acres to accommodate the new Railway Works. A hundred were held in reserve, and the rest sold to speculators at ten times the buying price, to pay for the initial investment.

There were no places for the navvies to lodge and they were forced to look after themselves. At first they bivouacked under tarpaulins, a tattered and aggressive army. As winter came on they built rough huts of mud and stone, thatched them with heather from the moors, tied the tarpaulins on top, and slept twenty to a hut like animals. Supplies were a problem, since the village had no shops. But this suited Len Babbage, who set up his own tommy-shop and charged his own prices.

The drinking capacity of the average navvy was legendary. He drank before, during, and after work. His wages were pledged in beer before he earned them. He drank to assuage his thirst, to keep out the cold, to spur himself on to greater efforts, to dull a pain or to celebrate an occasion. The consumption of a gallon of beer a day was one of the marks of his calling. He also ate 2 lbs of bread and 2 lbs of steak. He liked a swig of gin on top of that.

Sniffing profit from afar, the publicans moved in and came to an agreement with the contractor. In lieu of wages he issued beer tickets. Gangers were given five shillings for every barrel of beer sold. And every nine weeks the men were paid in a public house, to save them the trouble of finding one.

Garth began to grow and change so radically that the original inhabitants found themselves overnight, as it seemed, in the midst of a little metropolis. By the spring of 1824 little of the former hamlet remained. The church spire of St John the Divine, the chimneys of the parsonage, poked forlornly above a landscape of war: a wilderness devoid of birds and trees, scarred by pits and trenches.

The corn mill and the bakery went together. The forge and the wheelwright's shop, which had existed side by side and stayed in the same two families for generations, were knocked down with a dozen other cottages in Garth Bottom. And Garth's one convivial drinking shop, which for two hundred years was called 'The Woolpack', had been bought up by a brewery who enlarged its premises, reshaped its image, and changed its name to 'The Railway Tavern'.

Hostilities between the *Clarion* and the *Post* increased with the years. To such eminence had Ambrose Longe's brainchild risen, in less than a decade, that it was no longer regarded as one more frivolous upstart but as the *Post*'s major rival, and the only independent voice in the Wyndendale Valley.

The two newspapers acted like cocks set in the pit to fight, but their battle was not to the death. Every attack infused them with fresh energy and purpose, and they sharpened their spurs that they might score again. Each paper honed its wits upon the whetstone of its opponent. 'THIS INKY GADFLY!' sneered the *Post*. 'THIS BLOOD-SUCKING PARASITE!' retorted the *Clarion*. The editors cut each other daily in the High Street. Their apprentices scuffled in the gutter. Their newsboys laid in wait for one another. Bundles of *Clarions* and *Posts* were always being stolen, muddied, torn, or mislaid on purpose.

This schism went so deep that Millbridge hostesses arranged their musical soirées and social assemblies in such a way that leaders of the two factions never met. Even Mary, falling in love with a handsome stranger, immediately fell out again on hearing that he subscribed to the *Post*. Even Charlotte, seeing the ironmaster mount her front doorsteps on a filial visit, tactfully slid her copy of that morning's *Clarion* under a cushion before she received him.

'Genius and Generous Patronage Fetch Wyndendale to the Forefront!' proclaimed the *Post* ecstatically, as the first rail of The Wyndendale Line was laid with great ceremony in the summer of 1824. 'This Visionary Enterprise will create New Work upon a vast and varied Social Scale, raise the level of our general Prosperity, and bring with it nothing but increasing Wealth and Opportunities for all. . . !'

Lord Kersall's influence was evidently on the wane.

The *Clarion* took up the challenge with zest.

'Had the Wyndendale Line depended upon the public spirit of the Rich,' it remarked, 'this Venture would have been Doomed from the start. For the landed Gentry will not have their Peace and Privacy disturbed, and the Manufacturers refuse to give up a yard of Profitable Space. Fortunately, the poorer members of our community have been more Obliging, and allowed their scraps of Garden to be Dug up and their Humble Homes to be Rased, in the interest of Progress. So all is Well, and because of their Self-sacrifice the Rich should eventually become even Richer. . . !'

The Cornishman remained good-tempered under fire, but the ironmaster always returned it with interest.

Sir! May I Sound a Note of Sanity in y^r Scurrilous Broadsheet? I feel it Incumbent upon me to Answer y^r allegations of Inhumanity, with regard to the Poor being Turn'd Out of their Homes to Make Way for the Railroad. Every case has been Fully Compensated, and Many have Profited by the Opportunity. Tho' it is Good Christian practice to Consider the People's Welfare no

Progress can be made Without Change. But, Sir, there will Always be Agitators!

The Wyndendale Railway Company is at present Investing Time, Work and Monies in a Local Project w^h we Believe to be of National Importance – as were the Canals in their Time. I Prophesy that in Years to come, Many of these Same People will not only be Employed upon the Railway but will also Broaden their Minds and Refresh their Bodies with Cheap Travel. What c^d be more Christian and Democratic than that?

Our Venture is in its Infancy, and like any Infant is Unable to Run before it can Walk! But You w^d Hold us Back even as we begin to Crawl! We are the Pioneers of an Age which will enable Everyone to enjoy the Benefits of Steam-locomotion. Pray give us the Chance to shew you what we shall do Tomorrow – rather than find Fault with what we do Today!

I remain, Sir,

y^r Perpetually Disgusted Correspondent,
William Wilde Howarth. Chairman.

Whereas the ironmaster considered himself to be a patron of the Steam Age, Hal Vivian was certainly one of its priests, and no amount of radical rhetoric would deter either of them. They committed themselves quite as passionately to the future of steam as Ambrose did to the future of parliamentary reform.

Yet the Cornishman preserved his friendship with Ambrose by accepting him for what he was and expecting him to return the compliment, which Ambrose did. So he could always call upon them, and be a part of the Longe family – welcome, even in his differences.

FOURTEEN

Coming Out

May 1824

Thornton House, with only one young girl to dress for the Ball, was in as great an uproar as Kingswood Hall with a flock of daughters. Mary had woken at six o'clock that May morning and written in her journal, 'Today, Cousin Sophy is Coming Out! I Strive to Imagine her Emotions! It must be Almost as Exciting as being Engaged or Married. I am Faint at the Thought!' She crossed this last sentence out and wrote, 'The Thought Stabs me to the Quick!' But this did not satisfy her either. After much quill-sucking she changed it to, 'I am Transfixed by the Very Notion!' And went on, 'From Today I shall call her *Sophia!*'

Then, spontaneously, 'Why couldn't I be called *Sophia* instead of plain *Mary*? A Name is So Important. *What's in a name?* says Shakespeare. I would answer *A Great Deal, sir! It can Alter a Woman's Fundamental Attitude towards Herself! . . .*'

At nine o'clock Miss Barlow came round, bearing the finished ball dress. She was a diminutive person with a large head and cold hands. She had a clipped way of speaking, as though she took her scissors to the conversation. Her elderly flesh smelled sour, and her breath of peppermint – which Ambrose uncharitably said was a cover for something stronger! And Mary could not bear the way she used her teeth to hold the pins, and then breathed hard through her nose. But she was the best dressmaker in Millbridge, combining flair with craftsmanship. The knowledge that Sophia's gown had been purchased in Paris was not even confided to Mary's journal, her feelings on the matter being far too deep and complex.

'Because you don't truly *care* about clothes, do you, Aunt Cha?'

'I like them well enough, and did so certainly when I was close on seventeen, as you are. I still remember a cinnamon velvet dress.'

'But you don't really love them *passionately*? Not so that you feel a wretched shabby creature without them and a goddess in them? Not so that you are *hungry* for them?'

'Oh, my dear child!' cried Charlotte, laughing. 'What a deal of suffering you make for yourself!'

Which Mary did not understand at all.

Now she stood very still on the footstool and contemplated her image in the cheval mirror, while Miss Barlow scurried round her with a mouthful of pins. The girl in the glass looked contemplatively back at her – slender and grave in her lemon-striped taffeta. On her pale neck glowed Charlotte's golden locket. Was the gown cut too low? Were her shoulders too thin and her breasts too small? Mary pulled up the pleated frill to hide her bosom.

'Don't do that, if you please, miss – you'll unsettle the line!' cried Miss Barlow, peremptory, muffled by pins.

And tugged at the frilled hem. The delicate half-moons reasserted themselves, and Mary fretted again.

'Are these too tight?' Miss Barlow demanded, inserting a rough forefinger under each short puffed sleeve.

Mary gritted her teeth. She could not bear to be touched by anyone she did not most desperately love.

'No, just right,' said Miss Barlow, satisfied.

The dressmaker straightened up, walked backwards, half closing her eyes, and took a long hard look at her young client.

'What about that, then?' she asked, in supreme satisfaction.

Mary's image smiled openly, radiantly, at the girl in the gown.

'That is perfectly beautiful!' Charlotte replied, from the doorway.

'Am *I* beautiful too, Aunt Cha?' Mary cried.

Sharp with the need for perpetual reassurance.

'You were until you started to worry about it,' said Charlotte briskly. 'Miss Barlow, I do congratulate you!'

I have forgotten Miss Barlow, Mary thought, who will never wear a ball dress of lemon-striped taffeta.

'Oh, Miss Barlow, I do *love* you!' said Mary.

Which was excessive, but true for the moment.

Something, buried long and deep in the elderly seamstress, surfaced under that careless, passionate blandishment. But she put it away from her and replied primly.

'Very kind, miss, I'm sure. I just do my best.'

She began to stick the pins carefully back into their stout tight velvet cushion. Pins were a luxury. That accomplished, she divested Mary of her finery, and disclosed to the mirror an anxious girl in a clean white shift and corset, with rumpled red hair.

'Fancy their coming back again,' said Charlotte, of the whale-boned stays. 'I remember how we used to tease my mother, because she clung to hers long after they went out of fashion.'

'Oh yes, they're right back,' said Miss Barlow in her clipped way. 'And waists are back. I like a waist in a lady myself. And skirts are getting fuller by the year. And day-sleeves getting longer and larger, more like legs of mutton than sleeves! By the time Miss Mary comes out next November we shall see a different style again!'

Thus ensuring a further order.

'Will Mr Babbage be calling in to dress her hair?' she asked.

For that pale, curled gentleman was much in demand before Millbridge parties.

'Yes, he promised us for five o'clock. Then she must sit with a sheet round her until it is time to leave.'

Miss Barlow said, 'Should you like me to call just after six o'clock and see that the dress is right?'

They both cried in unison, 'Oh, that would be *most* kind!'

'Well,' said Miss Barlow, shyly, excusing herself, 'we have only one first Ball in a lifetime, don't we?'

Dick Howarth, sitting on the edge of a parlour chair, said, 'Our Alice were right enough for three days after you come last Wednesday. But then it all started to go wrong, and she's struggled on until this forenoon. Then I said, "No. I'm going to ask our Charlotte." So I come. Because you allus know best, our Charlotte.'

His sister leaned forward and pressed his hands lovingly, gently.

'Have you eaten?' she asked. 'Would you care for anything at all?'

'Nay, I can't put my mind to my victuals, somehow. I want nowt, thankee – except to get our Alice up and about again.'

'Then stay here awhile,' said Charlotte. 'I believe we should call in Dr Standish. Are you willing for him to come?' He nodded, dumbly. 'Then I will tell Mary.'

Alone, he removed his neckerchief, wiped his face with it, stuffed it absentmindedly in his coat pocket.

'Our Dad would've thrashed me for getting all them babbies on her,' he remarked, in bitter self-reproach.

Mary was sitting raptly, eyes closed, the better to contemplate her inward self. A clean old sheet, in the final stages of retirement, cloaked her finery like a humble toga. Mr Babbage had framed her face in russet curls, and drawn a bunch of shining ringlets over one shoulder.

As Charlotte entered the bedroom, Mary smiled. It was one of those moments in life when the dream becomes reality. She felt beautiful within. Her voice was richer, softer, more leisured, speaking from the centre of her being.

'When I move, Aunt Cha, even the littlest bit,' said Mary, sharing the reverie, 'the taffeta whispers. And when I walk up and down it goes surra, surra, surra, as if it was talking to me.'

She opened her eyes slowly, divining the meaning of Charlotte's silence without knowing the cause. One hand went to her mouth, the other warded off bad news. All the colour and joy fled her face.

'Oh, my dear love,' said Charlotte, 'I wish with all my heart it were not so, but we must fetch Dr Standish to see your mother. Father is waiting downstairs, my love. And Alice is very ill. Very ill.'

The girl rose from her chair, white and mute. Wordless, she began to untie the knot upon her shoulder, rigid with disappointment and terror. But Charlotte put both arms about her, and held her until she relaxed and began to cry softly.

'There's my love,' she murmured, stroking the shining hair. 'There's my brave girl.'

Polly came in quietly for once, saying, 'The carriage is here from Kingswood Hall, Mrs Longe. What should I tell them?'

Then Mary stood back and wiped her eyes, saying pitifully, 'Help me change, Aunt Cha. I can't manage the hooks.'

'Tell them to wait. Dick has come on his horse. Not thinking we should come back with him. They can take us as far as Garth.'

'There's that blooming doorknocker again afore we can turn round!' cried Polly. 'It's either everythink or nothink in this house!'

'Tell the carriage to wait,' Charlotte repeated emphatically.

'Has mother asked for me?' Mary cried.

'Mrs Longe! Mrs Longe!' Polly called up the stairs. 'Prue's back, and Dr Standish is out on a call, and Dr James has come instead.'

Mary made a gesture of despair. For all the ingredients of the dream were there: the warm May evening, the glory of a carriage drive down the watching High Street, complete with liveried footmen, Dr Jamie riding alongside. But none of them would connect. Her first Ball was being folded away with the taffeta gown, before it had begun.

'I'll ride on, Mr Howarth,' said Jamie to Dick. 'We must waste no time. Whereabouts is your farm, sir?'

He had never been called so far down the valley before. They nursed their own on the fells, having neither money nor faith in doctors.

'Straight on until you get to Garth, sir,' said Dick, red with concern, 'then the first turning to the right, opposite the church, and a mile up the lane. Kit's Hill's the first farm to your left. You canna miss it. All t'lights are on, and there'll be somebody on t'look out.'

He was feeling a little more hopeful with all this help and support, and mounted his big gelding nimbly.

'Follow me! I'll show thee t'road!' he cried to the ironmaster's coachman, who touched his shining hat in cold salute.

Then they were off. They quickly lost sight of Jamie, who drew away as soon as they crossed the river and cantered down Millfields at a great rate. Dick had lit his horn lantern against the encroaching dark. It bobbed from the saddle stick, shedding slivers of light upon the gelding's chestnut coat, the farmer's muddy boots, and the uneven road. At a safe distance, the ironmaster's glossy black carriage followed him, its four matched greys trotting in unison, harness jingling. From time to time they tossed their heads as though they were bored with this everyday pace, for their speed was famous and country folk would run out to watch them gallop down the turnpike road. The white-wigged footmen stared solemnly ahead of them, liveries ghostly in the twilight. The coach lamps glittered. Charlotte and Mary held hands and did not speak.

Now residential Millbridge gave way to industrial Wyndendale. Mill chimneys, lighted factories, back-to-back houses marked the one-time villages of Charlotte's childhood. Flawnes Green, Brigge House, Thornley. Then they were into the Whinfold-Childwell coal belt where King Billy reigned, still unsold, over Swarth Moors. To their left, the sky was lit at regular intervals for miles around by the cupola fires of Snape. And high on Cunshurst Hill the Hall had all its gas lamps lit, and was on the look out for a very different reason.

It seemed to Mary that splendid music floated on the evening air. In her mind she saw Sophia being led out like a princess for the first dance. All white and gold gleamed the ironmaster's daughter in her Paris gown. And the gentleman who danced with her, and had been waiting for this moment to begin paying court, belonged to a diamond dynasty. True, he was only a younger member, but time would improve his status, and he was rich enough even by the ironmaster's standards. To be embraced by love, youth and money upon one's coming-out must be the finest dream of all. His first gift sparkled on her slender neck, and Sophia danced in diamonds, her Paris gowns assured.

Garth was the end of the valley, a dormitory suburb of workers. The air which had been reeking of dye and sulphur now stank of oil and smoke. In place of rock and thorn, up the steep hillside, houses were being built in red-brick terraces by the hundred: built half a brick thick, quickly and cheaply – run up, as it were, to accommodate a population which had risen from just under three hundred to just over a thousand, and was still rising.

'We can't go further, madam,' said the coachman to Charlotte, in stiff apology. 'They're widening the road here, and it's all rubble.'

'There is no need,' said Charlotte promptly. 'My brother will take us to the farm. And would you give this letter to Mr Howarth as soon as you arrive at Kingswood Hall? It is both important and urgent.'

'Yes, madam. Certainly, madam. Good evening, madam and miss!'

He saluted them with deference. One footman jumped down and helped them out. Dick waited for them, lantern glowing in the dusk.

'Hop up behind me, Lottie,' he said, almost cheerfully. 'Mary, you'll have to walk, love. Will you be all right in them thin shoon?'

'Yes. The ground's quite dry,' she answered, practical.

Now that they were by themselves, and the grand carriage had gone, a burden seemed to be lifted from them.

'Lead on, Macduff!' said Mary, lifting up her skirts, picking her way by lantern light.

In these realms of the wind, trees and hedges bent in continual obeisance. Barbered and crook-backed they marked his highway, and the world below was forgotten. Nature still ruled over water and stone.

Candles stood sentinel throughout Kit's Hill, and Mary smelled the familiar hot stench of tallow as soon as she walked in. Susan was lifting the kettle off its iron hook. The younger children sat round the scrubbed table, eating their evening porridge in unaccustomed silence. They greeted their elder sister shyly, like a stranger. And Susan, normally so friendly, merely gave her a curt nod.

'How's Alice?' Dick asked at once. And was answered briefly.

'Badly. Doctor's been up there ever since he come.'

'Ah!' he said, and gave a long shuddering sigh, looking restlessly towards the kitchen door, holding his hat to his breast.

'Here, take this up for t'doctor,' said Susan, having mercy on him, giving him the kettle. 'You'll want to see her for yourself.'

Then she moved close to Charlotte and embarked on a long story, speaking softly so the children should not hear.

'. . . but Doctor thinks summat's been left behind, after t'babby were born, as is poisoning her. He canna feel nor find it, so he's been trying to sweal it away. As if she hadn't had enough already!' She remembered the hospitality of the house. 'Can I brew you a pot of tea, Mrs Longe? You're more than welcome.' Charlotte shook her head, and thanked her. 'Well, sit you down, then. And you, Harriet, move up and let Mary sit by you.'

She noticed Mary's elegant head, stared at it for a moment with disdainful curiosity, and continued their catalogue of woes.

'We've had a right year of it, Mrs Longe. What with our Ned getting wed in haste, and losing her and the babby soon after. Then t'scarlet fever running through Garth last summer, and t'four youngest catching it, and t'littlest lad dying – poor little Walter, not two year old! Our Judith near died, as well. She don't hear as good as she did. Then our Willum goes off to Swarth Moor, to be a collier, like our Ricky did two year since! And he wasn't there above a month when t'roof caved in, and him and Ricky were trapped for nigh on three days. We'd given them up for lost, and that upset Mrs Howarth more than owt since our little Walter died. She makes favourites of her lads, do Mrs Howarth! (Well, you don't need me to tell you that! We've all got us faults.) Then they've no sooner got *them* out than our George joins the army and goes off for a drummer-boy!

'Well, there's nowt for farming folk these days, is there? I say to Mr Howarth sometimes, we're like a lot of hens scratting to make do. And what wi' the new babby coming, and not being able to take trouble like she did, Mrs Howarth's been low for months. But this last lot. . . .'

Dick stood in the door, grey-faced.

'Lottie, I think you and our Mary should come up,' he said.

Jamie Standish was rolling down his sleeves as they came in. He looked young and harassed. A fourteen-year-old girl was clearing away basins of stained pink water and soiled cloths. The customary fire roared up the chimney-back as it did during all confinements. The room stank of tallow, sweat and blood.

He took Dick aside and spoke softly, apologetically.

'There is nothing more I can do at the moment, Mr Howarth.'

He meant that he could do nothing at all.

'Meaning no offence, sir,' said Dick slowly, 'but would t'other doctor be able to do summat for her?'

'He could try, sir!' Hesitating over what must be said. 'But your wife's condition, at the moment, is such that a further examination would do more harm than good.'

Dick ruminated over this statement.

'It's her life, you see,' he said.

Jamie consulted his brief experience for advice and comfort, and found none.

'Might I ask how old Mrs Howarth is, sir?'

'Three-and-forty come the end of December.'

'And how many children has she borne, sir? Living and dead.'

Dick counted them upon his fingers. He had not forgotten, for he loved them all, but the number was great.

'This'un makes twelve,' he said finally.

'You see, sir, the lady is exhausted,' Jamie explained, as gently as he could. 'The organism cannot respond to treatment.'

Dick looked at him without comprehension.

'But could t'other doctor – meaning no offence – not do summat?'

Jamie hesitated again. But there was no point in offering false comfort, nor in sending his uncle on a twenty-mile round trip to no good purpose. Besides, time was not on their side.

'Sir,' said Jamie, steeling himself, 'I regret to tell you that I believe your wife to be already beyond our help. I can only prescribe an opiate to ease her suffering.'

Dick's eyes were very blue, his face very red. He could not take in the enormity of the news.

'I will endeavour to ease her,' said Jamie, in despair.

He administered a generous dose of laudanum. He spoke to Charlotte, as to the only person present who would understand him.

'Mrs Longe, there is nothing more to be done, and I am sorrier than I can say. I will leave this with you. I believe Mrs Howarth will sleep herself out, but if she does wake and is in pain – twenty-five drops.'

Charlotte nodded, accepting responsibility. She slipped the little dark jewel of a bottle into her pocket. Dick sat by the bed and took one of Alice's lax hands in his, and stroked it and stared into her face. Mary stood at the foot of the bed, caught in an old trap.

'Here's our Lottie and our Mary come to see thee, love,' he said softly, willing Alice to open her eyes.

Which she did, wearily. And turned her face to see them with such an effort that they were sorry to trouble her. Then she ran her dry tongue slowly over her lips, swallowed once, and kept her eyes fixed upon them while she debated the reason for their coming.

This was their second visit within the week. The first had been one of congratulation, even on the birth of a twelfth child. But what did a night drive with a doctor portend? She shaped her own conclusion.

'I must be badly,' said Alice to herself.

'Nay, nay, nay. We'll have thee better in no time,' said Dick, unable to face the truth.

She did not heed him. She focused upon Mr Babbage's coiffure. She spoke weakly but clearly, with a hint of roguishness.

'Our Mary's had her hair done,' Alice observed, 'like one of them French dogs at Kingswood 'all!'

Mary smiled ruefully. Her mother's humour had always been of the scathing variety.

'You had a head of hair like our Mary, and thicker and curlier nor hers,' Dick reminded her lovingly, 'when I first met thee.'

Alice considered this compliment with great satisfaction.

'None so ginger as her, neither,' she said. 'She gets that from Grandad Wharmby. And he were nowt but tongue and temper.'

Her words and images fell upon Mary like stones. She was degraded by them. And yet it was only honesty and rough wit.

'A nut-brown maid as stepped like a queen,' said Dick, recollecting their courting days.

Alice said, suddenly downcast, 'Eh, my dear lad. Them days is gone long since.'

In the hooded cradle the latest Howarth mewed fretfully,

and the spent woman on the bed made a final effort.

'However are you going to feed her?' she asked, and one tired tear rolled down her cheek. 'Cow's milk don't suit.'

Dick put both hands over his face and gave a terrible sob, and Mary felt herself torn apart by the strangeness of the sound, as though he fetched up his very soul. Charlotte moved quickly between husband and wife, seeking to comfort both.

'Alice, you must think of yourself, my dear, not worry about the baby. Susan tells me there is a woman in the village who will suckle your baby as well as her own for a shilling a week. I will go and see her myself if you wish me to. But rest for now, my dear. Rest.'

Alice was quiet. The laudanum was dulling her. Dick wiped his eyes and reached again for his wife's hand. The infant, now well awake, squalled with hunger. Charlotte came round to Mary and whispered.

'Go downstairs and ask Susan to take the child away, Mary, and to make the necessary arrangements with Lettie Pycroft.'

'I'll take it down myself,' said Mary, oppressed. 'I'm not wanted.'

'I think,' said Charlotte, of the dying woman, the stricken man, 'that there is nothing any of us can do here.'

Mary nodded. She bent over the cradle and looked at the scarlet infant with distaste. She lifted it up carefully. A fist, waving at random, struck her lightly on the cheek.

'That's right,' said Mary softly, sarcastically, 'belt me!'

But the comment drew Alice back from eternity.

'Mary!' she commanded, weakly but firmly. 'Mind you take care of her like I would. You're in my place now.'

'Yes, Mam,' Mary replied, automatically, sullenly.

She was back at the beginning, without hope.

'And Mary, you're to come home and look after your father and your brothers and sisters like you should. And Mary. . . .'

'Yes, Mam?' In bitter resentment.

'You can have the naming of her.'

Mary considered the bribe, and dismissed it.

'Can I?' she said grimly. For Alice should not have it all her own way. 'What about Philomena, then, for a nice name?' she asked.

There was a short silence, during which Mary felt momentarily ashamed. Then Alice spoke again, in the same light weary tone.

'Just like her Grandad Wharmby. All tongue and temper.'

'Well then, I'm sorry!' Mary cried, throwing aside all restraint and good diction. 'But you drove me to it!' She came round to the other side of the bed, jogging the infant in her arms out of habit, speaking to her mother face to face. 'I needed you to love me, don't you see? And you wouldn't let me. You're forever slapping me down and making nowt of me. And I'm not nowt. I'm summat. Why didn't you love me? Why couldn't you love me even as much as you love our Harriet and our Judith? How did *I* come to be left out? Whatever could I have done to *you*?'

'Mary!' Dick cried dreadfully.

He rose, an enraged giant, wiping away his tears.

'Nay,' said Alice, surprisingly. 'Let her be. She's right.'

They saw that she wanted to speak before she slept her life away, and were silent for her, waiting.

Alice looked at her eldest daughter without mockery or dislike.

'You allus had to be different,' she said honestly. 'That's why. And I did try. But I couldn't. And *I'm* sorry, and all.'

The final stone killed all resentment.

'That's fair enough,' said Mary to herself, damaged and purified. 'We'll leave it at that.'

She could break her heart over it many times, much later. Now she hushed the infant absently, gently.

'That – fancy – name,' said Alice, more weakly. 'What – were it?'

'Take no notice,' said Mary, attempting nonchalance. 'I

was only having you on.'

Alice's eyes were attempting to repair a lifetime's estrangement.

'Do *you* – like it?'

There was no need for pretence or obedience now.

Mary said, 'I think it's beautiful. It means *I am loved*.'

Alice nodded once, twice.

'Right,' she said. 'Tell it – to your father – so's he'll know.'

Mary looked at Dick, colourless with disbelief.

'Philomena, Dad.'

He bowed his head. He cared not a whit one way or the other. The core of his life was being cut out.

Mary stared down at the baby, who was endeavouring to suck anything that came within reach of her ravenous red mouth.

'*I'll* tell you what's in a name!' she said to herself.

She could have laughed out loud for joy, but held Philomena to her, and wept.

A commotion on the stairs presaged the appearance of Susan, bearing good tidings.

'Mr Howarth! Mr Howarth! There's a message from Kingswood 'all. T'ironmaster says not to fret. He's sending his own doctor as fast as the gentleman can ride!'

'Nay,' cried Dick proudly, 'if that isn't our William all over!'

Hope soared like a lark in the morning air. The ironmaster had spoken. All would be well.

'Alice!' he cried joyfully, bending over the huddled woman. 'Did you hear that, love? You're going to get better. T'ironmaster's doctor is coming to see thee!'

But she had not stayed for the honour.

FIFTEEN

Picks, Shovels and Gunpowder

On 27 September 1825, the first public railway in the country was opened between Stockton and Darlington, and great crowds collected all along the route – some to cheer, some to jeer, and many in the hope that the locomotive would blow up. But apart from the chimney overheating all went remarkably well, and the No. 1 steam-engine *Locomotion* drew a train of thirty-eight vehicles safely and steadily from one town to another – a distance comparable to that of the proposed Wyndendale Line.

George Stephenson, the designer and company engineer, was at the controls. And among the hundreds of privileged passengers travelling in the wagons at the back were William Howarth and Hal Vivian, holding on to their hats, since the speed several times reached twelve miles an hour. And afterwards they met and shook hands with Mr Stephenson, a shrewd and likeable fellow, with whom they had some conversation.

Of course, it was heartening to see the amount of public interest shown, to hear that others were thinking and working along the same lines, to know that it could be done. But the Wyndendale Line was far from completion. The two men were beset by different problems, nursing separate grievances, and close enough to blame each other.

As they jounced back to Millbridge in the stage-coach, the ironmaster opened the debate.

'I suppose you heard them say that they'd had to cut their costs on the railway lines, Hal? Even though Mr Stephenson, like yourself, recommended malleable iron. Well, it stands to reason when you think of the expense.'

'Let us see how their rails wear before *we* start

'cheese-paring,' said the Cornishman, determined not to budge.

The ironmaster diplomatically changed course.

'Still, they arrived at the same conclusion as we did about the track-gauge, Hal. Four foot eight and half inches – the standard wheel width of a wagon.'

'Mere commonsense,' said the Cornishman, unwilling to be placated.

He had been brooding on other matters.

'I tell you what occurs to me, sir,' he burst out. 'Here we are with the prospect of a *single* railway line which is not yet laid down, and there is Mr Stephenson already talking about constructing a *double* line between Liverpool and Manchester.'

'Twice as much money,' said William flatly. 'Nor have we the potential traffic of Liverpool or Manchester.' He began to be annoyed in his turn. 'Besides, Mr Stephenson must conquer the quicksand of Chat Moss before he is able to construct even *one* line between them. Let us see how he deals with that little problem first.'

'But surely, if we plan to carry goods and passengers on a regular basis, we need two steam locomotives and a double line!' cried the Cornishman. 'Else, in another few years, we must start again and do what should have been done in the first place.'

'Apparently I have not made myself clear,' said William, very hard and cold. 'The proposed line between Liverpool and Manchester will be four times as long as the Wyndendale line. And the joint population of those two towns is more than six times that of Millbridge. We are not talking about the same proposition.'

The Cornishman changed his tack.

'Well, I disagree with the Stockton–Darlington company's division of haulage. To carry goods by locomotion, and draw passengers by means of horses, will slow down the work of the railroad. And one service must stay off the single line while the other is being operated.'

'Why concern yourself with a passenger service at the

present moment?' William demanded. 'It will be years before ordinary people wish to travel by rail. Passengers are a side-line.'

Hal Vivian caught him up neatly.

'But my concern does *not* stop at the present moment, sir. I look to the future, and I deplore the way you are setting limits on our original concept. I believe you should reconsider my idea for a tunnel, to take the railroad out through Garth and into the next valley.'

William's tone was now openly sarcastic.

'Ah yes, the tunnel. I did mention the matter to Mr Stephenson, if you remember. I wonder that you did not hear his comment! He said that he would be prepared to eat any locomotive that ever came out of it!'

As the ironmaster grew louder and redder with each exchange, the Cornishman became paler and cooler.

'On the basis of such a prejudiced and inaccurate account as the one you gave him, he could come to no other conclusion. You made my tunnel sound impossible, sir, and I resent that bitterly.'

'Damn your tunnel, sir!' shouted the ironmaster. 'We are not halfway through this enterprise and already we have had to borrow money, at an infamous rate of interest – *I* would not have borrowed at such a rate. And one would think Snape was your private property, the way you call upon it for materials. Neither iron nor money grows on trees. For all your fine promises to watch expenditure you have spent almost double the original estimate, and frankly there is nothing to show for it but chaos and disruption. Wyndendale is a mess from one end to the other, sir! A – big – damned – expensive – *mess!*'

Haughtily, the Cornishman withdrew his attention and stared through the coach window, while the ironmaster shook out his newspaper in wrath, and glared at its contents.

By and by Hal Vivian's face softened. Other men's triumphs, and other men's bank balances became of small account. None could know what astonishing visions he conjured up; but would have guessed, from the light in his grey eyes, that every one of them outdistanced the Stockton-Darlington railway.

At Upperton in the district of Wroughton, a mile beyond the ironmaster's residence, Len Babbage's men were cutting their way through clay, and blasting it through millstone grit.

Just outside Millbridge, Tom Hosking's men were building an embankment half a mile long and thirty feet high, sixty feet in breadth at the base and twenty feet at the top. Every wagonload of earth had been dug and brought in, every spadeful lifted and placed by hand. The labour was prodigious, the spectacle magnificent. And, making play on the name of the district through which it passed, the *Clarion* had already dubbed it 'The Great Wall of Babylon'.

At Snape and Belbrook ironworkers were casting the parts for two iron bridges, to span the River Wynden. In the worksheds of Garth skilled mechanics were assembling Hal Vivian's locomotive, *Pioneer*, while others made wagons. The passenger coach had been put out to an old firm of coachmakers, who elongated a traditional design but painted it a different colour, so that the finished product resembled a couple of yellow Royal Mail coaches stuck neatly together.

Wyndendale was, as the ironmaster remarked, a mess from end to end. And all his enemies rejoiced.

Now the *Post*, who had been conducting a paid flirtation with the valley's industrial magnates, returned to the bosom of the aristocracy and spoke for Lord Kersall instead.

'RAILROAD CAUSES VALUE OF NEIGHBOURING PROPERTY TO FALL'

This leading article was based mainly on the indignant evidence of Squire Brigge who, being very poor, had reneged on his agreement with the other squires and secretly approached the Railway Company with the offer of land at a high price – only to be turned down because

204

they had already bypassed his estate; whereupon another buyer was able to snap it up for a song.

'MORAL TONE OF VALLEY LOWERED BY SCANDALOUS BEHAVIOUR OF NAVVIES'

Excited evidence of an elderly Millbridge spinster who wished to remain anonymous, proving that a lady could be accosted on the street in broad daylight. Strolling past the great earthworks at Babylon Mill, she had castigated a navvy for blasphemy – while pointing a furled parasol in his direction. The gentleman concerned, being known among his mates as 'Dirty Dicky' with good reason, had put forward a number of imaginative suggestions as to what else she could do with the parasol – which had the effect of making several single ladies stroll past the navvies, in case the same opportunity arose again.

But 'WYNDENDALE RAILWAY COMPANY GOES BANKRUPT!' brought an instant and savage retort from the ironmaster.

Sir, In Reply to the Infamous Suggestion in y^r columns Regarding the Finances of the Wyndendale Railway Company I w^d like to State that the recent Suspension of Working Operations was due Solely to Foul Weather. Far from being Bankrupt, we are Delighted to Announce that Investments and Loans are Plentiful. Fortunately, sir, Some among us have the Vision, Wealth and Enterprise to see Further than our Noses!

As a final blow he submitted an extremely late and quite unexpected bill for the steam-driven printing press.

But the halt in construction had indeed been due to lack of funds; so close a shave as almost to cut the Company's throat. And only the intervention of a venerable firm of Quaker bankers, fortunately connected to the ironmaster by marriage, had saved them.

The *Clarion* mounted quite a different attack.

HOSPITAL CHARGED FOR HEALING RAILROAD WORKERS!

Since work on the Railroad began, just over two years ago, three Navvies have been killed and one hundred and seventeen so Seriously injured as to require Hospital treatment, while the number of minor injuries is Uncounted. One member of Millbridge Hospital staff, formerly an Army surgeon, likened the Casualty Rate to that of a Battle-field, and believed we sh^d Question the Safety of the present Working Methods. But the most Immediate question the Hospital must ask is a Financial one. Dr Hamish Standish, Director of the hospital, tells us that the Cost of treating railroad workers last year Alone was over £100, of which the Wyndendale Railway Company paid £5 and the Contractors £5.10s! He – and We – w^d like to know How the Hospital is expected to Find the Difference of £89.10s? And if it does Not then will the Ratepayers be asked to Pay the Bills . . . ?

SIXTEEN

A Fine Lady Upon a White Horse

Since her mother's death the previous year, Mary had endeavoured to take responsibility for Philomena. It was she who rousted out poor Lettie Pycroft on the midnight of Alice's passing, presenting her with a squalling hungry infant to be fed at once, and laying the first weekly shilling on the table. It was she who proposed herself as godmother, and supervised the doleful little christening ceremony. Then, making the supreme personal sacrifice, she had offered to return to Kit's Hill and take Alice's place.

Susan immediately and most fiercely resisted this idea, and was backed by the younger members of the family down to the last child. Hurt and astonished, Mary turned to her father for support. But Dick had trouble enough of his own, and would take no part in the quarrel. So Mary went back to Thornton House and tried to bring up the baby from a distance.

She studied late and rose early in order to encompass the dual demands of Charlotte and Philomena. Most of her small allowance was spent in hiring horses to get to Garth. When it was gone she begged lifts in carts and carriages. Once there, the baby cradled in her arms, she questioned Lettie minutely as to its progress. She was both selfish and generous, short-sighted and perceptive, in this new love.

The Kit's Hill Howarths did not mind a whit, so long as she left them alone. Ambrose and Jeremy were alternately amused and annoyed by her passion for the child. But Charlotte was deeply concerned, and confided her misgivings to Zelah, who talked to the ironmaster, who came up with one solution. He gave his niece a pretty white mare, put it in the Royal George livery stables, and had the bills sent to him. Thus he solved her problem of transport, and gained her loyalty for life.

Sophia had long since danced away with her diamond merchant, leaving a wardrobe of clothes behind her like discarded plumage. So Mary was able to cut a dash, that cool autumn morning, in her cousin's green cloth riding habit. Its matching pantaloons, hidden by the full skirt, were neatly strapped over black leather boots, like those of a man. A yard of veil made sure that her hard top hat did not blow off.

Mary consulted the reflection beyond hers in the mirror.

'Now tell me, Aunt Cha, how I am to thank Lettie Pycroft for taking care of Philly all this while – though I disagree with most of her methods. Should I give her money or my old Paisley shawl, or both together. I want everything to be just so.'

She brought the veil down under her chin, and tied it in a bow.

'What a mercy that Sophy and I were the same size,' she went on, smoothing her cousin's gloves over her fingers. 'I remember when Livvy married, and her dresses weren't a bit of use to anybody because she was such a Maypole.' Her thoughts ran off in another direction. 'Goodness me, I hope I don't meet Jamie Standish on my way to the Royal George. I am always bumping into him. Whatever must people think?'

Charlotte did not laugh, but must smile a little to herself.

'I daresay you will carry off any embarrassment,' she remarked.

Fortunately for her self-esteem, Mary was hailed and complimented by a number of Millbridge acquaintances, and made a tremendous impression on two ostlers and an old waiter at the Royal George. Best of all, who should be hiring a mount but their itinerant friend, the Cornishman, who journeyed thus from end to end of his railway line. Hands on hips, standing with his back to her, he was haranguing Fred, the head stable-lad.

'For though I am no jockey,' he was saying, 'the horse you gave me last time – Speedwell, was it? – did not speed

208

well at all. Indeed, she had two speeds – slow and stop – and drank like a fool at every trough we passed. Now you used to have a chestnut called Red Nell who suited me nicely.'

'Bless you, Mr Vivian, sir, Nell's been dog's meat these three years past! And you did say as you wanted a quiet 'un.'

'Aye, quiet, not dead!' cried the Cornishman, with dry humour.

'Then try Champion, sir. He's a proper gentleman's horse, he is.'

At the mention of Champion Mary marched forward, clutching her whip like a weapon, saying, 'Have nothing to do with that horse, Mr Vivian. He kicks and shies at anything.' Then, turning on the stable lad, 'What in mercy's name are you thinking of, Fred?'

'Well, miss, I'm doing my best. We're a bit pushed this morning.'

'Here, I will choose you a mount,' cried Mary, and paraded down the stalls, inspecting their occupants.

Fred made a face of despair. The Cornishman laughed outright.

'What about Firefly?' Mary demanded, from the end of the stable.

'Ordered for eleven o'clock, miss, by the editor of the *Post*!'

At the mention of this newspaper rival her partisan spirit rose.

'Oh, but you should give Champion to Mr Thwaites,' she called, clear and sweet. 'For he is a proper gentleman's horse.'

Mentally consigning that poor man to a ditch.

'If it weren't for t'ironmaster's custom ...' Fred grumbled to himself, as she led her choice out. Then, 'Saddle up Firefly for Mr Vivian, Jemmie, and look sharp about it!'

'And now – good morning to you, sir!' cried Mary, vivid and triumphant. 'To what part of your railroad do you ride today?'

He lifted his hat courteously, replying, 'To no part at all, madam. I am expected for the weekly consultation with your uncle at Kingswood Hall. Your own errand, I presume, is in Garth?'

'Yes, sir. And afterwards at Kit's Hill. Philomena changes homes today, being fully weaned, and I wish to see her happily settled.'

'Then may I have the pleasure of your company as far as Wroughton?'

'Certainly, sir!' Graciously. 'Fred!' in quite a different voice, 'Is Caprice saddled?'

'Yes, miss. Ready *and* waiting,' said Fred, with some emphasis.

Hal Vivian cupped his hands gallantly. Mary set her little boot in this human stirrup and sprang neatly into the saddle.

'You really are becoming uncommonly pretty, Miss Mary,' said the Cornishman, smiling up at her as she smiled down at him. 'But do not marry too soon! When do you come out, by the by?'

'Next month, sir. Uncle William is giving me a supper ball. Have you forgot your invitation?'

'No, no!' Hal Vivian lied. 'It was the date that escaped me.'

She watched him mount Firefly. Her expression was critical. Like all true Howarths she was a good rider and a fair judge of horseflesh.

'Are you not fond of horses, sir?'

'Not particularly.'

'How strange,' said Mary. But recollected her manners. 'Shall we go, sir? And you must tell me what you meant by saying I ought not to marry too soon.'

Artless in her vanity.

'By Gow!' cried Dick, as his daughter clattered over the cobbled yard. 'Here comes Queen Caroline! We haven't seen *you* for a while.'

He ignored the fact that she had not been welcome. He

hugged her in his old loving fashion. Then held her at arms length, the better to admire her.

'Come and look who's here, Susan!' he called.

The housekeeper approached, hands folded in her apron. She and Mary had not met since their confrontation over a year ago. They nodded a greeting, eyes guarded.

'You've seen Lettie Pycroft then, have you?' Susan asked.

'Yes, and she said she brought Philomena up after breakfast this morning, but Philly made no end of a fuss.'

'Oh, she's shaping nicely now,' said Susan briskly. 'She's asleep by the kitchen fire so's I can keep an eye on her.'

Then she looked directly, meaningfully, at Dick.

Awkwardly he drew her arm through his, patted her hand.

'Susan and me,' he said, 'have summat to tell thee, Mary. We're getting wed next month!' He tried to explain. 'It's a while since your Mam died, and the little 'uns need a mother. We're hoping as you and our Charlotte'll come to't church and wish us well, lass.'

Mary wanted to cry out, to hit them both, to gallop away shouting, 'Traitors! Traitors!' and never set foot in Kit's Hill backyard again. But she thought how Charlotte would like her to behave. She thought of her eighteenth birthday, when she would be completely grown up.

She said, a little stiffly, 'Of course I wish you joy. And of course we shall come to the wedding. I think it is a very good idea.'

She thought of Alice lying in Garth churchyard, to whom joy and sorrow were nothing.

She was heartbroken.

Dick hugged both women at once, kissing his daughter fondly and his future wife shyly. For he was always a gentle and chivalrous man.

'Shall us go in and fettle t'dinner then?' said Susan cheerfully.

'Aye, and call me when it's ready,' said Dick, relieved.

211

Philomena had fallen asleep, exhausted with crying. Drops of sorrow and bewilderment clung to her lashes and sparkled on her cheeks.

'Oh, poor love,' said Mary softly. 'Oh, little love.'

Tears came to her own eyes in sympathy.

'Eh, don't fret yourself,' said Susan hardily. 'She'll soon get over it. It's the change of place and face as does it. She's used to Lettie, you see. She'll soon muck in with us.'

'Suppose,' said Mary, remembering, 'that she doesn't?'

Susan glanced sharply at her.

'She'll have to,' she replied flatly. 'There's no room for moaners and skrikers in this house. We've neither time nor brass to study *her* likes and dislikes!' And having settled that question she said loudly, 'Side up that table, Hattie! We're nearly ready!'

'Can I do anything to help?' Mary asked, subdued by her tone.

'Just keep out o' t'road,' Susan answered.

So Mary sat in the corner by Philomena, and watched her mouth open and her hands uncurl as she slept. She had often sat with her brothers and sisters by that same cradle, and observed their solid slumbers in childish hatred. But this last late fruit of a long marriage bore none of the Howarth's usual characteristics. She was small-boned, dark and solemn. Her air was poignant, the product of grief.

'Susan,' said Mary humbly, 'I know you have a lot to do, but when she cries it's always for a good reason.'

'She'll not go short in this house.'

'I know. But sometimes she cries for reassurance.'

'And what's that when it's at home?'

Mary kept her pride and anger down, and her manner pleasant.

'She just needs to know that you're there and you like her. And if you hold her and speak to her a bit she's all right again.'

Susan faced her, arms akimbo. She had waited for such an opening.

'Just you mind your own business, Mary,' she said. 'I

were here when your Mam had her first babby, as well as her last. What I don't know about childer you could write on a sixpenny piece and find room left over.'

Having established that point she moved on to the next.

'Lettie Pycroft's told me all about you, Miss High-and-Mighty! Riding up at all hours, finding fault with this and that and the other. Do you know what she said? She said, "Every time Mary Howarth knocked the door I could feel my milk drying up!" Well, I'm not being badgered like that, and I'm mistress here now. So if you don't like it you know what else to do – here's your fancy hat and there's the door!'

Mary was dumb with shock. She kept her face averted and rocked the cradle, pretending not to notice that the younger children tittered.

'Judith! Fetch your father and the others!' cried Susan, informing them all by order and tone that she would reign absolute.

Then she spoke to the girl again, but more quietly.

'Now listen to reason, Mary,' said Susan. 'You chose to leave here. You're not one of us. That child is. And how I fetch her up is my business. If you want trouble I'll give you full measure. Or we can get on as sweet as pie. It's up to you to decide.'

Dick, coming in, found his eldest daughter sitting silent and colourless by the fire.

'Are you all right, love?' he asked uncertainly.

She nodded vigorously, unable to speak.

'You needn't fret yourself about our Philly,' he continued, trying to guess at her disquiet. 'She'll soon perk up, won't she, Sue?'

'I've told Mary as she'll muck in with us,' Susan replied firmly. 'Now let's stop mithering about her, and eat us dinners.'

At Thornton House where they dined fashionably late, all four of them sat long over their coffee.

'I am surprised that Dick said nothing to me,' Charlotte

remarked, a little hurt, for she had always been his confidante.

'Perhaps he thought you would disapprove of his choice,' Ambrose suggested, leaning back in his chair until the hindlegs creaked.

'But I do not. I think it is a sensible solution on the whole.'

Mary had been sitting silently, pleating her napkin, head bent. She spoke with sad philosophy.

'Susan means to run *everybody* at Kit's Hill. I've earned the dislike of the children. That's fair enough. But she'll make my father wary of me, and eventually she'll turn Philomena against me.'

The other three looked at one another in despair.

'Be that as it may,' Charlotte replied, 'I think it a thousand pities that poor Alice spoke as she did.' Her tone was resolute. 'If she had not, you would never have given that child a second thought.'

'But it is too late to say that now,' Mary answered. 'Philly and I are part of one another. She knows and loves me, and I love her. Even so, I could bear to lose her if I thought Susan truly cared about her, but she does not. Lettie Pycroft told me that Susan only enquired about Philly if they happened to meet, and hardly ever saw her.'

'Lettie Pycroft has been telling tales and making trouble on *both* sides, apparently,' said Charlotte drily. 'And whatever faults Susan may have she is basically a good and decent woman.'

'How can you say so, after the way she has treated me?' cried Mary, her sense of justice violated.

'You threatened her position,' Charlotte answered. 'Kit's Hill is the only home she has. She was a child of twelve when my mother brought her up from the village to be trained. She has served there faithfully ever since. She has never known any other life. She has nowhere else to go. What would you have done in her place? Think, before you condemn her! You have been fighting for an idea; but Susan has been fighting for her very survival. Now tell me where my sympathy should lie!'

The two men glanced at each other, rose, and made a quiet excuse to depart. Charlotte in this mood was not to be gainsaid.

In face of her idol's sharp judgement Mary was silent for a minute or so. Then she spoke again, quietly and more thoughtfully.

'You talked of survival? Kit's Hill is concerned with nothing but survival, and when you cannot survive any longer you die. Philomena is the twelfth child of middle-aged parents. She is not robust like the others. She needs particular love and attention, which Susan is not prepared to give. She'll fret, and she'll die. And yet, with a little care and understanding, there is so much she could have, so much she could be. And I care what happens to her. I do care.'

'What are you asking of me?' said Charlotte, thoroughly disturbed. 'That I bring her here to live? That I offer to adopt her?'

'That you take her in, as you took me in, Aunt Cha. Please, dear Aunt Cha. I shall look after her myself. She won't be any trouble. I promise. I promise.'

'Oh, my dear child,' said Charlotte, and rose and paced the dining room as she used to many years before, when problems would not let her rest. 'My dear child, I feel for you and her, but you do not know how deeply you are committing yourself. Better by far that you let her take her chance. They are good people. She is one of them.'

'No, Aunt Cha, she isn't. She's little and dark and quick.'

'Listen to me carefully, Mary. You are nearly eighteen. You could be married within a year. Suppose your husband does not want her? The child cannot be put aside as though she were a doll you had outgrown.'

'Then I will not marry him,' said Mary, stricken but determined.

'Forgive me, I do not wish to hurt you, but you must understand yourself better than this. You flower in the company of *any* man. You would never refuse a dance, let alone a proposal of marriage!'

Mary was crying silently, the tears running down her face, but still she said, 'I would tell him so, Aunt Cha. I should have to.'

'Then even more strongly must I insist that Philomena stays where she is. I shall not take her in. I cannot allow you to hamper and spoil your life in this manner. I am sorry, love, but I am resolute.'

She touched Mary's hair gently as she passed, leaving the girl to grieve in private. On her way upstairs, feeling for once that every step was a yard high, and every limb weighted with lead, she remembered Dorcas saying, 'I am too old for trouble!' and knew for the first time what her mother had meant.

SEVENTEEN

A Great Occasion

The matchmakers of Millbridge had long since decided that Mary should marry Dr Jamie Standish. The two young people were well suited in every respect, and in the matter of temperament could be called complementary, since Mary was explosive, unpredictable, and passionate; and Jamie quiet, reliable and gentle.

'Just the proper husband for her,' whispered aging ladies over china teacups.

They even regarded the vexed question of Philomena with undoubted approval, not concerned of course with the child itself but what it meant in terms of maternal instinct. Who would have thought that Mary could soften so? It was a good sign, a sure sign, that she would settle down in time. With an eagerness which said much about the emptiness of their own lives, they awaited her fulfilment.

Like most girls of her age Mary's need for masculine attention and admiration was paramount, and she fell in and out of love with great ease and regularity. But her fondness for Jamie remained steady, and she openly delighted in the knowing nods and glances which attended their most casual meetings.

For Mary's coming of age, Zelah and William planned a supper ball with exquisite taste and tact: making it grand enough for the girl to queen her occasion, but sufficiently informal to include all her friends and relatives. To which they also invited every newspaper editor in the valley, so that she could record the event afterwards by pasting their sparkling comments into an album.

For her part, Charlotte asked the dressmaker to spare

neither talent nor expense on Mary's ball gown, and Miss Barlow came up with a dream of white tarlatan enhanced by flounces and rosebud trimming.

Richer members of the family were guided towards gifts of an enamelled watch, a pair of white chalcedony and gold earrings, a carved ivory fan, silk slippers, French evening gloves and a blue velvet cloak.

Finally, Mr Babbage created a special coiffure in Mary's honour, to be kept secret until the very evening of the ball: the hair to be parted in the centre, some piled into a silken knot on top of her head, the rest fashioned into ringlets on either side of her face, and the whole tastefully ornamented by artificial rosebuds to match those on her gown.

For once, Mary could not have asked for anything more. She stood on a pinnacle of singular importance, with the future stretching out before her and her little world at her feet. This time fate chose to intervene three days before the event, in the shape of an uninvited guest.

All the ironmaster's carriages bowled up the High Street at high speed, and came to a halt in front of Thornton House. For Zelah had been gathering her daughters and their children from far and wide, with the excuse of celebrating Mary's birthday. So quite a flock of first and second cousins swept into the hall and filled the front parlour. And a great deal of kissing ensued among the ladies, which was sedulously dodged by the ironmaster's grandsons.

'Why, what news is this that brings everyone out on such a cold day?' cried Charlotte, puzzled but hospitable, smiling round at the handsome assembly. 'May we offer you some refreshment?'

Zelah shook her head, unable to find words. Impatiently her troupe urged her to speak. She endeavoured to smile. The smile wavered. She gave a small apologetic sob, put her hands over her face, and wept.

For a few minutes all was commotion, as her daughters endeavoured to comfort her, Charlotte ordered wine and *sal volatile*, and the boys surreptitiously kicked each other in embarrassment. Then Zelah dried her eyes, accepted the offer of a chair by the fire, called her grandsons to order, and became herself again.

'Those were tears of gladness,' she said. 'Oh, my dear Charlotte, we bring thee news indeed. Oh Charlotte, my dear, Anna is coming home!'

In the seven years since the end of her engagement to Hal Vivian, Anna had corresponded only with her mother, though sending dutiful good wishes to the ironmaster in a postscript. For the relationship between father and daughter had been strained almost to breaking-point. The girl had invested too much in love, and expected too much of it, to survive its dissolution. Her letters ceased to record the state of a pretty girl's heart, and began to mark the progress of a soul.

Zelah alone had understood the conflict, and kept, and most lovingly answered these letters from afar: finding meaning even in their stained and travelled pages, re-reading the words her troubled child had penned. Such intimate disclosures could not be common topics of conversation, and Zelah merely passed on tales of India: of strange gods and pagan festivals, of a sun too hot to bear and rains that washed villages away, of dark princes riding upon elephants.

So the picture others formed of Anna's life was an adventurous and exotic one. Her freedom, compared to that of her sisters, seemed untrammelled, limitless. Privately, they envied her. Socially, they were inclined to boast. And all of them believed that her call to Quakerism was a temporary comfort. They fully expected that she would come to her senses, marry a nabob, and return home – heralded by trumpets, hung with jewels, surrounded by dark servants who spoke in strange tongues.

'No wine, I thank thee, Charlotte,' said Zelah, putting it away from her. 'We shall not stop longer than it takes me to tell thee the tale. For we are such a band! No, no tea, either.

I need nothing.' She added quietly, 'I have everything I could wish for.'

'Anna's coming home will make no difference to your supper ball, Mary,' Livvy assured her. 'Except, of course, that it will seem a greater occasion than ever!'

'Oh, we are not so selfish,' Zelah said, shocked at this implied slur on their hospitality, 'as to forget thee, love!'

She would have liked to continue, but her daughters took the story away from her, each detail tripping over the feet of the next.

Tibby. 'The Friends are bringing Anna home in stages. We do not know exactly when she will be with us. . . .'

Kitty. 'They spoke as if we should have heard from India. But we had not. And this letter was dated some days ago. . . .'

Livvy. 'Anna has been so ill that she nearly died, Mary! And they say that she must never go back to India again. . . .'

Sophy. 'Mama ordered the carriages immediately we heard. . . .'

Molly. 'So that we could share the news at once. . . .'

Ruth said, 'And we descended on the Inferno in full force!'

'Oh, my dear child,' Zelah reproved her gently, 'do not call thy father's ironworks an inferno! Oh but, Charlotte, I have rarely seen William so moved. . . .'

'We descended on Uncle Caleb, too!'

'In fact, we have managed to rouse the entire valley in the past hour. Even the navvies gave us a cheer as we drove by. Though they had no notion what they were cheering about, of course.'

'What did they mean, Mama,' Ruth began, 'when they shouted. . . .'

'My dear child, pray do not repeat their blasphemies! Though, heaven knows they are not wholly to blame. How can they learn when we all treat them as outcasts? Surely the churches have a duty towards these poor fellows? Christ said that it was not the righteous but the sinners He called to repentance.'

Here some restlessness was evident among her grandsons. She rose at once, kissed Charlotte and Mary fondly, and stressed how much they were all looking forward to the supper ball. Her family followed suit, down to the youngest miniature ironmaster.

Mary stood at the parlour window, watching the carriages drive off. Her face was troubled, her heart in conflict. Guessing what doubts and disappointments must be tormenting her, Charlotte said nothing. But was surprised when the girl finally spoke.

'Do you know, Aunt Cha, when I was eleven years old – and living at Kit's Hill – we all went to one of Uncle William's Christmas Eve parties. It was the time when Mr Vivian was courting Cousin Anna, and Herbert interrupted them by sitting on her lap.

'Mother told me to go and fetch him, and I stood on the outside of a conversation they were having, afraid to interrupt. What they were actually saying didn't matter. They were loving each other with words. Do you know what I mean, Aunt Cha?'

Charlotte nodded, and there was a little pause.

'In that moment,' Mary went on, 'Cousin Anna *was* everything, and *had* everything, that I could ever desire. It happened seven years ago and I have never forgotten the feeling of being ugly and awkward and shut out. Of guessing what it must be like to be inside their world.' There was another pause. Then she said, 'I thought they were the two most beautiful people I had ever seen.'

They were both silent.

Then Charlotte said, 'It will be a shock for Hal and Anna when they meet, however long it is since they parted, however well they think they are prepared. For neither of them has found anyone else.'

Mary did not answer, and when she spoke again it was to continue her train of thought.

'Herbert had misbehaved himself, of course. He wet

Cousin Anna's lap and she had to go away to change her gown. Then Mr Vivian noticed me standing there. At first he treated me like a child – offering me mince pies, and making jokes. But when he saw I was unhappy, he started to talk to me properly. It was the first time any grown-up person, except for you, had tried to understand what it was like to be me.

'When he came back to Millbridge again, three years ago, I thanked him for that kindness. Not being silly, or trying to make him notice me – as Ambrose always says I do – but truly thanking him. And, do you know, Aunt Cha, he couldn't remember the conversation at all. He couldn't even remember me.'

Charlotte's clasped hands tightened. Recently she had begun to feel that other people's suffering laid her open. And every effort she made to comfort them drained her of strength. As though life itself were seeping away. Yet she must comfort.

'Well, my dearest, as you said, he was in love with Anna, and people in love are very selfish. They only really notice each other.'

Millbridge in the November dusk was too poignant to contemplate. Mary let fall the curtain and turned away.

'I cannot think how I came to feel so sorry for myself,' she said, seeing that Charlotte looked white and tired. 'I think I shall go and read a little Latin. I find it a good corrective for self-indulgence.'

But at the doorway she stopped, and cried as though the question were torn from her, 'But is it not sad, Aunt Cha, that something so important to the receiver should be so unimportant to the giver?'

Anna arrived at Kingswood Hall that same evening, escorted by two elderly Quakers whom Zelah had known in her youth. And the mother wept first over her child, and then at the sight of these old friends. The ironmaster, too, shed tears quite unashamedly, and his daughters joined him – so that Anna was borne into the house on a flood of family emotion, and clung to the arms of her travelling companions almost in terror.

'Anna is still weak,' Jane Lilbourne explained, helping the girl to a chair, 'and wearied by the long journey. Though thy hearts are full thee should not tax her strength.'

Her spectacles glittered beneath the narrow brim of her black bonnet. As tears and exclamations continued to flow she permitted herself a crisp reproof.

'I am surprised thee should allow such a Popish scene as this, Zelah Howarth!'

Which effectively dried everybody's eyes.

Calmer now, her sisters divested Anna of her outer clothing – permitting themselves no more than a smile, a loving look, a touch upon her cheek – and settled her by the fire. She accepted their attentions passively, stretched out her hands to the blaze and seemed to absent herself from the company.

'Let her be, Zelah Howarth, and do not fret thyself or her,' said Rachel Fox kindly, as Zelah's eyes filled again and she tried to attract her daughter's attention. 'She will heal herself thus. She hath improved even in the past week . . .'

Anna remained silent and motionless, warming herself. Tabby ordered tea to be brought in. Kitty showed the Quaker ladies to their rooms. Each daughter took upon herself some hospitable task so that William and Zelah were free to sit together, holding hands for comfort, and looking on the changes that seven years had wrought in their third child.

The Kingswood Hall Howarths were good at organising family events, and Mary's coming-out ball was faultless in every detail, but the spirit which would have exalted even the humblest celebration was missing. The guests did not know whether to wear a happy or a solemn expression. Should they congratulate the healthy girl downstairs, or ask after the convalescent woman upstairs? Would it be callous to enjoy themselves, or rude to seem half-hearted? They attempted to fulfil both obligations, and the party failed to come alive.

One guest had sent an honest excuse and stayed away. No one was surprised at that. The situation was difficult enough without the Cornishman pretending that nothing was the matter.

Only one man present was too concerned with his own affairs to notice what was going on around him. As Charlotte had said, people in love are very selfish. It was scarcely the adjective to apply to such a good-natured, hard-working fellow as Dr Jamie Standish, but he was wholly preoccupied with the problem of getting Mary alone.

She, realising what was afoot, had already refused an offer to sit out one dance, and another to see the plants in the conservatory. She had seldom felt more frightened and miserable in all her life.

By nine o'clock, unable to manage her himself, Jamie rounded up possible allies. He asked permission from her father, consulted Charlotte, and sought advice from the ironmaster. Twenty minutes later he found himself confronting a cornered girl in Zelah's private parlour.

He stammered out his feelings, though Mary tried to persuade him not to do so. He made a formal proposal. She attempted to evade the question. He insisted upon an answer. She refused him gently. He begged her to take time, to reconsider. The last of her energy had gone.

She began to cry, silently at first, and then with the abandon of the utterly wretched. He tried to comfort, then to restore her. She could not stop crying. He ran for assistance, and returned with a dozen female Howarths. They tried smelling salts, cold compresses, mulled wine and kind words, but she could not stop.

She wept for deferred hopes and broken promises, for virtues unnoticed and sacrifices unrewarded, and for the most terrifying thing of all: that feeling of being forever outside the lighted window, and knowing that happiness lay within.

The news sifted through the party in whispers. The evening, which had been faltering, now halted completely. The Millbridge contingent gathered in corners. The Howarths, when they were not consoling Mary, stood round in discomfited groups. At half past ten o'clock, his hopes effectively doused, Dr Jamie thanked his host and hostess stiffly and stalked off with his uncle. They were followed at once by a crowd of sympathisers. The Kit's Hill contingent, relieved to be let off the social hook, also excused themselves, saying they had to be up early for the milking.

Mary came out at last, accompanied by Charlotte, and no one could have said which of them looked the worse. More concerned for his mother, Ambrose helped her into the waiting carriage. Sitting opposite them, shaken now and again by a hiccup or a sob, knowing she would not be forgiven, the forlorn girl plucked artificial rosebuds from her hair, and saw that it was coming out of curl.

In the early hours of the morning Mary suffered an attack of asthma to crown all others, and Dr Hamish was hurried up the High Street, tucking the tails of his nightshirt into the top of his trousers. Though sorry and angry for her treatment of his nephew, he remained compassionate, and her trouble somewhat soothed him. As she clutched his hands, and gasped and wept her apologies, he spoke philosophically.

'Maybe it's just as well, lassie. Red-headed folk are queer cattle and that's a fact. Two red-headed folk together might be asking too much of Providence.'

And so departed, to tell Jamie that the decision had cost Mary dear, and in his opinion the young man was well out of it. But the shy fellow had been grievously injured in his affections and his pride. He would have nothing more to do with Thornton House, avoided all social events in which he was likely to meet Mary, and became quieter and more reserved than ever.

Millbridge now called Mary wilful and heartless, and

made her aware of its supreme displeasure. In public, the Howarths and Longes kept up a united front. In private they all told Mary she had behaved badly. The only person who did not scold her was the Cornishman, but then he had other things to concern him.

General disapproval did nothing for Mary's peace of mind but much for her character. She deeply repented her part in the affair, and was unable to explain it even to herself. Was Jamie Standish only a dream, and did reality make him vanish away? Or was the dream real, and Jamie Standish only one of its guises? Whatever the answer, he was not the man. But his proposal had shorn her silliness away. She had indeed come of age, and found it a sobering business.

Part Three

Destinations

1826-1829

EIGHTEEN

New Growth

For the first time in many years, the Howarths did not gather at Kingswood Hall to celebrate Christmas Eve. Reasons were vague, but understood. Zelah had her invalid to nurse, who was said to improve daily, though not yet ready to see visitors. There were further tensions between Kit's Hill and Thornton House. And the ironmaster had business problems. A vast financial bubble of speculation had burst in the city of London, very nearly fetching down the Bank of England. The market was glutted with goods, and capitalists were calling in their loans.

Like many others, the Wyndendale Railway Company, existing on borrowed money, was forced to find repayment, and William called upon every member of the committee for help lest the venture should founder entirely. They had all been hit by the sudden recession, and the cotton manufacturers were in a particularly bad way. But they had too much invested in the railroad to be able to draw back, and Wyndendale could hardly be left in its present state of chaos. So, cursing this cruel turn of luck, each magnate sold everything he could lay his hands on, and sold it cheap.

Grimly, the ironmaster headed the list of rescuers at considerable sacrifice to himself. But the Cornishman emptied his pockets gladly. He was the only one to think more of the railway than of his money.

Then the rain set in. Throughout that miserable winter work was frequently halted either by bad weather or lack of capital. When that happened there was nothing for the navvies to do, and nowhere else for them to go. They huddled in their huts and shanties, playing cards on the earth floor, drinking and quarrelling. They crowded the local taverns. They picked fights with each other and anyone else they fancied. And whereas they might enjoy a little poaching on knock-off Sunday, they now took down their guns, called their bullhounds and lurchers to heel, and poached in earnest. The valley groaned under the yoke of their idleness.

'If we had started to blast out the tunnel they could work inside it,' said Hal Vivian impatiently, staring out of the library window at the pouring rain.

For he had spent this spare time in perfecting his design.

'We are not *having* a tunnel, sir!' cried the ironmaster. 'Because we do not need it and we cannot afford it! Even *you* reckon it will cost £30,000 and take three years to build. Which means £60,000 and six years, at the very least! As for blasting, sir, I begin to wish I had shares in gunpowder. I should have made a fortune out of our project alone.'

He spoke with some bitterness, not especially concerned with the price of gunpowder but with the on-going problem of Upperton cutting.

Since the railway sheds were situated at Garth Fold, they had decided to start the track from there. Railroads, unlike ordinary roads, should be both straight and level. So the Cornishman was only able to take the line a mile and a half from Garth to the other side of Coldcote before he had to think again.

Beyond there lay heavy industries, which made the land expensive, so he chose to cross the River Wynden by means of an iron bridge, over to Medlar. Here he was on the outskirts of the ironmaster's realm where the line was welcome, except that it ran into trouble on the steep slopes of Upperton and could not level out again until it reached the lower parts of Belbrook.

The ironmaster had been emotionally distracted at this point on the map. He stood, chin in hand, looking back into his youth.

'Belbrook,' he said meditatively. 'I shall never forget that

Saturday when I discovered the old foundry at Belbrook, Hal. I can still feel the sun on my shoulders. The brambles tore my shirt to shreds, and your mother. . . .' Here he paused, a little afraid but the Cornishman was in a receptive mood. 'Your mother scolded me,' he said, and gave a shamefaced grin. 'Scolded me and set me to rights. Belbrook! Aye, aye. It still has the old wooden bridge, you know. I promised myself that I should build an iron bridge there, Hal, when first I found it; but the river has flowed under it for nigh on forty years, and still it stays.'

'But it would be an excellent idea to cross the river again at that very place,' cried the Cornishman. 'For beyond Belbrook on this side the land belongs to Lord Kersall, while on the other side it is the property of committee members who will use the line for haulage of goods.'

'Well, well, well!' said the ironmaster, entranced. 'There shall be an iron bridge after all!'

He brought himself back with some difficulty.

'What was the trouble with Upperton, Hal?'

'I can see no way round it. We must go through it, sir. We must make a cutting a mile in length.'

He knew they would encounter problems seen and unforeseen, that the labour would be prodigious. He expected a long and fruitless argument, an order to survey other territory, and much discussion. He was wrong.

'We must design a pretty bridge, Hal,' the ironmaster went on. 'Strong but ornamental. And Belbrook shall cast it.'

'As you please, sir. But what of the cutting at Upperton?'

The ironmaster was mellow, prepared to listen to reason.

'Well, as you say, we cannot go round. So we must go through, Hal. Upperton cutting it shall be.'

Only when work began did they discover the magnitude of the task.

March came with daffodils and new lambs on the fells, cool sunlight and washed cotton clouds, pale blue skies.

The ironmaster rallied, bullied and persuaded.

231

The Cornishman, who had been travelling half-heartedly between Manchester and Millbridge for three months, dining alone off mutton chops on Christmas day, received news that more money had been raised, and caught the next coach from Market Street.

In the shanty towns, navvies tumbled out of their bunks, swore at the old crone sitting on a chair near the beer barrels and cuffed her a little – not too much, since she acted as unpaid housekeeper. They donned their moleskin trousers and canvas shirts, their rainbow waistcoats and velveteen square-tailed coats. They laced their hob-nailed boots and clapped their white felt hats to one side of their heads. They reached for their picks and shovels.

As usual, the weekly conference at Kingswood Hall had begun amiably and ended in argument.

'It is not the first time you and I have disagreed over the subject of expense,' the ironmaster cried, 'nor, I suspect, will it be the last. But I must impress upon you, sir, that I am at present risking my own enterprises in order to pay for your damned railroad – and that is the only reason why you are able to continue.'

The Cornishman thought this statement over, and reached an inevitable conclusion.

'Then, sir, the sooner we complete the railroad the better for all of us, say I.'

'Aye, you would,' growled William. 'And when shall that be, sir?'

'We could not have known about the weather, of course,' Hal Vivian began, 'which has lost us months of work.'

'Damn the weather, sir! When shall we be done?'

In his mind, Hal Vivian became the railway line. He thought himself out from the Millbridge end.

'Tom Hosking's men have finished the embankment. It is a fairly straight run from there to Whinfold. . . .'

'Ah! your straight run is another point of contention, sir!' William broke in. 'As soon as the ground is made ready for track laying you go along with your theodolite again, and fuss over every yard of it. Telling them to dig deeper here and mount up the earth there. . . .'

'Sir, I am an engineer. Each site presents its own problems. When we have dug it, or blasted it, or filled it out, we must then *level* it. I cannot pass any part of the line for track laying until it is *level*. The mean-gradient should be 1 in 1380. . . .'

'We are constructing a railway line, sir, not a billiard table!'

'By God, sir!' cried the Cornishman. 'My line shall be one long billiard table before I am done. Wait, before you rant and rave, sir!' As William showed signs of doing so. 'I will present the facts. On the level, a locomotive is able to draw 67 tons. On an incline of 1 in a 100, it draws only 50 tons. At 1 in 12, sir, it will not draw at all! Does that answer your question?'

They both paused for breath.

The ironmaster turned his back upon the company engineer, and stalked to the window. Had he been of a philosophical turn of mind, he might have asked himself whether this was the price of love? Instead, he reflected how deeply his empire was mortgaged.

Hal Vivian, guessing that his father's dark face concealed dark thoughts, endeavoured to lighten it with optimism. He temporised.

'I should say, sir, at the present rate of construction, that we could think of opening the line next autumn. Say, October 1827?'

'When do the Bolton-Leigh railroad plan to open?' William growled, realising he was defeated.

'Later than that, I believe. Sometime in 1828!'

'I suppose,' said the ironmaster, preparing to encounter other financial emergencies, 'that we can hang on until next year. . . .'

Hal Vivian made his farewells quietly, crossed the room swiftly, opened the library door, and startled a small woman who had evidently been listening on the other side.

She skipped back, smothering a laugh.

He would have passed by her with an apology, without another glance, but the laugh touched the deepest part of his being. He stopped and looked at her closely.

She wore a fine wool gown of Quaker grey, and a little white linen cap. Her eyes and mouth smiled in unison. Her hair shone silver-gilt.

For a moment they stood quite still and silent.

Then the Cornishman said, 'Anna!' and held out both hands.

Which she clasped. And laughed again.

'I was listening at the keyhole,' she admitted.

She withdrew her hands, but her smile mantled him.

'I knew thee was expected,' Anna said, 'and wanted to find out for myself how thee fared. Thou hast not changed, Cornishman – still battling for thy visions and hopes and expectations!'

He bent his head in acknowledgement.

'But how my father hath changed,' she continued, speaking of him with great affection. 'He puts thee even above himself. Thee should not be too hard upon him, for the love he bears thee.'

Her voice was warm. She looked at him frankly, spoke directly. And yet she seemed to be at a great distance from him.

'Where art thou going now, Hal? To work?'

He was searching for the girl he loved, and she had gone away, leaving this silvery Quaker spirit in her stead.

'To work?' he repeated absently. 'Yes, I suppose I am. Though this afternoon is supposed to be free. But we are having trouble with the cutting. . . . Anna, can we not talk together for a while?'

'Yes, if thee will wait for me,' Anna said, 'I must fetch my cloak, and then we can walk in the garden.'

He sat down on a frail pretty chair when she left, and put his head in his hands. He felt faint and empty.

Though his sorrow was no longer poignant, Anna had filled his private thoughts for seven years. The desire for a woman could be appeased by a visit to one of the professional charmers of Flawnes Gardens; the need for feminine company was filled by the ladies of his present acquaintance; but in his heart he had worshipped Anna's image.

He must have stayed like this for several minutes, because she stood beside him again, and touched his shoulder gently. And, looking up at her, he saw she comprehended.

'All experience is valuable, Hal,' she reminded him. And as he nodded dumbly she added, with a smile and a sigh, 'That is why we pay so high a price for it.'

They walked arm in arm through the gardens, and saw the green haze on trees which promised to leaf.

'Are you quite better?' he asked tenderly.

'Quite better, I thank thee. Death took my arm, even as thou hast done, and I wanted to die. But he let me go again, and I woke to a new world. So every minute of life is precious.'

'And what were you doing in India?' he asked, watching this new Anna. 'Teaching? Preaching?'

She laughed aloud, throwing back her head in her old manner, and said, 'Teaching, preaching, and engineering, Cornishman!'

This time he laughed too, and stopped to look at her, wondering if she were serious. She nodded emphatically, and they strolled on.

'Thee would be surprised how useful I have become, Hal. There is a Roman proverb which sayeth that an empty belly hath no ears. A few of us, all of the Quaker faith, went out to India to bring light to their souls. And found we must first look to their bodily welfare. I am no expert, Hal, but I can show thee how to build a mud hut and dig a well.'

He laughed again, and she joined him.

'Did you convert them to Quakerism?' he asked, curious.

'We met together in a loving fellowship, but not a Christian one.'

'What happened then?'

For the first time she lost her air of quiet contentment.

'The village was washed away by the rains.'

They were silent for a minute or two. Then they talked of the family and of the railroad, until the Cornishman took out his watch and consulted it ruefully.

'I fear I must look into the weighty matter of some 20,000 lbs of gunpowder, Anna!'

'It sounds a highly explosive matter to me!'

'We are dealing with a mass of gritstone, and blasting is the best way to move it. Normally, I would let them get on with it, but Babbage's navvies are a reckless crew and Hamish Standish is complaining about the number of casualties, and the *Clarion* is on my back.'

'Ah, your navigators,' said Anna. 'I thought, now I am better, that I could come and speak to them on Sunday.'

He was appalled at the notion.

'Dear God, Anna,' he said, 'no decent woman should go near them. No one has a greater admiration for them than I, for they are the finest workers in the world – heroes, in fact – but savage heroes, wild and lawless fellows without respect.'

'My mother will come with me,' said Anna, as though the question of a chaperone were his only concern.

'No, she must not go either! I shall speak to your father. He shall forbid it. He must forbid it. I have never heard of such a thing!'

'Well, we shall see,' said Anna.

Her tone was equable but her chin was firm.

'And above all, not this Sunday,' said the Cornishman, recognising the firmness, 'because they will just have been paid, and they are particularly drunken, obscene and quarrelsome at such a time.'

Now she smiled on him again, saying, 'Very well, Hal. It shall be as you say. Not *this* Sunday. Shall we go in, now?'

From the terrace of Kingswood Hall, at this leafless time of the year, the whole of Wroughton could be clearly seen.

Just below sprawled the dark and fiery realms of Snape Foundry, from which the ironworkers' houses radiated, rank on brick rank, across the black hillside. It was a busy, gloomy spectacle, but there were oases even in this industrial desert. Here lay the Howarth Public Park where folk could walk on fine Sunday afternoons, or sit and listen to music played by Wroughton Brass Band in the ornamental iron bandstand, or drink from the iron fountain. There, neat rows of winter vegetables marked the workers' allotments. Elsewhere, the few green fields of some lone farmer stood out against the march of progress.

Far down to the right was all that remained of the former village of Upperton: the dwelling known as Bracelet, in which Dorcas Howarth had spent her final years. Once a demure and orderly house in a country lane, it now perched on the edge of a precipice, seeming to hold back its skirts in terror, while the little garden clung behind it; and eighty feet below, as if a giant had scooped out the landscape with his trowel, lay the path of the Wyndendale railroad.

NINETEEN

Victors and Vanquished

The time when the ironmaster could frown his breakfast table to silence had passed. He sat with his sister and sought comfort.

'When she was a child I used to find much of myself in Anna,' said the ironmaster ruefully. 'Then, when she came home again I saw Zelah in her. But in truth, I believe she resembles our mother more than anyone. There is a confounded obstinacy about her which will not be denied. Her very bonnet looks like one that Mrs Dorcas wore when she was visiting the sick and poor in Garth. And if Mrs Dorcas believed something to be her duty, she *would* do it!

'Anna will not listen to me now, and Zelah is just as bad. It is as if the very devil had got into the pair of them! I shudder to think what they must have heard and seen in those confounded shanty towns.'

Charlotte said lightly, seriously, 'When I was on the convict ship we were visited by two good Quaker ladies. A few of the women prisoners were rude and blasphemous, and resented them. But the rest of us were glad to see them. They brought hope where there was none. And they were very practical. They fetched us blankets as well as bibles.'

Heedless, he continued his own monologue.

'And now I am being asked to provide schooling for the navvies' damned children, and a welfare scheme for the damned navvies. All this on top of the railroad! And my son. . . .' Here he paused, remembering the pure young ears of Mary, who was writing a letter at the escritoire. He continued in a less intimate manner, 'Nothing moves fast enough for the Cornishman. He is onto the next idea before we have half done with the present one. It is too much, Lottie.'

238

She placed a thin hand upon his strong one.

'Are you well?' he asked, afraid. 'You must not be ill, Lottie. Too many of us depend upon you. Do we not, Mary?'

The girl's face was sad, her eyes pensive. But she reassured him.

'Oh, Aunt Cha is much better since the sun came out. We have all found the winter trying.'

And as if to underscore her point, she dipped the quill into its inkwell and scratched away briskly.

'I am much better now,' said Charlotte as heartily as she could.

'You let folk drain you,' William warned, finding a convenient excuse for her pallor. 'You always did, Lottie. I have told you many a time that all these friends of yours come to take, not to give. They are always asking something of you. I never visit you, without I must chase someone away. You should refuse to see them.'

'What? Even though I love them, and might help them just by listening?' Charlotte asked, with a hint of irony.

Her eyes met Mary's for an instant and they exchanged the merest spark of a smile. But William missed the subtlety of her remark.

'Take a leaf from my book, Lottie,' he said, glad to advise her, 'and don't allow folk to waste your time. No one comes tattling to me, I can tell you; I have too much to do.'

Later, when he rode away down the High Street on his tall black horse, the two women burst out laughing.

'But Aunt Zelah has always been concerned with charitable works,' Mary said, 'and he never minded before. So what has disturbed him now?'

Some reluctance she could not explain made her shy of mentioning Anna, and so far she had managed to avoid meeting her. Which Charlotte had observed. Which she let be.

'William likes his charities to be socially acceptable,' she replied, 'and he likes to see instant results for his money – the poor widow's rent paid up, the orphans scrubbed and fed. The navvies cannot fulfil either of those requirements. I always know when Zelah has stopped listening to him, because he grumbles to me instead, and it makes me smile to see the puzzlement behind that iron facade.'

Mary, who had been standing at the window while they talked, gave an exclamation of surprise. For her uncle was riding back again, with the Cornishman close behind him, and their urgency was causing a small commotion in the street. In her old impulsive fashion, she ran to the front door and flung it open, crying 'Oh, what has happened?'

'Mary, be a good girl,' said the ironmaster, pale and stern on his tall horse, 'and try to find Jamie Standish for us. I am off up to the hospital to fetch Dr Hamish and anyone else they can spare. But Jamie is out on his calls somewhere in the Old Town.'

Mary clasped her hands in terror, brought back upon herself.

'Oh, but why must *I* find him? How shall I know where to start?'

'Knock on every door in the High Street,' ordered the ironmaster, 'tell him there has been an explosion on the Belbrook side of Upperton, and we need him as fast as he can get there.'

And as she stammered something about fetching her bonnet, he shouted, 'Never mind that nonsense, miss! There are lives at stake. Go as you are, and go at once!'

Polly appeared as she was wont to do in moments of crisis, put an old cloak about her shoulders, and gave her a little push.

'Off with you, miss. I'll look after Mrs Longe,' she said.

Mary ran to the first house and hammered on the door, distraught.

The navvies had begun work that day in Upperton cutting much as soldiers join battle: prepared, imperilled, and summoned by bugles.

When blasting was necessary, the Cornishman usually made sure that he or one of the assistant engineers were present, and that company regulations were observed. But the ironmaster had told Len Babbage that time cost money, and Len knew that regulations cost time.

'Cut corners wherever you can,' William had said.

Babbage did. His navvies worked double and treble shifts, by night and by day. And to keep them going he let them have all the beer they wanted. When they ran out of money he issued beer tickets, so they could drink the wages they had not yet earned. For a small consideration he allowed publicans to tour the line offering drink. The publicans gave the gangers a tip for every barrel of beer they bought. The gangers sold the barrels to their men.

Babbage cut another corner in the matter of safety fuses. He reckoned they were a waste of both time and money, and that if a man could not run fast enough to save his skin he was not worth hiring. Besides, with a few extra charges of gunpowder, this last explosion would open the way through to the ironworks at Belbrook, the river and the new bridge.

This last obstacle between themselves and Belbrook was a treacherous mixture of sandstone, millstone grit, shales, slate and clay. They bored a colander of holes, sowed them freely with gunpowder, and tamped the charges down with iron stemmers.

('Workers must use copper rams, in the interests of safety. . . .'

'Copper rams cost money. Besides, you've always got a length of iron handy. . . .')

The buglers blew their brassy notes of warning. The men lit the fuses and ran for cover. In the little hush that followed they could hear a blackbird singing.

The boom when it came was deep and muffled, as though nature attempted to contain her outrage. Then the earth trembled and shook, the rock face split asunder, and two hundred thousand cubic feet of Wyndendale spouted into the morning air. The mass seemed to hang momentarily over them like some horrific genie. They flung their arms over their heads, fell upon their knees and faces before it. Were bombarded, broken, crushed and pinioned by the avalanche of spoil.

Shown into Mrs Vincey's front parlour, Mary confronted Jamie Standish in full consciousness of her awkward situation. To begin with, the news sounded so dramatic that they would think she was exaggerating, not an uncommon fault in her. Then, why should she be the messenger unless she hoped to gain something by it? Would not a girl of delicate perception have refused, even fainted at the prospect?

Mary did wish that Mrs Vincey and her sister were not there, noting every change of tone and expression. On the other hand, she would not have been alone with Jamie for a hundred gold guineas. So she begged all their pardons, and clutched Charlotte's old grey cloak to her, and repeated exactly what the ironmaster had said.

Jamie's face was as red as his hair, but he thanked Mary formally, begged the ladies to excuse his haste, and left the house straightway.

The bird of news flew from mouth to mouth. Ambrose and the editor of the *Post* headed for the stables of the Royal George, and were off on a couple of hired horses within minutes of each other. At the rectory, Cicely ordered the trap to be brought round, and packed her box of medicines and bandages. On her way through Millbridge she called at Thornton House to tell Charlotte where she was going.

'Oh, let me be of help,' Mary begged. 'Let me come with you!'

'No, love,' said Cicely. 'It will not be a fit place for a young girl. Besides, you have no knowledge of nursing.'

'But I could do a hundred things else. I have a horse. I could ride with messages. I could hold basins. . . .'

'Basins!' cried Cicely. 'I knew I had forgot something!'

While Polly ransacked the kitchen cupboard, Mary renewed her pleas.

'This will be no place for youth and innocence,' Cicely repeated.

But Charlotte said, 'No, Cissie, let her help if she can. I believe that youth and innocence should be informed about life rather than sheltered from it.' She spoke firmly to the delighted girl. 'Mary, you are now solely responsible for yourself and your actions. Weakness or silliness on your part will steal time and care from those who need it. Monitor yourself. If you feel faint, sit down and put your head in your lap. If it is too dreadful for you to bear, come back at once. If you feel you cannot ride safely, then go to Kingswood Hall and stay there until they can bring you home. And if you cannot behave like an adult I shall not treat you as one – and that I promise you. And, Mary, put on your *old* riding habit. This is not a fashionable occasion!'

Shortly afterwards Cicely whipped up her pony and trotted off, a-jingle with old basins. Behind her rode Mary. And behind Mary, in any convenient vehicle they could summon up between them, came other ladies of like spirit, who had never bound up more than a cut finger but were ready for the worst.

At Kingswood Hall, Zelah and Anna had already set out.

Upperton looked like a battlefield. Debris was scattered for hundreds of yards on either side of the cutting, and littered the track for half a mile ahead. Beneath and beyond it, new broken ground had been churned by wheels and boots and hooves into a quagmire. Those who came to help left their horses, carriages and traps at the Wroughton entrance and picked their way forward on foot.

The bitter fumes of gunpowder smoke lingered in their nostrils. The groans and shrieks of injured men violated their ears. Though the ladies lifted their skirts almost to knee level, the hems were draggled with dirt and wet. Those who wore pattens stuck fast and had to be rescued. Those who wore slippers lost them. The men, better equipped for such expeditions, merely ruined their trousers and muddied their boots.

News of the accident had spread, and people converged upon the scene. Some were the navvies' wives and women from the shanty town near Medlar, who wailed and screamed and swore and tore their hair. Others were idle spectators, treating the disaster like a sideshow. A few made themselves useful.

The ironmaster took magnificent command, and thought of everything. He even made sure that the crowds on the sides of the cutting were held back by ropes lest they fall over the precipice. The Cornishman was in charge of the rescue operation. The two doctors removed their coats, rolled up their sleeves and organised their voluntary medical team.

These good women now found themselves in a new, exhilarating and terrible world. Navvies who had escaped the worst of the blast began the herculean task of bringing out their wounded and dead: blaspheming over every boulder, rallying trapped comrades with obscenities, and cursing each other on to greater efforts. Zelah and Anna were used to their profanity, but for the rest it was an education in the art of bad language. Nor could they translate the private rhyming slang they used instead of speech. And the fact that their nicknames were their names was a hopeless business. For how could a lady address any man as Randy Bill, Jimmy Redcap or Bristol Mac? But they did their best because social niceties seemed of small account compared to anguish and terror.

Like Charlotte, Dr Hamish began by warning the squeamish not to be a nuisance. Since they had been delicately nurtured this came as a novel idea. However, they stiffened their resolve, and were afraid of nothing that day except to be found wanting in courage.

'And what in God's name are *you* doing here?' Hamish shouted, as Mary's bright head and white face bobbed towards him.

She was as frightened of his shout as of the blood on his hands.

'Come to help. Take messages. Anything!' she

stammered, trying not to see the shattered limb he was binding.

He gave her a hard shrewd look. Then nodded.

'Have you come on horseback? Good. I want you to ride straight back to Millbridge hospital. Tell them I shall want twenty beds at least. In the hall, the corridors, on the floor, anywhere. Tell Mr Bailey to make ready for surgery. Say – it's chaos! Tell them to send more bandages and splints and another wagon to convey the wounded. And if you come across the hospital wagon on the road – it was supposed to be following us – tell it to hurry up. Can you remember all that?'

'Yes, sir,' said Mary, and was off at the fastest pace she could manage, somewhere between a hobble and a hop.

She concentrated on Dr Hamish's orders. She did not dare to register the sights and sounds about her. She knew she could deal with the situation provided she did not identify with it.

At the Upperton turning she met the covered hospital wagon drawn by two horses, and gave the driver and his companion brisk directions, advising them to leave the vehicle there. They began to negotiate the mile of mud on foot, clutching a stretcher.

Though the afternoon was now well advanced, the disaster some hours old, there was no rest or refreshment. The navvies still sweated and swore, and pulled rocks free with their bare hands, and dug like maniacs with their shovels, to find limp or swearing comrades in the debris. They fetched them all out, whole or in pieces, human bundles of rags. The medical team worked on, in blood to the elbows.

The dead were shrouded and put aside. The living were divided into groups, diagnosed and temporarily treated. Serious cases, requiring surgery or more intensive care, were despatched to hospital one by one. Their removal was slow, their waiting period long, for every stretcher must be carried nearly a mile either way, and the jolting journey to Millbridge took over an hour. There were many more cases, shocked, bruised and gashed, who must be patched up and left to mend themselves – lying in the squalor of a hut, or in the warmth of the boiler-house, until they were well enough to work again.

'They should fetch the Edinburgh medical school down here, Jamie,' said Hamish with grim humour. 'There's a lifetime's experience to be had in one day. Blast burns. Simple and compound fractures. Broken and crushed and dislocated bones of every sort. Internal injuries. Concussion . . . stand aside there, woman!'

She was a tall gaunt figure with wild black hair and wild black eyes: impressive, despite her tattered clothes and the livid bruise on her jawbone. Ignoring Hamish's order, she bent over the man he was tending, and asked a question. Her voice was deep, her words few and rapid. They could scarcely understand what she said.

'Is he bad?'

'Bad enough,' Hamish replied. 'Is he your husband?'

She chewed her lip, frowning, trying to assess the man's condition.

'You could call him that,' she said. 'I've had six brats by him, and buried three. What's up with him? He looks all right to me.' And here she thrust her broken boot into his side, crying, 'Get up, you lazy bastard! What are you lying there for?'

'For God's sake, woman. He has been crushed. He's bleeding to death inside. Get away with you. Someone take her away! You!' he shouted, seeing a scared female face come into view. 'Do something with her!'

Mary set down the copper hot-water jug she was carrying, and a basket full of tin cups.

'Tea,' she explained. 'From the lady who lives at Bracelet! And she's cutting bread and butter for us, too.'

She laid one trembling hand on the woman's dirty arm, and said timidly, 'I daresay you could do with a cup of tea, couldn't you?'

But the woman pushed her away, crying, 'If you waved a mug of gin under the bugger's nose he'd get up fast

246

enough!'

And she lifted her broken boot and kicked him again.

'He is dead,' said Hamish factually, and closed his eyes, and moved on to the next patient.

The woman paused as if frozen. She toed the giant gently. He moved at her behest. Then she opened her mouth as wide as it would go and howled like a wolf. Mary and another woman hurried to her. She threw them off. She flung up her arms to heaven and sank on her knees in the wet and trampled soil. She clawed up handfuls of mud and daubed her cheeks and forehead. She clasped her arms about herself for comfort, and rocked to and fro on her haunches. Then, punctuating the monologue with sobs and curses, she embarked upon a long profane litany of grief.

There was nothing Mary could do for her. She left the woman to mourn, squelched along the cutting, and climbed the hill to Bracelet to fetch the promised bread and butter. She had elected herself as general errand runner, but was amazed how quickly everyone realised it. Her legs and back ached, her riding habit felt hot and dirty, but her pantaloons and boots were invaluable. Looking round she saw Millbridge ladies in far worse states: hair straggling, skirts tucked up like those of a servant girl, working in their stockinged feet. Countless times she trod the muddy mile, and each time she hoved in view again it was, 'Mary! Will you do this?' 'Oh, Mary, I was waiting for you!' 'Mary come here!' and 'Mary, go there!'

She became aware of something else, too. Despite the horror and harassment, their voices were warm, their eyes friendly. For many months she had endured the snub of politeness or silence. Now they liked her again. The ironmaster patted her cheek and called her a good girl. The Cornishman, seeing her struggling with buckets of water, roared at Len Babbage to round up the boys who did the menial jobs on the site so they could help her. And Babbage hurried to obey him.

So she found herself in charge of a gang of lads, ranging from five to twelve years of age, who came with her to borrow and fill and carry receptacles of water. On her own initiative she begged for food and blankets and home-made bandages, and discovered how generous people could be in a crisis, how eager to help.

Before evening came, everyone who could be got out was got out. One man had been trapped by both legs, and four of his mates tried all day to release him. Hamish Standish sent for an amputation saw in an effort to cut him free, but there was no way he could perform the operation. The navvy screamed until his voice gave out, then had to bear his pain in silence, and so died.

His name was Dublin Rory, and his woman had known better days – running away from a respectable family to share a hard and wandering life. She paid for a small headstone to be put up in his memory. But as no one knew his real name, and Dublin Rory seemed unsuitable, she asked the stone mason to chisel a simple statement. So the navigator lies outside the wall of a Wyndendale churchyard, beneath an inscription which reads, 'A Stranger from Ireland'.

Ambrose toiled with the rest of them until the last stretcher went to the wagon, which was more than could be said for the editor of the *Post*. Then, human duty being done, he mounted his horse and returned to the *Clarion* as an eyewitness, to set up tomorrow's news.

Hamish Standish thanked Mary last of all, and most beautifully. She had taken off her jacket and subsequently lost it. She did not feel the cold as yet, but the warmth of Hamish's arm round her shoulders was comforting in every sense.

'You're a grand lass,' said Hamish. 'And you've done a grand job!'

He gave her a kiss as well as a hug, before hurrying off.

It was a signal for the others to add their own words of affection and praise, to kiss her cheek or give her a little handshake. Mary was glad of the encroaching dusk because it hid the tears in her eyes, and she was still anxious not to be a nuisance.

All day she had been aware of Anna, had run errands for Anna, and thanked God for the work which prevented any intimacy. Now Mary's heart misgave her, as her cousin came up to speak. Was it relief that she felt, in the knowledge that Anna was no longer beautiful as she had been? Or fear, seeing an inward beauty which could be set upon a pedestal? For the Cornishman's devotion and admiration were manifest. And nearby, obviously charged with fresh hope, hovered Jamie Standish. Oh, she was weary of them all! She would have liked to turn away and find a bed, and sleep for ever.

She held out her hand to Anna, but had not the energy to smile.

'Cousin Mary! I have not seen thee since thou wast a child, and had great converse with the Cornishman on Christmas Eve.'

'Oh, you remember!' Mary cried, momentarily revived. Then she recollected that the less said about that occasion the better. 'I am glad you are so well,' she said. 'I am sorry not to have seen you. The winter has been a trying one for us all. We should have met before.' She heard her mechanical phrases with distaste. She gave up social pretence. 'I think I had best go home now. Aunt Cha will be waiting for me.'

'Stay for supper with us,' cried the ironmaster. 'All of you come to supper. I will send a message to Charlotte, so she does not fret.'

'Oh no, please,' said Mary, nearly crying. 'Just let me ride home, Uncle William. I am poor company. I am very tired.'

There was a slight contretemps between William and Jamie, one of whom wanted to send her back in a carriage, the other to ride with her.

'Please to let me go home by myself,' Mary pleaded.

Anna gave her a long perceptive look. She slipped her arm through that of Hal Vivian and took him aside.

'Mary hath had enough for one day, and is afraid that young Dr Standish will propose to her again. Wilt thee not

249

go with them?'

'Miss Mary,' said the Cornishman, returning to the circle, 'you must not ride alone in the dark. I am returning to the Royal George in any event. So Dr Jamie and I will accompany you.'

Her face brightened a little. She nodded and thanked them both.

'If you will excuse me for a moment,' he added, 'I must have a word with the contractor.'

Like everyone else, he and Babbage had been working side by side all day without talk of anything but the task in hand. Now he intercepted the man as he endeavoured to slip by, speaking in cold quiet rage.

'You damned villain!' said the Cornishman. 'Why did you order that blasting when you knew I could not be there to oversee it?'

'Nay, it were that ganger, O'Leary,' said the contractor, blaming the safely dead. 'The daft bugger must have used too much gunpowder.'

'He did not do it without you instructed him, sir. I shall see you get no references from me. I would prosecute you if I could.'

'Well, you can't, Mr Vivian,' said Babbage factually. 'You know as well as I do that this here accident is the company's liability. So least said, soonest mended. Give the widows £5 apiece, and forget it, Mr Vivian. We've all suffered. There's horses been killed, wheelbarrows smashed, picks and shovels lost, a crane damaged, and a hell of a lot of track buckled and bent. That rubble'll take a mort of clearing up. And we're short o' men now. Still,' he added, with sincere pleasure, 'we've got summat to be thankful for, Mr Vivian. It weren't all for nowt. Take a look over yonder.'

Beyond the heaps of spoil, now clearly visible in the light of its cupola fires, lay the ironworks of Belbrook, a silver slip of river, and an ornate iron bridge.

TWENTY

A Breath of Fresh Air

The autumn of 1826 took its toll of Charlotte's health, and she crept into the spring suffering from an increasing number of ailments. Never robust, the flesh was at last overcoming the spirit. Bronchitis plagued her at every change of wind and weather. A new foe beset her in the form of rheumatism. And her eyesight was failing to such an extent that she could read only in the best of lights with strong spectacles. On bad days and nights she sat propped up with pillows. On good days she lay downstairs on the parlour sofa. Gradually, Mary took her place in Thornton House and presided at the head of the table with youthful dignity, while Polly devoted herself to her mistress and scolded everyone else.

Some events cannot be sidestepped nor rendered harmless, but must be met head-on. The strength of Mary's devotion to Philomena exasperated Susan, who would torment the girl until she retaliated, and then forbid her to visit. But their last quarrel had been so savage that Mary was banned from October to March. The thought of missing those precious months of the child's growth brought her to grips with asthma again, but this time she did not feel she could trouble anyone else. So she lit a candle to keep herself company, and tried to lower herself into that deep mythical pool in which Hamish Standish had such faith, and fought it out alone: coming down next morning for breakfast red-eyed and shaken, but quietly victorious. She told no one, keeping the knowledge to herself as a talisman against future attacks.

'A breath of fresh air is what you need, my dear Charlotte,' cried Hamish Standish.

He spoke in his most professional tone, only adopted when he came to the end of his resources and wished to hearten his patient. And the family had gathered in the parlour to join in the deception.

'Why, in these days of fast and furious travel you could set off after breakfast and be at the coast in time for luncheon.'

'Aye, the coaches are disgracefully fast,' said Ambrose.

'But in this case will serve their purpose,' Hamish continued. 'Yes, I wonder that you have not visited the seaside before. The benefits are quite extraordinary. There is physic in the sea, you know, Charlotte. I hear of poor folk walking the forty miles from Manchester to Blackpool for a mere three or four days' holiday. And they will drink as much as a quart of sea water at a time, for their health!'

He saw the dismay on her face and added hastily, 'But that is not necessary in your case. A change of surroundings, sea air, and a bracing climate, will do you a world of good.'

Charlotte's eyes filled with tears at the thought of the effort.

Hamish interpreted her distress.

'You shall not go alone, of course,' he said. 'That would be a dreary business. No, no! You should have Mary with you for company – she looks a wee bit peaky herself – and take Polly along to look after the pair of you. What do you say to that? And don't give me any of your *buts*, Charlotte!'

Nevertheless, she must do so.

'But who will look after Ambrose and Jeremy and the house?' she asked, feeling disagreeably helpless.

'We shall fend for ourselves, as we have done before, mother,' said Ambrose, brooking no nonsense.

'The house won't fall apart in your absence, Mrs Charlotte,' Jeremy added. 'And Prue can take Polly's place for a while.'

'But Polly will not like that,' Charlotte protested.

'Oh yes, she will,' said Polly, coming in so opportunely with the tea tray that they knew she had been listening at the door.

'But Prue has only cooked under your supervision, so far. Suppose she burns the dinner?'

'Then they're going to have to buy theirselves a pie apiece from the bakehouse, ain't they, Mrs Longe?' said Polly callously.

'It is not too expensive,' Hamish went on. 'At Dickson's, for instance, which is the finest hotel in Blackpool, you can live in luxury for five shillings a day.'

'And is Blackpool the most salubrious place?' Ambrose asked, before Charlotte could protest again.

'It is the county's most favoured resort, but I should tend to avoid it for that very reason. They cluster on the beach like flies in high summer. Southport used to be quiet until Manchester discovered its attractions, but now is just as noisy. I think my choice would be Lytham. It is nearer home than either of the others, and only twelve miles or so from Preston. You could visit her there.

'In another year or two it may be spoiled, but at the moment it is a pretty little place, with one wide street and a handful of dwellings. A patient of mine used to spend his winters in Lytham, and walked daily upon the beach in all but the coldest weather, with great benefit. I can recommend his landlady, who has a house overlooking the sea.'

'Pick me a mount, Miss Mary,' begged the Cornishman, as she walked resolutely into the Royal George's stables, whip in hand. 'You know how they treat with me, else. Besides, I like to see the rascals beaten down by your combination of beauty and bullying.'

She held out her hand, delighted as always to see him. He had never sat in judgement upon her, and the events at Upperton cutting had wiped out a certain patronage on his part. He loved to tease, but no longer treated her like a child. Her fighting spirit rose.

'Fred!' she commanded, winkling the little man out of the gloom.

'God 'elp me!' said Fred to himself, recognising defeat. Then to the stable lad, 'Give Mr Vivian whatever bloody 'orse Miss Mary fancies, even if bloody King George ordered it.'

'If you do not mind my mentioning it, sir,' Mary began, watching Hal Vivian ride out, 'you seem easier with steam engines than with horses.'

He laughed spontaneously, for he found her honesty amusing.

'Aye, you're in the right of it there. And the moment I can replace the horse by some personal steam engine I shall do so.'

She looked at him curiously, saying, 'I have never known a Howarth who did not love horses.' Then turned scarlet, crying, 'Oh, I could bite out my tongue! Pray do forgive me. Ride on without me, if you wish. I would not blame you, sir.'

He did not laugh this time, but smiled to himself wryly.

'How long have you known about *that* old scandal?' he asked.

'Oh, what a fool I am!' she chided herself. 'I beg your pardon, sir. It is common knowledge, though not common gossip, in our family.'

Then some gracious ancestress prompted her to say, with great spirit and emphasis, 'And we are very proud of the connection. So I hope you do not feel yourself disgraced by *us*, sir!'

'Well, I'm damned!' said the Cornishman, and drew rein.

His eyes were clear grey, crystalline – as though he saw her for the first time. She did not notice, preoccupied with her blunder.

'I suffer from impetuosity, and an unruly tongue, Mr Vivian,' Mary confessed, coming to a halt at his side.

She was flushed and troubled, but gracious still.

'Yet I do recognise these and other faults in myself, and strive to correct them. And though I deserve all the scoldings I get, sir, I do sincerely repent. So, pray forgive me if I caused you pain.'

A gang of Tom Hosking's navvies were laying the line at Flawnes Green. Seeing their company engineer with a pretty girl they drew their own inevitable conclusion, and assailed Hal and Mary with whistles, oaths, and advice of the bawdiest kind.

'Why is it,' Mary asked herself, anguished, 'that whenever I am discussing serious matters I am mocked by fools and madmen?'

Her earnestness struck the Cornishman as supremely comical. He shook his head at the navvies, but chuckled to himself as they urged their horses on and cantered down the Black Road.

'Of course,' he remarked, when they were once again riding at a more leisurely pace, side by side, 'you are Anna's cousin.'

She glanced quickly at him, her face shadowed by a peculiarly female expression. She had not entirely accepted Anna.

'I always admired her, of course,' said Mary, noncommittally, 'but she was grown up when I was a child. I was closest to Sophy and Molly, because they were much of an age with me.'

'You have a similar, and very charming, inconsequence of speech, which Anna used to have,' said Hal Vivian, watching her downcast face. 'But your attitude is entirely different. At your age, Anna believed she was destined for happiness of a high order. Whereas you have always given me the impression that you found life a difficult business.'

'Well, I daresay that if *I* had been brought up at Kingswood Hall,' said Mary, with some bitterness, '*I* would have thought happiness was my birthright.'

'And now I have hurt *you*,' he said penitently, 'and did not mean to – so must ask your pardon, in my turn. I make mistakes too, you see. You are not alone with your faults, cousin.'

She flushed with pleasure at the title, and smiled beautifully.

255

'Yes. We are cousins too!' she told herself, with satisfaction.

'Shall you call me cousin? Between ourselves, of course!'

She was radiant at the suggestion.

'I should like that more than anything, Cousin Hal! Best not mention it otherwise,' she added, slightly alarmed. 'Or they'll know I've been jabbering again, and putting my foot in it.'

'Oh, quite so,' said the Cornishman, and smiled to himself.

They rode on in a delightfully amicable silence. Then he asked after Philomena – for he guessed the purpose of her errand.

'Did you know that Susan refused to let me see her all winter?' Mary cried, her sense of grievance roused again. 'Oh, it is nothing new. I fear, in spite of my best intentions, that we do not get on together. Well, Aunt Cha and Polly and I are going away to Lytham on Wednesday, and I must say goodbye to Philly for the next three months. So, though Susan said I wasn't to come until they'd got the hay harvest in, I'm not taking any notice of her – for once!'

'Might she tell you to turn round and go home?'

Mary nodded, and compressed her lips.

'Surely, your father would not allow that?'

'He's married to Susan, and he likes a quiet life,' said Mary without reproach.

He saw that she was resolute, though much afraid of anger and humiliation, and looked at her very kindly.

'I admire your courage, cousin, which is apparently of the moral as well as the heroic sort. Suppose I come with you, and we make it a short and formal call? She can hardly send the pair of us packing, now can she?'

The girl was vivid with hope, crying, 'Oh would you, sir? And you could charm her, as you do all the ladies. And I shall not have to be on guard, as I usually am. Oh, would you do that, cousin?'

Hal Vivian said, 'The railroad will have to wait an hour or so. Well, I have given it five years of my life!'

256

Susan was pregnant, a state which had not been obvious on the previous visit and altered the situation entirely.

Mary jumped down from her horse, saying, 'Forgive me, Susan. I know you are too busy to receive visitors, but Mr Vivian and I have only stopped by for a few minutes. I am going away with Aunt Charlotte to the seaside next week, and shall be there all summer.'

Susan, realising that she was outmanoeuvred, dropped a clumsy curtsey to the Cornishman and sent a lad off to find Dick.

Mary whispered in her ear, 'I didn't know about the baby. I'm very glad. It'll be company for Philly.' And again, 'We shan't stay long.'

She felt sorry for Susan. And always her life was thus: that when the table was set in the presence of her enemies she knew herself to be unworthy of their abasement.

Susan whispered back, impressed, 'Your Dad'll want to see you. I didn't know you and Mr Vivian was so friendly. You're very welcome.'

For once Mary curbed her honest tongue and allowed Susan to think what she liked. She scooped up Philomena, who was trotting towards her, short arms outstretched, and cried, 'Ah, my littlest love!'

So that the child crowed with delight, and girl and child were one. All of which the Cornishman saw, and registered, with that new idea crystallising in his eyes and mind.

'Honoured to meet you, sir,' said Dick, coming up slightly breathless. He wiped his hand on his breeches and held it out to Hal Vivian. 'Hello, Mary. Give us a kiss then! How arta? You see how things is wi' us?' Nodding in the direction of Susan's swelling belly.

'Yes indeed. And I wish you both joy. When is . . . ?'

'September,' said Susan briefly.

And wondered whether she might die as Alice had done. For she was six-and-forty and this was her first child.

'I shall find something splendid for him – or her!' Mary

257

cried, always at her best when her sensibilities were aroused. 'I am delighted for you both. And *you*, little miss,' rubbing noses with the small dark child in her arms, 'will have your wicked little nose put out of joint! And serve you right for all your shocking behaviour!'

Dick said quietly, 'How's our Charlotte, Mary?'

The girl seemed to take upon herself a mantle of maturity, and to act and speak from its shelter, so that the Cornishman was quietly amazed at the transformation.

'Dr Hamish doubts that she will survive the coming winter.'

'Does our Charlotte know that?' he asked in a full voice.

'Of course she knows,' said Mary proudly. 'But she is keeping up our spirits by taking the doctor's advice, and pretending that a holiday is all she needs to make her well again.'

'When are you off, lass?'

'Next Wednesday, father.'

'I'll drop in a'Saturday and see her.'

'Oh, she would like that above all things.' She handed Philomena back reluctantly, but with her smile intact and resolute, 'We must be off, I fear. Mr Vivian is very busy with his railroad.'

'Aye!' said Dick, with a steady blue look at the Cornishman, 'You've made some changes round here, sir. I hope it's all for the best. We was glad when them navvies moved off, I can tell you! And we're still cleaning up the mucky camp they left behind them, and all.'

'Well, sir,' Hal Vivian replied, just as frankly, 'my ideas may not agree with yours, but I am sorry you have been inconvenienced. Perhaps, one day, the railroad may serve you well. I do hope so. For I have done *my* best, as I conceive it.'

Dick nodded, once, twice. Satisfied by the man, if not by his answer. He turned to his daughter.

'Mary,' he said, and held his wife's arm so that she should know he acted for the best, 'Susan's been none so smart the last month or two. I wonder if you could see your way to helping us out?'

Mary waited, knowing that her cup was about to run over.

'It'd be grand,' said Dick shyly, 'if you could take Philly off to the sea-side wi' you. We're not asking for charity. We can pay us way. But Susan gets dragged down wi' the little lass running about so much. And she's none so young as she used to be . . . .'

Mary said, 'Aunt Cha wouldn't dream of being paid, Dad, if that's what's bothering you. Anyway, children don't cost much to keep. If Susan wants me to, I'll look after Philly and fetch her back as fat and brown as – as a Kit's Hill sausage!'

She waited, not daring to look at her father's wife. There was a long struggling pause. Then Susan nodded: the nod of the conquered, who can offer no further resistance.

'Then I'll fetch the little lass wi' me, shall I?' said Dick. 'When I come to see our Charlotte a-Saturday?'

'Yes, father! Oh yes! Yes!'

She hugged him with all the love she felt for him. She shook Susan's hand cordially. She kissed Philomena with passionate tenderness. She turned mutely to the Cornishman for help.

Who took the situation over with his usual aplomb, bowed to the Howarths, and said he had been delighted to meet them, and hoped that this would not be the last time.

Dick said again, 'Honoured to meet you, sir!' and shook hands.

Mary could tell that he was wondering what relationship she shared with the Cornishman, apart from that kinship which could not be acknowledged socially. But she was not prepared to enlighten him either. Susan stood holding Philomena, and no one could have told what she was thinking, except that it was sad and without hope.

They mounted their horses, and rode away.

'All right, all right! I'll look after Phillermeen while you make a fool of yourself in the water!' cried Polly, out of all patience. 'You won't be satisfied until you've been drownded and catched your death of cold. I told you how it would be, Mrs Longe.'

They had helped Charlotte into the invalid basket carriage, and were now arguing over her while they adjusted her shawls.

'Dr Standish particularly recommended me to try sea bathing, Aunt Cha!' said Mary. 'And if Polly takes an old cup and spoon down to the beach, Philly can play in the sand and be no trouble at all.'

'And how are you going to get all them fancy seaside clothes off you, without me to help?' Polly demanded.

'I'll manage. If you will undo the back buttons.'

'And a proper sight you'll look. Coming down the steps of one of them machines in a flannel bathing gown and cap. As if you was in your nightwear in broad daylight. And carried, what's more, by a man with a flat red nose, like a drunken prize-fighter. And being ducked under like a blooming Baptist! I wonder you allow it, Mrs Longe. I do indeed!'

'My dear Polly,' said Charlotte mildly, 'we must move with the times. Mary will be no more indecorous than anyone else. And Mr Hicks is a most respectable person. A Methodist teetotaller. He told me so himself, only yesterday. All the ladies speak highly of Mr Hicks.'

Polly's sniff consigned Mr Hicks and his lady clients to oblivion.

'And how's she going to dry herself?'

'I can but try, Polly,' said Mary. 'Now do come on, or the tide will be out. And besides, you are tiring Aunt Cha with your tattle!'

'*Me* tiring her? I tell you this much, miss. If Dr Standish had just sent the two of us off we'd not have been worritted with neither Mr Hicks nor your Phillermeen. And that's the truth!'

The little party was not alone in its summer of sand and sea. Visitors came and went. Ambrose and Jeremy made the journey half a dozen times by stage-coach, and were put up by Charlotte's landlady for the weekend on two sofas. Ever ready to espouse new causes they used these opportunities to check on the alleged ill-usage of horses, the scandalous speeds of stage-coaches, and the subsequent dangers to all travellers and pedestrians. And were personally involved in one incident, which they reported as: 'RECKLESS DRIVERS COLLIDE ON HIGHWAY!'

The ironmaster came with Zelah and Ruth in his private carriage, and for a fortnight they stayed at Dickson's Hotel in Blackpool and drove over to Lytham most days.

And one visitor arrived unexpected and unannounced. So that Mary, carried forth like some flannel-clad sacrifice by the dependable Mr Hicks, shrieked even before she was plunged into the boisterous sea. For there was the Cornishman, top hat in hand, bending over Charlotte's invalid carriage in friendly conversation.

'First you can't wait to get in. Then you can't wait to get out again,' Polly grumbled, towelling Mary's hair. 'It's men, men, men, all the time with you. If you're so fond of 'em why didn't you marry that young Dr Sandwich and be done. They're all alike, you know.'

If she had struck the girl she could not have produced a greater effect. Mary's pleasure vanished. She saw herself as an object of derision – an eager, awkward, anxious spinster. For she thought of Hal Vivian as her special friend, and was proud of their mutual liking and trust. The notion of love between them brought her nothing but anguish and embarrassment. Her colour and temper flared.

She pushed Polly away, crying, 'How dare you say such a thing about Mr Vivian! Don't touch me! I can manage by myself. Anyway, Philly must come back to the house for her luncheon and afternoon rest. So fetch her to me, if you please!'

'Without saying so much as a how-de-do to the gentleman?' Polly demanded, for she had not been serious in her remark. The Cornishman was nearly fifteen years older than Mary. 'Where's your manners?' Polly asked. 'Has the cat got them again?'

'Hold your tongue!' cried Mary, in tears. 'Why do you torment me?'

'Well, I'm blessed,' said Polly, watching her run off like some bedraggled Naiad, wet red hair flying.

Hal Vivian kissed Charlotte's hand respectfully, as she sat in her basket carriage upon Lytham beach, and asked her how she did. She looked almost transparent now, as though she were literally fading away, but her eyes and smile shone forth.

'I find myself much improved, I do believe. This good sea air will set me up for the winter.'

But winter was the edge of a precipice over which she could fall, and she turned away from it to speak of other matters.

'How nice to see you, Hal!' she cried, 'Now what can be of such importance that you would leave your railway line?'

There was a touch of irony in her humour, but he did not mind. He was watching Mary's flight across the sands.

'Oh, I had a meeting with my partner in Manchester yesterday,' he answered lightly, 'and finding myself free upon a Saturday morning, decided to play truant for a while. I have not had a holiday in years, and wondered whether I might take lodgings here for a couple of nights? Or, failing that, I can catch a coach back this evening, and no matter. At least, if you will permit me, I can spend the day with you all.'

'But how kind of you to think of us! You are welcome to stay as long as you please,' said Charlotte, wondering. 'As to lodgings, there will be no difficulty, for we are almost alone here now. It is the end of the season.'

At her feet sat Philomena, spooning sand into an old cup with fierce concentration, and tipping it out to form lopsided mounds. The beach was deserted. Mr Hicks, his morning duties accomplished, had retreated to his cottage. Lytham's two bathing machines stood, forlorn castaways, at the edge of the sea.

'I cannot offer you a chair,' Charlotte said, 'but if you

262

spread one of those rugs upon the sand you may sit down in picnic fashion.'

'First of all,' continued the Cornishman amiably, making himself as comfortable as he could, 'I wanted to see how *you* were, though everyone fetches back good reports. We shall be glad to have you home again. Millbridge is a sorry place without the ladies of Thornton House – a sentiment with which, I feel, Ambrose and Jeremy would agree!'

His shoe here accidentally came in contact with one of Philomena's sand moulds, which promptly collapsed. She stopped in the midst of her labours, stared at the shoe with dark displeasure, and struck it with her wooden spoon.

'Oh, Lord! I beg your pardon, little miss!' cried the Cornishman, all contrition. 'Were you building a sandcastle?'

Her reply was as neat and precise as herself.

'No. Pies,' said Philomena briefly, and pursed her lips.

'Shall *I* build you a fine big castle?' he asked, anxious to make amends, but she shook her head grandly. 'With a moat? And bridges?' Attempting to ingratiate himself. She turned disdainfully away from him and began to refill the cup. 'Shall you not even let me help you, Philly?' he begged. She cut him dead.

'How old is she now?' he asked, amused.

'She was three in May; but she is an old-fashioned little soul.'

'And whom does she resemble?' Intrigued.

'Oh, she is Mrs Dorcas all over again,' Charlotte replied. 'Quite uncannily so. I feel that time has played a trick on me, and fetched my mother's childhood into my old age. And though she is Mary's darling, I must confess to taking a quiet delight in her myself.'

Here Polly came up, grumbling over Mary's wet bathing gown.

'Miss Mary's in a funny mood. And she says I'm to take Phillermeen into the house for her dinner and her rest, Mrs Longe.'

'Not so early, surely?' said Charlotte, tired but firm.

'Tell Mary that Mr Vivian is come and we should like her to join us. And shall you fetch us out a jug of Mrs Harvey's lemonade and a barrel of biscuits?'

The Cornishman had laid aside his hat and coat. He found a suitable piece of driftwood. He marked a wide circle with the ferrule of his cane. He began to dig.

The child, aware of his movements, glanced quickly and covertly at him. Then, as he seemed to be unconscious of her, she ceased patting and ladling, and observed him intently.

Charlotte laughed and lay back on her cushions, watching them.

Now Hal Vivian – first asking permission of Charlotte – removed his jacket, rolled up his shirtsleeves with theatrical gestures, and set to work in earnest. A rough hillock emerged, surrounded by a rough trench. He straightened up and slapped his waistcoat pockets, looked all about him, saying, 'I wish I had a cup. Or a spoon!'

Philomena's face reflected her thoughts. She drew her brows together, determined not to yield, but her mouth quivered. In a moment or two, as though her mind were upon higher matters, she stuck the wooden spoon into her pinafore pocket, scrambled to her feet, stared at some point miles beyond the Cornishman, and ran towards it. As she came level with the sandcastle she tossed the spoon wildly into the trench like some comical blessing from heaven.

He played his part superbly, crying, 'Why, here is a *spoon!*'

She stopped in mid-course, smiling secretly to herself. She ran back again and fetched the cup. Again she trotted swiftly towards that far horizon, again bounced her gift at the feet of the Cornishman. But this time, as he cried, 'Why, here is a *cup* . . . ' she could contain herself no longer. Throwing her arms wide, she ran round and round in ever-decreasing circles until at last she fell down laughing.

So that Mary walking shyly, and Polly carrying

lemonade, merged into the little group without embarrassment, with spontaneous delight.

Hal Vivian turned to meet them, but looked only at Mary. Sea, sand, sky, rushed away from her, rushed towards her. The moment crystallised in her eyes and his. It was too much. She saw Charlotte become aware, Polly look triumphant and knowing. She faltered.

He returned them both to earth. He held out his hand, smiling like the old friend he was. Saying, 'I have been trying to please miss!'

Amazed at her composure, Mary heard herself laugh and reply.

'Oh, miss is very hard to please!'

'Yes, look what I have had to do to scrape an acquaintance.'

'But how splendid, Mr Vivian!'

She knelt to admire the sandcastle, which had been built by a fine engineer. She dared to look at him again. And found herself inside that private world she had yearned for so long ago. They smiled on one another in an understanding which was mutual and complete.

They heard Polly say, 'Are you feeling the cold, Mrs Longe?'

They heard Charlotte reply, 'No, I am entirely content.'

They knew she meant she was content with them.

TWENTY-ONE

An End and a Beginning

An understanding had been reached but not established. The Cornishman departed for Wyndendale two days later, leaving an impression both joyful and indistinct. His note of thanks to Charlotte was warm. He stressed how much he looked forward to seeing them early in October. Yet the matter of himself and Mary was left open.

On the other hand there was no doubt about the intentions of a blotched letter from Kit's Hill, which arrived in the same post.

'Is it bad news, Aunt Cha?' Mary asked, seeing her turn suddenly white and weary.

Charlotte handed it to her across the breakfast table.

'There is a decision for you to make,' she said quietly, 'as I feared there might be. And at the most inopportune time.'

Mary looked from the letter to Philomena, and back again, as pale as her aunt.

'What I say to you now I shall never say again, love,' Charlotte began, 'for I have not the strength either to argue or to discuss the matter. So listen carefully, make your own decision, and then abide by it. Whatever you decide to do, I shall accept.

'You know, of course, what your father is asking? And that he has not thought the matter through to its logical conclusion? But then, Dick was always short-sighted where people are concerned.'

Mary temporised.

'He only asks us to keep Philly for another month or two, while Susan recovers and the new baby grows stronger.'

Charlotte said sternly, 'If we are not to speak the truth to one another we may as well be silent. I have no use for pretence.'

'Very well, Aunt Cha,' said Mary, after a pause. 'Tell me how you view the letter, and then I can answer you.'

Charlotte spoke drily and directly.

'Susan nearly died in childbed and will be an invalid for the rest of her days. The infant is sickly, and mercifully might die also. Young Harriet is trying to run the household and has her hands full. They have neither the energy nor the time to cope with Philomena, and would be obliged if she extended her visit indefinitely.'

Mary considered this statement with a rueful countenance.

'That is not exactly what he says, Aunt Cha.'

'It is exactly what he means. And though he talks of "us" looking after the child, he knows very well that there is no question of "us". I cannot even look after myself! He means *you*, Mary. He is asking you to take full responsibility for Philomena. At best for some months, more probably for life. He would, of course, be shocked if he realised exactly what he was expecting. Fortunately for him he can evade the issue. But evasion is a luxury which neither you nor I can afford. So what are you going to tell him?'

The girl cried, 'How can we deny him, Aunt Cha? What will happen to Philly if we send her back?'

Charlotte said inexorably, 'They will find they can manage.'

'You know I cannot do that. You know I have no choice, Aunt Cha!'

'I think you have. And I believe that on this first decision a second may depend, which will be even more difficult. As I told you once before, a future husband may not take kindly to the idea.'

'Oh, that is hard. Very hard, Aunt Cha!'

'I warned you it would be.'

'But what would you do in my place?' Mary demanded.

'I am not in your place. You have to make your own decision.'

Mary considered this too, and liked it no better.

'I have no firm ground upon which to base this argument,' she said, trembling, 'but if you are thinking about ... the Cornishman ... he is very fond of Philly, and very sweet to her.'

'He wishes to please you,' Charlotte replied, 'but I do not know what his reaction might be if he found she was a permanent dependant.'

Trapped, Mary cried, 'Surely, he sees that she is part of my life?'

'He sees her as a much-loved guest, and accepts her as such.'

'But you cannot judge how he will behave!' Angrily.

'Nor,' said Charlotte, 'can you.'

Wearily, at length, Mary said, 'Well, I must take Philly and the consequences, Aunt Cha. I cannot do otherwise. Do not blame me for it.'

Charlotte summoned up the last of her strength.

'Very good. Now I know your mind I can tell you the arrangements I have made. And I have discussed them with Ambrose, so you need not worry about him. He is quite content.

'I shall leave Thornton House and its contents to you, and an income sufficient to keep you. No, love, do not speak. Do not thank me. I have so little energy, and I must finish. There are provisos. Ambrose and Jeremy can picnic anywhere, but they have no home. I ask you to allow them to stay in the house until you marry or come to sell it.'

Mary nodded vigorously.

'And I leave you the responsibility of Polly's welfare. She is too old and set in her ways to be Ambrose's housekeeper. Pray take care of her for me. Now, and when she can work no longer.

'You will find all this in my Will. Nick Hurst helped me to draw it up a few years ago, when I realised that *you* had become a permanency. Since Ambrose is not in the least practical I have tied up the capital I am leaving him, but it will bring him a good and steady income. So he has no

268

reason to feel that you have robbed him of his inheritance – not that the idea would occur to him, anyway.'

She had finished.

She said, 'Please to ring for Polly. I shall not sit on the beach today. It is too cold. It is the end of the season.'

Charlotte and her small entourage were fetched back from Lytham in the ironmaster's carriage on the first Thursday in October, but Hal Vivian was not able to call until the Saturday, though he had left a visiting card to greet their return. Nor was he surprised to hear that Charlotte still lay abed at four in the afternoon, but said he would pay his respects to Miss Mary instead. And, walking cheerfully into the front parlour, he found that young lady romping on the carpet with Philomena.

While laughter subsided and Mary attempted to tidy her hair, the child provided a focus of conversation beneath which a more important conversation might conceivably flower.

'Welcome home, cousin!' said the Cornishman, kissing Mary's hand with great gallantry. 'And good day to you, Miss Phil!' Putting out a finger for her to grasp.

Philomena ignored the courtesy, but they saw her smiling to herself, and so could smile at each other over her small dark head.

'And when does miss go home?' he asked, lifting his coat-tails, preparatory to sitting in Grandfather Wilde's armchair.

Mary did not reply at once, but occupied herself by ringing the bell and asking Prue to bring in the tea. And found it a difficult matter to meet his pale gaze, for more than the usual reasons.

'Oh, do you not know the news from Kit's Hill?' she cried.

As he shook his head she rattled on, 'Well, Susan is recovering but she will be a good while getting better. The baby is very weak. And my sister Harriet has taken over the household and is working wonders. Well, she is a hearty healthy girl of sixteen, and well pleased with her present importance. Very like my mother used to be, before time and children brought her down . . . .'

'So Miss Phil will be with us until Christmas?' Hal Vivian said.

'Oh, longer than that. She will not go back before Easter. She will winter with us.' Integrity compelled her to add, 'In fact there are no plans to return her at all, at present.'

The Cornishman became thoughtful, and contemplated the child. Talk languished. Prue's appearance with the tray was a relief.

'And how is Mrs Longe?' he asked pleasantly, accepting a biscuit.

A certain light in Mary's countenance was fading.

'My aunt did not travel as well as we had hoped. We took the journey in easy stages, and Uncle William's carriage is most comfortable, but she went straight to bed when we got back. And has not got up since.'

He spoke now with his old kindly mockery of her.

'So you are mistress of Thornton House in her stead?'

'Yes, I am captain of the ship – as Ambrose says!'

'And how does your aunt feel about this latest arrangement over Philomena?'

For he knew of their controversy in the past.

'She left the decision entirely to me, sir,' Mary replied, low in voice and spirits.

He mused on the girl's tumbled coiffure. It had begun the day as a double knot upon the crown with loose side curls, but was now the worse for a game of bears. His expression was one of tenderness, and regret. He refused a second cup of tea.

'Well, I must take my leave of you both,' he said. 'If Miss Phil is still with you in June of next year, you must fetch her to the opening of the Wyndendale Railway, and ride from Garth to Millbridge on my locomotive, *Pioneer*. What an adventure that will be!'

Mary's expression was now so sorry as to be noticeable, but Hal Vivian kept up his easy demeanour.

'Pray give my best wishes to Mrs Longe, and say that I will call on her again as soon as I can. I do not know when that will be. We are busy on the line and in the workshops. But there, you know me of old. My time is never my own.'

He offered a finger to Philomena, who shut her eyes very tight and opened her mouth very wide. Mary rose also, picking up the child so that the Cornishman could not kiss her hand. He bowed gravely. They looked away from each other in pain.

'Take care of yourself, cousin. God bless you,' said Hal Vivian.

And was striding down the High Street before the front door had closed behind him.

Polly, coming in to light the candles, found the girl sitting with the child in her lap, staring sombrely into the fire.

'I'm a-going to tell you somethink afore it's too late, Miss Mary . . .' she began, hands on hips.

But Mary turned such a sad little face towards her that Polly swallowed the advice, and left her to rock the child and weep in peace.

Charlotte needed little nursing. She retreated faster than life itself, spending much time in a dark and bright world of her own, coming back in mild amazement to the best front bedroom at Thornton House, and whichever loving face watched by her. Her normal conversation had given way to cryptic messages, as though the secret bourne to which she travelled were equipped with a Delphic oracle. Otherwise, she ate and drank frugally, submitted to their ministrations patiently, and awaited her release.

The ironmaster took charge of the situation in his own way of course: sending fruit and flowers out of season, specialists from London, and a regular messenger from Kingswood Hall to bring back the latest report on her state of health.

Dick brought fresh eggs and butter on market days. Cicely walked down from the rectory each morning. The

Reverend Jarvis prayed for her each evening. Grandchildren and nieces and nephews came and went. Callers knocked at all hours to ask how she did.

Mary was entirely taken over. She supervised the household, cared for the child, played her part in the night watch, and met everyone's needs and demands. So that the ache in her heart became the ache in her bones at three o'clock of a cold morning, and the emptiness at her centre matched the void which Charlotte approached with so peaceable a mien.

Polly divided herself between the old mistress and the new. She was fifty-seven come Candlemas, and the greater part of her life would depart with Charlotte.

Mary's birthday, on the twelfth of November, was acknowledged rather than celebrated. In spite of her winsome face and ebullient spirits, in spite of her wardrobe which benefited from Sophia's Parisian castoffs, she had attained the age of twenty without acquiring a husband. In Millbridge there were rumours that the Cornishman had been interested, but his matrimonial hopes had not survived the burden of Philomena. The matchmakers whispered over their teacups that there was no hope for the girl now, unless she found a middle-aged widower with a large family. Mary was inclined to agree with them, but mentally rejected the widower. So she was desolated, at the end of this grey birthday, to see the Cornishman mount the front steps and lift the knocker.

'There is enough to do without visitors,' she cried sharply, as Prue intimated that the gentleman awaited her commands. Then, accepting this as she accepted all else nowadays, she added. 'But show Mr Vivian in, of course. And bring in the sherry. And two glasses.'

They had not met since that decisive autumn afternoon, six weeks before, and Mary felt sorry that Philomena was being put to bed, for the child would have acted as a shield between them. However, she held out her hand and greeted him calmly, though she could have wept.

He seemed both pleased and awkward at finding her alone, and made a great show of warming his hands at the fire and asking after Charlotte.

This time she answered frankly, 'You know that she is dying?'

And he answered just as frankly, 'Yes. So I hear from Hamish Standish. That is partly why I have come. I should like to speak with her if it is possible.'

So they were both wiped clean of social flummeries.

'And how is Miss Phil?' he asked nicely.

'Oh, she is better than any of us, for she does not comprehend the situation. We draw comfort from her happiness, which is innocent.'

'And how is your stepmother, and the situation at Kit's Hill?'

Mary thought deeply and carefully for a moment, and then gave him the facts. For he must do what he would with them.

'The infant died, and Susan is as well as she will ever be. Harriet is the heart of the household now, and has more than enough to do.

'Forgive me if I seem to speak too plain, sir, but I am not telling you anything that the family does not know already. When my aunt dies I shall inherit Thornton House, and a modest income which will give me independence. I have reason to believe, in those circumstances, that an offer on my part to adopt Philomena would be accepted.'

He sipped and thought: as careful and as forthright as herself.

'And you will make that offer, will you, Mary?'

The use of her Christian name, in such a natural and spontaneous fashion, almost reduced her to lies and tears. But she resisted this temptation and answered as truthfully as Charlotte could have wished.

'There has never been any question in my mind about that.'

He was silent. And accepted a second glass of sherry.

'Aunt Cha saw this coming a long while ago,' said Mary,

who had no more to lose, 'and deplored it as being too great an imposition. But you see, cousin, Aunt Cha did the same for me as I hope to do for Philly.'

She had pondered this problem over and over, during the long night watches. She knew both questions and answers. She spoke as she had learned, from her inner self.

'My grandmama, Mrs Dorcas, whom I can just remember, once told Uncle William that we are given nothing without return. Seven years ago, Aunt Cha took me out of bondage – that is not too strong a term for it – and gave me freedom and an education. I hope to do the same for Philomena. I look upon her as my payment for that privilege.'

He said, with difficulty, 'It is a costly payment, Mary.'

'I know that,' she answered, 'but I would not be in debt to life.'

He set down his glass and paced the room, fetching up at the window from which he could watch the slow descent of dusk.

'How much of my scandalous story do you know, cousin?' he asked.

'Oh! . . . that Uncle William was a handsome young blacksmith with great ambitions, and your mother his widowed housekeeper. Her name was Hannah Garside, and she confided her secret only to Mrs Dorcas, who gave her a hundred gold guineas to help her to make a fresh start. Which was what your mother asked, since she thought it would be best for everyone if she went away. And that, years later, she married your stepfather who gave you his name. That is all I know, cousin. Except,' she added, 'that folk called your mother "the good woman of Flawnes Green"– which has always intrigued me.'

'Because the title does not sound like a housekeeper who obliged her handsome young master?' asked the Cornishman drily.

'No, heaven forbid!' said Mary. 'How can you say such a thing? She did not oblige him, she loved him. Loved him enough to leave him when that was necessary, without counting the cost to herself. And loved you enough to take responsibility for you, rather than expose you to a lot of gossip or make Uncle William marry her – which he should have done, in my opinion. But then, he is a child, my uncle the ironmaster. He roars and blusters and runs industrial empires, but he knows he cannot manage without a good woman. Look at Aunt Zelah – and he has caused her a deal of grief. She left him once, you know.'

Mary stopped, since this was another old scandal which ought not to be discussed, and endeavoured to smooth matters over.

'That sounds ungrateful to Uncle William, for he is generous to a fault. And he has been so kind to Aunt Cha! Lord above, what it must have cost him in fruit alone! And I love him very much, in spite of everything. Oh, Lor'! Pray do forgive me, cousin, I run on, as Ambrose says, like a hen with its head cut off!'

He had heard and understood.

He said, 'Your judgement is sound, Mary. Over the years I have pieced my mother's story together from those who knew her. She had never travelled further than a few miles in all her life. She was four months gone with child, and knew no one and nowhere outside the valley. Yet she took a coach to Liverpool. And for what? So that she might struggle on her own to raise me, and hopefully give me a good start in life. I imperilled her good reputation, her ability to earn a living, even her devout Methodist soul. She, who would lie to no one, lived a lie for me!

'I spoke with Mrs Boulton, who employed her. She said my mother left her cottage scrubbed and clean, and her cooking pots in payment for past kindnesses, and a letter of thanks. I have seen (for, to give him credit, he has kept it!) the letter that she wrote to my father, the ironmaster. I heard her voice again, as I read it. It was the letter of a brave and loving woman. I marvel at the courage of women.'

He looked uncannily like the ironmaster in figure and posture – hands clasped behind his back, chin well up. His voice had the same timbre. His glossy black hair was that of the ironmaster's prime. But he was more perceptive, more aware, than the ironmaster would ever be.

'I lack that sort of courage,' he said in a lower tone.

The pause was so long that Mary, half-inclined to tears because of his tale, and half to asperity because of his vagueness, spoke up.

'How should I reply? Like many men you praise our sex. But I dare swear, like every other man, that you thank God you are not a member of it! What can I say to you? That you have your own sort of courage? Well, so you have, but *tant pis*! That your mother found her happiness in you? Would that relieve you of further worry on her account? Why sir, you are no better than your father! And I say thank God for Mr Santo Vivian, who took upon himself another man's responsibilities, and worked and cared for you both, and made you his son. But, of course, it is easier to praise others than to improve oneself!'

Now I have lost him indeed, she thought. My tongue, my tongue!

Well, he has caused me enough grief, and deserves to smart!

Oh, God forgive me for a vengeful shrew!

The Cornishman gave a grim chuckle, brushed his sleeve across his pale eyes, and turned to face her.

'You are one of the honestest people I have ever come across, Mary. If only you could learn to dissemble a little, your truths would be less abrasive. But you will come out into the conversation like a boxer from his corner, squaring up to an opponent. The amiable Dr Jamie has been spared many a spoiled breakfast . . . '

'Oh, how unkind!' she burst out, and now tears shone in her own eyes. 'I honoured you because you never scolded me about that affair.'

'I had not finished what I was saying,' he said, with such authority that she was silenced.

A smile glimmered at the corners of his mouth. Her own mouth was sulky, but tightly closed.

'I was about to remark that the amiable Dr Jamie was simply not up to your fighting standards. And I never scolded you because I thought him a fool for taking you seriously. It should have been obvious to everyone that you were simply practising your youthful charms on any man who happened to be near at the time.'

'You are insulting, sir!' cried Mary, all aflame.

'No, I am honest. As honest as you, madam. All girls go through these courtship rituals. How else should they learn? It was all very well for you to beguile Jamie Standish, but he should not have been so silly as to offer himself up for a lifetime's deception.'

Mary wept with rage, crying, 'I shall tell Ambrose what you have said, and he will shoot you!'

'You know very well that he would laugh and agree with me. Mary, Mary . . . ' as she stamped her feet alternately, and sobbed aloud in sheer frustration, 'I have not come here to discuss Jamie Standish, nor to belittle you, nor to criticise you in any way . . . '

'Nevertheless, you are doing all those things most successfully!'

The Cornishman seized her shoulders and shook her until her teeth rattled.

'I am trying to propose to you! Damn you!' he shouted.

She choked on the next sob, and began to cry in earnest, saying, 'Well I dislike the way you are doing it. And if I wasn't honest I'd say *No!* As it is, just in case you change your mind, I accept you. And the first thing I am going to do is to quarrel with you . . . '

He began to laugh. He folded his arms round her, and she put her head on his chest and wet his shirt front with tears of protest.

'I did not forget your birthday,' he offered gently, 'I have brought you a most frivolous gift. . . . '

'You made me think you had only come to see Aunt Cha . . . !'

'I did not intend to. But I should like to ask her permission to marry you, since she is your guardian.'

'I am accountable to myself, sir, and can make up my own mind!'

'Mary, Mary, you know very well what I mean. And –

277

though his part in your life has diminished – should we not approach your father also, and discover what he thinks of me?'

'It is what *I* think that counts, sir!'

'It seems I cannot say anything right today,' he observed, smiling. 'I meant only to show consideration towards those who love you, Mary.'

'"Many a spoiled breakfast," you said!'

'That was uncommonly foolish of me,' he remarked with grave humour.

Mary laughed and cried together, but had not quite forgiven him.

'And you did not come outright with your proposal, but hesitated – do not deny it – because of poor little Philomena.'

'My dear love,' he protested, 'the prospect of taking on *two* strong-minded women would daunt a braver man than I! But I shall devote myself to both of you, and endeavour to hold my tongue at all times.'

He could not tell whether the sound she made was a giggle or a hiccup, but hoped he had amused her.

'And you know that I am very fond of miss,' he added.

This time she lifted her face and looked radiantly upon him.

'Oh, Mary,' he said. 'Oh, Mary, Mary mine. . . .'

So that in a short while she clasped her arms shyly, lightly, around his neck, and smiled and was at peace again. And he comforted and loved her as Santo Vivian had once loved and comforted Hannah, stroking her bright hair and speaking words of endearment which she would remember in the times he was absent.

Charlotte gave her blessing to the engagement with quiet pleasure, with relief. She made no prognostications and offered no advice. She was leaving the business of life to the living. The excitement quickly tired her, so Ambrose and Jeremy held an impromptu party downstairs in the front parlour, with the aid of two bottles of old Malmesey and the remains of a heavy fruit cake. And on that loveliest of evenings, Polly, Prue and the scullery-maid joined the family and toasted long life, health and happiness to the Cornishman and his lady. Their joy, though subdued, was great. Even the manservant from Kingswood Hall was regaled with wine and news as well as the evening bulletin, and rode back full of goodwill.

No immediate plans were made for their wedding. Charlotte's illness and the Wyndendale railway ate up almost all their time. So they must steal an hour here and an afternoon there.

'I have noticed very often,' said Mary wistfully, 'that everything wonderful in my life comes hand in hand with sorrow. It is as though I was never meant to be completely happy. As though God said, "No!"'

'He doesn't say "No!"', Hal Vivian replied. 'He says, "Not yet!"'

Snow came early that year, transforming even the meanest streets, turning the old town into a fine white citadel. Inside the handsome houses, however high they banked the fires, there were chill places near doors and windows, and everyone sought the inner circle of warmth and stayed there.

In Charlotte's room the fire blazed night and day, and copper warming pans came up hot and burnished every few hours, but she grew colder. Morning and evening, when Polly and Prue had made the bed, Polly lifted her mistress up and held the washbasin and proffered the towel, since Charlotte still liked to conduct her own toilet. The gestures of ablution had become more perfunctory of late. Often Polly had, surreptitiously, to do some small services over again.

On this morning, a few days before Christmas, Charlotte woke up clearer in mind and stronger in body. The expression on her face was one of quiet delight, as though she felt new energy flowing through her. With solemn concentration she rolled the ball of sweet-smelling soap between the palms of her hands, and laid it aside in the china dish. She anointed her cheeks and forehead, and bent over the bowl of warm water.

'Half a minute, Mrs Longe,' said Polly, 'I ain't wrung out your face-flannel yet.'

Charlotte took no notice, but rinsed her face and hands without the aid of the flannel, and came up smiling in triumph. Slowly but thoroughly she dried herself.

'Feeling chirpy today, ain't we?' said Polly.

Charlotte was not yet satisfied. Her eyes were eloquent.

'A clean nightgownd?' Polly guessed aright, and signalled Prue to fetch one out of the chest at the foot of the bed. 'Do you want your hair brushed now, Mrs Longe? Or shall you have it done later?'

For all these were great efforts on Charlotte's part.

'You'd like it done now, eh? There's no stopping us this morning!'

And as her mistress sat immaculate in the immaculate bed, 'Would there be anythink else, Mrs Longe?'

Charlotte pointed.

'She wants her hand mirror,' Prue guessed, and held it up.

With an air of satisfaction, Charlotte contemplated herself in the little glass. Then she motioned it away, smiled on them both, folded her hands, and died.

TWENTY-TWO

All Aboard!

There had not been such a public celebration since Waterloo, thirteen years before. Even the two leading newspapers in the valley set aside personal politics and vendettas to join in the general enthusiasm.

'WYNDENDALE LINE BEATS BOLTON–LEIGH RAILROAD TO THE OPENING!' cried the *Post,* rejoicing in the discomfiture of rivals.

'TODAY WE ARE ALL *PIONEERS* OF THE RAILROAD AGE!' proclaimed the *Clarion,* making a neat play on the name of the steam locomotive.

On that fine morning in the late spring of 1828, the hopes and plans of the past six years had come to fruition. Hundreds of homes had been rased, thousands of people displaced, and over a million tons of earth moved. Tooth and claw the ironmaster and the Cornishman had fought for its being. Inch by inch navvies had hewn it, levelled it, laid down its rails with sweat, with blood, with their very lives. The earth had yielded up its iron, quarries their stone, businessmen their fortunes.

Until at last the single-line wrought-iron track gleamed on stone sleepers from Garth to Millbridge. And waiting in its special shed at Garth Fold stood the Cornishman's latest vision, *Pioneer:* a steam locomotive weighing seven tons which, with God's grace and Hal Vivian's ingenuity, should draw fourteen wagons and a coach loaded with passengers a distance of some nine miles.

Lord Kersall was quite out of the festivities. He had been the committee's chief stumbling block, but was too important a personage to be overlooked. So they had invited him to the ceremony, and asked if Lady Kersall would name the steam locomotive. He declined the invitation for both of them, saying they would be travelling on the continent.

The committee's second choice was the ironmaster's wife, since William had been chief instigator of the project. Zelah did not shrink from social duties, but preferred to avoid such a public performance if that were possible. This the ironmaster reported back, and they thought long and carefully, since ladies of distinction were in short supply.

'Aye, well, I'm sorry about it. But we oughtn't to put on Mrs Howarth, if the lady isn't willing,' said a coal magnate gallantly.

Arnold Harbottle sat, cigar in mouth, staring into the mahogany mirror of the table like some industrial Narcissus.

'D'y'know,' he said, at length, 'this here opening ceremony has been more bloody trouble than the whole railroad put together.'

Their murmur of agreement was heartfelt.

'I never knew how vicious folk could get until we started picking them out for places on the first trip,' another coal magnate observed, looking round at his fellows. 'I've been offered money and fancy women. I've been threatened with arson and personal assault. I've had anonymous letters. You wouldn't believe what lengths they'd go to . . . !'

Oh yes, they would. Everyone had a tale to tell. Everyone had suffered. Everyone wanted to say his own particular piece. Until the ironmaster called them to order.

They were silent again, glancing at each other on the sly, secretly considering and rejecting the wives of those present. Then Arnold Harbottle spoke with a degree of sympathy which no one thought he possessed, with surprising perception.

'There *is* a lady as'd do the job damn well, and enjoy doing it, what's more. And I think we owe her something, on account of the fact that our railroad has pushed her to the back in the last few months. What about Mr Vivian's lady, his wife-to-be, Miss Mary Howarth?'

The ironmaster was amazed, was quietly gratified. He agreed to ask his niece at once. In fact he pledged her answer, which fortunately coincided with his own. The problem was most beautifully solved.

On the eve of the great day every hostelry and tavern was full. Public and private vehicles of every kind brought spectators to Millbridge from all over the country. Enthusiasts too poor to ride or drive had walked as far as sixty miles to get there. Lodging houses were packing three makeshift beds to a room, and four visitors to a bed. The Royal George had put up its prices in order to maintain its standards, and were providing a cold buffet luncheon, with roast beef at three shillings a plate.

Since the navvies could hardly be spirited away they were incorporated into the occasion. All the Irishmen were sent up to a tavern at the far end of Swarth Moor, to drink themselves into a stupor at the Company's expense and keep out of the way. The Scotsmen were posted singly at intervals along the line, to make sure that everything ran smoothly. The Englishmen were divided into guards of honour, one at each end of the railroad. Hal Vivian addressed them all personally, asking them to enjoy themselves without spoiling the enjoyment of others. And that was the best anyone could hope for.

At dawn, people began to gather along the route to ensure themselves a good view. Some hardy fellows had slept in their chosen places overnight, and were brewing tea and breakfasting cheerfully by the side of the line like so many gipsies. By the time the sun rose, the road was a moving stream of carriages, traps, wagons and gigs. Occasionally some equipage far grander than the rest would have a servant trotting ahead of it, crying, 'Make way, if you please! Make way! These ladies and gentlemen have seats on the *Pioneer!*' Then everyone drew aside, staring hard at those who had been so honoured.

The Cornishman had slept at Kit's Hill, and was up before their cock crowed. He made the final check of

Pioneer in his old clothes, and then rode to Kingswood Hall to change into something more formal, and to breakfast with William and a tableful of scientific notables. He did not see Mary, who was eating apart with a full complement of Howarth womenfolk. Long before the others had finished, Hal Vivian mounted his horse again and made his way back, pale with apprehension and excitement.

By this time Garth looked like a racecourse. Village lads, seeking the best vantage points, were standing on headstones in the churchyard and sitting in the higher branches of its yew trees. A great dais had been erected for committee members and their wives, and before it stood Wroughton Brass Band, playing a selection of light music to while away the time. As each person mounted the platform they were given a rousing cheer, which they acknowledged gravely or delightedly according to mood.

The haberdashers of Wyndendale must have been quite sold out. Every gentleman wore a green and white silk favour in his buttonhole, every lady was aflutter, every worker sported a ribbon in his hat, and the little girls were like so many butterflies. Flags flew from spires and pinnacles. Banners hung from windows.

The appearance of Mary on the ironmaster's arm caused a pleasurable commotion. She was vivacious in apple-green silk. Ostrich plumes nodded on the crown of her straw bonnet. Her cream parasol was edged with lace.

After them came the grave grey Quaker, Caleb Scholes, escorting his sister Zelah at the head of her family.

Here were the scientific gentlemen and practical engineers, who had come from London, Birmingham, Liverpool and Manchester. There, the Mayor and Council, the Committee members and their wives. Such a concourse of notable men and fashionable women! The comments of the crowd were audible. Their eyes roved everywhere, fearful of missing something.

At five minutes before eleven o'clock Wroughton Band played the opening verse of 'God Save the King', which everyone sang heartily whether they liked him or not. Then they all waited for the new clock in Garth market-place to chime the hour.

Upon the last stroke the doors of the shed were opened, and there was a long soft 'aaah' from the crowd.

Myths and rumours had proliferated during her construction and subsequent trials, so they had expected a metal mammoth. Whereas this was a little iron horse, sturdily built, with a round belly and a long spout of a neck. Every inch had been most lovingly polished: her body glowed, her copper pipes shone, her wheels glittered. She seemed to pause at the threshold, to look upon the assembly of well-wishers, to wonder at the beauty of the morning sun, at the adventurous rails which could carry her to places she did not as yet know. She gave a preliminary clearing of the throat – a chuff. And then another. And two together. And chuntered sedately up the track, trailing seven wooden wagons and a gamboge-yellow coach behind her.

'Hurrah for *Pioneer*!' cried her subjects, enraptured. And then, 'There he is! There's the Company Engineer! Hurrah for Mr Vivian!'

The Cornishman was driving: his face absorbed, intent upon his task. He stopped the engine exactly opposite the dais. Beside him stood Edgeworth, outraging his wife by acting as fireman in his best clothes.

A megaphone boomed out.

'Silence, everyone! Silence, if you please!'

They all craned to see Mary, very pink and frightened, standing on the platform with a garland in her hands. The Cornishman became human, whipped off his top hat with a flourish, and smiled at her.

The megaphone spoke again.

'Silence for Miss Mary Howarth. Mr Henry Vivian's lady!'

They hushed each other.

Mary stood as tall as she could, but the garland trembled a little. She had written the speech herself, using Ambrose and Jeremy as both critics and audience, refusing to let Hal

285

Vivian hear it before the official opening. She addressed the crowd in order of importance, and the list of dignitaries was long enough for her to lose her nervousness. Her voice was light and clear, and they let it be heard.

'... and today we are helping to make history in Wyndendale. I hope I may say quite truthfully, without offending anyone, what our valley is *not*. It is not very large. It is not the centre of Lancashire industry. It is not noted for any particular craft or trade. And yet Wyndendale is large enough to contain all the most important trades, crafts and industries in Lancashire, and to be a centre of new ideas. Today, as a result of vision, courage and enterprise, we have produced one of the first steam-locomotives and one of the first railroads in the country. And though it has taken up a great deal of Mr Vivian's time...'

Her tone, her momentary pause, caused an eddy of amusement.

'... now I see the results I cannot wonder at it!'

They laughed with her, and applauded.

'So I am greatly honoured to be given the naming of the locomotive, on this historic day.'

She moved forward, lifting the scented tribute, saying, 'These flowers are hers, and I name her *Pioneer!*'

Obligingly, Edgeworth stepped down to receive the garland, which he attached to the flue. Everybody clapped and cried, 'Bravo!'. Mary bowed and smiled: well pleased with herself, as was the Cornishman. Then the ironmaster, escorting his niece, led the notables to the yellow coach. Edgeworth resumed his duties as fireman. Hal Vivian turned his attention to the controls.

'Ladies and gentlemen,' the megaphone invited, 'pray take your seats on the train!'

Wroughton Brass Band played a triumphal march until the élite were settled. Then they emptied the spittle from their instruments, climbed into the last wagon, and waited for orders.

'All aboard?' the megaphone enquired.

And the ironmaster, sticking his top hat out of the coach

window, answered, 'All aboard!'

Pioneer huffed and puffed this time with a note of impatience. For now she was going to show them what she could do.

'She's off! She's off! She's off!'

She was. The band struck up a jubilant march though their eyes goggled over their shining instruments, and they were plainly unused to playing on the move.

Boys were running alongside, waving their arms, shouting.

Faster and faster spun the wheels, glinted the piston rods, as she trundled resolutely down the line towards Coldcote, gathering speed. Faster, faster. The men took out their stopwatches. Six, seven, eight miles an hour.

The boys were falling behind, outrun, exalted. They stood, panting for breath, watching the back of the gamboge coach grow small. Herds of cattle in the passing fields scattered and ran. Horses whinnied and galloped away. Birds clapped out of trees. Dogs barked and chased, until they too fell behind exhausted.

Pioneer approached Medlar iron bridge at a rattling nine miles an hour. In the open wagons the ladies held their hats and screamed as they saw the river flowing beneath, but the engine made nothing of it – was over the other side and away. She passed Snape sidings, where foundry workers were standing rank on rank, cheering her progress. And headed for Upperton.

Every member of the household at Bracelet stood outside, cheering. A Union Jack flew from chimney. Both sides of the cutting were lined with spectators, waving handkerchiefs by the hundred.

Past Belbrook sidings and more foundry workers. Clattering over the ornate iron bridge, with sentimental ironmaster leaning from the coach to take in an old dream, eyes watering in the wind. Another river crossing, another scream from the ladies. Rattle, quiver and skim. And they were in the heart of the coal country. Colliers in holiday clothes crowded the route.

'Sixteen mile an hour, by George!'

The factories in Thornley, Brigge House and Flawnes Green had not ceased to work. The long chimneys smoked, but the mill windows were all mouths and eyes.

Onto the embankment, with the spire of St Mark's Church in the distance. On one side flowed the broad river. On the other flowed the branch canal. Even the barges had been decorated with flags and bunting for the occasion, and their occupants came out to watch and wave and shout through cupped hands.

Millbridge suburbs ahead! The engine was slowing down perceptibly. The throng grew thicker, wilder. Faces flickered past. Another official rostrum came into view, bearing a reception committee whose welcome had become a delirium of hats and hands. Millbridge!

Pioneer chuntered and chuffed, drawing to a halt. She gave a final shriek and snort of triumph. She awaited the acclaim she deserved.

The second set of speeches and addresses being done, Hal Vivian prepared to put his engine through her various paces.

There were some remarks, one could not call them complaints, about the considerable jolting experienced by the passengers. Which the ironmaster immediately reported to the Cornishman, while railwaymen attached a further seven wagons to the train.

'It was no worse than a fast mailcoach for most of the way, Hal. But when we picked up speed on that last stretch after Belbrook, we were jostled like sacks of flour. If we hadn't been packed so tight we could have been knocked about quite unpleasantly. As it is, Zelah has a great bruise on her elbow. . . .'

'Perhaps it will be better with the extra wagons, sir?'

'Well, well, it is no great fault, Hal. But I thought it worth mentioning. Worth looking into later on. . . .'

But if he had bawled his criticism through the megaphone no one would have taken the slightest notice.

Old and new passengers were all too busy pushing to get aboard. And on the return journey *Pioneer* drew fourteen wagons, all filled with waving cheering travellers – who, in their turn, were cheered and waved the entire length of the course. The brass band played with tremendous aplomb as they travelled along, their music pouring away behind them, until they drew into Garth Fold with not an ounce of breath to spare.

Then the passenger service was suspended, and *Pioneer* showed what she could do as a goods train, taking on six wagons and twelve tons of coal, delivered to her at Swarth Moor by Hal Vivian's first primitive steam-engine *The Cornishman*, and pulling them at twelve miles an hour.

Finally, at the end of the day, when everyone else's demands were satisfied, Hal had all the wagons removed, and took the locomotive by herself up the line from Garth and back, to see if she could reach twenty miles an hour. On this journey, despite the delicacy of her costume, Mary came up on the plate between the Cornishman and Ted Edgeworth, to share the triumphs and hazards of such a run.

The weather had been kind to them for once. The evening light healed a scarred landscape, and wrapped it in purple and gold. Roofs and chimneys turned to black paper silhouettes. Cupola fires from Snape and Belbrook flushed the sky at intervals.

Sparks flew from *Pioneer*'s spout of a chimney. The coal in her belly glowed white and red with heat. She gained momentum and fairly hurtled along the track. Mary clasped both arms round Hal's waist, and shrieked with fear and exaltation. She saw Wyndendale dash up to meet her and whip away again. She lost her parasol in the coal bunker and her bonnet to the wind. She was covered with smuts. But the Cornishman and Ted Edgeworth, looking at each other over her blown hair, shouted, 'Six-and-twenty miles an hour, by George!'

And did not know whether to laugh or cry at the wonder of it all.

TWENTY-THREE

Many a Spoiled Breakfast

Soon after *Pioneer* was launched, Hal and Mary had their first serious quarrel, which arose from the sale of King Billy though it did not concern him.

Hal Vivian's hundred inch pumping engine had been advertised as 'A Wonder of the World' but the world showed only a sporadic interest, and nobody wanted to buy him. For six years the monarch stood idle on Swarth Moor, greased and boarded up, a silent reproach. Then a coal magnate in Durham, with an abandoned mine and notions of grandeur, offered £2000 for him: a mere fraction of his cost. Reluctantly, the offer was accepted. So now workmen must labour to dismantle him, and horses strain to haul the massive parts away: an arduous task, and in many ways a sad one. For King Billy was magnificent, but would always be more trouble than his upkeep was worth.

So the Cornishman needed sympathy of a rare order that morning, and stole off to Thornton House to be comforted. He was, in a sense, losing a beloved and unappreciated child. But Mary, too young to have been part of this first dream, simply saw the pumping engine as an expensive disappointment. She congratulated Hal on getting rid of it, even for such a pittance, and said how relieved he and the ironmaster must be.

The Cornishman's countenance became overcast. Unconsciously he set out to annoy her. Which was all too easy, for Mary's stock of patience had been used up by the Wyndendale railroad.

'Well, as you say, Mary, it is a great relief. And now I must get back, I fear. I only came to tell you the news.'

Her face expressed her feelings with painful clarity.

'But you are not going back this moment, surely? You have only just come!' And his kiss had been preoccupied, perfunctory.

'Unfortunately, yes. Your uncle and I are having another discussion about my future. Over which we are somewhat at loggerheads.'

'Your future?' she repeated. 'I thought all that was settled. Have you not enough to do here, perfecting the railroad?'

Since this was what the ironmaster had said, Hal Vivian became even more aggrieved.

'My ambitions go beyond tinkering with one locomotive. We must progress. Your uncle wants to collect his profits, and let matters lie.'

Mary knew he was punishing her, though she could not understand why, and she answered back sharply.

'He cannot collect profits until the original investment has paid for itself. And I happen to know that is not the case.'

'I see that I shall get no help from you, Mary. I had thought otherwise. Never mind. I must be on my way.'

'One moment, sir,' she cried, deeply angered, deeply hurt. 'I am not a *sidings*, to have your problems shunted onto me when you can go nowhere else. But why do I say that?' As months of neglect mounted into one inflammatory moment. 'If I *were* a sidings I should see a great deal more of you than I do! I had thought, sir, that when *Pioneer* was launched we should have time to arrange *our* future. But it seems that only *yours* is important!'

She was terrified, but would not draw back now.

'I am ready to be married as soon as you wish,' said the Cornishman, eyes pale and cold. 'There is nothing to arrange apart from the date and place of the ceremony. It is merely a matter of moving my things from the Royal George to here.'

She was choked with rage, because he had brought up another issue.

'But, Hal, I have been saying to you for some time that I

did not want to live here after we were married.'

Which he knew very well, but spoke in a patient tone as if she were being unreasonable.

'In that case, we must discuss where else to live.'

'But you know that Uncle William wants to give us a beautiful site and our own house as a wedding present. And has offered Bracelet to us, while we build. And Bracelet comes empty at Michaelmas. Which means we could be married in October.'

He looked at her with keen displeasure.

'Evidently, I did not make my views clear. To my mind, though not apparently to yours, the ironmaster is a metaphorical boa constrictor. He would like to swallow us whole, and the most sensible action to take is to remove ourselves as far as possible from his vicinity.'

She was so shocked that her voice rose, became clamorous.

'How can you say such a thing? He has been so kind and good. . . .'

He overrode her, speaking loudly and deliberately.

'The prospect of our wedding, on top of the success with *Pioneer*, has quite turned my father's head. He thinks that I am bound and gagged and given over to him for life. And he is trying to organise our marriage, from the reception at Kingswood Hall to our first home at Upperton – just under his nose. The beautiful site you talk of is half a mile from him, on Cunshurst Hill. Can you not see his purpose? Why, the very thought of that old despot breathing down my neck every minute of the working day, and then encroaching on our private time together in the evenings, makes me feel like taking the first ship to Venezuela!'

Mary burst into tears. He fidgeted, unrepentant. She flung words at him from the depth of her being.

'You are a prevaricator, Hal! Why you ever proposed to commit yourself to me I shall never know. For you are quite happy to go on as we do. Forever on the brink of life, but never having courage to drink!'

'If that is what you think of me, I wonder you accepted.'

She turned and ran from the room, sobbing. He snatched up his hat from the hall table and let himself out.

They did not communicate for three days, stoned by the truths they had hurled at each other.

Then Mary wrote a letter, in which she set down the main points of the argument, and suggested they talk it out. And Hal saw a bonnet in the milliner's which whispered 'Mary' to him in satin and velvet, and he bought it. So that she, running down the steps of Thornton House to post her letter, and he, hurrying to her with the striped and be-ribboned band-box, collided in the High Street.

Mary laughed and wept simultaneously. Hal made no secret of his delight and relief. The polite society of Millbridge passed by on the other side, smiling a little, as the couple made up their quarrel. Then Mary and Hal picked up the band-box and the letter, and took them inside the house to inspect their contents.

'As I see it, and you so succinctly put it,' said the Cornishman, admiring Mary, as she admired her new bonnet in the parlour mirror, 'we have three main problems: my work, our future home, and the ironmaster.'

'Oh, poor Uncle William!' Mary said, but had to giggle.

'Will you let me explain myself, love, so that you may understand my feelings? Then you shall put forward your own case and between us we can come to some sort of compromise; else it will be like the other day: we shall be no nearer to a solution and we shall only hurt each other.'

Remembrance of the quarrel cast a shadow over both their faces for a moment. His voice shook very slightly, but he finished firmly.

'And since marriage is concerned with two people living in harmony and honest fellowship, the sooner we begin to learn it the better for both of us.'

'Harmony and honest fellowship?' cried Mary, aghast. 'Dear God in Heaven, Hal, you make it sound like a Methodist meeting!'

He smiled then, amused and renewed.

'No doubt you will improve upon my description and

the concept, but for the moment it will serve. Yes, the double bows at the back are very fetching! Mary, Mary . . . pray kiss me in another few minutes when we have resolved this matter, if you please! Well then, kiss me now and be done! And sit with me while we talk.'

'But I shall crush my bonnet!'

'Then take the bonnet off.'

'Oh, here is Prue with our tea. . . .'

'I have never before drank tea with a lady, who is sitting upon my knee and wearing a bonnet,' he remarked, ten minutes later. 'Is it possible to conduct a serious discussion under these conditions?'

'Yes,' said Mary, without hesitation.

But she had taken the comment as a rebuke. She slid off his knees and made a pretext of toasting bread over the fire, most of which burned. When she did speak her voice was heavy with disappointment.

'Uncle William promised I should be married from Kingswood Hall because Aunt Cha is not here to arrange anything else. And Kit's Hill would not do at all, even if they could be bothered.'

The Cornishman watched her, hands clasped between his knees.

She wiped her eyes and scorched the bread.

'And I always loved Grandma Dorcas's house at Upperton, for it seemed just the right size, and so perfect in all its appointments. And then to have a home with such a pretty name as 'Bracelet'! I thought it very thoughtful of Uncle William to offer it.'

'Take off your bonnet, love,' said Hal Vivian gently, 'or that will burn, too! And give me that toasting fork and the bread. Don't cry so, Mary. We can find a way if we try.'

'And he promised that I should have exactly what I wanted in the house he will build for us. And that Mr Field – who designed Kingswood Hall and rebuilt Bracelet – would be at my disposal. And I love Aunt Zelah, who would be near to me, and has been like a mother to me since Aunt Cha died. And I was very good – though perhaps I should not say so – about your *Pioneer*, and thought that I deserved a lovely wedding.'

She untied the ribbons of her bonnet, placed it carefully in its box, and wept openly.

'For it is very hard that your engine should have all the world to see it, and a reception at Kingswood Hall before and after, and that I should make do with nothing very much.'

'Well, that is understandable,' he said quietly. 'Though I had not looked at it in that way, I must confess.'

'And though you would be happy enough to live here after we were married, I should not. And neither would Polly. I want my own house.'

'This *is* your own house,' he observed reasonably.

'It is my property, which is not the same thing at all. Aunt Cha was making sure that I should have a degree of independence, so that I was not obliged to go back to Kit's Hill, or become a governess, or marry out of despair. But how we shall live with Ambrose and Jeremy I cannot imagine. For you and they are fighting for different principles, and you might quarrel if you shared the same house. And I should be in the middle, which would be horrid. And heaven knows how I shall deal with all your different hours and meal times! For you work from five o'clock in the morning to five in the evening, and they work from noon to midnight! And it will be nothing but pother and fuss.'

He thought. He nodded. He made up his mind.

'That I do see. You shall have your own house, love. But not at the ironmaster's end of the valley, and he is not paying for it. In fact, I do not want to build a house, as yet. The future is too unsettled.'

She was sorry for the ironmaster's disappointment, and her own fears for the future increased, but she had no choice.

'What will you do with Thornton House?' Hal Vivian asked. 'Keep it as an investment, or sell it?'

Mary dried her eyes and blew her nose.

'Oh, I could not sell it over the heads of Ambrose and Jeremy. That would be too unkind. It was Ambrose's house in the first place, you know, before Aunt Cha came back; but she left him money instead.'

'Then no doubt he will offer rent, and that will give you some financial independence apart from my income. Meanwhile we cannot expect to find a suitable home, furnished or unfurnished, in five minutes. And we are not accepting the offer to live at Upperton. That would be the thin end of the wedge.'

Mary nodded slowly, saying, 'We must look around us, then.'

'Well, that is a couple of things settled,' said Hal Vivian, buttering toast and offering it to her.

'I should be doing that!' she cried, penitent, taking the toasting-fork from his hand.

He broached the sorest subject of all.

'As for our other problem, Mary, I shall endeavour to strike a balance between home and work. It will be a difficult transition, but you must keep me to the mark, love, and we must always be able to discuss matters calmly and openly. Remember that work has been both goal and way for me, all my adult life. I cannot change a habit overnight, but I shall not cease to try. And you were the best girl in the world over *Pioneer*, and have every right to say so – and I love you for that and many, many other reasons.'

She cried, 'I thought you did not love me very much.'

'How could you?' he asked, astonished.

'Well, you are all the world to me, Hal. But I am only a little part of yours. I loved you from that evening at Kingswood Hall, which you don't even remember. And you can manage alone, you see.'

He said honestly, 'Yes, I can manage alone, but it is an empty business. And I do love you. And I want a life made whole by you. But I am a poor hand at expressing those feelings, and you must forgive me for it. I shall learn.'

He raised her hand to his lips. The bread flared.

'Oh, put the damned toast down!' he cried, laughing, and kissed her long and soundly.

They knelt side by side on the hearthrug, and he held her close, and felt her cheek hot and damp with grief against his own.

The ironmaster accepted his defeat with good grace, knowing which quarter it came from, and had the sense to let them go about the business of house-hunting without help or hindrance. This was more difficult than they had anticipated, and in August they quarrelled again when the Cornishman disappeared for three days to attend the opening of the Bolton-Leigh railroad. Mary became feverish and cross with despair. However promising each house sounded, the reality was always a disappointment in one way or another. And their friends' advice tended to complicate matters.

Hamish Standish, for instance, was so adamant on the subject of good sanitation as to rule out nine-tenths of the market.

Then, the location was strictly limited. Hal Vivian had rooted objections to anywhere less than three miles from Kingswood Hall, and added Flawnes Green as an afterthought because his mother used to live there with William.

Mary refused to consider the far end of the valley because it was too near Kit's Hill, and anywhere on the moors and fells because it would be too isolated.

It also seemed absurd to move from one part of the Old Town to the other, though 'Beech Grove' was up for letting, and would have suited them very well. Nor did either of them care for a new house in the industrial suburbs, so that ruled out Millbridge.

'I thought love made people happy,' Mary said pitifully, as they made up their second quarrel, 'but I have never cried as much in all my life. And when I gave my speech I was right to say that Wyndendale was not very large. It is even smaller than I thought.'

The Cornishman had his own problems.

'If the ironmaster does not make up his mind to finance further improvements to the railway, I shall pack up and go back to Manchester. I have had other offers. . . .'

'I do not want to leave the valley just yet!' she cried. 'It will be too many new things happening at once!'

'Then what do you suggest, love?'

'Oh never mind. Just let us not quarrel. Just let us sit by the fire this evening and make friends again, for it is too terrible!'

September came. Mary suffered attacks of asthma, some mild, some severe, but happening all too frequently. Four-year-old Philomena, whose state of health always reflected Mary's state of mind, ran high temperatures and caught one drizzling cold after another. Even Polly drooped beneath these new responsibilities. While Ambrose and Jeremy, feeling unwanted and unloved, offered to leave. It was ebb tide.

William Howarth rode up the High Street on a tall black horse. He favoured tall black horses, and had long since forgotten why: the reason being that his earliest impression of power was the sight of Zelah's father, the Warwickshire ironmaster, similarly mounted. At Thornton House he tied the animal to a hitching post, and knocked with his usual air of supreme importance.

A red-eyed Polly said, 'Miss Mary's been poorly again all night, sir. She's laying on the parlour sofa, a bit down in the mouth like.'

'Then I shall cheer her up!' cried the ironmaster, walking in.

Polly heard him say, as she closed the door, 'Mary, I know of a house which will suit very well indeed.'

The Brigges, though not rich and noble like the Kersalls, were old-fashioned gentry. They could trace their ancestry back to the days of Queen Elizabeth, who had given John Brigge a small manor. This was their first and last piece of good fortune. The present suburb of Brigge House used to be their manorial estate, but imperceptibly they had retreated over the centuries.

From time to time the late Squire Brigge had engaged in some public enterprise which gave him a brief reprieve, but he was no businessman. His last effort had been to offer land to the Wyndendale Line. Their refusal caused him to lose face and money. Shortly afterwards, he died in his sleep.

His sons had sensibly left home long since, and gone into the Church, the Army and the Law. His widow lived on at the Old Hall, shutting up most of the rooms, keeping only one servant to tend her. Hospitality became a thing of the past. She was solitary, keeping a wolfish hound to hold visitors as well as intruders at bay. There were rumours of starvation and madness. Then she ailed, and called a doctor in who found such a neglected old woman in such a neglected place that he ordered her family to make some other arrangement.

'. . . which I happen to know includes letting or selling the Old Hall,' said the ironmaster, drinking his tea with gusto. 'So I had a word with the Brigges's solicitor, and if you look sharp about it – and the house suits you – it is yours for the asking. What about that?'

His own delight with himself was so evident that Mary kissed him heartily. She loved him, faults and all.

'You will slop my tea over, miss,' he cried, very pleased. 'Now there is one more matter to mention, so give me your full attention. I know how things stand with Hal, so do not tell him of my part in this. The house seems right for you in every respect, apart from dirt and damp. Scarcely two miles from Millbridge, and well away from me. He can pay his own rent and live under his own roof, and need never know I had a hand in finding it. I give you my word, Mary, for your own peace of mind, that I have no interest of any sort in the property. If it suits *you* then I am content.'

'Oh, uncle!' said Mary sadly. 'Oh, dear uncle!'

'Well, well, no need for you to fret,' he said cheerfully.

'We shall come to an understanding eventually, Hal and I. These things take time. And I know he has been thinking of leaving the valley. Well, I cannot say more at the moment, but I have been nosing around. I think there will be something to make him stay here, very soon.

'So put on your bonnet, miss, and walk down the High Street. Here is the solicitor's name and address. He is expecting you, and will drive you out to see the Hall. I would offer to take you myself, but it is best not. There, there, no more tears, miss. It is the day for smiles!'

Everything happened at once. Ignoring its condition, Mary fell instantly in love with the Old Hall and decided they should live there for ever. That same evening the Cornishman was driven off to inspect the premises by candlelight – not that his opinion mattered – and by ten o'clock had signed an agreement to rent it furnished for a year. At the end of this time they could either buy the property or take a long lease at a higher rate.

Hal Vivian was so plainly unused to dealing with these matters that Mary quietly brought in their own solicitor for future reference, and kept the ironmaster secretly in the background as a second opinion.

There followed the time which Polly later described as 'scrubbing our blooming fingers to the bone', when she supervised the cleaning.

The Old Hall had intended to be E-shaped, in compliment to the monarch who made it possible, but the Brigges's coffers never matched their ambitions. So it was a long house with a deep gable at either end, pleasingly modest in size and appearance, its timbers sound and good.

Two men started work on the roof at once, and two others began painting and tarring the outside of the Hall. A labourer with a scythe tackled the jungle of garden, and shortly found the mossy remnants of a lawn, the suggestion of a border, a tangled shrubbery, and various urns and small statues of broken stone.

Inside, terrible things came to light. Curtains being taken

down for washing fell to pieces. Furniture, being moved, either followed the example of the curtains or was discovered to be riddled with worm. Sofas and cushions housed nests of mice. All the wallpapers were either peeling or holding up the plaster, and breeding bugs of every description. Worn carpets covered holes in floorboards. Pictures hung askew on rusty nails: their backs cobwebbed and scuttling. The kitchen quarters had been taken over by cockroaches, and the attics by spiders. The conservatory was an insects' paradise. Nothing was what it seemed, and everything hid something worse.

Polly scolded, the cleaning women grumbled, but Mary was undaunted. Her asthma disappeared, her zest for living returned. She no longer noticed the hours Hal worked, for she worked the same herself, and sometimes longer. Thornton House became a mere lodging, in which she and Polly ate and slept whenever they happened to be there.

'Quite like old times,' said Ambrose and Jeremy, amused.

As Mary improvised with her future home, certain articles of furniture disappeared. A set of fire irons, a footstool, Charlotte's little escritoire. Later she became more ambitious, and dismantled and moved the entire contents of a guest room, including a four-poster bed. Polly was as acquisitive as her mistress, and Prue grumbled dreadfully as she looked for saucepans which no longer lived there. But Ambrose and Jeremy never noticed, never knew.

'Well, miss,' cried the ironmaster, invited to admire a major improvement, 'when is your wedding to be? Do you fancy April as a month? Zelah and I were married in April!'

'Oh, why should we wait so long? We have been engaged almost a year! The house is scrubbed from top to bottom. The roof and outside work is done. The rooms we need for the present are ready, and we can do the rest at leisure. We could move in well before Christmas. Why wait?'

'I will give you one good reason,' said the ironmaster,

smiling on her dismay. 'A wedding such as you hope for takes some months to plan, and Zelah and I will be living in London for much of the winter. April will be the earliest month that we can manage.'

She said, after a hard minute, 'Then April it must be, of course.'

She watched the expression on Hal's face mirror her own feelings. He won his minute's battle, as she had done, and made a great show of admiring the new curtains – taken from a back room in Thornton House.

'April it must be, of course,' said the Cornishman.

She loved him then in a new way. Not with desire which, despite her innocence, she already experienced as an unknown hunger, but with a knife turned against herself. She suffered his suffering, and suffered for him. She wanted to give him the world, and to protect him from it.

'No, it must not,' said Mary, her mind made up. 'Our wedding is a private commitment, not a public entertainment. We can be married as soon as we please. Tomorrow, if need be! Uncle William will understand, and anyway it will save them a lot of trouble and expense.'

She added with perfect sincerity, 'What a good thing I did not wear my new autumn gown! It is pretty enough for any occasion!'

So at half-past eleven o'clock one late October morning, Mary and Hal met in St Mark's Church at Millbridge, and Jarvis Pole married them without pomp, but reverently, lovingly, and with great dignity.

Only the family were there, though they were quite a crowd – from Thornton House, Kingswood Hall, Kit's Hill and the rectory. Dick Howarth wiped his eyes on his sleeve, just before giving his daughter away, but that was in memory for she had left him long ago. Philomena lay down in the aisle at first, but got up again when she found she was being ignored, and behaved very well. Polly and Prue cried quietly at the back of the church. And at the Royal George afterwards, Florrie Tyler outdid herself in the variety and quality of her glazed game pies, while the landlord ransacked his cellar and came up laden with fine old claret and covered in cobwebs.

October was the genteel season at Lytham. Mr and Mrs Henry Vivian stayed at the Clifton Arms Hotel, paying seven shillings a day for complete and luxurious privacy.

Even in a year the resort had changed, and was changing. Soon there would be gigs, horses and carriages for those who wished to hire them, livery stables for those who came provided. There would be more streets, all of them named and well lit; more houses, all of them clearly numbered. There would be a market square and a clock. A public reading room. A row of bathing machines.

They walked at leisure in the evening light. The cool dark sands stretched ahead of them, empty and at peace. The sea pegged out its lace upon the shore. They were one night and one day old.

'Why is it,' said Mary pensively, 'that whenever I am absolutely and most beautifully happy I think of things that make me sad?'

The Cornishman laughed and put her hand to his lips. They stopped to watch the endless toiling of the sea.

'What makes you sad, love?'

'I can't quite think at the moment but I want to be comforted. Is it improper to kiss you back so much?'

'I have no idea, but it is extraordinarily pleasant!'

'I do like the way you hold me, Hal!'

In a little while they strolled on again, arm in arm. For this was not the first pause in their evening walk. Mary smiled mischievously up at him. He smiled quietly to himself.

Reading his mind, she said, 'I must make sure that my motives are always for the best, Hal. Otherwise, I might tend to exaggerate a little so that you could make a fuss of me. And that would never do! Oh, there is the place where Aunt Cha used to sit, in her last long summer. . . .'

'Yes,' he answered, 'I remember very well. What was it

303

she said to Polly that was meant for us?'

'"I am entirely content!" Oh, and I am, I am!'

'Well, so am I,' said the Cornishman.

TWENTY-FOUR

Grand Designs

On their last day at Lytham Mary left her husband to walk ahead while she lingered along the shore, finding shells for Philomena. And coming up unnoticed, knotting those translucent treasures into her handkerchief, she discovered him drawing in the sand with the ferrule of his cane. Her former chagrin rose, her new-found confidence faltered, as she looked down on the sketch he was attempting to erase. Then she mastered herself, slipped her arm through his and spoke teasingly.

'So my charms have ceased to enchant you, sir?'

His answer was a silent one. Rapidly he drew two hearts transfixed by one large arrow.

'Too late, sir!' Mary cried, restored by his impudence. 'I saw your locomotive first!'

She laughed. He joined her. And begged her pardon.

'Oh, you are not alone in your abstraction, Hal,' Mary said. 'To be quite fair to you, I must admit that for the past half hour I have been turning the back parlour into my private sitting room, and choosing a pretty paper for the walls. Running side by side with those thoughts has been a programme of education for Philomena. Also a firm resolve to make jam next summer from the blackcurrants in our kitchen garden. So I think, love, that our honeymoon is indeed at an end. We are ready to go home now, and begin our life together in earnest.'

They indulged in an embrace, from which they emerged refreshed.

'Our honeymoon is not over,' said the Cornishman. 'Merely postponed. From time to time, as the fancy takes us, we shall escape for a few days, and begin it all over again.'

Then he began exultantly to draw in the damp sand, to explain, forgetting her lack of knowledge.

'Your absence left my own mind free to wander. Look, Mary, I have improved vastly upon my design for *Pioneer*, by means of a tubular boiler. This will extend the heating surface, and enable a rapid and continuous rise of steam, in order to keep up a high rate of speed. And by contracting the openings to the two blast-pipes I shall increase the draught. Mary, she could reach four-and-thirty miles an hour!'

She squeezed his arm, uncomprehending but proud.

He said, 'And I shall call her the *Mary Vivian!*'

Halcyon days.

The Cornishman was an early riser and liked to be about his work by the time day broke. So Mary, who preferred to face the world at eight o'clock and drink a cup of hot chocolate in private, rose at half-past five that first winter and prepared his breakfast herself. It was not a tremendous undertaking: two slices of wheaten bread, a piece of cheese and three cups of tea set him up for the day.

With a delicacy for which she was seldom given credit, Polly made enquiries as to whether she should perform this office. But, on hearing that it was a labour of love, stayed abed until her usual hour of half-past six and thanked God for married bliss.

'He ain't a troublesome gentleman, neither,' Polly remarked. 'Not like Mr Ambrose. A-dirtying of all his shirts without telling me, and a-stuffing of them back into the drawers. And then expecting them to be washed and ironed in five minutes!'

Polly was right. Hal Vivian's domestic requirements were modest. His expressions of gratitude for hot suppers and clean linen were touching. The reverse side of this character coin was clearly one of omission. He did not make demands because he was usually thinking of something else, and the gratitude was mere good manners.

In order to sustain her at the hour of dawn, Mary had bought a delectable white morning dress and matching cap, the whole being trimmed with sky-blue ribbons and cotton lace. In this ensemble she would sit at the breakfast table, trying to turn yawns into smiles, so that Hal should go to work with her image engraved upon his heart. A long time afterwards she realised that he must never have noticed.

Charlotte had taught her a great deal. With subtlety, tact and praise, Mary lightened Polly's load so that she could rule this new roost without being overworked. The elderly housekeeper took great pride in her kitchenful of fresh-faced maids, but was inclined to make a favourite of the gardener.

They now had a stables of their own, and Mary soon dispensed with the services of Fred at the Royal George, for which he was truly thankful. With the help and advice of her father, she bought Hal a horse to his liking at Preston Fair. It was a handsome gelding with a mulberry coat, called 'Bramble': not too fast, not too slow, and sensible enough to turn in at the Old Hall when the Cornishman – in an unusual fit of abstraction – was heading back to his old quarters in Millbridge.

Time passed quickly. Mary gave Philomena her lessons, discussed the day's duties with Polly, continued her own education, kept her journal, and enjoyed a bustling little social life.

What a delightful thing it was when any of her Kingswood Hall cousins came visiting – apart from Anna, whose presence still disturbed her. But to pour tea from her own silver teapot, and ask Tibby or Kitty or Livvy how much cream they liked; to giggle with Sophy or Molly over clothes and husbands; to give matronly advice on affairs of the heart to fifteen-year-old Ruth; all this was heaven on earth. Or Cicely might come, and bring the dark and lovely young Dorcas. And sometimes she had visitors from Kit's Hill, but that was not often.

Then, as the afternoon waned and her guests departed,

she would stand at the window to watch the evening come in, and wait for her husband. The best part of the day began at that time, with the candles lit and the curtains drawn against the night.

Perhaps it had been Hal Vivian who, first and last, made Mary's wilderness flower. Perhaps, as Charlotte once said, she flowered in the presence of any man. But as Mary Vivian she became a veritable garden.

She had taken to love-making as to a natural element. It was an ultimate compliment, a supreme intimacy, which satisfied something deep and earthy in her. Mary's training as a lady had come late in life, and her flesh was all Kit's Hill. Too many lusty girls in the Howarth dynasty had been tousled in the hayloft, and enjoyed it, for Mary to pretend maidenly modesty. Once her initial shyness was over she excelled her husband at the love-feast. There was a niceness about Hal Vivian's banqueting; Mary tended to lick her lips.

People were quick to notice the difference. Her voice softened and slowed. Her thin body rounded. There was a seductiveness in the way she walked or sat, a languor in the way she smiled. She had a voluptuous air which Millbridge ladies found slightly coarse, which made Millbridge gentlemen envy her husband.

Sophy expressed the general opinion in acceptable terms.

Remarking with a smile, 'Goodness! How very *married* Mary looks these days!

Halcyon days.

Though the launching of *Pioneer* had been so successful, the investors were anxious to see signs of getting their money back. Hal Vivian was juggling with his commitment to Mary, his plans for a new locomotive, and the teething troubles of the new railroad. The ironmaster was attempting to hold his son by raising more money on a project as yet unproven. Momentarily, the two of them slackened their grip; and in a little flurry of excitement and panic the Wyndendale Railway Committee attempted the unknown.

'Why concern yourself with a passenger service?' the ironmaster had said to the Cornishman, back in 1825. 'It will be years before ordinary people travel by rail.'

The response on Opening Day had made a fool of this prophecy. There was a positive clamour for a passenger service. Taking the chairman's place, during William's absence in London, Arnold Harbottle suggested that they let out this service to a contractor, charging him tolls for the use of the line and the yellow coach, and setting certain hours of the day apart when he might use the railroad.

'And that way,' said Arnold, satisfied that he had covered every aspect of the question, 'we make a steady income without mithering ourselves.'

The resolution was passed unanimously, and within a month the Wyndendale transport system was tangled like a skein of wool.

'Devil take it!' William roared, banging the emergency meeting to order. 'I have never seen such a damned great mess in all my life!'

'Aye, well, we couldn't know as the contractor was going to sub-contract, you see,' said Arnold. 'There were only *one* coach.'

'Aye, only one coach,' said a coal magnate profoundly.

The others murmured agreement, and looked ashamed. For what would they have done in the contractor's position? Paid rent and run one coach, or let out the use of the line to a number of interested parties and provided further coaches?

'*Sub-contract?*' cried the ironmaster. 'That is an understatement of such magnitude that a new word should be invented for it. The man has *splintered* his contract into a thousand fragments, and is making a profit on every splinter! I wish I were in his place, sir!' To the unfortunate

Arnold Harbottle, 'I should not be beating out my brains, trying to improve our present situation. I should be able to *retire!*'

And here he flung himself back into his chair, and thrust out his bottom lip in a pet.

Returning to Millbridge in the spring of 1829 in an open carriage, the day being fine – doffing his hat at the sight of each acquaintance – the ironmaster had noticed significant looks and smiles, heard the odd jocular comment, as they bowled along. He saw a group of people waiting at the railway terminus near the Cornmarket, and another group at Middletown. He rested his chin upon the silver knob of his cane, and pondered. Then he poked his coach driver in the back.

'Mogg!' he ordered. 'Follow the railway line and drive slowly.'

While he was away a regular string of stopping places had sprung into being. The main ones followed the old line of villages which he had known in his childhood, each of them about a mile apart: Flawnes Green, Brigge House, Thornley, Whinfold. There were others in between such as Flawnes Gardens, for instance, where he took care not to acknowledge a handsome showy woman, who smiled to herself and sauntered on. And at each of these places stood the inexplicable groups of waiting people.

The official halts were conducting their own business. Mind you, he counted the number of coal wagons waiting at Tarbock incline and found three more than there should be. And *Pioneer* seen from the side view, chuntering across Belbrook bridge, was already hauling a full load. He must look into that. You could never trust folk to do as they were told.

Then, 'Stop!' roared the ironmaster, and his four matching greys halted like one horse.

He stood up in his carriage, white-headed, dark-faced, and swollen with fury. Everyone knew him, stared at him, was prepared to placate him if possible.

Only Zelah dared to say, 'Pray love, do not disturb

thyself so much. Thee knows what the doctor told thee!'

He ignored her.

'What?' cried the ironmaster, pointing his cane. 'Is *that*?'

Swaying and trundling along the track, a few hundred yards behind *Pioneer* was a most extraordinary vehicle, drawn by a huge cart-horse who plodded between the rails. It resembled one of the more cumbersome stage-coaches, and had been given a hasty coat of paint. There were people sitting on top, and others now poked their heads out of the window. As it drew nearer William could see faint traces of its original identity. LA.CASH.RE D..IG.NC. BO.T.N, B..Y & R.CHDA.. A strip of paper had been pasted on both sides, on which was scrawled, 'GARTH FOLD TO MILLBRIDGE CORNMARKET' and 'MILLBRIDGE CORNMARKET TO GARTH FOLD'.

'It seems to be some sort of passenger coach, love,' said Zelah mildly, and concealed her amusement.

At this moment *Pioneer* hurtled past and drowned the ironmaster's shouts of rage with thunder, smoke and smuts. Thirteen wagons later William got deliberately from his carriage, stood in the path of the oncoming trachyderm and shook his cane at it in a threatening manner.

'Whoa!' said the driver, and the horse stopped gladly. 'Art coming aboard, sir?' he asked, uncertain of such an illustrious passenger.

'No, I am damned well not! Take this rubbish tip off my railroad instantly. What the devil are you about?'

'Begging your pardon, sir,' said the driver, touching his hat at every other word so that the ironmaster should know it was not his fault, 'but I canna do that. This here passenger service belongs to t'landlord of t'Railway Tavern in Garth.'

'Passenger service?' William roared.

'Yes, sir. And if we dunnot get on we shall be holding up all t'others. Yes, sir, t'others. Drive on, and thee can see for thysen.'

Behind the old Lancashire Diligence, straggling along at respectable intervals, was a motley collection of ancient horse-drawn stage-coaches and a funeral hearse in flimsy disguise. Each had been renovated with a hurried coat of paint, baring glimpses of its former name and destinations, and now advertising new halts along the valley railway. In order to tempt passengers aboard, various sub-contractors, all landlords of local inns and hostelries, had attempted to cater for different halts along the route. One battered monster, travelling between the main cotton mills from Thornley to Millbridge bore the exotic legend 'HELL'S GATE TO BABYLON'.

'What a sight for your Chairman to see!' said the ironmaster to his committee. 'What an insult to any shareholder! What a return for all my efforts on this railway's behalf!' He paused sorrowfully. 'What a welcome home!'

They accorded him the silence he expected before they replied. Then Arnold, as the guiltiest party present, cleared his throat.

'I'm not saying as it hasn't got a bit out of hand, like. But Harry here took the trouble to tot up the fares. They've got a good business going there, Will. They're making a small fortune. I'm thinking we should have held on to it.'

The ironmaster's expression told them nothing.

'Who rented our yellow coach?' he asked.

'Ben Tyler, at the Royal George. And he's charging a shilling each way, wherever you get on, to keep up the class of passengers. The others, they're looking for big trade and quick profits, they charge according to where the passengers get on, and they let them have up to 14lbs of luggage with that, and all. Ben charges extra for luggage.'

'And he gets plenty of customers?'

They nodded solemnly. Benjamin Tyler was not the landlord of a fine and thriving hostelry without knowing how to get plenty of customers.

'Then there must be a need for both kinds of passenger,' said William. He shifted position. 'Of course, I should like to make it clear that my remarks in no way reflect upon the service itself, which is a good and necessary thing, but upon the way it is being conducted.'

Oh, they assured him, they understood exactly how he felt.

His next remark made them glance hopefully at each other.

'In fact, Mr Vivian happened to mention the matter to me this morning. That is to say, with regard to the way such a service *should* be run. Not this present chaos! Suitable coaches could be built to our specifications. One sort plain and practical, the other more luxurious, to cater for both classes of passenger.'

'Or we could build them all the same, which would be cheaper, and charge a shilling to the inside passengers, and sixpence to the outside ones. Like the stage-coaches do!' A coal magnate suggested.

'No, I think not,' said William, who had discussed the problem at length with Hal Vivian. 'Unlike the road coaches, whose speed is regulated by horses, the speed of rail coaches depends upon the locomotive. We must reckon on travelling very fast indeed. It would not be safe for passengers to ride on top.'

They waited for the next move, which they could now guess.

'In fact, this business of drawing the passenger coach by means of a horse,' said William, quoting the same source, 'is nonsensical. We could make four times the number of journeys with a locomotive. What we need is another train to carry passengers. I believe Mr Vivian would be prepared to look into the matter for us, if we were interested.'

'There's just two small problems,' said Arnold Harbottle, meaning there were two big ones. 'Folk want to travel at all hours of the day, which them passenger coaches are doing – though not supposed to. Now, if we want to make good profits we must give an all-day service. But at the moment *Pioneer* has right of way, and anything else on the line has to push off into a siding. I've heard of journeys lasting over two hours because of that. Now, if we have a second locomotive, the two engines'll be criss-crossing each other on the line, and shunting in and out of sidings for ever more, and nobody'll get anywhere!'

'You take my point exactly,' said the ironmaster, smooth and bland. 'We need to put down a second railway line by the side of the first.' They opened their mouths to protest. 'Fortunately, Mr Vivian foresaw our needs and made room for another line, should we require one.'

'Of wrought iron, I daresay,' a rebel remarked.

'We can discuss that later,' said William coldly, 'if, of course, you are interested in expansion and profit.'

'I daresay we could find the initial capital,' said Arnold Harbottle, looking round cautiously for approval.

He received it, equally cautiously.

'I am pleased to hear it,' said the ironmaster, clinching the matter, 'because I have not been idle in London. I believe I can interest other investors outside the valley.'

They smiled on one another again.

'In the meantime,' said Arnold Harbottle, 'what do we do about them old coaches?'

'Oh, we call in our passenger service contract,' said William grandly, 'and buy up the vehicles cheap. Make them look decent, paint them all one colour, find better horses to pull them, and work them until our new locomotive and passenger coaches are built!'

Nature gave Mary six months in Eden, and then reminded her there was a price to pay for apples.

'I thought it might be so,' she said philosophically, as Dr Hamish Standish advised her on her condition.

She felt very cheerful, apart from being nauseated by the smell of food, and unable to eat anything but oranges.

'And when might it be. . . ?'

'As far as I can judge – your monthly courses being somewhat irregular – early next January.'

'1830!' Mary said, absurdly pleased. 'A new year and a new decade!' She added, a little apprehensively, 'Oh, I do hope it doesn't clash with the opening of any railways!'

With a robustness which set Millbridge ladies whispering over their teacups, Mary soon overcame her

314

sensations of nausea, and ate to make up for the diet of oranges. Pregnancy, like love, suited her immensely. There was no need to beg her to take care of herself. She gave up early rising and took a nap on her day bed after luncheon.

Now fourteen-year-old Margery Bowker prepared the Cornishman's frugal breakfast, and puzzled him one morning – standing at the table pouring his tea, dressed in a humble grey gown and clean apron.

'I could have sworn,' said Hal Vivian, 'that you wore something different, Prue! Margery I mean, of course. Margery! Yes. Thank you, Margery. We must see that Mrs Vivian rests all she can. . . .'

For some reason he had thought the girl wore a white dress trimmed with blue ribbon. But forgot it, soon after. He had never been busier.

That winter the ironmaster had raised more money than ever before, and raised it comfortably. The possibilities of the Wyndendale Railway were becoming probabilities, would become certainties. The speed, ease and cheapness of steam locomotion was going to lead to national public transport. Best of all, it would be profitable beyond even their greediest dreams.

On behalf of himself and the committee, William thanked and congratulated the Cornishman on the swiftness with which he had produced his plans, their undoubted quality, and the range of his vision.

But it was Arnold Harbottle who summed up the future attitude of all sensible businessmen.

'This here valley is done with farming and home weaving! We're in the age of iron and steam, whether we like it or not. And it's like a tide-race, I tell thee. We either go with it – or we go under. And I know what *I'm* going to do, by God!'

The navvies had returned to Wyndendale in full force. This time they were under the aegis of Tom Hosking, and another contractor of similar nature and reputation – Mike Aspinall; for Len Babbage had been refused the option.

In the opinion of the valley this was a minor concession. Whoever the contractor might be, navvies were navvies. Wyndendale had been free of them for nine months, cleaned up most of the mess they left behind them, and begun to feel like itself again. Now the termites were back. Public opinion expressed itself through the two leading newspapers and all the peripheral ones. And according to the local press, the public was none too pleased.

Garth was to be doubly-honoured, or twice-plagued, according to which spokesman spoke. In the extended Railway Works the Cornishman and his assistants were constructing his new passenger locomotive, the *Mary Vivian*. While, at the far end of the town, Tom Hosking's men began to blast out a tunnel which would bring them into the next valley. The Cornishman had got all his own way at last.

'For you see, gentlemen,' said Hal Vivian, addressing the attentive committee, 'railway lines, like canals and coachroads, will eventually join towns and cities all over the country, and we must prepare to become a part of this grand design.'

Their valley had shrunk to the size of a map upon the library table. He pointed to Millbridge.

'At this end, in Lancashire, we are ready to meet the equivalent of a Leeds-Liverpool railroad!'

He traced the line down to Garth.

'While here we shall be cutting a tunnel one and a half miles long, which will enable us to connect with routes as far apart as York and Carlisle. . . .'

The Wyndendale Railway was running on oiled and twinkling wheels, despite occasional tragic incidents. Folk both admired and feared this new invention, and had not yet come to terms with it. Watchers stood too close, crowded and pushed each other, fell off bridges into the river, misjudged the speed of *Pioneer* as they crossed her line. For she went faster than they expected, and could not halt quickly. Once, her boiler blew up. Two or three times wagons were derailed.

The *Post* reported every accident in detail and with tremendous relish. The *Clarion* – was it kinship, rivalry or a liberal view? – tended to tone down criticism, to praise progress, and to take up the lighter-hearted side of following the rail.

'IS LORD KERSALL "GAME" ENOUGH TO TAKE WYNDENDALE LINE TO COURT?'

'It has been brought to our Attention that one of Lord Kersall's Partridges flew into *Pioneer's* cinder-box at Belbrook yesterday, with Lamentable Results. By the time the Locomotive reached Millbridge the Bird was Cooked. Whereupon the Engine Driver, being of a Practical Disposition, Ate it. The Creature was well Out of its usual Habitat, but it is not Possible that his Lordship could Sue the Company for Poaching whilst "on the Run"'...?

The Cornishman was more often away than at home. When it was not this railway it was another. In the September of 1829 he attended, but did not enter, the trials at Rainhill, ten miles from Liverpool. *Pioneer* was not, in his opinion, up to the mark. The *Mary Vivian* was not yet built. He watched that humble genius, George Stephenson, take the prize of £500 with his steam-engine *Rocket* – and saw, with personal chagrin, with professional delight, that Stephenson's improvements were similar to the ones he himself had sketched in the sands of Lytham beach the previous autumn. The greatest triumph of all lay ahead. For Stephenson had floated a railroad across Chat Moss, and the double line between Liverpool and Manchester would be finished within a year.

Meanwhile Mary had been left to herself: not an unusual state of affairs and one to which she was growing accustomed. While Philomena, perhaps realising that

Mary's attention was no longer focused quite so intently upon her, had been suffering from a series of colds and was at present sitting up in bed convalescing from the latest.

Mary was not unhappy. She was enjoying excellent health. She did not feel neglected. Was it the poignancy of autumn which came upon her? Whatever the reason, she was suddenly seized by an unaccountable desire to see her old home. Forbidden to ride at this stage of her pregnancy, and having no carriage of her own, she was puzzled how to get there. Until she remembered the Wyndendale Passenger Service.

'Polly!' she cried, bouncing into the kitchen much as Polly used to bounce into the front parlour at Thornton House. 'Polly, I'm just going to pop over to Kit's Hill for the afternoon. Will you keep an eye on Philly for me?'

'Not by yourself you ain't,' said Polly firmly. 'Not in your condition. And I can't come if I'm keeping an eye on Phillermeen.'

'Oh, there's no need to fret. I can take Margery Bowker with me. Her mother lives in Garth. It would be nice for them to have an hour or two together. But hurry!'

Mistress and maid walked over the stone bridge to Brigge House Green and caught the first-class coach to Garth Fold. The journey was interrupted by a bustling *Pioneer* no less than twice, and took one hour and forty minutes to complete.

Together, mistress and maid trod the weary mile up Garth Fells, stopping to rest when Mary got short of breath. The rows of red-brick houses, already turning black with soot, came to an end. The landscape grew harsher, cleaner, the air purer and colder. They opened the gate at the end of the lane and entered another world.

She was still there. Kit's Hill. Sitting in the September sun, windows glinting: like some hale old woman with bright spectacles, wrapped in a gritstone shawl. Though the courtyard was as slippery and pungent as usual, the place looked cared for. The sounds of female voices inside were brisk and young and cheerful.

Mary knocked at the back door with some misgivings. Even invited she had not been entirely welcome. A surprise visit might be disastrous.

A buxom lass of eighteen, with the Wharmby's russet-brown eyes and Alice's nut-brown braids of hair, opened the door. For a moment the two sisters stared at one another speechlessly. Then Harriet fairly screamed with delight, 'Eh, look who's here! It's our Mary!' into the recesses of the farmhouse. And Mary, overcome by the easy tears of pregnancy, was brought inside weeping for joy.

'Well, I never,' said Harriet Howarth, arms akimbo. 'You're a proper stranger, our Mary. We've not seen hide nor hair of you since Susan's funeral last February. Hello, Margery! Do you want a cup of tea or do you want to run down and see your Mam? Right! I'll take care of Mary – Mrs Vivian, that is. When do you want her back, our Mary?'

'The coach leaves at six o'clock from Garth Fold. Oh, Hatty! Hatty! I just had to see you all! How's our Dad?'

'Fine as fivepence,' said Hatty, putting the black kettle on its hook. She shouted at the top of her splendid young voice, 'Judith!' And as Mary jumped, accustomed to thick carpets and soft tones, she added, 'I have to yell me head off or she don't hear me. She's been bad since she catched the measles all them years ago.' Then, eyeing Mary with a rollicking brown gaze, 'Well, I can see what you've been up to – you pisey cat! When's it expected? November?'

Mary corrected her estimate.

'My word, you're big for six months,' said Hatty frankly.

But Mary could no longer be irritated. She laid aside her fine manner and lapsed into the comfortable speech of Kit's Hill.

She said, 'The house looks grand, Hatty. Tell us what's been happening to you, then. My word, this tea tastes good!'

The thick blue mugs had been bought from the packman, who still plied his trade in the outlying farms, walking the old tracks with his donkey and two bundles of goods. And the sisters propped their elbows on the kitchen table while they drank, and flung back their heads to laugh, and talked woman to woman.

'Our Dad gets a bit mopey, now and again,' said Hatty drily, 'but I'm not sure whether he frets for our Mam or Susan, or just a woman to wait on him. I wouldn't be surprised if he married again – if anybody'd have him. But he's getting on a bit. He were fifty-four in May.'

'What would you do if he did?' Mary asked, interested.

Poor Judith crept in, and fingered the stuff of Mary's gown as they talked, smiling all the while, reading the conversation from Hatty's lips. She seemed backward for a ten-year-old, simple, but the simplicity might have been due to deafness.

'What would I do?' said Hatty. 'I'd leave our Dad to make a fool of himself, and marry Fred Tunstall of Shap Fold.' She translated Mary's expression. 'Oh, our Judith'd come wi' me.'

'Well, it won't be the first time we've married into that family over the years,' Mary remarked. 'But isn't Fred the youngest son?'

'Aye! And there's no room for him on their farm. We should have to go somewhere else. Fred says we should go to America. That's why I hope our Dad'll behave hisself. Then Fred and me can live here, and Fred'll take some of the work off Dad's back. None of our lads have stayed on t'farm. Our Herbert says he wants to be an engine-driver!'

'Do you and Fred really like farming?' Mary asked, wondering. And caught herself up as she saw her sister flush with resentment. 'Nay, I'm not being pisey! I mean, do you *choose* it?'

'I canna think of owt better,' said Hatty with supreme conviction. And could not resist adding, 'We're not all steam mad, you know!' She said, looking curiously at Mary's bountiful form, 'Are you sure it's expected in January? Well, I'm blessed! I tell you what, our Mary. The Wharmbys, on our Mam's side, was allus big breeders

And they used to have twins in that family, and all!'

Hatty had made Kit's Hill her own. Every shining brown rope of onions, every copper saucepan, the very scent of new-baked bread, proclaimed her supremacy. But who would have thought, Mary pondered, that out of Alice's great brood, out of all those beloved sons, the second daughter should inherit? For she could see Hatty ruling Fred and their family of little Tunstalls, contentedly, firmly, with Dick sitting in the chimney-corner as he grew old.

The meaning of inheritance stirred her. And she began to reflect upon the way man strives to shape the future in his own image: and the curious ways in which Providence fulfils and denies him. In his passion for continuity, for a grand design, William Howarth had created a kingdom. But who would reign over it in the end? Not his son, who lived in a world of ideas. Not one of his seven daughters – each queen to another king. Not his wife, who would embrace her faith again when she had no one but herself to please. No, the dream would vanish upon the closing of his eyes, become merely a valuable property to be sold and portioned out among his dependants.

But that inheritance which he sowed so carelessly all those years ago, in a back bedroom at Flawnes Green Forge, would fulfil his dream in its own way. Not taking his name, nor stepping into his shoes, nor acknowledging in the slightest what love or fealty it owed him. And yet remake, renew him, take him further. In his son lay the ironmaster's inheritance. The Vivian inheritance.

Mistress and maid picked their way down to Garth Fold. At the trickle which had been Garth Bottoms brook, Mary gathered a little bunch of wild flowers. They had half an hour to wait before the yellow coach took them back to Brigge House.

The former lych gate, the country hedge, had gone. A brick wall and railings now enclosed the church of St John the Divine. Mary opened the new iron gates into the graveyard. She found the Howarths, rank on rank, grey stones in the late afternoon sun. She put her scarf on the damp ground so that she should not catch cold. And knelt, and covered her face with her hands. Margery wandered tactfully away, leaving her to commune in private.

'I don't know how to put this,' said Mary to Alice in homely fashion, 'but I'm right sorry we never got on. I can understand things a bit better now. I used to think you were hard on me, but it can't have been easy for you neither. I've brought you these. They're not much. But then, there's not much I *can* do for you now.'

She laid the flowers at the foot of Alice's grave. The difficult part was over. She could speak easily, cheerfully, as she had spoken to her sister that afternoon.

'Well, you can see how things are wi' me,' said Mary, 'and I'm all right, Mam. I've got a good husband, and I'm thankful for him. He's famous, and all. Mind you, he takes some looking after – what you might call a full-time job – but he means the world to me.

'Our Philly's doing nicely. She'll never make old bones, but she's wick enough. Proper old-fashioned. She were five at the end of May.

'Did you know that our Herbert wanted to be an engine-driver?

'Eh, I wish you could see our Hatty. She's got Kit's Hill sorted up a treat. She's you all over again, Mam. And d'you know what she told me? She told me there was twins in the family, on the Wharmby side! I never knew that. Mind you, I never listened much! But I'm as big as a house already! Whatever should I do wi' two at once? Well, I suppose I'll manage somehow.

'It'd be nice if I had one of each sort, wouldn't it? But if it's a lad then his name'll have to be Santo William Henry. I don't suppose Dad'll mind one way or the other. He's got a grandson called Richard, any road. But if it's a girl then she's Hannah Charlotte Alice. And, I tell you what, if I ever have two daughters the next one'll be straight *Alice*.

promise you that, Mam. Alice Vivian.

'I'll tell you summat else, as well. You said I allus had to be different, and I am different. I wanted to take a long look back today, just to see how far I'd come from Kit's Hill. And, Mam, I found I'd never been away.'

The ground was cold. The clock in Garth market-place chimed three quarters of six o'clock. Margery was walking slowly but purposefully towards her, a silent reminder that they should take their seats in the yellow coach.

Mary said, 'It's been grand, talking to you! I don't know why I couldn't have said all this before!'

For in saying it, she felt she had been given leave to go.

9 December 1980 – 11 February 1982